TH
SCEP
MORTAL

To the parents of the author:
Donald, Gwendoline, Herta and Philip

The Sceptre Mortal

Derek Sawde

ORIFLAMME PUBLISHING
London

First published in Great Britain 1985
by Oriflamme Publishing Ltd.,
60 Charteris Rd., London N4 3AB

Copyright © 1985 by Oriflamme Publishing Ltd.

No part of this book may be reproduced in any
form without permission from the publisher,
except for the quotation of brief passages in
criticism. All rights reserved.

ISBN 0 948093 00 5

Phototypeset in 10 on 11 point Linotron Plantin by
Input Typesetting Ltd., London SW19 8DR
Printed and bound in Great Britain by
Cox & Wyman Ltd., Reading

CONTENTS

Pronunciation and Orthography	vii
Map of the Isle of Misen Taïrail *or* Helland Holme	x
1 The Festival of the Lamps	1
2 The Story of Melandir	6
3 Last of the Black Lords	18
4 The Quest	33
5 Valley of Eternal Shadow	45
6 The Ruby Caverns	56
7 Aldel Morn	69
8 Melurin	84
9 Belengar	97
10 The Empty Lands	109
11 The Sceptre Mortal	122
12 The Great Goddess Ral	133
13 Lord of the Pines	145
14 The Wild Hunt	160
15 The House in the Forest	171
16 The Loss of the Sceptre	186
17 The Ice Castle	198
18 Sagoth Son of the Morning	218
19 Battle of the Treeless Plain	231
20 Wizardries of War	244
21 Pit of the Werebats	259
22 The Festival of the Ice Fire	270
Map of the Empty Lands and the Forest of Sorcery	277
Appendix: The Count of the Years	279

PRONUNCIATION AND ORTHOGRAPHY

Proper names in the Northspeech have been translated into English, or at least Anglicized, and should therefore be pronounced as English, e.g. Alban (both vowels short), Amray (to rhyme with 'say'), Lerod Anth (all vowels short), Peiri (Peer´-ee), and Melurin (Mell — yoor´ — in). Many names in other languages can also be pronounced in this common sense way, e.g. Alat, Anrith, Arnorin and Rethrind.

The other names are for the most part in the High Speech (Peirian), or in Elvish. For these, the following rules of pronunciation apply:–

Vowels:–

Vowels may be long or short; long vowels should properly be indicated as such by the use of a long sign over the letter (ā, ē, ī, ō, ū). These signs have, however, been omitted in the text, as they are felt to be alien to English readers.

a as in *cat* (short) or *father* (long)
e as in *pen* (short) or *fair* (long) — not as in *green*
i as in *fit* (short) or *see* (long) — not as in *fine*
o as in *hot* (short) or *sought* (long) — not as in *boat* or *boot*
u as in *put* (short) or *moon* (long) — before 'r' the short 'u' is pronounced as in *fur*
(N.b. In the speech of the Sylphs long vowels are signified by a double letter)

Diphthongs:–

ai as in *sky* and *high* — not as in *fair, fear* or *say*
au as in *cow* — not as in *laud* or *lord*
ei as in *day* and *rain* — not as in *hair, hear* or *lie*
oi as in *coin*
ou as in *go* and *stone* — not as in *cow, rough* or *through*

Consonants:–

ch and sh — as in English
c (in Elvish and Fayish words only) — as English 's'
dh — the soft 'th' sound as in English *the* and *then*; not the hard 'th' sound of *thing* and *three*. 'Dh' should never be pronounced as 'd'.
g — always hard, as in English *get*
kh — as in Scottish *loch* or Welsh *bach* — an aspirated 'k' sound

zh — a softened 'sh' sound, as in English *azure*
(N.b. In the speech of the Sylphs trilled 'r' and hissed 's' have double letters)

Some Common Names

Aldel Morn	Al´ — del (short vowels) Morn (as English)
Andrai	An´ — dry (to rhyme with *fly*)
Belengar	Bel´ — en — gār
Dargul	Both vowels long, first syllable accented
Elandril	Ell — ān´ — drill (note the long 'a', accented)
Eldhoril	Ell´ — th (soft) — o (short) — rill (note the soft 'th' rather than 'd' sound)
Erathrir	E — rāth´ — reer (the initial 'e' is short as in *error*, the 'a' long)
Fandorel	All vowels short, including the 'o', which is accented
Fermilondath	Fair — mill — on´ — dath (short a)
Filindrin	Fill — in´ — drin (all vowels short)
Grathgel	Long 'a', accented; short 'e'
Iksalai	Ick — sāl´ — eye (long 'a', accented)
Iroi Girindhouz	I´ — roy Gi — rin´ — those (all the 'i' sounds are short)
Karandar	Ka — ran´ — dār (only the last vowel is long)
Khulgrakh	Chul´ — grāch ('u' short, 'a' long; both 'ch' sounds as in *loch*)
Kruakh	Crew´ — āch (long 'a'; 'ch' as in *loch*)
Melandir	Mell — and´ — eer
Misen Taïrail	Miss´ — en Tā´ — i (short) — rile (note that the first 'ai' combination is not a diphthong, but long 'a' followed by short 'i')
Niaherz	Nee´ — a (short) — hērts (e long as in *hair*, 'z' pronounced 'ts' as in *tsar* in this word in Black Speech)
Nyaroth Khrathril	Nya´ — roth ('ny' as in *banyan*; both vowels short) Chrāth´ — reel (long 'a', accented; 'ch' as in *loch*)
Ral	Short 'a'
Relnar	Rel´ — nār (short 'e', long 'a')

Sagoth	Sā´ — goth (pronounce more like Sar — goth than Say — goth)
Sart Emig	Long 'a', other vowels short, 'e' accented
Selenthoril	Sell — enth´ (hard 'th' sound) — o (short) — rill
Talak	Both vowels short, accent on the first
Talarnidh	Tal (short 'a') — ārn´ — ith (soft 'th' sound, *not* 'd')
Tasarnil	Tass — ārn´ — ill
Telmirandor	Tell — mi (short 'i') — rand´ — ōr
Tharang	Thār´ — ang (first 'a' long, second short)
Turnalordath	Turn—al (short 'a') — ōr´ — dath (short 'a')
Wenyaltrir	Wen — yalt´ — reer
Wenyorel	Wen — yo´ (as in *yon*) — rell (note the short 'o', accented)
Werendilren	We (as in *wet*) — ren — dill´ — ren (all vowels short)
Wirdrilded	Weer — drill´ — ded
Wondrith	Won´ — drith (note 'won' to rhyme with *gone, on* etc)
Yeselwir	Yess´ — ell — weer

Accented, or stressed, syllables have been indicated by an acute accent (´) after the last letter.

Sindle
Marnouf
Garmell
Sarmish
PELDEROUN
LOTHCHEN
Kōrngāl Point
Keseryeth
Adānyeth
Mt. Granyāsh
Mount Delemnādh
Castle of Selenthoril
Lake Khrāth emrin
Nyaroth Khrāthril
Mt. Kachadh
Giants' Castle
Cape Grudel
Mt. Rálnadh
Nal Vorod
Mount Rethrileth
ALĀT
Mount Parileth
The Dārgūl
Ir Angornyekh
Mt. Guldūrin
Glacier of Parileth
ALDEL MORN
The Dārgūl
Lerod Anth
Grāthgel
MELURIN
Ice Wastes
MORTHALN
The Island of
MISENTÄÏRAIL
or Helland Holme
Causeway of the Teeth

CHAPTER 1

FESTIVAL OF THE LAMPS

Under all the over-ripeness of a late choking autumn full of shrivelling heat and musty white decay, Iksalai of the Western Ocean spread its goldness in the morning sun. The high north waves of salt deceptive coolness mocked its sunburnt strand. Fat languid farmers leant on their gates weeks after harvest, or slept in the stubble fields like their beasts. Townsmen and villagers neglected their trades. The markets were loud only with flies, and the timbers of galleys and barques were warped as they lay in the ports. Only warm rain falling late on the enervated soil had saved the withered windless trees of bronze and sunshine gold.

Lethargy brooded over the shadow court of decayed and ruined Telmirandor and her exiled ageless princes. Only reflected glories of worm-eaten halls recalled her splendours, as ancient rituals distilled the sick sweet juice of faded time. The ghosts of kings looked on in sunny shrouds, and waited for their afterglow to end. An eternity was ending that summer, and worlds awaited the winter coldness to come.

The Festival of the Lamps was due, and the anniversary of the Dragon Slaying. Old men looking back remembered Werendilren the Fair and the Mighty. They remembered the Festivals of the Lamps they had seen, every hundred years, back into the past. For the Peiri, the men of the High Race, were nearly immortal. Once they had ruled the world, and did so no longer. A few still lived who remembered the Garden of Eternity. They had seen the making of the High Kingdom and the Nine Realms, and the eternal struggle with Sagoth, Son of the Morning. Others remembered only the great years of power and Empire. Some could not remember beyond the long season of exile and faded splendour on the island. But all had fought against Ral, the Witch Queen. All had heard, in the War of the Sceptres, the echoes of the ancient might of Wenyaltrir.

In Iksalai was still a Prince of Wenyaltrir. After all the wars, after the reign of the Black Lords, and the returning might of the Sceptres, Talarnidh, son of the Emperor, lived on, the rightful lord of all the tottering remains and cold unearthly ruins of Telmirandor, lost realm of Wenyaltrir. In Talarnidh and in the lords of the High Race, in their replica court in the humble halls of Alban, the elder glories remained. The High Race was lessened and few, but Wenyaltrir lived. Her ceremonies still recalled the dusts of long ago.

The Festival of the Lamps was a ceremony as timeless as the rituals of life. In the old days in Werendilren, in the age of the Empire of Telmirandor, and then in the times of war and darkness, and finally in exile and decline, the Festival had come and gone, once in every century, commemorating forever that first day of the High Race in the Garden of Eternity. Then the Nine Kings and the Nine Queens, and the High King and the High Queen, bearing the Jewels of the World Tree, had kindled the myriad lamps of the High Race, newly created in wonder. That first shining procession, giving thanks for their birth in their birthplace, had wound on through the centuries. Once the kings of the world had walked barefoot in vast concourse and kindled the Royal Fire within their lamps. Still from the realms of the Northlands came emissaries to the Festival on Iksalai. The splendours were not wholly forgotten, as the princes of newer kingdoms paid homage to Talarnidh's lineage, though no more to his power.

From Sindoris, Queen of Azantul, nearest land to Iksalai, came two ships bearing five lords of that land. Each of the princes of Alnaron, saving only dark Gurmol, had sent ten knights. And from Chamley, between the forest and the mountains, the king had sent his son, the young prince Relnar, descendant in true line of Jaran, dark-skinned warrior of the south. After the Festival Relnar was to stay and serve as squire in Alban. To represent Amray came one of the merchant princes of her great city, Zerakhtror. He told of a fleet following under the city's victorious admiral, Andrai, charged to make treaties with the westward realms. From the new kingdom of Melatin, strong in men and wealth, came the king's justiciar, and from Iriel far away on the shores of the Sea of Mlindolorou came one of the sons of her viceroy.

In Morena, river realm of the desert, reigned Parvaloril of the High Race, son of one of the Nine Kings of Wenyaltrir. After the War of the Sceptres he had restored the kingdom of his father, and strengthened the ancient alliance with the Elvenkind. When the fury of the cruel new Empire of Drarkh swept out of the south, Morena became a refuge for those who fled. It became a land of Elves and Dwarves and Men alike, mingled together and united under one king of the Peiri. To the Festival of the Lamps the lords of Morena came. Fandorel and Wondrith brought their ships, winged lords of the Elven race, skilled with bow and spear, great in song. It was they who had saved Parvaloril in the years of exile, and brought him to the woods of the Elves whose armies he was soon to lead. They alone of all those at the Festival remembered the Time Before Time, for they were of the Old Elves, almost the last of their kind, that came through the Gateway To Time from the place of Zehrvan. Wondrith was a great wizard, one of the few among the Elves, while Fandorel was the greatest of the Elven archers that still dwelt in the world. In the third ship of Morena came Karandar, but he was not its captain. For he was a Dwarf, and Dwarves do not love the sea. Karandar was sturdy, firm of will and resolution. He had pitted his sinew against the rock as a prisoner of Ral, and freely in the deep halls of the Dwarves. All three, Karnadar, Wondrith, and Fandorel, had been of the Immortals, the Sacred Band, that had guarded the Emperor of Telmirandor. Karandar had been the closest friend of the Emperor at the very end, in the downfall of Werendilren, and was the last to see him alive, after all the rest had gone. The Dwarf Lord had ever been in the closest councils of the Peiri.

Other guests also sat down at the high table in the stone and wooden palace of Hirenon in the port of Samain on Alban, called Iksalai of the High Race. There also was Tasarnil the One-Eyed. He was one of the thousand sons of the King of the Sun, who guard the Gates of the Sun in the meadows of the East of East, where one of the ways to Heaven lies. When the fleeing lords of Wenyaltrir returned from the Overworld to the Midworld, they came first to this land of Kourala, where the sun rises. Two of the Sons of the Sun guided their band to settled lands. For this, the enemy of the High Race, Ral the Witch Queen, lay an awful curse upon the two, by which (men thought) one of the two brothers was slain. But Tasarnil survived, and was accounted strange and fearful. For the Sons of the Sun have but one golden eye, set in the middle of their forehead, as if it were the mark of the sun. Tasarnil was the only one of his people abroad in the world of men, and the Peiri and the Elves had long welcomed him in their halls.

Beside him was Relnar, king's son of Chamley, and on his left sat Filindrin. Filindrin was a man of Alban. Yet he had been born years without count beyond the memory of any living man of the islanders. The tale is told how, with Talarnidh's help, in the times of tumult after the War of the Sceptres, Filindrin was led to the Deepest Well, where he drank of the Waters of Life. Thus he gained immortality, and had ever been as one with the High Race. But he often travelled from their halls into the unknown, nor any knew whither he journeyed.

At Talarnidh's right was a man known to few of the guests, save by name and repute. He spoke little, yet often the eyes of the great lords fell upon him. This was Melandir, which means 'Angel of the Sword'. A man of unknown race or father, he was fabled to have come from beyond the heavens, from the Outer Worlds whence none return.

Fermilondath and Turnalordath were also there. Lords of the High Race and, like the lords of Morena, warriors of the Sacred Band, they had taken a great part in the aiding of the young Prince Talarnidh in the days of the downfall of Empire and the centuries of ruin. They were brothers, and born of the second generation of the High Race in the founding years when they had left the garden of their origin. Time had aged them differently across that vastness of years. Fermilondath had long been a mighty warrior, famed for his valour. Yet many times he would have rushed to certain gainless death had it not been for the hand of his younger brother. Turnalordath had grown in unchanging honour to equal his brother. He was content to rule his simple folk from wooden palaces, while his beloved prince reigned over him. Fermilondath saw only the splendour humbled, and the greatness made a mockery. All men held him in awe. Yet the bond between the two brothers was such that it could not be broken.

Among all the lords of Alban and the princes and knights of the Northlands only to one emissary, that came from Drarkh, were the doors barred. For the great and conquering power of Drarkh had spread its cruel empire into the Northlands. It seemed that Drarkh was become the new enemy of hope, and faced by its power men forgot the old witch of the northernmost forests, that men call the Forest of Sorcery. The watch on the

Hills of the North grew weak, as all eyes turned south to the menace of Drarkh.

Wide thrown were the oaken doors bronze-bound, and into the great hall streamed the surging crowds as the smoky torches were quenched at the sunrise. The people of Alban paid momentary homage to their lords. Then they turned to the breakfast feast. The palace was theirs to make free of. Sweating servants rolled in endless rows of ale tuns, and jovial farmers helped in the bearing of piles of meat from the steamy kitchens till the hall was decked with food and drink to gorge an army. The palace of Hirenon was filled with laughter as the morning passed in revelry and mirth. Only the twenty-seven lords who sat at the raised table were constant. They ate little of the foods set before them and seemed silent as the throng seethed all around. And now the wanderers in the palace and the orchards and the gardens and courtyards were steadily trickling into the great hall. The casks of ale were renewed and most of the mass of people sat down or sprawled themselves about the floor so that the hall was filled to overflowing and latecomers crowded the doors. The High Steward was about to rise, his white rod held ready for silence, and for the second part of the Festival. Three times he smote on the floor and cried:

'The morning of the Festival is done. Be still for Talarnidh, great Prince of Wenyaltrir and Telmirandor, that he may ordain the Telling of Tales.'

The silence in a moment was complete. For the custom was that one of the lords of Wenyaltrir would tell a tale, and until it was told the Festival of the Lamps should not proceed. Often in the past it had been a tale of the ancient days from the long chronicles of the High Race or the Elves, but in this, the twelfth Festival on Alban, there would be a difference.

Talarnidh spoke:

'Subjects and Lords of Telmirandor, it is decreed that this day there shall be a Telling of Tales, as there has been and will be, that the rite of the Festival of the Lamps be fulfilled. Arise and hail, Lord Melandir, for it is thine to speak, and thine alone.'

And so Melandir rose, and told this tale.

CHAPTER 2

THE STORY OF MELANDIR

My tale is of how I came from one of the Outer Worlds, in sombre space, the way no man had trod, to Tharang in the world of Faerie, first-created of all worlds. I have known strange adventures and seen far wonders. Strike a quiet note, harper, for I tell of things unheard before, and now my tale begins.

There were three of us who sailed south in those days when I dwelt in the Outer Worlds. That was in the days before I won this sword and with it the name Melandir. My companions I will call Erathrir and Yeselwir, for those were the names they were given on our journey. The ship of steel bore us across the ocean to a city on the coast of the white sands in a land of few cities. We stayed only long enough to hire a guide and bearers before setting off again towards the shadowy mountains and far-echoing jungles.

At first all went well, but our path was little-frequented and soon the farms and fields were fewer, until we were walking through a grassy emptiness inhabited only by lank cattle. After a few such easy days there were more trees. The greenery became lusher, and there were a myriad insects as we entered the dank green shadows of the forest. Noises were all around us, and the air was full of abrupt shrieks and distant wailing cries. Trailing creepers, as thick as a man's thigh, hung across our way, while luxuriant undergrowth spread in wild profusion out of the slimy earth to clog and tangle the air with rotting greenness. All the while great green insects flew about us on heavy wings, phantoms in the half-light haze, and tiny mindless mites feasted on our flesh.

We became lost, and in that pathless world misfortune followed us. Four of our bearers fled with what they could steal, and then most of our remaining baggage was lost in a wide and treacherous marsh. Our guide urged us to go back but we would not. Then he and the others left us and we were alone. We stifled in the heat and clinging dampness. We wandered without direction.

Our food was gone and there was no pure water. Every day we grew weaker, and nearer death.

When all hope had gone we saw sunlight again through the trees. We pushed through the undergrowth and stood in the open in the morning sun. We found to our wonder a spring of untainted water, and only after we had drunk our fill did we look about us. Behind, the forest ended abruptly near the brow of a low ridge on which stood a line of rocks spaced huge and black against the sky as if they held back the forest. Sloping down before us the land was wide and clear to see, glistening with brilliant colours as if newly-created. A breath of wind blew on our faces and it somehow carried a faint suggestion of the seaweed smell of ocean's shore. Then the air became still, but it held a silence of expectancy, as if that place had been made for that moment.

Talking and laughing we followed the stream. Almost unnoticed it became a river, and on its bank grew flowers and stately trees. We found fruit in abundance as if from all lands and all climes growing there together. We ate, and found everything sweet and ripe and more sustaining than we had ever known before. Days passed in that land, where we walked slowly through shady groves and grassy meads by riverside, and our lost strength returned. Eventually the river flowed into a great lake, where none was charted, more blue and brilliant than any waters I have seen. In its middle was an island, and misty in the distance beyond it we could just make out the farther shore. When we swam in the waters it seemed that the pains and vileness of the jungles were washed from us.

The day after we came upon the lake we found a boat moored hard by the shore. It was golden in colour and made of metal, yet in the form of timbers, as if the planks themselves had been turned into heavy gold. There were no sails nor oars, nor even a rudder. Yet under the deck-boards we found cloaks and jerkins, clothes such as the sailor of Alban might wear. They served us better than our own tattered rags. But as we changed our clothes aboard the boat, the vessel gave a lurch and rocked in the gentle swell. When we looked over the side we saw all around us the wide flat blueness of an unbroken sheet of water. The shore where the boat had been moored was gone as if it had never been.

Far ahead was the island, and it was as distant from us now

as when we had first seen it from the land. Our vessel was moving over the waters, for its bow furrowed the surface and its wake was racing behind us. Yet, though we eagerly watched the island, it drew no nearer, though the hours went by and though we rushed through the waters. The sun remained unmoving at the same spot in the sky. Fear welled up inside us. In the very brightness of the day and the clear waters that sped by us we felt something older and stranger. We fled on unmoving in the unearthly brilliance of a sea of silence. An endless age went by as we crossed the unknowing ocean.

At last a speck of darkness moved in the changeless sky, coming from behind. Now it was above, circling around and about and falling, an albatross, storm-winged and grey on the unbearable brightness. Then it was at our bow, moving forward and flinging the air in our faces with its massive wings. Faster and faster it flew, and faster our boat sped after it. A wind roared about us and storm clouds scudded above. The sun was sinking blood-coloured in the sea behind us. Darkness fell and the gold of the ship rang upon stone.

We slept that night in the deep sedges on the hillside of the island. The next day revealed it as a land like that we had left behind, a wide place of woods and orchards and grassy meadows, all rising to a single central hill. The hill was crowned with a single tower, a hundred feet high and thirty feet about. It was perfectly made of smooth stone with no sign of gaps or mortar. From the farthest horizon, and now through all the sky, came a great light, but there was no sign of the sun rising. We climbed the hill until we stood at the base of the tower. Beyond the island we saw the waters stretching away as far as we could see, but we could not see the land we had come from, nor yet the farther shore of the lake. For the lake was now an empty sea.

From the base of the tower there flowed a spring, running straight and swift and silent down the hill. When we saw its waters we realised our thirst, and Yeselwir at once knelt down to drink. But even as he raised his cupped hands to his mouth there came a great wind blowing through the trees, and a voice spoke to us out of the tower, saying:

'This is the Drink the Gods Desire. Do not touch these waters!'

Its words, I think, were not in our own tongue; they were in that tongue which is now called by men the Sorcerers' Speech, which is the first speech of Men in all the worlds. Then I knew nothing of that, nor had any of us heard that language before. Yet we understood the words that were spoken to us, and from that time we spoke in that tongue amongst ourselves; also the Twenty Great Tongues of Tharang were implanted in our minds from that moment. We could not forget them, and we spoke them as if we had known them from birth.

We stood in amazement and disbelief. We were afraid, and talked much of the thing, but our thirst grew, and the lake around was salt. Yeselwir finally knelt again, and from cupped hands drank from the spring. He started to rise, then fell to the ground. Erathrir and I ran towards him but as we stooped to pick him up he whispered:

'Sleep! The Drink the Gods Desire . . . Sleep!'

And so he fell into the deepest sleep. As we stood by him the same voice spoke again:

'One has drunk of the Drink the Gods Desire. Now he shall sleep. Yeselwir is his name. It means: "He who will die in Tharang". In Tharang he will sleep forever.'

The voice ceased, and we saw that a door, till then invisible, had silently opened in the base of the tower. There was little we could do for Yeselwir. We entered the tower, and found there only stone steps, spiralling upwards. We started to climb the stairway. The light was left behind but we chose to go on, feeling our way by touch. Round and round we climbed until our legs were weary and our minds dazed. Far below now we could see the dim light of the doorway we had entered, but above was only blackness. It was as if the dark windings went on for ever and ever. I cannot tell why we did not go back. It always seemed that at any moment we must reach the top. But inside its walls it was as if that tower went on through all eternity.

Almost when hope had passed, Erathrir felt cold stone over his head. The endless stair had ended. We pushed with all our strength against the stone until the slab lifted and fell crashing over. We stumbled out into daylight. Our eyes blinked in the light, but when we could see again we looked back at the stairway we had climbed for so long. We saw the last few stairs slowly crumble into tiny grains of dust and fall grey and smokelike into the darkness below. Our way back was gone.

In the shock we turned our eyes from the stairwell to the summit of the tower. It was flat, open and unprotected. All around was only the air. Cautiously we went to the edge of the tower. We lay flat and gazed over. We looked into an abyss. Below us were clouds. They parted, tossed by the winds, and as if through a haze of blue-black light we saw the rim of the world. The spinning orb was patterned with oceans and approaching night as the sun tracked blood behind it. Somehow the tower had grown or stretched till it reached to the edge of the void, and the air was suddenly cold and fiery in our lungs.

'I offer you the Drink that Men Desire', said the voice again, — behind us as we squirmed back from the dizzying heights. A man now stood on the tower with us. I can recall little of how he chose to appear to us then, though I knew him again afterwards. I can only say that we were afraid. We understood little, in an unknown place. The man held a thin-necked bottle of blood-red liquid. Erathrir, my companion, took it. I did not. He drank, cried out a fearful cry, and fell at my feet. The man unknown said:

'He has tasted the Drink that Men Desire. This is Knowledge. He has seen all eternity in a moment. When he awakes he will not remember, lest he should die. But days will come, and one day above all. Then, on those days and on that day, he will need knowledge. His name is Erathrir, "Seeker after Truth". He will be the Guide through the Final Darkness. Leave him now with me. You must go on.'

Though I can describe nothing of what befell on that tower, I can yet recall every word that the man unknown spoke to me then. And now, as he spoke to me, he pointed outwards into the void beyond the tower. Somehow — I do not know how — I walked, halting and stumbling, fearful as a child, by my own choice, out into the empty air. As I stepped from the tower I felt it shake and the stones crack and split then fall away. And I was alone, stood in the air and the whiteness.

There was one thing only to be seen. A sword buried deep in a great stone. The part of the blade I could see glinted dully, as did the hilt, and about it were set jewels, red, blue and green crystals of great size and brilliance. Around the blade was coiled a sword-belt of black leather studded with gold, and a long sable scabbard hung from it. A great cold was on my limbs. The heavens seemed alive about me. I walked forward, took the sword belt, and buckled it around my waist. The blood within me beat on my senses and I felt a moment of great choice upon me. The universe swayed, and stars moaned in the wind. The great jewels of the sword flashed together, dragon eyes, ice-blue, fire-red. I pulled once upon the sword and it quivered in the stone. I pulled again and the stone trembled. A third time I pulled, and power flowed within me, — a third time and the sword was mine. Free from the stone it was glistening upraised in my hand.

I looked up, holding the sword. Behind me was the sun. Before was my world, among the stars. I stood in space and gazed out. As I watched a change came over the face of the world. In the northern lands the clouds became black, and blacker with every minute. They spread apace, billowing high and cutting off the sun. There were sparks among them, gusting into the sky, sudden points of red, seen briefly then lost. But soon came more, spreading far and wide in the north and south alike. Lurid fires now shone through. Destruction rained on the world, and cities fell and crumbled into the burning dust. The winds were of fire, the forests blazed, and the seas ran black with blood. I saw the smokes of the funeral pyres blend into one.

I cannot tell how long I watched as the blackness spread over the world and the long night began. My world lay dark in the dark of the void. The sun shone on my back, and my knuckles were white as I gripped the sword hilt. Beyond time, the darkness deepened. The sun was gone, and I felt a bitter chill. In the coldness I looked out past my dead forgotten home. The stars were going out. One by one the lights vanished until all were gone and the night was utter and absolute. Alone in evernight I cried out, then fell into the folds of darkness.

When my sense slowly returned, I felt that a very long while, an immensity of time, had passed. I was bemused and without clear understanding and, though I remembered with perfect clarity all that I had seen, at first I wondered if it had all been dream and illusion. For I lay on a low homely couch in a sparsely-furnished room. Sunlight flooded in through a wide unglazed window. I rose, and saw that the sword hung on the wall. The sword belt lay near it, and the clothes we had found in the Golden Ship. I knew now it had been no dream, and the memory was a cold heaviness within me.

I dressed myself, buckled on the sword (for it seemed right to do so) and went out from the room into the open air. Beyond stately groves and meadowland I saw water, as far as the eye could see. I walked round the house. Now, on a hilltop, I could see a tower — or rather the stump of a tower, with its stonework broken and blackened and ruins about it. I had no doubt that it was the tower I had climbed with a man named Erathrir.

I turned back to the house, and saw that a man now stood at the door awaiting me. He wore similar clothes to mine, and his hair and beard were white and his face marked by age. Yet his eyes were young and alive. He seemed ageless, and I felt I had known him for all my life. He bade me eat with him and while we ate he answered all I wished to know and told me much more beside. His name in the Northspeech is Ask, and in the Peirian tongue of Wenyaltrir it is Padhpadir. He is the Allfather, the first man that ever was of all Men.

He told me how for immemorial years he had guarded that island, which is called the Island of the Stars. It is the gateway from the Midworld to the Outer Worlds in space. For the Midworld is in Faerie, first of all worlds, where the Garden of Eternity lies, and which is held up by the World Tree. Yet between Faerie and the Outer Worlds lie the Sundering Seas. I learnt that many had passed that way in the Ship of Gold to people the Outer Worlds, pausing only at the island-in-between, called the Island of the Stars. There are people who dwell on the island, — those who over the years have been lost in the waves of the Sundering Seas. They live there forever, called the Children of the Sea, and Ask is their lord.

And now Ask spoke of his sons and their sons through a myriad generations, who had gone out among the stars from the Midworld. But this he told me also: that three men alone, of all the men created, were destined to return that way. Two of them he had already sent on their way to Tharang the Midworld. They were my companions, Erathrir and Yeselwir. I was the third and the last. He told me that I would be named Melandir when I came to Tharang. This had been ordained since the worlds began. The name means: 'Angel of the Sword'.

I was glad that my comrades had not died. I questioned Ask whether all that I had seen was real or unreal. But it was all true. He told me that the Island of the Stars is beyond all worlds yet in them all. Yet now the Outer Worlds were falling, and I had seen, with true sight, their stars burn out. For Sagoth, Son of the Morning, great avatar of evil, had come from the Outer Darkness, beyond time and space. He had entered the universe, and his coming had broken the balance that held it together. The stars were dying, and only Faerie remained. Now the Sundering Seas would lead out from the centre only into darkness. And the Island of the Stars would stand on the edge of Evernight.

Then Ask bade me shew him the great sword. On its blade of iron he read its name, Wenyorel, though I could see no letters there. And that in the High Speech means: 'The Sword of Fate'. He told me that while I bear this sword I can suffer no bodily harm, for it is an enchanted blade, and this is its history:

The sword was the sword of Talmond, Emperor of Telmirandor. It came into the world when he came, and of its origin no tale is told, save that it is said to come from before time and beyond creation.

At the time of its coming, Sagoth, Prince of Darkness, dwelt in Tharang, and he bore the Sword of Doom, twin of this sword. The Nine Kings could not contend with the fullness of his power, and they called on the Mendoral, sprung from the very World Tree, as the High Race had called before. It was in answer to their call that Talmond came, and he bore Wenyorel, the Sword of Fate.

Its bearer can suffer no hurt or harm, and it has given me immortality, even as the Peiri are immortal. It is forged of iron, harder than steel or diamond. When Talmond brought it, it was unadorned, but the Nine Kings of Wenyaltrir each placed in its hilt a jewel of great worth. Talmond also placed here on the crosspiece a Star Sapphire, alike to the stone of the ring of the old High King. That ring also was given to Talmond, for the High Race held these jewels to be the royal stones of their people, and the stone of the ring of the old High King was a stone of destiny.

For a hundred years the Emperor led the High Race in war against Sagoth. The Prince of Darkness fled to the Northlands and his grim holds of Aldel Morn. The High Race know of the evil that befell in that time thereafter when Sagoth came to another Festival of the Lamps long ago. It is a bitter tale nor will I tell it here. But Sagoth fought with Talmond, Sword of Doom to Sword of Fate. Long was their battle and much in doubt, until the power of the Sceptres was put forth. Then Sagoth rose up in all his power and majesty, but in the moment of his glory, when the union of Sceptres was sundered, then Talmond clove him with the Sword of Fate. By this sword fell

Sagoth, Son of the Morning, and his spirit fled away from this world and all worlds, out to the Outer Darkness.

He left behind him the Sword of Doom. The High Race could not destroy it, for it is made of the same stuff as my sword and there is no power to break this iron. But they sheathed it, and bound it to its sheath by spells. Even so, it was Sagoth's sword and the evil remained. Though sheathed, it became Ral's sword, and she was the ruin of the High Race. For after the great years of Empire came the rebellion of Ral. She it was who marred the wholeness of the moon and spread renewed evils over the earth. Though she was defeated once, yet her power and guile increased and the High Race did not know that she deceived them. She came again with the Black Lords. Werendilren was ruined, and Telmirandor downthrown. Talmond went down to the vaults of the dead, and was never seen more. His sword and ring passed out of the knowledge of men.

But from Ask I learnt how a man came to him in those years on the Island of the Stars. He brought with him the Sword of Fate that he set in the stone beyond the ancient tower. He brought also the ring of the old High King and the Imperial Standard of Wenyaltrir. The ring and the standard were given over to Ask himself. He was told that soon three men would come back from the Outer Worlds, whence none came ever before. One would not ascend the tower. To him Ask was commanded to give the standard, and the name Yeselwir. Another would ascend the tower and would take from him at its summit a certain drink. To him Ask was commanded to give the ring of the old High King, and the name Erathrir. The third would draw the Sword of Fate from its stone. Ask did not know, or would not tell, what manner of man it was who bade him do all this, but it was done. And so the Sword of Fate, the sword that has the power to banish Sagoth, has returned.

This then is the history of the great sword. It is also in part the tale of the ancient ring and of Talmond, father of Talarnidh, who bore both sword and ring. I have told that part of the tale because it is close to the hearts of the men of the High Race who dwell in the halls of the Emperor's son.

Much more I learnt from Ask, and the long bright day of the island wore on, brilliant yet lit by no sun, unless it was the myriad suns of the Outer Worlds that even then were dying as I had seen them. The time came to depart. The Golden Ship stood by the shore of the Sundering Seas. The Children of the Sea came down, and threw the fragrant flowers of the island into the ship. One last thing Ask, the Allfather, told me. He said that my companions, called Erathrir and Yeselwir in the High Speech of the Peiri, had already been borne to the Midworld. But though they sailed before me, and the ship had already returned, the journey across the Sundering Seas is a journey through time where its currents flow strange. For me that boat sailed swifter and I came here to Alban five years before my companions should ever arrive. Today is five years since that day. I wonder yet if the Golden Ship will sail into Alban from the stars and bring them to me.

There, as I boarded the boat on the island, the light was fading. The boat rocked on the waves and then I was cast loose on the Sundering Seas. In that moment night fell and I saw the island no more. I felt the motion and speed of the vessel. The sky was utterly dark above me, the waters a void beneath. I lay down in the bed of flowers and slept. Behind me, my long-lost home receded further into the mists of memory and distance.

I do not know how long I lay unconscious, for when I awoke the boat still sailed that sea of darkness. Yet now I felt a vague unease, and there seemed to be chill currents and eddies in the air, with unknowable odours upon them. Then there came a great rushing sound and the beat of vast unearthly wings upon the wind. I saw a shape coming from behind in a torrent of speed. The heavens were grey around it as it flew formless like a grim winding sheet blown across the sky. A dull sheen rippled on it, like a fluid thick with oils, red, blue, green and shining black. As it came over me I crouched in the ship and gripped the sword.

I looked up into a form of unutterable terror. Choking fetor hung about it, and its monstrous colours blended into a vile darkness, with only fiery eyes that pierced the night and gazed upon me with hideous desire. It was such a creature that to look upon it alone was torment. I do not know whether it truly saw me. It flew on, fainter and dwindling. A shrieking sound, shrill with many screams, followed it. I had no doubt that I had seen something from Hell, and I sat long awake and trembling before I could sleep again. The creature was that which men name Sagoth. I saw him flying to Faerie.

When I could finally sleep again my peace was unbroken for

a long long time. It was the sound of the keel on the ringing rocks that woke me, — that and the light. A moon, larger than I had ever seen, and bluish white, hung over me. Its light was on the long sea spaces behind, and inland, before me, was the moving darkness of sable woods between the moon-struck hills. I took my sword in my hand and climbed over the side of the Golden Ship onto the shores of Faerie across the Sundering Seas.

I walked up the hillside through sedges and groves where the sea smell mingled with the scents of my new home. On the hilltop I gazed out to sea. Gold on the silver sea, my ship was drifting away. Far in the distance it slowed, and without sound or shock settled in the waves. The bow dipped into the foam. Silently the Golden Ship sank into the sea and was gone. The last link was broken.

The rest of my tale is well-known to most in this hall. Walking among the fragrant pines searching for the first man I might meet on Tharang, I heard the clash and uproar of a deadly struggle. I came upon a wide clearing in a cleft in the hills. I found there the Lord Turnalordath, assailed by a Dragon and fighting for his life. He had gone there alone by night to fight the beast, Kirnoun, in his lair under Wyrmlow, whence none had returned since the Dragon awoke. The people of Drakedale had called on their lord, and Turnalordath had gone up to do battle.

I came on him sore beset. My hand went to the sword hilt and the blade seemed to spring uncalled to my hand. In the light of the Dragon flames it flashed redly. The beast was huge, coiling between the tree trunks and smashing down branches with its tail. Already the small figure of the armoured man had twice assailed its green and scaly hide, only to be flung back by the whipping tail. Then Turnalordath fell, and the massive snout was over him on its arched neck, with dripping flames all about its flickering tongue.

I raced forward and thrust at the jaws as the head darted down. The blade entered its mouth, and the Dragon blood gushed. The creature reared, and fire went about me. I did not die, as any mortal man would have died. I felt no pain. The words of Ask were proved true. The bearer of the Sword of Fate can suffer no harm while he wields it. Again and again I wounded the creature. It was as if my sword could pierce any armour. It died with a thrust through the eye into its brain, rearing up and then crashing back among the ruined trees.

Turnalordath and I came safe back to his folk who awaited afar off. He brought me then to the Prince, and to high honour in Alban of the High Race. Every year since then, that is for five years, we have celebrated the anniversary of the Dragon Slaying. This year it falls by chance upon the day of a greater festival, for today it is the Festival of the Lamps. At the last, then, I leave this thought with you all, to bring my tale full circle:

It is five years since I sailed away from the Island of the Stars. Yet the Golden Ship had already carried my comrades away to Tharang before me. Ask told me that it would bear them five years into the future. If his words are fulfilled, as all his other words have been, today is the day that Erathrir and Yeselwir will come to Faerie from the Outer Worlds.

CHAPTER 3

LAST OF THE BLACK LORDS

It was a journey of five years past that Melandir remembered in his tale at the Festival of the Lamps, five years to the day since he saw the Ship of Gold sink. Yet the paths of time are strange in the Sundering Seas. Before ever the ship bore Melandir to Alban, it steered a different course to Faerie Tharang. Faster than the rushing years it sailed, and from the Island of the Stars it carried two men from the Outer Worlds. Only three would ever make that journey. Erathrir and Yeselwir were the first. Melandir would be the last. Faster than time the Ship of Gold sailed, till it reached the shores of Nyaroth Khrathril, called Enchanter's Isle, bearing Erathrir and Yeselwir. Then it would sail back through time to bear Melandir to Alban.

Erathrir stood up, and peered over the side of the Golden Ship. The great pale blueness of the sea was almost white, and somewhere unknown it merged with the silver sky. Erathrir revolved in his mind all that Ask had told to him and to Yeselwir. He knew that somewhere far away his friend, now named Melandir, trod a dangerous path. He wondered how Melandir fared, while he and Yeselwir were carried, as Ask had foretold, across the Sundering Seas to Tharang, the Midworld, in Faerie. His old life had already gone, and the new seemed strange and only half real. Faerie he knew of from the tales of Ask, but though its light was already in him, and its tongues were his tongue, yet it was not his home.

A whole day they had listened to the Allfather, and he had told them of the world that was to be theirs. Then he had given Erathrir a token, a silver ring set with one star sapphire, the ring of the old High King. And then at last Ask had led the two down to the shore among the Sea Children, and watched as they sailed away. Erathrir thought of many things until, as he stood, the brightness became too much for his eyes, and he lay down again and at once slept. The boat sped on, unknown to space and time, until it entered Faerie far away.

The next time Erathrir awoke, it was with a sudden start. Something had changed. Yeselwir was already looking about, wide awake.

'What is it?' he asked.

Erathrir could see one difference. The utter light of the island and the Sundering Seas had gone and the sky was now draped with gloom. He paused a moment before the realisation came to him.

'We're not moving,' he cried.

They had come to Faerie Tharang.

'So, somehow we have arrived,' said Yeselwir. Then, hoisting himself onto the gunwale of the ship, he dropped over the side. There was a splash, and muddy water flew up. Erathrir followed him more cautiously, climbing over near the bow. He brought with him the rolled and wrapped bundle given by Ask to Yeselwir — the Imperial Standard of Wenyaltrir.

Stretching before them almost to the horizon was the marsh, a vast brown-green expanse of mud, interspersed with stagnant pools linked by brackish canals. Even the turbid water was the same brown as the mud. Thin sickly-green plants straggled and clustered, and tufts of half-dead grass floated rootless amidst decaying hulks of long-foundered trees. In the distance the marsh gave way to a pallid sheet of water, its surface unbroken by any ripple. The air was wholly still, without a breeze to stir the limp marsh plants or scatter the palpable stench of decay. Overhead, an unbroken mass of dark cloud warned of approaching night. All around, the surrounding waters merged into a grey mountain of mist. There inside the mists nothing moved. In the brooding stillness it was as if nothing had ever breathed that air before from the beginning of time. The two men were alone and suddenly afraid. It was thickly and damply cold. They shivered.

'This is Tharang', said Yeselwir. 'A world of the dead. This is not what Ask described . . '

'The Golden Ship brought us here,' answered Erathrir. 'Yes, — this is Tharang.'

He paused, uncertain. Now both realised that Ask had said nothing of what they were to do. There had been many tales, but little advice. They bore a ring and a standard as tokens, but they did not know of what, or for whom.

'If we board the ship again, it might carry us on,' said Yeselwir.

'No', Erathrir answered. 'Look over there.'

He pointed and, some distance away from them, still half hidden by the ship, they saw a tall structure built on a low hill, the only feature amidst the marshland.

'A castle,' said Yeselwir. 'Three miles away, maybe a little more. Do we make our way there?'

'I think we have to,' Erathrir replied. 'I have a feeling we are on an island, and most of it seems desolate. It also seems to be surrounded by mists. The one thing assured is that if there is any life here it has to be in that castle. So we have no other choice — whatever we find does live there.' He smiled. The gloom and foreboding of that place had not yet dampened the unreasoned happiness left over from the Island of the Stars.

'It is becoming darker fast,' he said, looking up at the gathering clouds. 'We had best hurry.' Yeselwir also looked up, and shivered once again.

'Of course. Come on, we don't want to be caught out here in the night and we need to move fast while we can still see where we are going.'

They started out eagerly towards the castle. After a while Erathrir turned to look for a last time at the Golden Ship. The mud beach lay empty and cold. His eyes swung up and looked out over the water. Everywhere was the sightless wall of mist, and there, sailing into the greyness, very small yet still bright as the sun, was the Ship of Gold that had borne them so far.

'Look, Yeselwir, the ship,' said Erathrir quietly. Yeselwir stood and looked for a long while.

'Now we are alone,' he muttered.

'We have been alone for a long time really,' Erathrir answered. The ship grew more indistinct, fading into the horizon of mists until it was gone. The Island of the Stars now seemed worlds away. The desolation pressed more heavily on them, as their eyes strained after a last glimpse of gold in the greyness.

Without another word they turned and walked on. No breath of wind disturbed the air and the clammy mist from the outside rolled in upon the swamp, closing them in more and more and adding to the gloom of darkening night. The two figures trudged across the clinging slime. For an hour or more they went on and the night was complete, with no moon or stars to break the cloud. Mist now spread about them and the cold had become deep and penetrating. Their direction became more uncertain and all the while a great fear of the unseen waste was growing on them.

They feared the unknown, but they feared more than that. For both men felt that something evil was there, — near to them.

Not far away, as it rose from the marsh, the creature sensed them. Deep within it there stirred an age-old hatred, a desire for killing. The Khulgrakh, the marsh monster from the darknesses of the past, reared its massive bulk erect and tore at the curtains of mist with the great curved sabres of its claws. It sensed that enemies were near, for all life was its enemy. It stood still for a moment, silent and searching, — then it smelt out the men.

A soulless wailing cry burst from its throat, hollow sounding in the mist, filling the island. The cry of death and battle rose to a shriek, and then stopped. The monster began to run. Now, after long years of sleep since the Black Lords' fall, it sought again to fulfill its ancient purpose. For it was created only to kill.

The two men stood transfixed by its cry, unprotected on the bleak marshes of an alien world. In each there welled up a nameless terror. Loping soundlessly across the marsh, the Khulgrakh came upon them. It towered over them, darker than the surrounding night, hideous and shapeless in its immensity. Its noisome stink enveloped them with untold ages of death and putrefaction in the swamp. For one timeless moment the monster stood poised for the kill, its claws high, its jaws showering fluid. The talons slashed down. Both men cried out, stumbling away from death on the muddy ground. Their voices were lost in the echoing roar.

But the roar was cut short. A beam of fire shone out of the darkness into the monster. Its outline grew indistinct and shimmered, surrounded by a pale glow. The black form diminished before their eyes. Then, enveloped in a curtain of light, it was gone, — not consumed but utterly vanished away. A sorcerous fire danced for a moment and then disappeared. Erathrir and Yeselwir slowly and uncertainly stood up. The nearness of death and the horrible suddenness of the attack had left them weak and trembling. The poisonous stench of the creature still hung in the air.

'Come on,' said Erathrir at length. 'We are still alive, and there is something here trying to keep us alive. We have to reach that castle. It cannot be too far now. We've come a good way.'

Yeselwir nodded dumbly. Almost in a daze they continued walking. They were already caked with icy mud and their falls were frequent. The way was treacherous, but at last the ground became firmer and then began to rise, leaving the marsh behind. As they climbed the mist lessened and the air grew clear, until they could see the sombre structure soaring above them. No glimmer of light came from the castle. The land lay silent far and wide. Below swirled the sea of mist. They ploughed wearily on as the ground became steeper still, and the hill proved higher than they had thought. They were tired and hungry as well as bitterly cold when they finally halted a few yards from the castle. Its appearance was ominous, a grim façade, windowless and broken only by a massive door studded with iron spikes like spearheads. But the door stood half open. The two men looked helplessly at each other.

'What else can we do?' said Erathrir. 'The thing that killed the creature in the marsh must be here, — and must be waiting for us.'

They slipped in through the doorway. Before them, down a vast chamber, stood a row of ten great columns of obsidian, soaring roofwards and spreading in intricate vaults at the summit. High on the ceiling near one of them was hung the only light, a white-flamed torch of great size. It lit the interior of that cavernous hall, but none of its light had spilled through the door. In its light, red jewels glinted from the black stone of the walls, inlaid in monstrous deep-cut carvings of alien form. Strange and haunting scenes of warfare and sacrifice overspread all the sixty feet of sheer walls, and strange shapes partly obscured by the shadowy columns shone redly down on them in the torchlight.

They walked the length of the hall, examining the reliefs as they went. Many panels shewed the Khulgrakh, the thing in the marsh. They saw its combats with tiny man-figures, set between the scenes of panoramic battles. They also saw yet darker creatures that wandered contorted landscapes, and all inlaid with precious metals, and all red-jeweled for blood. There was a long-vanished evil portrayed on those walls as vividly as life, and it worked its way on their minds. The fear of being watched grew on them. The silence became oppressive, and their steps, the only sounds, echoed among the endless vaults. Blind engraved eyes stared at them from either side, and sudden freaks of nature appeared red and black on the walls from out of deep shadows. At the far end of the hall, nearly two hundred feet from the great door and almost hidden by the pillars, was another door, richly set with silver. They almost ran the last yards of the hall to the silver door, and when they reached it pushed it open at once.

They entered a small narrow room, at the end of which, turned away from them, was a chair. A figure sat there in a long robe of heavy red stuff. It had once been rich, but was stained with dirt, and layered with dust. A hand like a claw rested on the arm of the tall chair. Slowly the figure moved. Its face turned on them, — fleshless skin hung on bone, lips drawn back from the broken stumps of blackened teeth: livid greenish-tinged, the face of a foul corpse. But the eyes stared with a hideous yearning, alive in the dead face. And they stared sightless, for they were pure white, bulging and rolling in the sockets. The men felt themselves held by those blind awful eyes, and they knew that the monstrous thing was looking into them, and seeing their very thoughts.

In the grim night of a lone castle, on Enchanter's Isle of the furthest north, Erathrir and Yeselwir gazed on the face of the last of the Black Lords. It was the night of the Festival of the Lamps on Alban. The tale that Melandir had told in the morning was coming to a new ending.

The Festival of the Lamps went on, as it had and would. But now it was on Alban's isle, for Telmirandor was fallen, and only Iksalai, Alban of the Northlands, remained. It was in the Northlands that the old evil was stirring again. Ral the Witch Queen, once called Ral the Fair, had long lived on, broken in power and hidden away in the great wide woodland named in fear the Forest of Sorcery. She it was that overthrew the realm of Telmirandor. Born of the House Imperial, yet cursed and raped and destroyed by Sagoth, Prince of Darkness; fair as a queen, yet an outcast from her own race, she had created the Black Lords by hideous perverted arts. Their life was bound with hers. They died and were reborn of her. She was the Great Goddess, fair and perilous, and the death and rebirth she gave them was a screaming and hideous torment. Yet they were great in their evil. Their being was compounded of fear and sorcery. Terror went before them, and death haunted their tracks.

These it was that Ral had used to strike down Telmirandor the Golden. After the great Crown was broken by Ral and the city of Werendilren in ruins, they passed over the world like a breath of plague. They came from their haunts in the cold wastes of the Moon and the pits of Aldel Morn. They fell upon the lords of Wenyaltrir, close by shattered Werendilren. Everywhere victory went with them. And so the Great Goddess Ral ruled in Tharang. Blood ran in her temples. She bore the sword of Sagoth and drank her power from it in foul embraces. She named herself greater than Sagoth. For he had made her an outcast, and she hated him more than her own race that she had destroyed.

Yet one of the Black Lords was to be her downfall. The first-created of her brood had grown great in necromancy. He was a cloud of fear in the night, a touch of clammy cold, a rotting of the bones. None ever saw his face. He was the Hooded One. Four times he knew Ral in the Love Death, and four times its agonies were written in his unseeing eyes. Called to a fifth death, the Hooded One, whom all men feared, was lost in dread. He fled the brazen face and beauty of his Goddess-lover.

But everywhere he fled her fury pursued him. At last he came into the Underworld. He found there a man and two women. The man was already dead, the others dying of thirst. One was Delwen, wife of the Emperor of Telmirandor, the other her daughter, Elandril. For reasons he could not understand, the Hooded One protected them. He raised up magic halls and phantom slaves in the Underworld, lit by sorcerous suns. He claimed that he was Banatem, who had been a High Magician. The Hooded One had slain Banatem in Kanmoun, and now he stole his name as well as his life. For the Black Lord found that he loved Delwen of the High Race, who was mother not only of Elandril and Talarnidh, but also, many years before, of Ral the Fair.

He found that the man who lay dead beside the women bore a great treasure. From him the Hooded One took the Sixth Sceptre of Wenyaltrir. Only one of great power himself could wield a Sceptre of Wenyaltrir. But, confident in his sorcery, the Hooded One claimed and wielded the Sceptre, and lived. The dead man had been one of the nine Guardians of the Sceptres, into whose hands the Sceptres were given after the death of the Kings in the fall of Werendilren. His had been the Sceptre Spiritual, which ruled the minds and souls, the emotions and thoughts, of all men and all beings. Its power waxed or waned with the power of the one that bore it. The Hooded One no longer covered his face. Now he could make all see him as he wished to be seen. He could make Delwen return his love. He may even have known happiness.

But his hiding place in the Underworld was found by Eldhoril, the Wizard of Wenyaltrir. Eldhoril had been the first of the Nine Kings, and had reigned, first under the old High King, then as King of his own realm, and then again under Talmond the Emperor. His very name meant 'Eldest King', and now after the downfall of Telmirandor he was the greatest living of the High Race. He had long been named Wizard of Wenylatrir, and the power of his sorcerer's staff was great beyond knowing. Yet that staff had been broken at the time when all the other Kings were slain and Talmond wounded (it seemed) unto death. For Eldhoril had been in the Throne Room when Ral put forth the might of the Crown of Sceptres, and the Crown and the city alike were ruined. Though his staff had saved him, Eldhoril lay as if dead, and was placed in the vaults of the High Race with the dead Kings and the Emperor. There he lay for nearly four thousand years, and there at last he awakened to learn of the ruin and chaos of the world. Slowly and secretly, still weak and without his wand, he followed the trail of his own Sceptre, like the others given into the hands of a Guardian by the last wish of the Emperor.

Finally, deep in the Underworld, he found the Guardian of Elemental, his own Sceptre, the Fifth Sceptre of Wenyaltrir. The Guardian gladly gave it to him. Eldhoril claimed his own, and the power returned. Now Eldhoril, with the man who had guarded his Sceptre so well, searched for Elandril and Delwen. Long years the two of them wandered in the Underworld, where all the while evil spread, and the Black Lords went about in the darkness, also seeking — as some said — for a renegade of their own kind.

At last Eldhoril came to the enchanted castle of the man who named himself Banatem and claimed to be a High Magician. By the power of the Sceptre Spiritual, it was a High Magician that Eldhoril saw and not the Hooded One. But the Black Lords had watched Eldhoril and his companion as they passed through the Underworld. For they watched all strangers in their own relentless search for the Hooded One. They followed Eldhoril to the castle, and so their search was ended. Now they attacked.

The attack was sudden, and Delwen, the Empress, fell prisoner to them before they were driven out of the castle. The Hooded One, and the Wizard of Wenyaltrir went out together against them. But the Black Lords called on Eldhoril, asking him who rode at his side. When Eldhoril named him Banatem, the High Magician, they laughed in his face and cried that in truth he rode with the Hooded One, called Niaherz in their tongue, once their brother, now a renegade.

Eldhoril heard their taunts, and remembered the power of the Sceptre that the man beside him bore. He knew that the Sceptre Spiritual could make that man appear in the guise of his choosing. But while Eldhoril was still in two minds, the Hooded One, full of rage at their taunts and fury as he saw his loved one Delwen in their hands, put forth the might of the Sceptre, and loosed on the Black Lords the monsters of the mind. So great was the power that they were driven mad by the phantasms and all died in frenzy and fear. So great was the power that he who had been Guardian of the Fifth Sceptre and now watched wounded on the battlements above also died from the horrors. And Delwen died.

Eldhoril alone had sufficient power to resist the potency of the images, though he too was partly under the spell. But as well as the monsters of the mind he saw the real monster at his side. For the Hooded One let drop the disguise that the Sceptre had given him, as he concentrated all his will on the destruction of his enemies. Eldhoril saw the blind-eyed hideous face, and knew the truth. The man who called himself Banatem was a Black Lord.

The Hooded One, Niaherz, knelt over the body of Delwen, and wept. But when Eldhoril challenged him and called him a Black Lord the grim foul creature turned, wild in his fury, torn with grief at the death of Delwen, full of hate for Eldhoril, needing to blame him for the body that lay there, its eyes still full of terror in its death. Again the power of the Sceptres was given full rein, and in his rage the might of the Hooded One flowed through the rod like a fire of vengeance. Eldhoril fled, and was broken.

Stricken with grief and anger, in the dimness of the Underworld, the Hooded One plotted his vengeance on all his enemies. Ral above all he hated, for he blamed her for the death of Delwen, and Elandril was a constant reminder of his dead beloved. He came out into Tharang, the Midworld, and thence to the Overworld, beyond the East of East, where the Guardians of the Sceptres were gathered. The Peiri were still weak, and hesitated to take any action. Talarnidh, son of the Emperor, and a few others had fought on through many dark years in the West, but his strength was always diminished. The lords of the High Race in the Overworld had long lost their Emperor, their cities and their power. They knew the Nine Kings were dead. They had no way of knowing that Eldhoril still lived. And now the Hooded One came to them as the last of the High Magicians from the lost Empire of Telmirandor. He told the Guardians of the Sceptres that he, Lord of the Sixth Sceptre and protector of Elandril, daughter of the Emperor, would lead them. They doubted and were afraid, but they saw him in all the majesty of his power, as he wished to be seen. Even their minds were swayed, and they named him Selenthoril, the White King; and thus he gained another name. He led the host of Wenyaltrir and the Guardians of the Sceptres to war. The Black Lords were broken by the firstborn of their own kind, and the revenge of Selenthoril was mighty.

The Northlands lay ruined, the goblin cities were razed, and the Black Lords themselves stood in their coffins of stone in Grathgel, City of Black Fire, in Aldel Morn. In his triumph Selenthoril had confronted Ral herself, and revealed to her that he was the Hooded One, Niaherz. She had fled to the Forest of Sorcery, Queen and Goddess no more. But her power was not utterly broken, for the sheathed sword, the Sword of Doom, was still hers.

In Nyaroth Khrathril, Enchanter's Isle, the Guardians of the Sceptres held high council over the stricken world, and in their council Selenthoril swayed the minds of all with the power of his Sceptre, Arlurin, the Sceptre Spiritual. But though his mind was strong, his body was weak, for, whether as a Black Lord or as a High Magician, his flesh was mortal. So it was that the Guardian of the Sceptre Temporal was persuaded to make for him a timeless place on Nyaroth Khrathril. And round that timeless place the fabric of the world itself was twisted and changed by the power of the Sceptres. None could come in to Nyaroth Khrathril who did not know the secret way. In his black castle on Enchanter's Isle, wreathed in mists, Selenthoril thought himself secure. But Eldhoril, the Wizard of Wenyaltrir, was still alive and he knew Selenthoril for what he really was. Stricken and broken in the Underworld, he had been succoured by Gnomes, Elementals of the Earth who served his Sceptre. Slowly his spirit was renewed and power flowed in him again. Through the dark labyrinths of the Underworld he searched for the false magician who had assailed him. The trail was cold and the Underworld full of evil things. His journey was long and hard before at last he came out into Tharang, the Midworld. And there he heard the tale on everyone's lips, — that Ral was overthrown by the Guardians of the Sceptres, and that they were led by Banatem, now called Selenthoril, the last of the High Magicians.

Flying on the giants of the wind he sped to Nyaroth Khrathril, the island in the mist. With his powers of sorcery the Wizard of Wenyaltrir found the hidden way and came to the Guardians of the Sceptres in council there. There he saw Selenthoril, as he had first appeared to him in the enchanted castle in the Underworld. Then Eldhoril cursed him for the Hooded One, last of the Black Lords.

But the Hooded One wore the robes of the White King, and the Sceptre Spiritual was in his hand. He sent forth its power, and changed the minds of the Guardians so that they saw Eldhoril as the Hooded One come against them. So Eldhoril it was who was taken and bound in bands of gold and thrown into the dungeons. Though the power of Selenthoril was strong over them, the Guardians had yet heard Eldhoril's words. They knew which Sceptre Selenthoril bore, and they began to wonder. The last of the Black Lords sensed their suspicions, and became afraid. In the night dark phantoms of the mind came to the Guardians in their sleep, and they all died screaming. On that night too the hosts of the High Race gathered on Misen Taïrail died in maddened frenzy, as Selenthoril cast wide the evil powers of his mind through the Sceptre he had stolen. One alone survived. His old enemy, Eldhoril, steeled his will against the mind monsters, and as day broke he was still alive.

A new day dawned on the scene of Selenthoril's triumph, but its light shewed the triumph was empty. The Sceptres he had intended to take for himself were gone. In his rage he came to Eldhoril, certain that he must be the cause of their disappearance. With the Sceptre Spiritual he looked into Eldhoril's mind, but found there only that the Wizard of Wenyaltrir had been imprisoned in his golden chains throughout that dreadful night. Selenthoril in his anger disbelieved the Sceptre. He raved of his triumphs, of the death of the Guardians and the slaughter of the High Race, and swore to wrest the secret of the Sceptres from Eldhoril. Going from the dungeons he prepared a necromantic potion to unlock the truth from his prisoner. In Selenthoril's moment of inattention, Eldhoril broke the bands of gold with his own wizardry, and called his Sylphs and wind giants to him. The wind creatures followed the path their master had taken, and burst through the mist maze to the castle.

Eldhoril was borne aloft, and assailed the castle with the Elementals. Selenthoril met the attack with the monsters of the mind called up by his Sceptre. Eldhoril was still weak and his forces of Sylphs and wind giants insufficient. Selenthoril strove to wrest their control from him, and maddened and terrified the Sylphs fled away southwards. Many were lost in the mist mazes around the castle, and Eldhoril himself fell from the hands of the wind giants, and was lost to the knowledge of Selenthoril and the world.

For a while he sent out searchers for Eldhoril and the missing Sceptres. But the conflict had worked a change in Selenthoril. His old precision of evil was gone. He could no longer bind the Sceptre Spiritual fully to his will. He was weakened by his struggles with Eldhoril and was haunted by the whispering shapes of the monsters of the mind that he had called up. He no longer need fear his own death or even ageing. And with him dwelt Elandril of the Peiri, the High Race. Long years he sat alone and forgotten in the timelessness of his island.

No news came south of his contest with Eldhoril, or of his treachery and the disappearance of the Sceptres. When Talarnidh and Fermilondath and Turnalordath came back from Werendilren and the West, they met the remnants of the host of the High Race from the East of East. But they could learn nothing of the Guardians of the Sceptres and their forces, save that they had destroyed the power of the Black Lords, but in so doing had disappeared themselves. The part of Selenthoril was unclear, but all believed him to have been the High Magician, Banatem. He too had vanished. The Isle of Nyaroth Khrathril where all this had befallen was itself lost in mists and seemed removed from the world, for none could find their way thither though many were sent to try and not all returned.

As the ruined Northlands were rebuilt, and men even walked again in the poisoned lands of Sart Emig, and built their villages on Misen Taïrail, Selenthoril's mind turned inwards, and became stranger and more twisted, part of him always the Hooded One who had known the Love Death in the Goddess, part of him almost in truth the High Magician that had loved a queen of the

High Race and still cherished her daughter. He became as an old man, frightened amidst the ruins of his evil.

Above all Selenthoril now knew fear. He was no longer forgotten. There were forces at work, shutting him in. There were stirrings out on the ice sheets by the City of the Giants; the Rethrind had been seen on the Pass of Anrith; and something had awoken in Wirdrilded. The creatures, freaks of the days of the Black Lords and beyond, had come again out of the waters of Lake Khrathemrin to the mud flats of Nyaroth Khrathril. The Khulgrakh that had attacked Erathrir and Yeselwir warned him that the revenge of Ral was coming ever closer to him. For Ral was still great so long as she possessed the Sword of Doom.

Deep in the vast woods that lie between the settled lands of men and the desolation of Sart Emig, she had rebuilt her power. More and more of the forest fell beneath her sway. The Dwarves fled their mountain mines, and in their place was heard the flapping of the wings of Werebats. Slinking creatures moved in the hills north of Chamley where the guard had long been neglected. Men looked south to the great new empire of slavery called Drarkh, while the creeping darkness in the north spread unnoticed. It spread from the forest to the caves of the Kalandian Mountains, to the ancient citadels on the coasts of Ithiaz-Keiden, and through Sart Emig to Helland Holme, once named Misen Taïrail, where Lake Khrathemrin lay. In Lake Khrathemrin was Nyaroth Khrathril, called Enchanter's Isle. Ral knew Selenthoril was there.

What was his refuge had become a trap for Selenthoril. The timeless zone was no shield against the death Ral planned for him. Where he had rejoiced to be forgotten, he longed now for aid. Beset all round, crazed with terror, and increasingly unable to use his Sceptre, he could not think of anything save the Great Goddess Ral, and the death that awaited him when he looked again on her brazen face. In his terror at last the resolve grew that he must kill her, so far had he come from the time he was her slave and lover.

He had known for many centuries what had befallen one of the Sceptres. In the days when he had searched for the lost Sceptres, his servants had captured one of the Merpeople. He had read in the mind of the Merman that the Sceptre Mortal lay in the Sea Caverns of the City of Kruakh. This Sceptre he had never seen. Its Guardian was not one of those he slew on Nyaroth

Khrathril. Its Guardian had taken no part in the War of the Sceptres. As he had lain dying beneath the ancient city, he had given the rod of power to a new guardian. A chamber deep in the winding ways, washed by underground tides, had been found for the Sceptre. It lay there yet. Its power was to kill. It could kill even Ral, by no more than the thought of its bearer. Selenthoril had sought for it once, and none of his messengers had returned. Then he had sought no more, for then he had no great need of it. Now he sought again. And all of his messengers died. Ral had let no-one escape from the mists surrounding Nyaroth Khrathril for a year now. Selenthoril could find no way of getting the Sceptre. For if he tried to leave the timeless place, he would be as dust in an instant.

At first he had thought that the two strangers on the marshes of the island were come from Ral. Then the monster attacked them. He slew it, and watched and waited as they walked into his lonely castle.

Both men screamed as they saw the monstrous face and were compelled to gaze at it. The horror in their eyes widened as the creature in front of them began to alter their thoughts. And then the fear was banished. Before them, rising from the throne of a High Magician, stood Selenthoril, fair to look upon, mighty in wisdom and magic. Yeselwir unfurled for him the Imperial Standard of Wenyaltrir. Gladly Erathrir gave him the token that he bore. In his hands Selenthoril now held the ring of the old High King, the ring also of the Emperor. He knew that whoever wore it could see and speak to all of the line of Talmond, Emperor of Telmirandor. He already saw how he would use it to bring about the death of Ral.

Erathrir and Yeselwir spoke their greetings to the first man of Faerie Tharang that they had met. They thanked him for saving them from the Khulgrakh. For they knew now that it had been his art that did so. They drank wine with him and he had food brought. He spoke much of the world of Tharang and of himself. He spoke of Ral and his hope to be saved from her.

'This is why you have come hither,' he told them. 'By the ring you have brought me I may speak across seas and lands to Talarnidh, son of the Emperor. I will tell him of my plight and he will remember how I encompassed the downfall of Ral long ago. I will tell him of Elandril his sister and he will rejoice that she is alive. Tonight, deep in the night, when Talarnidh and the lords of Wenyaltrir are all alone, I will call to them and summon Talarnidh to my aid. For now, at last, I have the means to kill the Great Goddess Ral.'

Images and pictures of the world of Faerie flooded into their minds, put there by the power of Selenthoril's Sceptre. But in all the images Selenthoril was fair and mighty. They could not see or remember the true thing that had met them in that room.

'We offer you our service,' said Yeselwir to him.

'It is as if we were sent here to serve you,' said Erathrir.

'I need only the service of the ring,' answered Selenthoril. But already he wondered if these two strangers from the darkness beyond Faerie might help his purpose in other ways. He had already chosen not to kill them.

'You will stand beside me on the tower when I call by the stone of the Emperor's ring to Talarnidh, son of the Emperor,' he said. And the hideous face, that they could not perceive, smiled in the candlelight.

CHAPTER 4

THE QUEST

Melandir's tale was finished now, and the halls of Hirenon had disgorged their concourse of people. The sun had just set, but its afterglow gave the red-clouded western sky a lingering brightness which gleamed also on the gold inlay of the highest tower of the wooden palace. The eastern sky was tinged with spreading purple. Over all the land was silence as the moment of the sign drew near. The spirit of Wenyaltrir shimmered and floated in the stillness, and half-forgotten memories took life. The moment was come. The last ray of the hidden sun struck the topmost pinnacle and kindled the silver star set there.

Each of the throng bore a lamp now, some no more than bowls of bronze or copper full of cheap and reeking oil, but most richly worked and made of silver. The nobles bore lamps of diamond-studded gold, the heirlooms of Wenyaltrir, and they now stood in two lines on either side of the doors, awaiting Prince Talarnidh. The doors of the palace were closed. All now looked towards them. The afterglow was dying away abruptly. Only the star still shone, a fainter silver, high above the palace, like a reflection of the newly risen Star of Evening, bright and big in the darkening east. The doors swung slowly open and the High Steward came out, robed in cloth of gold that glowed and rippled like a sheet of molten metal. He took his stand on the left, and on the right was Fermilondath, who was Priest of the Festival, once the right of Eldhoril, the lost Wizard of Wenyaltrir. He was clad in the robes of priestly crimson, woven with intertwining dragons, blue and gold.

Last Talarnidh came forth, white in the hero's robes, his sword girt on. He bore the royal lamp carved from one great sapphire and shining with stars of blue and whiteness. The musk-odoured liquid, translucent in the gemstone's hollowness, was Royal Fire that Tyrvaz brought to the Garden of Eternity long before — a celebration of the life of the High Race and death to its foemen in other days.

The taper in Talarnidh's hand sprang to light of its own accord, burning with a dark blue-green flame, but with no sign of being consumed. He lit his own rich lamp, and from it the lamps of the Priest and the Steward. Then each of the nobles in due order received light for their lamps, passing it to the crowd till the whole courtyard was a close-packed galaxy of lights. As the star on the palace was quenched, ten thousand were kindled below to take its place. A mingled column of scented smokes rose upwards, thick with aromatic spices. Strange shapes flickered on the trees of the gardens and faces in the crowd were suddenly lit, then lost in gloom and shadow.

Fermilondath began the ancient chant, the slow and rhythmic hymn to the Star People, and the throng joined with him, intoning the phrases they could not understand. Yet they felt the power and mystery of the Old High Speech, and its words spoken first in the Garden of Eternity. Fermilondath's voice continued strong but trancelike and now he was echoed by the notes of the great bell in the palace that tolled for the procession to begin. Everyone had donned the tall silvered hoods. Only Talarnidh's head was uncovered.

Down the palace steps, attended by the lords of Wenyaltrir and the Northlands, Fermilondath at his right, Melandir at his left, but both one pace behind, into the body of sound he came, and the waves of the chant beat upon him. The way lay through the iron gates out of the small town and up the hill road towards the cave. The three leaders were walking with measured pace, never looking back, stiff and upright in their ceremonial robes. And behind them at the set distance followed the procession. It filled the road with a stream of scattered lights, swaying in waves to its echoing chant.

The road was steep and dusty, still hot underfoot from the autumn sun. The flame of Royal Fire, itself akin to starlight, burnt in Talarnidh's lamp, unwavering as it led the way. Fermilondath's voice was hoarse now, but the chant was nearly finished. They halted at the cave mouth in the hillside by the road. The stream of magic light moved liquid into the clearing by the cave, until all the People of the Lamps were there. The chant ceased. They raised their lamps as homage to Talarnidh's fire.

Talarnidh raised his lamp, like the others but brighter far. A full minute he held it above his head. All waited and wondered in the rustling silence. With one movement the sapphire lamp was upturned above his head. The fire fell about him.

Slow, like a silver dust falling in a sombre liquid, the particles of fire hung in the air and then drifted down about Talarnidh's head and shoulders. The crowd gasped its horror. The Prince's head was an orb of fire, his features lost in silver, too bright to see. Then all at once his form was become one pillar of starlight, human no more, but made of fire.

All in a moment it had happened. Fermilondath gave a great cry, and at his signal the people were running, rushing and jostling each other, away in all directions over the hillside, a scattering starburst of light. The space before the mouth of the cave was cleared and the myriad lamps were dim now, or hidden in the woods or behind the rocks. Only a few remained, in a half circle around the clearing. Their bearers watched Talarnidh and waited. His face was like a mask of newly-hardened silver in which his blood was seen flowing in veins of molten light. Fire were his eyes, and flames were in his mouth. The Royal Fire had burnt in him, but he was not consumed. This was the ritual: he died but was not dead. Such it had been for the old High King, the Nine Kings, and Talmond the Emperor. The fire had not harmed them. The fire now would not harm the Emperor's line. When the people returned they would find Talarnidh living, their past and future lord.

Talarnidh turned, slowly and with difficulty, and entered the cave. In the circular chamber was a stone block, the length of a man, and on this he lay down. Fermilondath took his stand with the priestly wand at the Prince's head, and Melandir with the hero's sword at his feet. Only nine lords were chosen by Talarnidh himself to be admitted to the Chamber of Royal Fire. These were Fermilondath, Turnalordath, Wondrith, Fandorel, Karandar, Tasarnil, Filindrin, Relnar, and Melandir. All others had fled to await the morning for their sight of the living prince. Tarmansur, Guardian of the Gate, stood, sword in hand, at the cave mouth to keep the curious away. The night wore on in whispers, as the fire in Talarnidh died down and slowly left him. The waiting lords stood or paced the floor, and watched the Prince. Fermilondath called the passing hours, one, three and five, of the ritual, and thought in his mind the proud thoughts of the Peiri, that the men of the Northlands call the High Race.

The first hour was called. Fermilondath's words of announcement rang hollowly in the cavern and echoed into an unknown distance of dark unthought-of stone. A haze hung in the air of the night, and a sudden wind rustled the stiff robes of the lords in the cave. Shadows flickered across the lustre of the deathlike Prince. The lords gazed at each other unbelieving. A voice without source echoed in the darknesses. The watchers listened, rocklike in their silence amidst the disembodied noises.

'Talarnidh! Talarnidh!' The voice of the unknown whispered its drawn-out syllables on the breath of a breeze from nowhere.

'Talarnidh, aid me! — It is Selenthoril that calls thee, from Nyaroth Khrathril far away. It is Selenthoril, last of the High Magicians . . . Talarnidh!' The voice was suddenly stronger, sibilant and swelling in the midst of far-off murmurings. And the voice was desperate and afraid.

'Talarnidh, Ral is risen again. Help me to fight Ral . . . Talarnidh! I need your aid . . .'

As the voice faded slowly into its own echoes there were suggestions of other voices, even fainter. There was a cry of surprise — a question in the voice of a maiden — the tongue of Wenyaltrir scattered by winds and indistinct. And there were harsher words, also a woman's voice, but full of anger and command, speaking the Black Speech. There might have been a third voice, but so distant that it seemed as if from beyond the world. Then the voices died, and there was only silence and echoes.

Anxious, the lords spoke in whispers. Time passed in doubt and uncertainty. The third hour came and was called aloud by Fermilondath. Again the air was shaken by unknown sounds. A hazy light formed into a shape like a ghost above the Prince. The form of Selenthoril spoke in their midst.

'Talarnidh, by the ring of the Emperor, I call you. You must aid me now. I am attacked by Ral.'

Now those in the cavern who had seen Selenthoril long years before in the days of the War of the Sceptres looked on his image and remembered. They also saw the ring of the Emperor on his hand, and that also was known to the lords of Wenyaltrir. In his hand the vision of Selenthoril bore the Sceptre Spiritual. All believed in the truth of the vision.

'I am alone here, O Prince. The Sceptre fades . . . The old danger surrounds me. There is one thing only that can restore my power and save the Northlands. If Ral destroys me, her power will be great as of old. You must aid me Talarnidh. I am alone here . . . with Elandril!'

Talarnidh moved, rising ghost-white and rigid as death.

'Elandril!' he cried. But the form of Selenthoril was already dissolving, fading back into the mists, and the only answer that came was:

'Danger . . .'

Once more the cry broke from Talarnidh's lips:

'Elandril!'

For out of the ways of darkness and the murks of time he saw, where the image of Selenthoril had been, the shape of his sister, Princess of the High Race, daughter of the Emperor. There were other shapes and hints also. All saw another woman's face, staring from nowhere at them, black hair falling on a dark robe. Anger stared in her eyes and hate was written in the line of her mouth. It was the face of Ral. Other shapes there might have been, but too distant to perceive. But no-one doubted that they had seen Ral and Elandril. Stiff and slow, Talarnidh lay back on the bed of stone.

'It is the ring of the Emperor,' said Karandar. 'Selenthoril is using it to call for help. The ring can reach even across the void. It speaks to any and all the House of Talmond.'

'Why have we seen these other faces?' asked Melandir.

'It must be that the ring indeed shows us all the living members of the House,' answered Wondrith. 'Remember that the Witch Queen is also a daughter of Talmond. Her and Elandril we certainly saw.'

'So it means that Ral and Elandril live,' said Melandir, 'though the tales of the Peiri tell that both are dead, — as they also tell of Selenthoril himself.'

'It means they live,' continued Wondrith. 'It is clear that this summoning means that the old danger is truly returning.'

'Then you do not doubt that it is Selenthoril?' said Turnalordath.

'It is Selenthoril,' replied Tasarnil the One-Eyed. 'He is as I saw him in the War of the Sceptres.'

'This is true,' said Fandorel. 'This is no false summoning. Ral is risen again, and Selenthoril and Elandril are within her grasp.'

'But it is not clear what the summons is,' said Wondrith.

'It is not clear that Selenthoril fully knows the power of the

Emperor's ring,' said Karandar. 'I do not think that he expected Ral and Elandril would also appear to us.'

'Their appearing is the surety of his truth,' said Fandorel.

'But a danger if he wishes to reveal his plans and purpose to us,' added Karandar.

'There is another thing we must consider,' said Melandir. 'This ring, the Emperor's ring, the ring of the old High King, was that given by Ask to my companion Erathrir. It must mean that he too has come to Tharang, as was foretold.'

'I think we must wait another while yet,' said Turnalordath finally. 'I feel that Selenthoril will try to reach the Prince again.'

They waited, and the fifth hour came. For a last time they saw Selenthoril. The shape formed and grew stronger. The ring on his hand was vivid blue and seemed to pull the figure of the wizard into the cavern. But the other shapes were also clearer. Beside Selenthoril, almost as solid as he, stood Ral. Her hand reached for the ring. Melandir stepped forward, and the Sword of Fate passed between the two forms. The vision of Ral screamed and faded. Selenthoril, Elandril, and the other shapes farther off, remained. The outstretched hand of Selenthoril, from across the distant seas and mountains, touched the hand of Melandir. The blue stone of the ring of the Emperor gleamed on his finger. This was the ring that Erathrir had brought to Nyaroth Khrathril from the Island of the Stars. Also from that island had come the Sword of Fate that Melandir bore. On its hilt shone the second of the Star Sapphires. The twin magic sapphires, one in the ring, one in the sword, met again across the distances of space and emptiness. Blue light and a roaring filled the cavern.

'Help me!' cried Selenthoril.

The cavern spun in bitter coldness. The world crashed away, and the distances were bridged. Elandril screamed in a moment of sickening shock, and fell into the arms of Melandir. The lords of Wenyaltrir stood in the Castle of Selenthoril on Nyaroth Khrathril. The fire faded from the Prince in their midst. Beside him, Selenthoril swayed in weakness. Erathrir came forward to support him. Melandir and Erathrir had come together again by the tokens they gained beyond the world.

The early snows of coming winter began to wrap the Northlands in their frosted cloak. The long warmth of autumn was fading fast. Over a month had gone by since that night when tradition was broken and the age-old ceremony left unfulfilled. For the lords of Wenyaltrir had fled away by night. There was no longer a prince in Alban of the Western Ocean, where the last fitful flame of Telmirandor's glories had shone. No-one knew whither or how the lords had departed, but in their departure long years had sighed and passed away. The north winds blew in the sedges of Alban and whispered the end of an age.

Away from Iksalai sailed the ambassadors of the North, with their message of a vanished prince. And in the far north, beyond the Mountains of Guard, in the Forest of Sorcery, things stirred, and slow fires were kindled. Unknown to the ambassadors and kings of the Northlands the first skirmishes of a new war were being fought. Ral had arisen behind the civilized lands and the forces of her foemen and her allies gathered slowly in the vast woods.

Talarnidh and the lords of Wenyaltrir had vanished into the dark and forgotten regions of far-off Nyaroth Khrathril, Enchanter's Isle that lies in Lake Khrathemrin on Misen Taïrail. Thither to Misen Taïrail also the ships of Amray were sailing, on their way to Azantul, new-found ally of that republic. Chamley too might join with them. But now she mourned for Relnar, the lost son of her king. Parvaloril also mourned in Morena for the lords of his land, Karandar, Wondrith, and Fandorel. But all these lands thought most about Drarkh, their newer enemy. None knew of the risen power of Ral.

Over fifty centuries had passed since Ral had seen her brother Talarnidh and her sister Elandril. Beyond Selenthoril's devising the ring had brought all of the House Imperial together, and Ral was of that house. She had also looked again on the face of Selenthoril, the Hooded One. The traitor of traitors, whom she had planned to snare and kill, had dared to challenge her again. Now her revenge would be greater, and would last longer.

The joining of the two Star Sapphires, had brought the lords of Wenyaltrir to Selenthoril. Talarnidh himself had come, and with him Karandar, Wondrith, and Fandorel from Morena, Fermilondath and Turnalordath, brothers of the High Race, Tasarnil the One-Eyed, Filindrin of Alban, Relnar of Chamley, and Melandir from beyond the stars. There also were Erathrir and Yeselwir who had brought him the ring. Yet the sorcery that had carried the lords of Wenyaltrir to him was not part of his plan. Only when Ral had appeared had Selenthoril realised that he could not speak of the Sceptre Mortal to them. But now he could unfold his purpose in his own halls. Yet those halls were far from Kruakh where the Sceptre lay, — and all around his timeless zone lay the ancient haunts of the power of Ral.

Selenthoril, the White King, the High Magician Banatem, the Guardian of the Sceptre Spiritual, received the lords on lonely Nyaroth Khrathril. Now he felt his power renewed, as he remade his ancient alliance with the High Race. As he remembered his victories over his brother Black Lords, Ral became less his Goddess, twice-betrayed, and more the old enemy that he had once defeated. To slay Ral with the Sceptre Mortal was now within his power. No more would he fear the death of a Black Lord in hideous union with her, nor the death of a mortal man at her hands. Ral did not know his purpose. She would watch the lords of Wenyaltrir, the chosen instruments of his plans, as they advanced towards her secret places. If she struck at them, their power was great enough to withstand her. He expected that she would wait until it was too late, and he had become the Guardian of two Sceptres.

As the days went by Selenthoril did not reveal his whole purpose to his guests. He slowly strengthened their trust, and played on their fears for the safety of the Northlands. They learnt from him of the Goblins and Trolls who had spread abroad again and roamed in the Empty Lands unchecked. He told of the growing power of Ral, and her tentacles of terror that stretched out from Thulgarn to hold the Forest of Sorcery once again. There in the Pit of the Werebats, at the heart of her realm, lay the Sword of Doom. Selenthoril spoke of it with hushed and shuddering voice as the ultimate source of her power. Talarnidh promised that, if Ral was defeated and the Sword found, it would be brought safe to Selenthoril, — and the Hooded One smiled a secret smile, for he dreamt of true immortality. But his immediate purpose was the gaining of the Sceptre Mortal and the slaying of Ral.

The lords of Wenyaltrir heard the fears of a great wizard, who, for all his power, was mortal and trapped in the timeless place on Nyaroth Khrathril. He was surrounded by foes he could not flee or fight, and the net of Ral was closing ever tighter. Finally he told them of the Sceptre Mortal, that the Merpeople guarded in Kruakh. He put his request to them. He bade them go to Kruakh to find the Sceptre and bring it back to him. He would claim it, and Ral would die at last by its power. One by one the twelve lords (for Erathrir and Yeselwir were now of their number) became the Quest for the Second Sceptre of Wenyaltrir, Arnorin, the Sceptre Mortal. All agreed that it should be brought to Selenthoril. The High Magician alone would claim the Sceptre and wield it. He was the last known in the world who still bore one of the Sceptres. He was the only one that all knew for certain had the power to wield the Sceptre Mortal.

Far away Ral knew nothing for sure, but guessed much. She could still see the mind of her first-created, and knew its dark workings well. She perceived that her death lay at the centre of his plans, and her mind was clouded by the thought. When Ral had first begun to close her hands upon Selenthoril, secure in the trap of his own making, she had not feared him. She knew his power and old magic were weakening, and his control of the Sceptre less sure. Once he had been able by it to conceal all his mind from her. Now there was only the centre of his thoughts still hidden. Her attention drew away from all her other purpose, and turned on him. For she could not see how he devised to slay her. She had seen Talarnidh and his companions carried north on the wings of magic more ancient than Selenthoril's. But they were men, however high their lineage, and she was a Goddess. To send them against her was not enough. She feared some other hidden menace. She resolved that these men must be killed as soon as they became a danger. But before that she would find their secret. Then she would turn to Selenthoril again.

The men of the Quest stood about a great table in the castle of Selenthoril. Before them lay a map of the Northlands, and another of Misen Taïrail. The High Magician lay his finger on the northern isle.

'We have spoken much of the way from Belengar, the Nowhere Road, and the Crossroads of Takunan at Kruakh,' he said. 'I fear that the way across the mountains of Misen Taïrail will be as hard.'

'The island was the home of Ral of old,' said Turnalordath. 'You have made it plain that she has renewed her power here.'

'What are the possible ways across the mountains?' asked Talarnidh.

'We sit on an island in a lake. The mists on the lake guard me here. They are a maze, but I know the path through,' answered

Selenthoril. 'Round the lake is a ring of mountains named Adanyeth. They were once part of a loftier peak, the like of which is no more seen in Tharang, and it burnt with fire in the youth of the world. Now there are many ways across the mountain ring, but none will be easy.'

'Here is the Pass of Anrith. Its summit is never free of snow, and in high winter it cannot be crossed at all. Even now a storm on the pass might bring death to travellers. Beside the path there are the Ruby Cliffs, and in them the Caverns of Emrurl Arnag. The Rethrind dwell there. Avoid the caverns. The Rethrind are creatures of Ral.'

Selenthoril moved his finger on the map.

'Here lies Wirdrilded, Valley of Eternal Shadow,' he said, 'named thus because its sides rise so high and sheer that even at noon no light enters there, and the stars remain in its skies. Here once marched the forces of the High Race at the time of the War of the Sceptres. They marched from Melurin on the sea towards Alat by the lakeside of Khrathemrin. There are tales told of their journey . . . The valley is long untrodden and empty now.'

He looked at Tasarnil.

'I do not think it is empty, Selenthoril,' said Tasarnil the One-Eyed, Son of the Sun.

Selenthoril continued:

'It may be at the height of summer that men could cross the Glacier of Parileth, where River Nirid has its source. But at this season of the year it is impassable. Beyond it are the Ice Wastes above the buried city. The Dragon Hills are nearby, and Ral may have awoken the Dragons.'

'What of Aldel Morn?' asked Fermilondath.

'It was the heart of the power of the Black Lords,' Selenthoril answered. 'The Lords of the Sceptres and I burnt it and scoured it a thousand years ago. It is empty forever of good and evil alike.'

'Unless Ral has re-occupied it,' said Karandar.

'I have the Sceptre,' Selenthoril replied. 'I would know if anything had entered that land. Even Ral could not prevent me knowing. I would sense the mind of an enemy.'

'So the Black Land is our best route,' said Fermilondath.

'Aye, but the Black Land . . .?' said Fandorel.

'Of old we have heard of Aldel Morn. I have trodden its soil,' his kinsman Wondrith went on. 'It is known to the Race of

Wenyaltrir by her warriors who died there. It is known to the Elves in tales of fear, and to the Dwarves and Men alike.'

'The Black Lords are all dead,' said Selenthoril. 'Ral has not re-occupied Aldel Morn. It is the safest way of all.'

'Then let us not delay for fear of shadows,' answered Fermilondath.

'We will divide into three bands,' said Talarnidh. 'Fermilondath will lead those who go through Aldel Morn. I will go to Wirdrilded. Melandir, will you cross the pass of Anrith?'

Melandir nodded his consent.

'I will take Erathrir with me,' he said.

'And Yeselwir?' Talarnidh asked.

'No,' said Erathrir. 'One of the three of us should remain apart.'

'It is true,' answered Talarnidh. 'There are three men alone from beyond the stars. I will take Yeselwir with me, Melandir.'

'I will also go with you into the Valley of Eternal Shadow,' said Tasarnil. 'You know why, O Talarnidh.'

'Very well,' said Talarnidh. 'I will send Relnar with Melandir. I also wish Karandar to take the way over the pass, if he will.'

'You think I may be of use in the Caverns of Emrurl Arnag,' said Karandar with a half smile. 'Well, I hope we never come there, and I hope the snows of Anrith are not too deep.'

Talarnidh laughed, but Melandir said to Erathrir:

'If anything does befall on Anrith, it is Karandar who will be our best aid. He is the last of the old kings under the mountains, and the only one of his race who is a Lord of Wenyaltrir.'

'Fandorel, will you come with me?' said Talarnidh to the Elf Lord. 'The power of flight may be needed in the valley.'

He stopped abruptly and looked at Tasarnil.

'Prince of Wenyaltrir,' said Tasarnil, 'I know the tale of that place. I know why one of the Elvenkind may be needed there. It is to put the tale to the test that I go there.'

'So, in Aldel Morn there will be Wondrith of Morena, Filindrin, my brother Turnalordath, and I,' said Fermilondath. 'It is settled then.'

'These three ways we have chosen come out on different parts of the island,' said Selenthoril. 'Fermilondath, you will bring your men to Morthaln, Talarnidh to Melurin, Melandir to Lothchen. You will find fishermen who dwell in each of these lands. Pay them to carry you to Belengar.'

'We will meet at Belengar one week from the day we set out,' said Talarnidh. 'If any of us are not there, the others will go on to Kruakh and the Sceptre Mortal.'

'Arrange that the fishermen meet you again at Belengar,' said Selenthoril. 'And bring the Sceptre back to me. — The Quest is ready. The paths are set.'

Ral had once reigned over half of the world from her citadels of Misen Taïrail. In Alat by Khrathemrin, the gateway land to Aldel Morn, her temple lay, where once the Black Lords had consummated her rites in the final sacrifice. Nearby, the Poisoned Marsh had enwrapped her creatures in the slime of forgetfulness for long years after her downfall. They had arisen again and stalked the mudflats even of Nyaroth Khrathril, — the Khulgrakhs such as Erathrir and Yeselwir had encountered there. From the buried city came hollow sounds again, ringing through the deeps of ice. From the Dragon lairs behind Mount Rethrileth great winged forms flew above the Golden Forest, and spied upon Adanyeth, high with snow. The Whispering Wastes whispered fears into the night, and lights were flickering in the windows of the Giants' Castle.

The spirit of Ral had come again to Misen Taïrail, called Helland Holme. The men of the Quest had forgotten her power; Selenthoril had forgotten that here had been the home of all her might. She was a Goddess, and her might and her vengeance were boundless. Ral knew the threat against her. Her creatures lurked again in the silences of Misen Taïrail. But the darkest messenger was the mind of Ral. Her will turned north, and siezed the island in a closing grip. Hideous things moved in the Caverns of Emrurl Arnag. She knew that the great darkness of Wirdrilded between Guldurin and Nal Vorod was not empty, and had never been, for all the thousand years since the War of the Sceptres. In Aldel Morn also were the remnants of her power. Somewhere beneath Grathgel, City of Black Fire, the Black Lords remained, unliving but potent in their coffins of stone. She bent her will to re-enter that land, but only there had she failed, she knew not why. But she was prepared for any who came out from Nyaroth Khrathril.

CHAPTER 5

VALLEY OF ETERNAL SHADOW

The men, who were now the men of the Quest, took their leave of Selenthoril, and of Elandril, Talarnidh's sister. Down to the edge of the waters they walked in silence, and then, in a small boat, put out into the lake. Behind them Selenthoril raised aloft the Sceptre which he had stolen, to bid them good speed upon his dark purpose. Talarnidh, who stood in the stern of the boat, drew his sword and held it high in answer, but only Melandir saw in a window high in the castle the distant form of Elandril, and bade her a silent farewell.

Imperceptibly the castle slipped into the mists that lay across the lake, and the clammy echoing greyness encircled them. Talarnidh heard in his mind the voice of the High Magician:

'Turn the steering oar hard to the right now.'

The boat swung round on its new course. Guided by the soundless voice of Selenthoril, Talarnidh steered them through the maze of twisted space shrouded in its undying mists.

When the mist thinned, they looked back into an impenetrable bank of grey cloud. The castle and the island in the lake seemed utterly lost, and a chill wind hastened round the edges of the deep fogs. They raised the sail, and the wind carried them over the scant ten miles of Lake Khrathemrin to the place by the mouths of the stream called Nirid where they would land. In a little more than an hour they had pulled the boat ashore in Alat. Before them was the north edge of the Dargul, which is the name of the mountains that guard the land of Aldel Morn. Farther away to the west were the tall peaks where the pass of Anrith and the dark vale of Wirdrilded lay.

'It will take us till noon to reach Ir Angornyekh from here,' said Fermilondath. 'I would depart now, my Prince.'

'Yes, the journey through Aldel Morn to Morthaln will be done before evening if we set off at once,' said Filindrin. 'Your journey to Melurin will be even shorter, my Prince. It is a fine land. The men of the village of Lerod Anth will surely take you to Belengar.'

'You know these lands, Filindrin?' asked Karandar.

'I know them. — We also will find fishermen in Morthaln who will take us over to the mainland.'

'What of Pelderoun and Lothchen?' asked Melandir. 'That is where we will come out from Anrith.'

'They are wider lands,' Talarnidh answered. 'Their men fare wider over the seas from their town of Sarmish. Amray is soon to extend its power and protection to them. You may even find a ship of Amray in the harbour there.'

'We will not cross Anrith and get to Sarmish today though, Melandir,' said Karandar. 'We will be fortunate if we are over the pass by nightfall.'

'But cross before dark you must,' Tasarnil broke in, 'and do not take too lightly the tale of the Ruby Caverns.'

'Very well,' said Talarnidh, 'Melandir, you and I and our men will set off now. We travel together as far as Nal Vorod.'

'We will meet again soon, you and I,' said Turnalordath to Tasarnil. 'Belengar is but a few days hence.'

'Turnalordath,' answered Tasarnil, 'you and I have a friendship of many years. Goodbye, Turnalordath.'

'What? Do you think that Fermilondath and I and Lords of Wenyaltrir have aught to fear from Aldel Morn?'

'May you all come safe from there. But my doom lies in Wirdrilded.'

Tasarnil turned, and went away with no other word. He followed Talarnidh and six other men of Selenthoril's Quest. But of the things he feared he said nothing more to anyone. Westward across the edge of the land of Alat they went till they stood at the foot of Nal Vorod, snow-capped shoulder of Ralnadh, the Claw of Ral. The path continued to the northward, rising steadily. The great peak of Granyash rose above it and ahead, almost ten miles distant, were the Ruby Caverns of Emrurl Arnag beneath the long snow-ridge of Keseryeth.

Talarnidh, Fandorel, Tasarnil, and Yeselwir watched as their four companions left them and began the long ascent toward the distant snows of the High Pass. Then they turned south and walked into the darkness.

High and sheer on either side rose the black rock walls that had never seen the light of day. The cleft between the two mountains, Ralnadh and Guldurin, was narrow, so narrow that in places two men might hardly pass in it. But its walls towered steep and sheer into unknown heights and overhanging fastnesses. Above, as the sliver of light from the entrance grew distant, the sky had turned from the pearl grey of the northern morning to mauve-dark, as if the day had gone and the sun already set. Then it became black, the sky of night, and they could see a star shining there.

'What wonder is this, lord?' Yeselwir asked of Talarnidh. But it was Tasarnil who answered:

'The light of day cannot enter Wirdrilded. Why do you imagine men name it so, — the Valley of Eternal Shadow?'

'I had thought it was from the shadows that move in the darkness,' said Yeselwir.

The one golden eye of Tasarnil glinted in the darkness, a darted glance at Yeselwir. The man of the Outer Worlds shivered, and shadows stirred in the valley.

The floor of the valley had once been paved with slabs that fitted the irregular twistings of the rock walls. The smooth way underfoot still remained, and all the years' passing had not disturbed the stones from their places, nor did any green thing grow through the cracks between them. The men could walk without stumbling, but now the night was total and they could see nothing.

'Halt!' said Talarnidh, who was leading. His voice did not echo, and the thoughts of Tasarnil dwelt on the strangeness of that. The Prince found the torch and lit it. The oil-soaked wood crackled and flame went up. It was the first light in the darkness for a thousand years. The huge shapes of the walls seemed to leap into existence above them, clear glistening shapes of dark rock where tiny crystals glinted, and cold to touch.

'The valley has not yet played us so ill, Tasarnil,' said the Prince.

'O Talarnidh, tell me two things,' answered Tasarnil. 'Why do our voices sound no echo in a place such as this? And why has the young man from beyond the stars seen the shadows that move?'

Yeselwir swallowed thickly, and looked at the torchlit shapes. The men themselves seemed strange, changed by the darkness and silence. And suddenly he perceived that this feeling had come upon all of them at the same moment, as if his companions had become ragged fearful things born in the night of that valley, like the shadows that lived beyond the torchlight.

'I can see the shadows also,' said Fandorel.

'It has begun,' answered Tasarnil. 'Do not look too closely at anything. Do not even look at one another.'

'Do you know what is happening, Tasarnil?' Fandorel asked quietly.

'Fear is what is happening,' came the reply. 'Fear is what dwells here.'

'Fear is just a word, my friend,' said Talarnidh. 'Let us at least wait until we have something to fear.'

He began to go on. Tasarnil and the others stood for a moment.

'You must name this fear for us,' said Fandorel to Tasarnil.

'It is a nameless horror,' Tasarnil answered.

Then he turned and followed the Prince deeper into Wirdrilded, where he knew the nameless horror dwelt. Yeselwir and Fandorel followed. Without a word spoken they had changed places so that it was the Elf Lord who now brought up the rear and saw most clearly the shadows that walked. At first they were only shadows and they had no shape or substance. They flickered behind, a greyness in the dark, and soon there were more and more until it was become a countless band of silent ghosts that walked the ancient way upon the huge stones laid there by a dead race.

It was better while the ghosts were silent, for when the noise of the empty feet and hollow bodies began to sound on the slabs, the men knew that the nameless horror was nearer, and the voices that they began to hear were angry and mocking, full of hopelessness. The faces they half saw, when they looked back, were drawn and grim, with no eyes and gaping mouths.

'Talarnidh!' Fandorel called, and the four men halted again. 'The Elves do not fear the ghosts of mortals. But what men are these that follow us?'

'Are they the nameless horror?' asked Yeselwir.

'These little ghosts are memories, reflections of long ago,' said Tasarnil. 'I see them clearer than you, for I can remember when they passed this way. They have no eyes for they were blinded. Their voices are thin like reeds, for the silence of this valley swallowed the sound of their passing. The only echoes here are the echoes of long ago.'

They looked at him, and his face was like the faces of the fluttering ghosts that grinned in their blindness behind them.

'They were the host of the High Race,' said Fandorel. 'I pray they are only memories, and naught dwells here of their souls.'

The host of shapes swayed and whispered its horror, and watery blood ran down from the maimed eyes of the ghosts.

They went on, and the floor of the valley began to descend. As they went down the darkness was greater, and this seemed no surprise until Tasarnil said, in a voice that would have been loud outside the darkness:

'Is the torch growing dimmer?'

They saw that it was, for, as they walked on, its light declined. It seemed as if the light was being sucked out of it by some hideous breath that inhaled all light and hope into its mouth of darkness. Slowly the flames flickered, turned into bluish glimmers and then only a dying ember. They stood in the darkness, and felt a great force nearby. Deliberately and thoroughly it was beginning to have its way with their souls. No other light they struck would kindle the torch. They went on in the darkness. They could not even see the ghosts that followed.

The sounds in the valley were no earthly sounds. There was a distance in them, like many voices heard down a long passageway. But these sounds of the ghosts were replaced in their hearing by another more subtle sound that stole upon their senses. First there was only a suggestion and when they strained their ears to hear they heard nothing. But in a while they all knew what it was. All around them, rhythmic and certain, was the beat of a giant heart full of vast and hideous force, so that the sound seemed to beat in their ears like storm waves, making them sick and giddy.

'Wait . . . stop! Make it stop!' Yeselwir called out.

Fandorel caught hold of him. They stood and waited, and there was silence. The silence continued until they began to walk forward again, and then the heartbeat returned. But the ghost voices had vanished now.

'They are afraid to come farther,' said Tasarnil to Fandorel. 'Even the ghosts are afraid.'

'But what are they afraid of?' asked Fandorel.

'Other ghosts. Fouler and more hideous ghosts, not flickering shadows. Ghosts that are alive in their rottenness. — Those and the living, — that is all they have to fear.'

Talarnidh still led the way, fumbling forward with a hand against the craggy wall, while the other three walked abreast.

Though the valley was wider it was overhung by rocks so that not even a sliver of the black sky was to be seen. They were completely blind. They progressed with painful slowness by touch alone. And the thing that lived in the giant heartbeat had returned. Its intensity had grown into a thing of monstrosity. They felt as well as heard each sickening pulse now for the rock of the valley pulsed in time to it, the very stone possessed by its monstrous rhythm.

The thing in the valley lived and breathed. They began to feel the sudden sharp gusts on their faces, the first suggestion of any wind they had felt in that place. It was a while before they became conscious of the regularity of the movement of the air, — even longer before they understood that the air moved in time with the shocking thud of the heartbeat that had possessed the very mountain.

Then they perceived the new sound, — the rasping choking sound, strange yet awfully familiar. And still they could not link together the things that were happening to them to make an explanation, however full of horror it must be. Only Tasarnil understood, and he did not name his thoughts for they were madness. The new sound grew louder, until it was louder than the heartbeat itself and more distinct. It was an animal sound. It was the sound of a fleshly mouth, of throat and lungs, but it was hideously and inhumanly vast, no more only a giant, but a thing too huge for the natural world. Wheezing and blowing it sucked in the air, and blew it out in gusty breaths. And when the air of that huge breath struck their faces it was warm and rancid. And the whole cavern shook about them with the breathing and the heartbeat of the nameless horror.

Yeselwir was not born of Faerie. He did not know the mysteries that lay in the night places of the first world created. He turned and screamed and began to run, stumbling and crashing back down the valley. And whenever his hands touched the cavern walls he felt the heartbeat pulse up his quivering arms. He felt it take his body and shake him in its savageness. From wall to wall he ran, bruising and bloodying his limbs, until it seemed that he was not able to go back farther. Everywhere he turned was the raw rock that moved like flesh and beat like a heart. He pounded against the rock with his hands, and though it seemed to yield to his pummelling his hands ran red with blood.

He leaned on the wall for a moment, half-sobbing, and suddenly the heartbeat had caught him into itself. It shook his whole body. His own heart leapt and he gasped for breath and felt a great weight on his chest, as the huge and monstrous heart of the thing in the valley beat through his own heart. He tried to move but his hands seemed glued by his blood to the rock walls, while his body jerked like a doll in tune to the huge heart.

When Fandorel reached him he was choking and screaming. As the Elf Lord touched his body he felt it twist beneath the force that controlled it. Yeselwir fell to the ground, but the floor of the valley throbbed to the heartbeat and Fandorel again felt him twitch and convulse. He seized the body and leapt upwards, hoping that the rock did not overhang too low. His wings spread, and he felt their shiny surface scrape the rocks. He twisted, but he could not fly far in the confined space and the inky blackness with the weight of a man in his arms. But Yeselwir no longer writhed under the hideous strength that had taken him. Fandorel descended, landing awkwardly beside Tasarnil and Talarnidh, directing himself at their voices. They found each other by touch. Fandorel had no choice but to let Yeselwir down onto the floor of the valley again, but the thing did not return to him. Yeselwir stood, shaking and gasping, as Fandorel told them what he had felt as it had possessed the young man's body.

'We must go back,' said Talarnidh.

'It would not let me go back,' said Yeselwir, his voice shaking with half-suppressed terror, for all around them the breathing and the heartbeat filled the air with a vile sound.

'No, it will not let us go back,' said Tasarnil. 'It can possess the very stone, — change it, shape it, make it breathe. Have you not seen this, Talarnidh? We are nearly in the middle of the valley now. We must go on to meet the nameless.'

He took the lead, and somehow they went on. Every step they took the sound grew louder and the shaking of the walls and ground grew greater so that at times they put their hands to their ears to drown out the sound, — until that brought them stumbling into the throbbing black rocks that felt like flesh. And then they took their hands from their ears and stretched them out in front, so that they might avoid more than the merest touch of the stone that breathed. For the touch of it was worse even than the huge and quivering sounds.

The men all saw the thing at the same time, and no word of

Tasarnil was needed to tell them that they had come to the centre of the valley. Five or six feet above the floor of Wirdrilded, before them, in their path, gleamed a single eye, yellow and pale, lidless and with a dark pupil in it. Behind it was a pall of darkness, darker than the night they had passed through. Unwinking the eye stared at them, and a strange unknown intelligence gleamed within it. From out of that darkness came the pounding of the monster's heart and the breath which beat on their faces like the reeks of hell.

'Clasp hands, my friends,' came Tasarnil's voice, suddenly loud and resolute over the swaying earth and surging air. They did as he bade, and in the light shed by the baleful eye they saw him step forward towards it, his form a dark shape facing the eye.

'I seek the Sentinel of Guldrokh,' said Tasarnil in the tongue of Wenyaltrir. And once again he spoke, in another tongue, the speech of the Sons of the Sun.

Weaving mists began to take shape in the utter blackness behind the eye. The light it shed grew greater, and in a moment the curtain of gloom was crumbling away. The heartbeat ceased. The gasping breath died into nothing. The silence was utter. The light of the single eye gleamed down on the face in which it was set. They saw a green and crumbling skull, rotted bones and gaping jaw balanced on the thin fearful neck, the cracked and broken ribcage beneath. Against nature the ancient hideous skeleton stood there. The skull shape changed and moved in the light of the great eye. It was as if the creature lived.

'We wish to pass,' said Tasarnil, though none of his comrades understood for he spoke his own tongue.

Slowly and with the sound of grinding bone the arm of undead bones rose. The skeleton hand was stretched out towards them, the rotten fingers splayed, — held up against them. The mouth in the skull, with its black teeth, moved for certain this time, — opened and closed, but no sound came.

'You are Feralnil,' said Tasarnil.

Again the thing tried to speak. A sighing sound came from the mouth without lips or tongue, but the skeleton could say nothing. Its skull shook and nodded forward. That was Tasarnil's only answer.

'Can we pass?' Talarnidh asked, and even his voice wavered as he spoke.

'Not yet,' Tasarnil answered. 'But it will do you no more harm. It is all that remains of Feralnil, that other one of my people who came from the East of East to guide the hosts of the High Race in the days of the War of the Sceptres. This is the curse of Wirdrilded. He must wait here, the Sentinel of Guldrokh, to guard the valley for Ral . . . To wait while the flesh falls from the bone, while the very bones crumble but do not fall — and only his eye stares on into the night . . .'

'Forever?' asked Fandorel.

'No, not forever,' Tasarnil answered. Then he turned again, and gazed at the staring yellow eye. Slowly he stretched out his hand and touched the upraised hand. The bones quivered at his touch.

'I have come,' he said. 'I am Tasarnil.'

From the eye in the skull to the eye of Tasarnil the One-Eyed there passed a hazy light. Tasarnil gave a low moaning cry and writhed, his body doubled up as if in great pain.

'Now . . . Now . . . Go forward,' came his choking voice, and from Tasarnil's bent and hidden face a strange and vivid yellow glow illuminated the floor and the walls of the valley.

They looked up again at the grim skeleton and as they looked the eye that gleamed there dulled and swam with liquid, red and grey. Then the eye had burst, and thick fluid rolled from it as, broken, it fell back into the skull. As it fell, the skeleton crumbled about it. The skull was spread across with cracks and then tumbled forward in pieces into the breaking ribcage. In a moment the bones had fallen into no more than dust, and from that ancient dust a great deep sigh rose up into the stillness.

'Go!' moaned Tasarnil.

The three still held their hands clasped. It was Talarnidh that jerked them forward. He and Fandorel ran forward, almost dragging Yeselwir between them. Over the dust that was all the remains of Feralnil they ran, but then they were stopped, for Fandorel had turned and he cried:

'Wait!'

They looked back. Tasarnil had fallen to the ground now and writhed and twisted, his hands clawing at his face, his whole body bathed in the yellow light, its colour like that of a corpse. Now they saw with horror that his fingers had made furrows in the flesh, that strips of skin hung down while blood ran down his neck in runnels. He began to cry out and they realised the torment that he felt. For a moment he took his hands from his face and reached out to them. They saw the remains of his countenance, that Talarnidh had seen so many days over so many years. As they watched the flesh fell from it in drops like melted butter onto the ground, where it smoked and dissolved into pools of fat and blood.

The fingers covered the face again, but they could see the nails fall from them and the skin wrinkle, crack, and break away. They saw bone through the skin. They saw the bone of his skull where the hair died and withered. They watched him rot and decay before their eyes, and a stench of decay came from the dying flesh. At last there was no flesh left, only a skeleton, stood up and clad in armour, its hands over its face, whence came a yellow light from the single gleaming eye that did not decay.

The leather straps of the armour broke, the last of his clothes were rotted. The very bones had turned green and brittle. What had been Tasarnil took down its hands from its face and they saw the ravaged and pitted skull with one staring eye in it. He had become as Feralnil was. A new Sentinel guarded the Valley of Eternal Shadow, and trapped in its rotten skull was the mind and soul and life of their companion.

Already a curtain of mist was drawing across the shape, but not before they saw the skull mouth open and a hideous wheezing breath come gasping out. It struck them like a wave of fetor. The fragile bones shook with a faltering heartbeat, and the walls of the monstrous valley shook in unison.

'We must go back to him,' said Talarnidh in a low voice.

'He is the possession of the monster,' said Fandorel. 'Do you not see, O Prince, it is the Curse that dwells here, in the rock and in the darkness.'

Talarnidh gazed at the Elf Lord for a long moment, his tears glinting in the yellow light. And then a thunderous heartbeat shook the cavern. The gust of the monster's breath, strong as a gale, swept upon them. They looked and saw the yellow eye set in a curtain of darkness.

'Run!' cried Talarnidh. 'If only for his sake . . .'

Talarnidh, Prince of Wenyaltrir, wept as he ran, stumbling in the light of the dead undying eye of Tasarnil, deafened by the crash of the inanimate yet alive which was the heartbeat in the stone, and sickened by the dead breath from the mouth of his friend. Fandorel too wept, for the fate of the undead is the greatest of evils and he knew Tasarnil for a good man. Yeselwir ran blindly, stumbling in horror, flinching from the haunted rock walls.

The journey out of that place was as long as the way in. There were no little ghosts to haunt them and the breathing and the heartbeats grew fainter and farther. But the darkness was total, and it was a web of fear around them. For they had seen the nameless horror, and now they must name it Tasarnil.

CHAPTER 6

THE RUBY CAVERNS

On Anrith the going was not hard at first, though the slope was a steady one and in time took its toll as they mounted the foothills and spurs that led up to the High Pass itself. Grassy hillsides began to give way to bare black rocks. There was no clear path for them to follow as that way was long untrodden. Before them the lofty ridge of Keseryeth grew steadily nearer, while to their left arose the peak of Granyash, greatest of the mountains in Adanyeth, the ring that encircles Lake Khrathemrin. Between Granyash and Keseryeth lay the pass, and already they were near it. But also near, under Granyash, were the Ruby Cliffs, in which were the Caverns of Emrurl Arnag.

The four men of the Quest paused to eat in a small glade. The day was already more than half gone and there was a new chill in the afternoon air, a reminder that they were in the far north and winter was coming on. Their way now became much steeper. Giants' teeth of boulders jutted sharply, and crags hung over them high and jagged. The birds and animals of the lower regions were seen no more. The only sign of life was an eagle wheeling high overhead, almost out of sight. Few thin trees grew in the cracks in the rock, and the tufts of hill grass were sparser. Though they could not help gazing up at the Ruby Cliffs, from them came no movement.

The snows of Keseryeth drew closer ahead, as Granyash towered above them on the other side, while Ralnadh and Karnadh hid the sun to the south. The pass was in shadow, and the shadows deepened every moment. They had been climbing for four hours and they looked with trepidation on the storm clouds that began to rise to the westward over the mountains, shutting off the sun completely. But the men were weary and as they came near to the snow line that marked the High Pass it was Karandar who called a halt.

'Well, how do you say?' Melandir asked. 'There is a storm gathering for sure. — Do we go on with the crossing now?'

'I am for going as fast as we can,' answered Erathrir.

'I would rather have it done now,' Melandir agreed. He looked up at the sky and then down to the Ruby Cliffs.

'Bad, — whether we are caught here or out on the pass,' said Karandar. 'The High Pass is three to four miles across. It will take us easily an hour or two, maybe more. With luck we might be on the descent when the storm breaks.'

Relnar had noticed Melandir's glance up at the cliffs and shivered at the thought of them. Though he was a Prince of the Men of Tharang, it was not required to ask his opinion in respect of his youth. Melandir looked across at him nonetheless.

'I would not like to spend a night under the holes of the Rethrind,' he said.

'So that settles the matter,' said Erathrir, grinning at him. 'We are all of a like mind.'

He stooped for his pack, and as he did so looked back southwards towards Ralnadh.

'Look there,' he said.

The others turned. Between the high shoulder of Nal Vorod and the grim peak of Guldurin a pillar of black mist stood up into the sky.

'It comes from Wirdrilded,' said Karandar.

'The Sentinel of Guldrokh?' asked Melandir, grim-voiced. Karandar nodded.

'You have heard that cruel story also . . .?'

'Then what are we to do?' asked Melandir.

'We can do nothing at all,' Karandar answered.

Melandir looked long at the Dwarf Lord, then nodded slowly. Without a word he turned and started up the slope again. The others followed.

'What is the story of the Sentinel?' Erathrir asked Karandar as the two walked together. 'Do you believe something has befallen Talarnidh and the others in Wirdrilded? They should have passed safe through long since.'

'Erathrir, man from beyond the stars,' Karandar answered, 'forgive me that I do not tell this tale now. There may be a better time later. But now I can only hope you are right. I hope they did come through an hour or more ago . . .'

They crossed the snow line onto the High Pass through the heights of Adanyeth. Already the wind was rising, and they could see only darkness coming out of the west.

'How far is it?' asked Relnar, after they had toiled a while through the snows.

'You know as well as we,' Erathrir answered shortly. It was already clear to all four that their decision had been wrong.

'Well, there is no turning back now!' Karandar's voice was a shout as the wind screamed past the summits.

An icy gust blowing in from the west struck through their heavy cloaks and brought the first flakes of snow. Thunder murmured afar and the snow came swifter on a wind that gained in strength every minute. It bore down on the exposed pass. The men tried to push on, but the full weight of the blizzard was upon them with unnatural suddenness. The clouds of storm closed above the chaos of snow.

The men's hands and faces were already caked with ice and their eyes blinded, as they were flung from side to side. Above came the crashes of thunder, almost constant, while lightning played on the peaks. All the wildness of the blizzard was bent upon that one lonely place. The men speedily lost all sense of direction. They stumbled on, numb from the blows of cold. The storm had expanded into proportions of immensity, and vast shadowy forms seemed to hang half-seen overhead in cloud and snow. Early night began to draw on.

Ral had already awoken the thing in the Valley, that she had used once before long years ago. Now she was using the storm. Its origins were natural, but she took it up and her power was in it, giving it a sorcerous half-life of its own. But as she contrived at the death of the men of the Quest on the pass a new and breathless wind was blown out of the south. Forms of elemental giants drifted shapeless in the upper air. A new power was in the storm, controlling it. The hints of sorcery in the screaming winds diminished. The gales sighed and began to fall away. It was still a storm of great fierceness, but its malevolence had gone.

Hidden beneath the snow the feet of the men found a rocky path, and out of the whiteness before them they could see dark rocks looming. Lost and weary they wandered close up against them and then clasped the bare stone in search of a shelter under their crags. Relnar's fumbling hands felt a place before him where there was no snow, a hole in the rock. He edged forward, crying out to the others:

'Over here! I've found a cave!'

Moments saw them safe from the dying storm's anger. But as

Erathrir, last of the four, entered, the curtain of snow was swept away for a few seconds. It revealed the hugeness of the summit of Granyash, silver crowned with fiery spokes of lightning directly above the cave where they sheltered. They had not crossed the pass at all. The drums of thunder rolled out again. Warmth returned to their limbs, and the numbness slowly began to ease. There also came time to regret their decision to attempt the pass. But they were too damp and chill for long regrets.

'Strike a flint, Relnar!' Melandir ordered the young prince.

His teeth chattering, and glad of any task to do, Relnar did as he was bidden and lit one of the two torches they had brought. He warmed his hands on its bright flame. In its light it had already become clear that they were in a great cave, many yards wide and higher than they could reach. They could see no end to the cavern which sloped irregularly down into the mountains. The rock through which it bored was black with a hardly discernible trace of red streaking it. The walls and even the roof were smooth, as if it were the well-worn passage of some swift-flowing ancient river.

'I suppose our luck is not wholly bad then,' muttered Karandar. 'I will take a look further in.' He pointed into the darkness.

'Shouldn't we stay together?' said Relnar. 'The storm will pass . . . and . . . we ought to be near the entrance.'

'You may leave that to me to judge,' answered Karandar curtly. Then he laughed. 'You need have no worries, my lad, on that score. I was hardly going down into *that* any distance. — Even Dwarves do not have cats' eyes.' He turned to Melandir. 'I will take the torch and go down fifty paces.'

Melandir nodded his agreement. The Dwarf Lord took the torch from Relnar and in the light saw the frightened look in the young prince's eye, but said nothing. He walked slowly down the strange tunnel. And, as the light receded from the three near its mouth, there came to Erathrir a sudden gust of air from the cavernous depths. It was heavy with the darkness of decay and death beneath the mountain. It was full of inklings of fear and unknown scents. It was a deep earth smell from places where unknown things moved lightless. He felt a sense of some impossible memory of that place stir in him, a memory that he groped for but could not reach. But he did not doubt its foreboding.

'Karandar! Wait!' he shouted.

Karandar too had felt the breath of evernight on his face and needed nothing to tell him that it was boded ill. But before him in the torchlight he had found another sign.

'I have ill tidings, Melandir,' he called. 'Come and see this thing.'

Melandir, Erathrir and Relnar hurried to where he stood.

'What is it?' asked Relnar, and Erathrir gave a low exclamation and pointed upwards.

The walls now glowed clearly in the torchlight, a dark deep-seated red. Set in them near the roof was a great red jewel, burning and bright. Relnar reached up. He could just touch the stone, and no more had he done so but it came loose and lay on his palm. Already too late, Karandar cried:

'Do not touch the stone!'

'Why? What is it?' gasped Relnar, spinning round guiltily to look at the Dwarf.

'This is Emrurl Arnag,' said Karandar. 'The Ruby Caverns.'

'How can it be?' stuttered Relnar. '— Why did you tell me to leave the stone? Come! Let us go back to the entrance!'

'That last is right,' said Karandar. 'Better the storm than these caverns. That stone is part of the horde of Emrurl Arnag. Jewels lie here like dewdrops, but long unseen. Once this treasure did not lack its seekers, but now it is accurst. The red of the stones is fire and blood. The places under the mountain are haunted by the Rethrind. Selenthoril told you of them. Let one stone of their treasure be touched, Relnar, and they will take vengeance. In the War of the Sceptres a company came here from their camp in Lothchen to cleanse the caverns. They were slain.'

'Then the red jewel is all the confirmation we need,' said Melandir. He turned at once and started towards the mouth of the cavern.

'What if they know already, lords?' asked Relnar, and looked wide-eyed at the red gemstone in his hand.

His fears were true ones. Before they came to the mouth a sounding crash split the air before them, and a rush of red dust and stone fragments flew up in their faces and clouded the air. All light from the outside vanished. In the flickering light of the torch, as the dust cleared a little, they saw that a great stone lay like a door across the cave mouth. Before the echoes of its fall had died away they knew that there was no way past.

'The touching of the stone was the signal for their trap,' said Erathrir. Karandar shrugged:

'So we will have to fight.'

'Will they come for us . . .?' Relnar asked.

'If they did not come we would still die from hunger or thirst.' Erathrir's voice was still level and calm.

'Is there any way out, Karandar?' asked Melandir.

'All the caverns of the Ruby Cliffs are said to lead to one dark passage through the very heart of the mountain,' answered Karandar. '— Certainly there are caves in the western face of Granyash, for the Rethrind have been known to prey by night on the folk of Lothchen beneath.'

'Then we can escape?' said Relnar, hopefully. But Karandar shook his head.

'I will tell unchanged the tale I have heard. — Ever downwards go the ways, deep into the roots of the earth and mountains, where creatures of stealth delve twisting tunnels in secret and in night. There are mazes and galleries, lofty chambers, and last there are the halls of the King of the Rethrind, at the Cleft of Fires. It was in these fires that the men of the High Race died. The Rethrind are a race of the deeps of the world. It is said that they were bred by Ral in the darkness as a mockery and jest to the Dwarves. They are akin to Goblinfolk. It may be that few survive now in the world. But here as of old they have a king and are powerful. They love to kill, and have no pity.'

'And our choice is to go to meet them in the heart of their dwellings or to wait until they choose to come to us,' said Erathrir.

'It is no choice,' Melandir answered. 'We must try to find a way through.'

'It is a faint hope, Melandir. Do not doubt that,' said Karandar. 'I am no guide in these tunnels.'

'I am,' said Erathrir.

Melandir and Karandar looked at him without understanding.

'On the Island of the Stars I took the Drink that Men Desire. It is the knowledge of all that was and will be. — I know the way through these caverns.'

'At the Festival of the Lamps, Melandir,' said Karandar, 'You told that the Man, Ask, prophesied that there would be moments when Erathrir had clear sight and remembered.'

'This is one of them,' said Erathrir. 'Though I remember

nothing else of what I was shewn in the moment I drank, — I do remember these caverns. Every path and turning. I know the way through.'

'So the prophecy given to you beyond the world is a true prophecy already,' said Karandar. 'Lead us on, my friend.'

' "Guide through the Darkness",' said Erathrir with a sudden smile. Then he picked up the torch, and the men of the Quest walked into the tunnels of night.

In his mind it was as if Erathrir could see the intricate network of caverns laid out before him. He walked fast, for the floor was still smooth and polished. Now and again he looked back in the torchlight to see the glint of armour on the short heavy form of Karandar a few paces behind. Once his eyes met the fleeting glance of Relnar, close beside Melandir, but always gazing around and about him in the flickering glow. All had drawn their swords.

Now reflected gleams of crimson were flashing back from the red rock walls, for they were studded with many a gem as fine as that which Karandar had found at the entrance. This time no-one touched them. The passage had begun to wind and curve, and many small burrowings joined it as the men went deeper in. Their sense of time became uncertain. Only Erathrir could tell the way, though they all knew that it was always downwards to the ever-dark of hidden rocks.

At first they neither saw nor heard any sign of life. But as they progressed deeper there came rustlings from the side tunnels, whisperings, and small white forms that fled in the light. Soon also the sounds came from the main passage, first only distantly before them, but then bolder and nearer, and also from behind. All around they could hear movement and rumour of voices, but they saw only fleeting glimpses. As the voices came nearer, and their owners lurked just outside the circle of torchlight, Relnar spoke to Melandir:

'Let us go back. They are near us . . . Awful things. Listen to them!'

Erathrir halted, and turned.

'There is nothing to go back to. And they are behind us also. They are closing in.'

Melandir tested the weight of Wenyorel, Sword of Fate, in his hand. Then he looked out into the darkness and back into the dark face of the young prince. Relnar had not been outside the wide fields and rolling hills of Chamley the Golden before. Caves to him meant the brilliant chambers of deep-delven Chamalat, blazing with the lamps of the Mountain Kings.

'So now we know it is to be the Rethrind,' said Melandir. 'We have no reason to fear them as yet. But we will test their will — and see.'

Karandar looked at Melandir and remembered the men of the High Race who had died in that place and the cruel fires of the Rethrind.

'The passage grows wider in front of us,' said Erathrir. 'Room to swing a sword. We can stop there if we are going to make a stand.'

Melandir half jerked Relnar forward and they ran down the passage, now resounding to their clatter. They came to the place where it was high and straight and no side tunnels entered.

'I hope you can use that sword,' Karandar grinned at Erathrir.

'It was you who taught me at the castle,' Erathrir answered.

'Erathrir and Karandar, the far end,' said Melandir swiftly. 'I'll take this end. — Relnar, between us. Two tasks, Relnar. Hold up the torch, — and take any of the Rethrind that come through. — But the torch is most important. In the dark we are as good as dead.'

Relnar nodded.

'I understand.'

Melandir released his arm, and turned to face the darkness. Four swords shone in the torchlight. The blades of Erathrir, Karandar, and Relnar were tongues of blue light, the dragon-steel of Wenyaltrir, but Wenyorel was dull iron, glinting bitterly.

'Here they come!' cried Karandar suddenly, and the Rethrind were upon them.

Small, half-human creatures they were, scarcely three feet high, and their skin a death-like bloodless white. Their arms were long, and claw-shaped hands dragged along the ground. Their bodies were unclothed, and a thick rotten stink was on their limbs. They might have appeared as some strange breed of ape but for the devil-light that shone in their eyes. These had once been the servants of Ral, and now they were about her work again.

In the light the Rethrind were not so much terrible as foul and repugnant. They were creatures without hope, aimless in their short cruel lives. They came, and in one rush a dense-packed howling mass charged at Melandir. Long fangs bared, and clawing hands flashed at his eyes. Wenyorel fell in a great arc upon the press of bodies just as they reached him. Hideous heads rolled and bounced against the rock walls, pink thin blood gushing and spurting onto the floor. Further down the cave Karandar and Erathrir also hacked and hewed at the throng, cleaving bodies and spilling hot entrails. The Rethrind made many charges, but their enemies remained unshaken and even unhurt amidst the blood and the dead.

Only one passed Wenyorel, springing with a cry of hate upon Melandir and sinking its poisoned teeth into his throat. Melandir felt a moment of dread, but the power of the sword was upon him. He knew no harm and felt no pain. Even as the creature howled its triumph he flung it from him, a clammy thing of slime. He thrust once.

But as the attack went on and on, Erathrir and even Karandar had begun to tire with the weight of armour on their shoulders and the heavy swords in their hands. Erathrir paused to wipe the blood from his face, only to jerk a weary arm back up to defend himself from some leaping horror of teeth and staring eyes, as a fresh and yet more violent assault broke upon him and Karandar.

One creature larger than the rest sprang at Erathrir. On its head was a cap of iron set with one red stone that shone with a fiery light of its own. And in its pallid hand, alone of the Rethrind armed with more than tooth and claw, it held a long metal spike. Screaming it thrust its short spear at Erathrir. The spear struck him over the heart and smashed on the steel of his breastplate. Erathrir raised his sword and struck with all his force. The iron helm was shattered, the skull cleft in two from crown to chin so that broken brains dribbled out. The claw-like hands clutched, already dead, at Erathrir's throat.

At this a shout of fear rose from the hordes of the Rethrind. For their king lay dead at Erathrir's feet. They turned and fled, leaving all their fallen. Karandar and Erathrir moved cautiously forward over the corpses, and from behind them came a sudden cry of fear. Turning, they saw Melandir go down. He had slipped in the blood and fallen. The sword was still in his hand, but a press of the enemy bore upon him.

'Relnar!' cried Erathrir, for only the young prince of Chamley was near enough to help in time.

Relnar gave Erathrir one frightened look. Then he spun round and sprang at the Rethrind, smashing the firebrand into the faces of the nearest and sweeping fiercely with his sword. His blows were wild, but they served their purpose. One of the Rethrind screamed in pain, blinded by the fire. Two others, howling from their wounds, released Melandir's sword arm. They had been struggling to wrench the sword from him, but now it thrust again and again as he regained his feet. Then Erathrir and Karandar were upon them. Suddenly the Rethrind had broken and were fleeing, all their attacks defeated, and their king dead on the cavern floor.

'Are you hurt?' Melandir asked the others. 'Your aid to me was timely.'

'A scratch at the most,' said Karandar. 'This blood on me is not mine.'

'Relnar fought well,' said Erathrir.

'I did nothing. I was greatly afraid,' answered Relnar.

'You played your part well,' said Melandir. 'And I do not count the aid you gave to me as nothing.'

'I think that no-one now will worry as to your skill with a sword, my friend Erathrir,' said Karandar. 'It seems I taught you well.'

Karandar lit their second and last torch from the remains of that which Relnar had borne. They wiped the blood from their clothing as well as they could, and cleaned their swords. One last thing Erathrir did. From the wrecked helm of the King of the Rethrind he took the red jewel and, with the gold wire that had bound it, did it onto his own helm. Then he led them again into the darkness. Their way was now a maze of winding alleyways and intersecting tunnels, all appearing the same. In and out and round many corners the path went, but it was still always downward. Sometimes they passed through wide halls, sometimes they almost had to crawl in dark burrows. The second torch burnt away as they came to the heart of the mountain.

As its light died the men realised that they were not in complete darkness. They linked hands, and Erathrir led on. From the walls, the roof, the very floor of the wide cavern they had entered shone a myriad points of faint redness. They passed down a great gallery encrusted with rubies, thicker than the stars in the sky. And as they went on the light from the stones became greater. They never knew whether the stones shone with their own light or by reflection. For ahead, at the end of that immeasurable gallery, there was another light that grew steadily greater.

The increase of light was slow, so that they were not blinded as it became brighter and brighter. Their bodies threw huge shadows across the glistening gems. Soon they could see as clearly as in daylight, though it was a darker, deeper, redder light there in the deep-earth places. With the light came a vast rushing noise and a heat that was already beating upon their faces. They came to the Cleft of Fires. A huge domed space opened out before them, and across its midst ran a chasm that seemed to gush with light, orange-yellow at its heart, and all edged around with crimson, too fierce to look upon directly. From time to time torrents of flame rushed redly up from the glowing depths to splash against the immense roof and then cascade down in gouts of fire. Over the cleft, where the flames lept up, the roof itself had become one great vivid jewel. Many great caverns met in the hall of the Cleft of Fires, and these were the chambers of the Rethrind, where the king had held his squalid court amidst the splendours.

'This way,' called Erathrir, shouting above the roaring of the flames.

He turned to the right, and they travelled along the wall of the cavern, as far away from the heat as they could. There were many curtained burrows high and low in the sheer wall, but no sign of the Rethrind. Then Erathrir led them upwards, a craggy, narrow and tortuous path that ascended the cliff side precipitously. Hours passed on the climb, so steep was the way. The cliff side began to curve round over the Cleft of Fires below, and the heat grew greater. They looked down into the intolerable brightness, and looked away half-blinded. They were almost at the domed roof of that majestic place. They could all see the bridge across the chasm.

They saw that it was many yards across, but that was all they could see, for it shone too brightly to look at. The bridge was made of ruby, its original stone changed by the fires of countless aeons until it had become a gem of impossible immensity, every facet and surface of it blazing with the light of the fires below. The light from the uneven surface flashed and darted in their eyes, dazzling and blinding them. They reached the beginning of the bridge, but could not even look at it.

'We cannot cross here,' said Melandir. 'It is a certain fall into the fires.'

'It is the only path,' said Erathrir quietly. 'We will cross.

Everyone come close. Put your hand on the shoulder of the man in front. I will lead across.'

'You will be blinded by the light of the bridge,' cried Relnar.

'You had best trust the Lord Erathrir,' said Karandar. 'He has led us this far.'

Slowly the chain of four humans moved out onto the jewel bridge, the other three following closely in Erathrir's steps, relying on touch alone to guide them forward. From below arose the roaring of the fires, the heat and the great brightness. They closed their eyes to the brilliance, and trusted to Erathrir. Every step was slow and tested, for the shining surface was like irregular glass. Like an insect the group of men edged onwards. They reached the top of the bridge, and descended the opposite curve. Erathrir stood on the rough stone of the ledge on the farther cliff and helped the others off the brilliant bridge one by one.

'How did you see, in the light of the burning jewel?' asked Relnar with awe in his voice.

'I did not see. I remembered,' said Erathrir. 'Every facet and contour of the bridge of ruby was in my memory. I relied on that alone.'

'So you could see nothing?' said Karandar, with a suspicious look at Erathrir.

All three stood, still running with sweat, and that not only from the heat. All three looked at Erathrir.

'For certain I could not see,' he replied, grinning. 'I had my eyes as tight shut as yours . . .'

There was a moment of silence, and then Karandar began to laugh aloud, slapping his knees in mirth. Melandir sat down, shaking his head.

'I am glad we did not know that before we crossed,' he muttered.

They rested for a few minutes, and then went up the steep tunnel that led away from the Cleft of Fires. On the far side of the bridge they had seen Rethrind scurrying, but none attempted to cross. For though the halls of the Rethrind are all about the Cleft of Fires, they rarely tread beside it, hating the light but needing the heat to stay alive. It was many years since any of the Rethrind had dared the crossing of the bridge.

The fire lit the way of the men of the Quest for a great distance. Then the path began to bend and they walked more slowly, again relying on touch in the utter darkness. The light of day came as a sudden faint glow after a series of maze-like turnings. They ran towards it and stood blinking and blinded in the light of dawn, beneath them the roar of breakers at the cliff foot, the blue-grey sea before them to the horizon.

CHAPTER 7

ALDEL MORN

Dark was the night neath the looming Dargul, but darker still the comrades' fears. They had taken a whole day to cross Alat, far longer than they had planned. Whatever paths there might have been, beside the River Nirid, had been swallowed up by the spreading of the Poisoned Marsh, a swamp that lay beyond the river and now encroached on its hither bank also. By the time they had made their way out to the higher ground, the morning and most of the afternoon had gone. By the time they reached the Dargul, close by Ir Angornyekh, it was near nightfall. The day ended with a storm coming down from the mountain ring to the northward.

Alat had proved a grey and dismal land, and their spirits had fallen as they crossed it. They camped there because Fermilondath who led them ordered it, judging it best not to enter Aldel Morn by night. It was he who stood watch while his brother Turnalordath of the High Race and also Wondrith of Morena and Filindrin of Alban, all Lords of Wenyaltrir, slept. He recognised the hidden menace of Alat, and guessed that the power of Ral was awake again in that land.

The new day dawned, ice-cold again, and when Fermilondath awakened his companions, their mood was as cheerless as the day. They ate hastily, then moved off towards Ir Angornyekh. Above them a grey sky drizzled unceasingly. Beneath their feet was the road of vast grey slabs, made even before the time of Ral, beyond the skills of the men of later days. They rounded an outflung spur of the Dargul, and saw before them the gap in the Rim of Fear, Ir Angornyekh, Gate of a Thousand Sorrows.

'This cannot be!' said Wondrith, and they stood and stared.

Black it was as the Dargul, high and sheer and iron-crowned, the gatehouse of Aldel Morn. An unchallenged fortress, its immeasurable dome of iron towered above them. Its immensity daunted their hearts, for the pillars which supported the ancient roof were the size of the hall in the little palace where Talarnidh had dwelt on Alban, and the gateway was a path of giants. The rock glistened like jet in the rain. The spears that glinted above the blue iron gates were the size of ten men. Stone and steel alike all bore the appearance of a fortress finished that morning, the metal unrusted, the stone unchipped, and all huge beyond understanding.

'I saw this place riven and smoking in ruin,' said Wondrith, '— a thousand years ago when the Sceptres destroyed the Black Lords.'

'It has been rebuilt,' said Fermilondath.

'There is no-one left in the world who could fashion such stones. This is the work of the Old Ones who have gone down into the darkness and the underworlds. This is the thing they built before even Ral conversed with them and learnt the echoes of their monstrous knowledge.'

'You are saying that sorcery has restored it,' said Filindrin.

'I did not even know there was such sorcery in Tharang,' answered Wondrith, and he was a mighty wizard among the Elves.

They looked up at the eerie patterns made by the immensity of the stones, but most they looked at the thin crack between the two doors that dwarfed both them and the whole land. Fermilondath motioned them to move forward and cautiously they came up to the utter blackness of the crack. Their way was made difficult by the tangle of creepers that flourished before the gatehouse, though none grew on the dripping walls. Their fronds were black and twisted and they moved as the men passed through them. They bore red flowers, though it was late in the year, and when the men touched the petals they found that the edges were sharp and cut them. They passed through the strange growths and, as they neared the doors, the silence became more pronounced, the only sounds a faint rustling from the writhing flowers and the pit-pat of rain on their petals. It was an expectant and waiting silence.

'These are the flowers of Ral,' said Wondrith. 'You have heard how she used them in the temple beyond the marsh.' The others nodded.

'Can you not feel the evil in the air?' said Turnalordath. 'We are awaited here.'

'Look, — on the door,' said Filindrin.

They saw there, beneath the jutting spearheads, carved in the iron, one vast sign in the middle of each door.

'It is the letter "S" in the High Speech,' said Fermilondath. 'I do not know its significance here. — I do not think we can wait to weigh up these signs. — We will have to go on. There are likely to be foes in here. I will enter first. — Follow at arm's length, one by one. Be prepared to defend yourselves.'

One by one they passed through the space between the great doors into the dark beyond. Filindrin entered last, and as he went he looked up at the huge letter 'S'. Even as he crossed into the gatehouse he saw it twist and change its shape, spreading itself into a word engraved into the ironwork:

'S A G O T H'

In the gatehouse the darkness was total. As each entered the light from the gap between the doors was blotted out utterly. But sounds were not. In the inky black every sound was magnified a thousandfold. Each heard his own breathing, the blood in his veins, the crash of his armour at every step, the banging of the grains of dust on the ground. Then they heard the screaming, fearful echoing screams that seemed to shake their bodies from side to side. They gasped and staggered, deafened by the uproar, a sound distorted into a gargantuan roaring, but which was still somehow recognisable as a man screaming in unknowable torment. It lasted no more than a few minutes, dying into an equally massive and vile groaning and gasping. But amid that human sound was another noise, not human at all but animal, the sound of an animal, or many of them, feeding. Filindrin, Wondrith and Fermilondath all tried to add their voices to the noise as they called to each other, but were defeated by the distortions and echoes and the strange giant quality in every sound.

As the groans of the man died away the light began to return, faint at first, a thin shaft of light like dusk or dawn behind them, and then a similar sliver far away before them. The light increased until they could see much of the vast hall. The gate where they had entered was behind them and now the crack between the doors admitted the wan daylight. Another doorway, similarly nearly closed, was far away. Above was the dome. Some distance towards the farther door, a tattered humped shape lay on the floor. Fermilondath, Wondrith and Filindrin approached it.

It was an armoured body, its cloak torn, its face in the dust. Fermilondath turned it over, and looked into the staring sightless sockets of Turnalordath's skull. As he lifted the head the skull came free from the stripped skeleton. It fell to the ground with a clatter of collapsing bones and armour. The high-crested helmet slid from off the skull. For a moment, Fermilondath held the death's head of his brother in his hand, his eyes widening into a sightless stare. Then, with a great agonized cry, he let it drop to the ground. Again and again he cried out, wordless shouts, his hands held across his eyes. This time no echo was needed to tell the horror of these cries. Only after a long while did Fermilondath cease to cry. Then he knelt beside the corpse.

'O my brother,' he said, and then said no more.

The light increased, and Filindrin, looking about, suddenly exclaimed:

'Look there!'

He pointed towards the farther door. A shape moved there, sluggishly along the ground. Their swords were still drawn, and Wondrith and Filindrin ran towards it. It tried to escape, but was caught between them. It turned on Wondrith, snarling and spitting. Wondrith looked into a great rat face set in a misshapen body. Its fur was matted and it gave off a vile stench. From its mouth hung the shreds of Turnalordath's cloak. Its teeth still ran with blood. Wondrith drove his sword between the tiny eyes and the creature writhed dying on the ground.

'There are others there in the shadows,' said Filindrin.

'We must get Fermilondath out of here,' Wondrith answered. 'Have you seen how light it has become?'

He pointed upwards. Across the immense dome there were places where the iron had become translucent. Somehow they could see the sky through it. The huge blocks of the walls also became unreal. They went over to Fermilondath. Wondrith took his arm. Unbidden the Lord of the High Race stood up. He took his hands from his face.

'It were better he had died in another place,' he said. 'You know how many years are ended here . . .? It is all my life. The old days . . . they are dying . . . and only grief remains — for us who live.'

He did not look again at the body, but turned and strode towards the farther doors. He did not seem to notice the changes in the gatehouse. Wondrith and Filindrin followed him out into Aldel Morn. As they passed through the door there came a muted roaring behind them. Both spun round. A cloud of mist or dust or something even less substantial arose all around the gatehouse. As it cleared they saw only a ruin. The great iron dome had fallen and was no more than rusted wreckage. The gigantic columns and blocks were smashed and crumbling. Ir Angornyekh lay as it had a thousand years before when the Lords of the Sceptres destroyed it.

Wondrith turned to Filindrin.

'Whatever is here, Filindrin, it is beyond my power,' he said. And Filindrin told him the word he had read on the great gate.

They chose to go on, for the power that dwelt in the gateway was now behind them, though they had little doubt that it lay in waiting before them also. They stood beside Fermilondath and looked out across Aldel Morn. Fermilondath alone did not turn to look back.

They stood on the edge of a wide flat plateau, all its horizons mountain-ringed. The land lay under perpetual twilight. No trees or grass grew there beneath the sunless sky. The soil was bare and arid, strewn with boulders and powdery white ash. Here and there deep-cut trenches scarred the face of the land. A stone road stretched out before them. It went to Grathgel, City of Black Fire. They could see the towers of the city in the distance. Their way led through its streets.

They walked unspeaking, — Fermilondath almost unseeing. His eyes were fixed on some unknown distance. The stillness of the bare land was like a cloak over all of them. The sense of great power, waiting within the very earth, grew on them. Their minds could not escape from the memory of Turnalordath, and the parody of his screams as he died. It was no longer Ral that they feared but something much older, something stronger and darker.

And far away in the Forest of Sorcery Ral turned her thoughts to the North, and fear gnawed in her heart. She had sent the snows upon Anrith, but they had only frozen the stones. Other forces had been at work, and her victims had gone without trace. In Wirdrilded she had awoken the old curse that she had used once before. One of her enemies remained there, but three had escaped. She took no joy in the stark bones that were her trophy in the Valley of Eternal Shadow. Aldel Morn had served her strangest of all. Long years she had gazed from afar on its towers of torment, and now she called up again her vestiges of power that slept there. But in a gust of coldness her stratagems were blown away. Another overmastering force denied the land to her. Impotent she watched by sorcery across the leagues of wasteland as the men of the Quest entered. The things of the tombs did not heed her spells. The shadows did not weave the shapes she summoned. She guessed at what might lie there, and shuddered for fear of that dark thing.

The three who survived in Aldel Morn knew that dark thing better. They felt its presence round every turn and behind every boulder. They breathed in its horror from the still air. In their minds it whispered that it was waiting, waiting for night and silence. They were drawn back into memories of the Time Before Time when creatures fed in the evernight deep in the Pit of the Worlds. For in Aldel Morn memories had never died from before Ral and before Sagoth. They knew what the thing in the Black Land was doing to them, but they could not prevent it. Their minds dwelt on the unknown and unnameable, and they knew that it stalked their steps and waited before them alike.

They entered Grathgel. The ancient structures of the Black Lords had been smashed by the hosts of the High Race and by Selenthoril, but the ruins were still huge beyond comprehension, full of alien shapes, the broken pinnacles of towers that had once stood higher than mountains, curved and twisted concourses and deep pits at their ends. Everywhere the massive stones were riven, and their fragments, shards of shapes already strange and unhuman, formed haunting vistas and cast unrecognisable shadows across the devastated city. As in the re-created gatehouse no windows were to be seen nor even doors. If the Black Lords had come out into the light their ways in and out were not those that men might use. The conviction grew on them that the lurking moster lay there in Grathgel.

In the centre of the city was a pyramid, skewed and unusually shaped so that at one moment it seemed ill-formed and at the next the designer's strange art was made apparent in its disproportion. Amid a city of stone it alone was iron. It was known to them, for deep within it the Black Lords had once held their hideous conclave. Around it there had been great slaughter when the Lords of the Sceptres swept over Aldel Morn. Now from it there went up a cloud of foreboding, but they could not pass by its black empty door. For out of the darkness came a voice.

'Fermilondath! Fermilondath! They have trapped me here. Deep down in the darkness . . , I cannot see, Fermilondath. My eyes are gone . . . I cannot feel or hear. Help me, Fermilondath! I do not know what they have done to me . . . I thought I was dead . . .'

Fermilondath stood like a statue, his face rigid and utterly white. The voice was that of Turnalordath. In a second he was running forward. Before Wondrith and Filindrin could move he had crossed into the doorway. Then they went after him. Inside they saw Fermilondath ahead of them, visible in the light from the door, running down a vast empty corridor that plunged steeply into the ground beneath the iron pyramid. Far away at its end was another light, so far away that they could have no idea of its source. For that underground way seemed endless. Wondrith leapt upwards and so massive was the place that he could fly as if in the open air. He sped over Fermilondath's head, and landed before the lord of the High Race. Fermilondath stopped. Then, seeing the Elf unmoving, drew his sword.

'Put your sword away, Fermilondath. This is madness,' said Wondrith, and as he spoke the word 'madness' he saw the uneasy light flickering in Fermilondath's eyes, and he realised that his words might be entirely true.

'Let me pass, Elf!' said Fermilondath.

'We will come with you, my Lord Fermilondath,' said Wondrith. 'If only for the love that we too bore towards Turnalordath, we would come with you. But he is dead, Fermilondath. You saw him dead.'

'I heard his voice,' answered Fermilondath. 'He is here. — I heard his voice here. Do not stand in my way, Elf Lord.'

Wondrith stood aside, and Fermilondath walked past him. At a little distance Wondrith and Filindrin continued to follow him. The grim light grew slowly clearer. They neared the end of the great passageway beneath the city of the Black Lords. They emerged into a chamber huge beyond comprehending. Box-like shapes stretched into the distance around the walls, all of them closed with stone. In the middle of the room a similar box lay unlidded, flat on the floor. From it issued the grim light that in some way diffused throughout the vault.

'Come Fermilondath! This is a trap,' said Wondrith.

But just as he spoke the uncanny voice came again, clear beyond any doubt. It was the voice of Turnalordath, and it came from the stone casket that lay in the middle of the great underground hall.

'Fermilondath . . . do not leave me here. They have taken everything from me, down here in the darkness, Fermilondath.'

Fermilondath ran forward, sword in hand, and gazed into the stone box. At first the light that came out of it blinded him. Then, as he began to see clearly, he gave a long groan, and the sword fell from his nerveless hand. Once again he was looking full on the sight of his brother's face. It was as he had seen it last, a staring grinning skull. But in his despair Fermilondath knew a new peak of horror from which he would never descend.

The dead mouth moved, and from the empty throat came the voice of Turnalordath calling his name. Then the pile of cracked and ruined bones was stirring. Against all nature the foul thing was lifting itself up. Hideous hands clutched at Fermilondath. Brittle fingers of bone pulled him, rigid and paralysed, down towards the awful head. The lips of the skull touched those of Fermilondath in a kiss. And from the mouth came an exhalation of utter foulness. For a long moment it held him without effort, and its charnel breath breathed into his lungs. As the clutching hands released him, he fell backwards. His face was already a livid green, his eyes bulging, his fingers grasping at his throat. Yellow froth surrounded his lips. He writhed and twisted. Wondrith and Filindrin ran forward to help, but in his torment they could not hold him. They watched in horror as he died, falling at last beside the stone coffin.

'It is as he said,' said Wondrith. 'Now at last the old days are passing. For the first time in a thousand years two of the Lords of Wenyaltrir have fallen.'

'Is it one of the things of Sagoth again?' asked Filindrin quietly. Wondrith looked at him sharply.

'So you too have seen to the heart of the evil. I believe it must be. I believe that he must have come here again, here in Aldel Morn where so many lie dead.'

As he spoke the word 'dead' he felt speech die in his throat, and the presentiment of evil became so pressing that he darted a glance behind him. But it was from the grim coffin that the voice came, timeless and distant and steeped in sin:

'Dead and dark as buried bone,
Cold and hard as deepest stone,
Here in sorcery enwrapt,

Deep in night eternal trapped,
Ye will pass your tortured years
And none will hear your pain-wrackt tears.'

There was a long silence, then Wondrith spoke quickly:

'Come! We are in a place with the mysteries of Hell.'

Filindrin glanced at the motionless form that had been Fermilondath.

'I must take his sword to Talarnidh,' he said. He moved to take it.

'Beware the thing in the coffin!' cried Wondrith.

Filindrin glanced quickly into the grey-green light from the coffin. Nothing moved. It was empty. The bones of Turnalordath, and the thing that had made them move, were gone.

'It is empty,' he said. And at once the voice from the pit took up its mocking echo:

'Empty lies the coffin stark,
Now the crypt is bare and dark,
Long have I in boneyard dire
Wrought for you this funeral pyre.
Ye will bear the balefire wyte
In charnel house of evernight.'

As the voice spoke the light changed into a sullen red glow about the coffin, fading every second. And then profound blackness. Filindrin felt Wondrith's hand clasp his arm.

'There is little hope for us now, my friend, and no help at all,' said the Elf. 'I only wish the end did not have to come in this place of sorrow.'

'Lord Wondrith, I fear the manner of our death,' said Filindrin into the darkness.

The voice spoke again, this time quiet and almost sensuous:

'Death will never woe abate,
Endless torment is your fate.
Fallen now beneath my sway
Hopeless ye will mourn for ay.
Soon draws near the time when all
Shall lie beneath the bloodstained pall.'

Slowly the red light returned, growing imperceptibly, not in the empty coffin but rather where Fermilondath lay. Flickering flames crackled and leapt about his body but did not burn it. The body was no longer as it had fallen. Wrapped round and about it, swathing it completely, were the winding bandages of a corpse, tattered and dripping in blood. The balefire moved up and down the swathed form. A smell like burning flesh came into their nostrils, but still the body did not burn.

The crash resounded through the cavernous vaults. The two survivors of the Quest started, gasping and fearful. All around those immeasurable walls the carven lids fell crashing and shattering from the stone coffins. Rows of haggard dead, fading into the distant shadows, stood silent, guardians of night. All had once been wrapped in shrouds as Fermilondath was. The tatters hung on them still, half-revealing taut parchment skins stretched over brittle bones.

'Look at the eyes!' Filindrin cried, and Wondrith saw that the shrunken, hardened eyes glistened with life.

'They are the Black Lords,' said Wondrith. 'Or their corpses. The thing here has possessed them.' He spoke, and already the flames about Fermilondath were dying. 'We were given that light to see the dead by,' Wondrith's steady voice went on. 'Now the real horror comes when the light is gone. See! The dead begin to move.'

Slowly, little by little, the corpses of the Black Lords began to stir. Ragged winding sheets fluttered across skin-bound ribcages. Stiffened limbs were raised. Whispers came from lips drawn back in fleshless grins. Creakings came from ancient bones. The stiff ranks of the evil dead advanced, and the light faded apace. Then the light was gone, and darkness filled the underground places. In the blackness the corpses came on unseen, grotesque and slow. Hideous hands stretched out towards the men.

Wondrith lifted his Elven bow and pointed it towards the far-off roof. He fired the arrow and as it flew spoke a sentence in the Wizards' Speech. The arrow kindled in its flight, with a flame of brilliant vivid white, too bright to look at. Once again Wondrith and Filindrin could see the dead, and they were near to them now, but they had halted — suddenly as if in mid-step. The arrow fell to the floor but continued to blaze. Only as its light began to fade did the first signs of movement return to the bodies of the Black Lords. The swifter the light died from its final flare, the swifter they began to approach again. Wondrith spoke quietly:

'These are not the undead, Filindrin. The corpses are moved by another power. And it needs the darkness. It cannot move them in the light.'

'Can you make light?' Filindrin asked.

As he spoke, the last flicker of the blazing arrow was extinguished. The rustling came of the corpses in the darkness. Wondrith drew a handful of arrows from his quiver. He stuck the first into the thick dust on the floor, speaking swiftly all the while. Then the other arrows were treated in the same way, until a wide circle was formed around them, and all the while the dead approached. Only when the circle was complete did he speak the final word. A ring of pearl white light surrounded them on the instant. It did not flicker and it did not fade. The arrows were not burnt, they only shone. For Wondrith was the last of the great Elven wizards. Outside the ring of light the dead stood stiff and unmoving in many ranks, entirely surrounding them.

'How do we pass them?' Filindrin asked, hope in his voice for the first time. Wondrith smiled.

'They are only poor dead bodies,' he answered.

He fitted another arrow to his bow, pointed it at the nearest of the silent dead, and let fly. The arrow kindled in the air, struck the chest of the corpse, and in a moment the winding sheet and the dust-dry body were blazing like a torch. Flames ran up the next of the dead Black Lords, and then three of them and four, and soon many of them were burning as they stood.

'Draw your sword!' called Wondrith. 'The passage we entered by is over there.'

Filindrin only paused for a moment. Then, rushing past the burning arrows, he hacked at the row of the dead which barred the path. The bodies caved in under the sweep of the sword, limbs rent, bones broken, dried out skin and flesh crumbling into bitter dust. Soon he was through their circle. Wondrith followed him and, as the two ran towards the massive corridor that led out to the light, the Elf Lord paused at intervals to drive an arrow into the dust. As soon as his fingers left it, it burst into flame. A path of light stretched behind them. The brightness grew all the while in the huge halls lit by the magic of the Elves and the last pyre of the Black Lords.

They came to the doorway of giants, and its blocks glistened in the white light, but the doorway itself was utterly black before them. The distant daylight did not show at the end of the tunnel, and in the magic fire the darkness seemed even blacker. Wondrith caught Filindrin's arm and paused. He seemed to sniff the air, then bade his companion go forward, but slowly. He placed no less than ten of the flaming arrows across the mouth of the passage.

'Come! Your fires will not hold the dead in check much longer,' said Filindrin.

'It is not them I fear,' Wondrith answered. 'Have you not seen how the light does not enter the passage? There is something in there. I sense it now . . . I have never known its like. I feel that it is vast . . . too great for this whole place. It is the thing of Sagoth, the thing we knew was here, Filindrin.'

'Then we still must die here?' cried Filindrin, disbelieving.

'I hope that it is only a matter of dying, but I know it is worse,' answered Wondrith.

Across the mouth of the immense tunnel something began to take shape. First a long, low shadow stretching back into darkness, dark itself. Then it filled out, greater, and every second clearer, the head of an unimaginable beast, a great black dog. Its substance was foul and changing, not natural, caked with slime and surrounded in a fetor beyond bearing. Its jaws worked and the sound of them sickened the two lone humans as they stood before one of Hell's monstrosities. Suddenly Filindrin, held as if in a trance by the staring animal eyes of the thing, realised that Wondrith was speaking to him.

'Listen, Filindrin! It is the Hound of Hell!'

Filindrin shook his head, not understanding. But Wondrith well knew what manner of thing it was. Far away beyond the Kingdoms of the Dead and the endless plains of the Underworld to the Gate of Hell, twined in the roots of the World Tree, the Hound had heard its name called, and it had stirred in its satiated sleep. Only once before had such a call come to it, and then it had been the death of the High King of Wenyaltrir. Slowly it rose once more from long dreams of blood and crossed the boundaries between its own unknowable existence and the worlds above. The bounds of the world were jarred as the Hound of Hell took shape in the land of Aldel Morn.

'Go back! Find another way out!' said Wondrith to Filindrin.

'You must tell the story of this if you escape. I will hold the creature here until I am slain.'

Filindrin began to protest.

'Do as I command,' answered Wondrith. 'What can you do here?'

Filindrin began to back away to the side of the great hall, his eyes darting about, searching for another door, but always his glance returning to where Wondrith stood. The Hound's snout filled the doorway, and its darkness began to expand into the chamber. Filindrin saw that Wondrith had doubled the line of flaming arrows and, as the Hound made its first move to cross, a great flash of light went up from the Elf Lord's hand. But even as it flared Filindrin could see the massive snout through it, and the darkness of the Hound seemed more visible than the light.

The creature moved its head from side to side and its panting seemed loud and hungry. The breath of it touched the flaming arrows. Their light turned from white to indigo and then a dull drab red. The giant paw stepped over the line of dim funereal light. The forequarters of the Hound grew even greater as they came into the chamber of the tomb. It assaulted the senses with its very being. It was not misshapen, for it had no real shape. Wondrith stood beneath its great jaws and looked into a pit of sentient darkness. He held his sword above his head and, as the light from all the remaining arrows turned into that same awful red, the Elf Lord himself shone with blue-white fire.

The great head of the Hound dipped slowly towards him. Fluid showered from its mouth and lay in green stinking pools in the dust. It seemed to savour its victim. Its eyes swam with blood and lust. A huge sigh came from the throat, that was the echo of a roar far away. The creature hated the clean light. Then Wondrith had leapt from the ground, his winged form shining and fair, into the mouth of darkness, the gleaming sword stabbing. Another sigh came from the mouth as he cut at it, hovering by its very teeth.

But it was his last act. From beneath the same teeth came a gush of slime, and there was no magic to guard against that fluid. The wings of his body shrivelled, his hair burnt away, and his eyes were seared out by the juice of vitriol. He fell blind to the ground, his flesh already turning grey with sudden disease. Twisting and tormented he felt the teeth close about him, not biting but caressingly. It lifted his body up and the deep mouth, slowly and with infinite delight, began to suck the soul and life from him. He had lived in the world through all the Aeons and before time began. He knew amidst the agony and horror now the full tale of his fate. What had been him would forever be a fragment, broken memories and long sorrow, a crawling senseless thing inside the great hound. The last of the dull muddy light died in the chamber.

Filindrin had stayed long enough to see his comrade die, held there by the horror of it. As the darkness fell, he began to run, for far away in the side of the underground tomb he could see the faint greyish outline of a door. He did not let himself think about what he had seen, or of the horror that lay behind him. It seemed time beyond measure before he reached the doorway and plunged through it. Before him stretched another of the massive corridors, no end to it in sight except the grey light far away. He ran until his lungs were bursting, counting the endless succession of gargantuan blocks that made up the wall, so that his mind could dwell on that alone.

At last he came to another smaller doorway set in the midst of one of those immeasurable blocks. A light came from it, grey like unbroken dawn and grim, but a light. Down a flight of black steps he clattered and when they ended fell forward, stumbling, onto his knees. He looked up. The quality of the light seemed worse now, like a cloak of mist that shrouded his sight. He found it hard to catch his breath, not only because he had run so far, but because the air had a clogging thickness that stuck in his throat. On the wall of a small square chamber was an eyeless image. He recognised it as Ral, the Great Goddess. But, before it, something stirred, a winged shape, no bigger than a man. Then it spread out the wings which had hidden its face, and the wings were awful, and the eyes of it were never to be forgotten.

'Filindrin, Filindrin! I have called you,' it whispered, and held him like a spell of horror.

It was the voice that had spoken to them in the tomb above, cold and clear and distant. Filindrin put his hand up before his eyes. He felt something touch it, the tip of a claw, hotter than molten iron. He wept, and the spell that held him was released. He turned and ran, stumbling up the steps and on and on down the endless half-lighted vistas of the corridors and galleries, on past their stones fashioned by the Old Ones who are vanished and the sickening statues of them that the Black Lords had made but feared to look on.

He came out into the light of livid evening, still running, guideless and unthinking across the broken land towards mountains that lay to the west. And as he ran he felt an undying agonising pain burning in his hand. He had not dared to look at it since that first moment when he had emerged from the caverns and read there, burnt and bleeding in his flesh, the single letter: 'S'.

CHAPTER 8

MELURIN

Slowly and with mists swimming before his eyes Talarnidh recovered consciousness. He saw a shape above him and, as his eyes focused, he realised that someone was standing over him. He struggled to his feet, reaching for the sword at his side.

'No, Talarnidh. It is a friend,' Fandorel's voice came from behind him.

He turned and saw the Elf Lord kneeling beside the form of Yeselwir. Soaring above them were the grim cliffs of Nal Vorod and Mount Guldurin, separated by the narrow black crack in the rocks where Wirdrilded lay.

'Where are we?' he asked, 'How is Yeselwir?'

'He is well enough, I think. Or will be when he awakens. We were all stricken when we came out of the darkness of the Valley,' answered Fandorel. 'As to where we are, our friend will tell you all you need to know.'

Talarnidh turned back to the figure he had first seen. A youth stood before him, no more than a boy; by his goatskin tunic and the staff in his hand, a goatherd. The boy's face was anxious, but half-smiling. Beyond the boy stretched green hills running down to the sea, the foothills of the great mountain ring of Adanyeth. On the coast he could make out the smoke from the cooking fires of a village. A fishing boat was nearing its harbour.

'This is Melurin, O great one,' said the boy. 'You have come from nowhere, and must therefore be the sons of heaven. I give you honour. My name is Talak, son of no-one.'

'I have told him whence we came,' broke in Fandorel, 'but he will not believe me. Assuredly he has never seen one of the Elvenkind, and none of us must make a common sight to such as him.'

Suddenly Yeselwir stirred and groaned.

'Listen, boy,' said Talarnidh quickly. 'Go to your village. Tell them what you have seen. Tell them we will follow you there. Say that one of us is probably hurt.'

The boy nodded at once, dropped his staff, and, turning, sped off across the hillside.

'Tasarnil!' said Yeselwir, sitting up suddenly, his eyes filled with fear.

'He is in the Valley, Yeselwir,' said the Elf Lord, and he knelt and held Yeselwir. 'We have come through, but he remains.'

'He had been my friend for many years,' said Talarnidh. 'He knew — from the first I think — what would await us in the Valley. Without him we would still be there in the darkness now among the ghosts.'

'Is he dead?' asked Yeselwir weakly.

'He is still alive,' Talarnidh answered. 'He has become the Sentinel of Guldrokh.'

'Can we help him?'

'One day, I will come back. All curses can be broken.'

'I will return with you,' said Fandorel.

'And I,' said Yeselwir.

He tried to rise, but was too weak. The effort brought fresh blood flowing from his hands and arms where he had been injured in the Valley. Talarnidh picked him up carefully, and they set off down the slopes to the village of Lerod Anth in the land of Melurin.

They were met by the villagers before they arrived. About thirty men came upon them. The boy they had first met was with them. Like him they were all clad in the skins of animals or in rough garments of coarse wool. All bore sticks and staves. Some had long fishing spears, and one, the only one amongst them who was not a young man, held a sword. The men of the Quest halted as the villagers silently encircled them. Then the man with the sword stepped forward, pulling the boy with him.

'These are the men,' the boy said.

'I see you, man of Melurin,' said Talarnidh in a loud voice, using the Northspeech.

'I see you, stranger,' answered the man, and the word he used for stranger also has the meaning 'enemy'. 'Tell me who you are, and why you come to my lands, and where you have come from.'

'I have come to ask help. You see my companion is hurt. Did I not send the boy to tell you?'

'The boy is likely in league with them,' said one of the men in the circle, a man who wore a coat all of sealskin.

'Have the people of Melurin changed so much that they will

not help the injured?' said Talarnidh. 'What harm can I do you when I carry this man in my arms and you see him bleeding?'

Slowly the headman of the villagers lowered his sword.

'What of the other one?' asked the man in the sealskins, his voice more unfriendly.

'I am of the Elvenkind,' said Fandorel. 'When have we done you ill?'

The headman sheathed his sword, and a noticeable sigh of relief went round the circle of villagers.

'Tell me your names,' he said. 'For I have decided you are not enemies. I am called Tor. I am chieftain of the folk of Melurin.'

'My name is Talarnidh,' came the answer. 'I am of the Peiri that you call the High Race. I bear in my arms a man called Yeselwir. For him I ask aid.'

'I am Fandorel of Morena,' said Fandorel.

They went together to the village that lay within its defensive stockade hard by the sea. The people were curious, but cautious of the strangers. One or two remained hostile. Melurin was not a safe place to live, beneath the shadow of the Dargul. Tor had taken a risk in trusting them. That trust was almost broken when Talarnidh answered his questions about where they had come from.

'I do not believe you have come through the Valley,' he said, 'for none ever have. So you are lying to me in my house. You have come secretly some other way.'

There was a long silence in the house of the headman. Then a voice said:

'But it was by the Valley I found them, right at the cleft of the rocks.'

It was Talak, the boy that found them, who spoke, and at once the man in the sealskins, whose name was Grel, struck him across the mouth, flinging him to the ground.

'Leave him,' ordered Tor. 'He speaks true. — I will not speak more of this, for I do not know what is right. But I will do this much, O stranger of the High Race. I will let you sail away from here tomorrow. You will pay us — as you said you would. We will take you to Belengar. — For I do not wish you to remain in Melurin a long time. I fear you.'

'That is all we ask,' said Talarnidh.

They slept deeply and well that night after the horrors of the day, and did not wake until the morning was almost gone. Tor briefly told them that the fishing boat in which they would sail had only just returned. Its catch must be unloaded and the crew must rest. They would not leave until the following day. Talarnidh and Fandorel readily agreed to this, for Yeselwir was still not fully well. The day went favourably for them amongst the villagers, as Fandorel told the tales of the Elves to the women-folk as they spun and to the small children. The boy Talak was one of those who sat listening, and when Talarnidh noticed him he spoke to him.

'I thank you for your service yesterday,' he said. 'Here, I owe you this reward.'

He offered a gold coin, worth perhaps more than the dreams of any villager. Talak shook his head.

'I am glad to serve you, O great lord. For I am the son of no-one, and of no account. Yet it was I that found you.'

Evening came and the men of the village came in to eat. But as they sat down in the great house, there came a call from the man who guarded the gate. The menfolk caught up their weapons and went out at once. With them went Talarnidh and Fandorel. From the gate in the stockade they saw a stumbling form move towards them across the fields in the twilight. Several times it nearly fell, and its path wandered from side to side. Only as the figure reached them did it look up. The two men of the Quest cried out in horror as they looked at the haggard face and staring eyes of Filindrin. He spoke no word, but looked at them for a long moment, moving his lips as if trying to utter words, and then his whole body writhed in some great torment. He fell fainting at their feet.

The people of Melurin took him to the house where Yeselwir had been lain. Their suspicion of the strangers in their midst had increased again. They returned to the great house, and left them alone. Filindrin recovered slowly, and it was not till the middle of the night that he was able to tell them the full tale of what had befallen in Aldel Morn. Talarnidh, Fandorel and Yeselwir listened in utter silence as, in stumbling halting phrases, they were told of the destruction of Turnalordath and of the things that had haunted the dark places and brought about the doom of Fermilondath and Wondrith. Filindrin told them nearly all, for every detail was imprinted on his mind. But he said no word of Sagoth, and he spoke nothing of that last thing that he had seen, for he could not bear to name it. Finally he ceased, and lay back exhausted. Almost at once he slept.

'So this is the ruin of our hopes,' said Talarnidh at last. 'The power of Ral is come back, greater than ever before. Already there are four of my truest friends dead in her domain. How many more of us, the mighty ones, can she destroy by the movement of her finger?'

He buried his head in his hands and sat in despair. Fandorel said nothing, but thought of Wondrith and the darkness where he had died. It was Yeselwir who spoke:

'I have not yet seen any of my friends die . . . I do not know if the same will happen to us, to the three of us, — but I think we all must still go on, my Prince.'

'We have to meet our comrades at Belengar. I pray there are still some to meet,' answered Talarnidh. 'Or have Karandar and Melandir died like Fermilondath, Turnalordath, and Wondrith? It is the end of our long sunset now . . . This is the real night.'

'But we will go on to Belengar,' said Fandorel.

'We will go on till we die,' answered Talarnidh.

On the following day at first light, before their departure, Talarnidh led Yeselwir and Fandorel to the foot of Nal Vorod again. There, in sight of the entrance to Wirdrilded, and under the grim peaks of Aldel Morn, they built a cairn to the memory of the three who had perished in Aldel Morn and the one who stood in Wirdrilded. Talarnidh chanted words in the tongue of the Peiri that told of the bravery and wisdom of Turnalordath and Fermilondath down through the countless ages from the Founding Years of Wenyaltrir. Fandorel sang in sweet tones of Wondrith, great wizard of the Elves, born of the Time Before Time, who now was dead. All swore an oath to lift the curse that ensnared Tasarnil, Son of the Sun. Then they returned to Lerod Anth. They found the boat almost ready to sail.

'I will fetch Filindrin,' said Fandorel. 'Sleep will have eased his torment now.'

But as he turned to go, there came the sound of angry voices from the boat. They saw a small figure dragged from off the boat by one of the fishermen.

'It is the boy called Talak who found us,' said Fandorel.

'We had best see what trouble this is. We must not be delayed now,' said Talarnidh.

They followed the man who had seized Talak over to the place where another of the large fishing boats was beached. There stood Grel, who of all the villagers had been most hostile to the men of the Quest.

'I found him hidden in the cabin,' said the fisherman, and pushed Talak before Grel.

'So my property wants to leave me,' he snarled.

'I wish to go with the strangers,' answered Talak, looking down.

'You are my property,' said Grel.' I own you. You may not even go out in the boats. You are a goatherd. Did I not whip you well enough yesterday when you left your herd to listen to the foolish tales of the Elf?'

Fandorel stiffened slightly. The three men of the Quest had moved close beside the group of villagers which had collected. Grel's words were intended to be heard by them.

'I want to go with them,' said Talak, and this time stared straight at Grel. This seemed enough to inflame his anger. A string of oaths burst from him, and he sprang forward and seized Talak. The boy's tunic was torn, showing a thin body heavily wealed with the slave lash. Grel spoke only the truth when he claimed ownership of Talak. The indifference of the other villagers indicated that such scenes of Grel's anger with his slave were common enough.

This time, perhaps because the men of the Quest were there, Grel's anger went beyond normal bounds. He had a knife in his hands, and he had now raised this — not the slave lash — over the defenceless boy. But the knife had no chance to fall on him. In one movement Talarnidh had drawn his sword and brought it up to smash the dagger from Grel's hand.

'You may beat the boy, but murder does not enter into your rights over him,' said Talarnidh in an even cold voice, his gaze fixed on Grel's eye.

Without letting his glance falter he stooped to pick up the dagger. Grel stepped back and looked round at the others. Anger still glinted in his eyes, but with it a measure of fear.

'May I not punish my slave?' he demanded, thick-voiced, of the gathering.

'Your right to beat the boy is not in question,' answered Talarnidh. 'But with a dagger . . .'

He glanced down at the knife in his hand, and when he looked up again Grel had more reason to fear what he saw in the Prince's face.

'This is a fine weapon, Grel,' Talarnidh continued, and he now held it clenched in his left hand as if at the ready. 'But it is not yours. I have seen it before. It is made of dragon-steel, and that betokens the work of Wenylatrir.'

Again Grel warily looked about him for support, for many of the men of Melurin had arrived there now.

'You see, O man of Melurin, this dagger once was mine,' Talarnidh said, and the menace in his voice could not be mistaken. 'I gave it to a friend when he set off into the Empty Lands. — It was nearly sixteen years ago now, I think. Here on the pommel is my mark, — the diadem of Alban. And here on the blade, finely cut, is the name of him to whom I made the gift.'

He handed the dagger to Fandorel, and the Elf Lord gasped as he read.

'Filindrin! The name is clear. Filindrin!'

Talarnidh's sword point rested at Grel's throat now. The people of Melurin said nothing, waiting for the outcome. Grel began to speak, a sudden gush of words.

'I took the knife from the hands of a dead woman, — one of my own clan. Her name was Bly, — one of the people of Melurin. It was in the year the Reavers came. They slew her, and I found her there on the beaches. She had only this knife and her new-born brat when I found her.'

'How did she come by the knife?' Talarnidh interrupted.

'There was another stranger then . . . She shared his house when he came here. My clan deemed this a disgrace. It was not lawful. He brought us ill-luck, — as you have. He left with the Reavers. Perhaps it was he that led them to us.'

'Do you think it might have been Filindrin?' said Yeselwir, half in a whisper. Talarnidh motioned him to be still.

'What of the child? Did it survive?' he asked.

Grel's mouth hardened. He looked at his people, but now they looked down. One or two began to move away.

'The boy survived, great one,' said one of the villagers. 'Since he was the son of no-one, Grel made a slave of him. He is the boy Talak.'

'Fandorel, go and bring Filindrin here,' said Talarnidh.

'Yeselwir, go to Tor, the chief of these people, and ask him to come also.'

Tor came at once and Talarnidh told him what had occurred, and that he now believed that Talak might be the son of their comrade Filindrin. Now Tor was afraid of this, for he knew his guests to be lords of Wenyaltrir, though he did not know that Talarnidh was the Prince of the High Race. And, if Talak belonged to them, the people of Melurin might suffer for the usage Grel had given him when he made him a slave. Tor also asked to see Filindrin, for he had not recognised him when he came to the village the previous night. Yet when Fandorel returned it was to tell them that Filindrin no longer lay in the house and was nowhere to be found. Talarnidh turned on Tor, and the headman saw what the Prince was thinking.

'This is not my doing, lordly one,' he said. 'Nor any of my people. — Now we will all search for this man of yours.'

The villagers split up and began to scatter out across the countryside of Melurin in search of Filindrin. With them went the men of the Quest. But Talak went to the house of Grel. He saw Grel's wife and went to her. She saw him, and spoke before he could:

'I recognised the man who came here. I knew him when I saw him yesterday. He is greatly changed, — and all for the worse. No-one else recognised him, but I did, for he was the man of my sister, Bly. He is your father.'

Talak did not answer at first. Then all he could say was:

'He has gone.'

'I saw him go, when the others were away. He went to the east.'

'Towards the Rim of Fear?' said Talak.

'Aye. Where it is low and there is a hollow in the hills. That is the place he made for. I watched him from the fence. I watched him for a long while.'

'I know it,' said Talak. 'It is Tewfell Valley. The grazing there is the poorest.'

Then, in a sudden moment, he had gone, racing out of the village, away towards the Dargul, which the men of Melurin call 'Rim of Fear'. He saw several groups of men searching but none questioned him. He ran as he had never run before. He crossed the stream and, still racing with all his might, began to climb the low hills that here made up the Dargul. From the top of one of them he at last caught sight of the man he now knew was his father. Filindrin was beginning to descend into the valley that Talak knew.

He also knew that the people of Melurin did not go there, not only because the grazing was poor, but because the far end of the valley opened onto the plains of Aldel Morn. Filindrin was moving slowly and haltingly. He had taken very long to come thus far, and Talak, as he ran on gasping for breath, hoped to catch him before he passed into that land. Once or twice again Talak glimpsed him, moving as if he could not see the obstacles in his path, his eyes fixed on some distant point of sky.

As Talak reached the valley he stumbled in his haste and fell onto the grass. Starting to rise he looked up, hoping to see Filindrin. Somehow he did not make a sound at what he saw. He pressed his body close against the ground again, only just daring to look. Before him was a level, nearly circular valley, with the white rocks breaking through the soil in the centre of it. Filindrin was certainly there. But it was the three other figures that he saw first, each of them stood at one of the points of the compass.

Eastwards stood a tall man, wrapped all about in a long winding sheet. His half-muffled face was pale and tinged with green, an unnatural and somehow fearful colour. Talak had seen a corpse before, and now he recognised one again. To the west what he saw was plainer. There stood the skeleton of a man, upright against all nature, broken armour hanging upon it. North was a vast half-formed shape, its contours changing and flowing, hard even to look on. The only feature clear on it was the great hound-head, the lolling tongue and its eyes. Continual sounds came from the shapeless mouth, like a distant wailing of countless people lost and tortured. The great jaws worked and poisoned saliva dripped from them. Talak lay rigid in a terror beyond anything he had known as he watched Filindrin take the empty southern place.

A long while he lay there, and there came no movement in that place. But as time passed he noticed a stirring of the dust in the midst of the valley. He thought he saw something there but could not be sure. The light had become strange and full of tricks to the eye. There was a mist or smoke condensing there, but its shape was ever changing and the forms it took were weird and inexplicably terrible. Finally he could not doubt that it was really there, a thing of hideous wings and eyes that seemed to stare into him and call him out to meet it. It spoke, and its voice was a thin reed, like a cry of an animal heard far away in the mist that makes men fear for no reason they can understand. It spoke to the four silent figures: the skeleton, the corpse, the Hound, and the man Talak knew to be his father, Filindrin.

'Turnlaordath, I have called you. Fermilondath, I have called you. Nyaqualtelk, I have called you.' (Thus the last name sounded to Talak, and the Hound stirred as it was spoken, but he could never recapture the foulness of its very syllables as it was uttered then in that place.)

'You know my purpose,' the thing of mist and awful wings continued. 'Do it . . . Do it!'

Then the shape swirled as if made of rags in an eddy of the wind, and its voice took on a different quality, full of heat and foulness and desire:

'Filindrin! O Filindrin! Wait . . . Wait . . . Wait for me, Filindrin. Be nothing! Be still! Be afraid! Wait, and I will come . . . Filindrin . . .'

The rags of mist spread wider on the air and the shape was expanding into the air of the valley. A lingering scent of the unutterable came to Talak, and suddenly he could move again. Clutching his hand over his mouth he turned and began to run. Despite what he had seen he did not move far. For his father that he never knew had been there amidst the monsters. He turned again and waited and watched as Filindrin, walking like one in a trance, came out of the vale and went falteringly across the hillside. Then Talak went up to meet him. Filindrin stopped and, though he looked straight at the boy, Talak could not be sure he had even seen him.

'When you were here before . . . you had a wife called Bly. The Reavers killed her. Do you remember, my lord?'

Slowly Filindrin's eyes focused on Talak. He shook his head from side to side slowly. Then he looked back towards the valley.

'Who are you?' he asked.

'My name is Talak.'

'I have come through a dark place. The thing . . . It will never leave me now.'

'I saw the thing in the valley,' said Talak. 'Let me help you.'

'You must never tell,' answered Filindrin.

'I am your son, my lord,' said Talak.

Filindrin looked at him for a long time, and then suddenly repeated, half in a whisper:

'Never tell! Never speak of it! Never again . . . It will want you too.'

Talak did not understand but nodded his head.

'I will do whatever you say, my lord. — Will you come back to the village with me now? The great ones and everyone search for you.'

Together they went back. Filindrin said no more. They were seen returning, and the scattered search parties were called back. In the centre of the village, surrounded by the people, Talarnidh held out the dagger towards Filindrin.

'Filindrin, my friend, what ails you?' he asked, when Filindrin stood unspeaking and did not take it.

'Sir, he is ill. He went towards the Black Land,' said Talak.

'Silence, boy!' ordered Tor. 'Nothing is yet settled, and you have no right to speak here.'

Once again Filindrin seemed to be making a great effort to concentrate his will. He took the dagger, and looked at it for a long time.

'Is it yours?' asked Talarnidh.

'I gave it to Bly. A long while it seems now . . . I never told you of it, my Prince. I married once. The Reavers slew her, and took me . . .' Suddenly he looked up and all around. 'It was in this place. This place is Melurin.'

'It is the same man,' said Tor. 'I knew him.'

Several murmured agreement. For the first time there was decision in Filindrin's voice.

'Where is my son?' he said. Talak went forward at once and stood before him.

'I am here, my lord.' Slowly Filindrin reached out and touched his face.

'If only it had been sooner,' he said.

'Is the matter yet settled, Tor, chieftain of Melurin?' asked Talarnidh.

'It is settled,' said Tor.

'What of my rights? I have lost a good servant,' said Grel.

Filindrin did not look at him. He drew a gold piece from his pouch and dropped it at Grel's feet. Grel at once stooped to pick it up, only to spring back as the point of Filindrin's sword struck the coin pinning it to the ground.

'If my son suffers injustice from you again, O man, there will be one come back to kill you,' he said.

'But I am coming with you, my lord,' said Talak.

'You will stay here! There will be gold to buy you a house and a share in a boat.'

'I want to come,' said Talak.

'No . . . no . . . You will not come,' said Filindrin, looking at Talarnidh.

'It would indeed be foolish,' said Yeselwir. 'Filindrin is right. The boy must do as he is told.'

Talarnidh nodded.

'It is a matter for Filindrin. I would take your son with us if you wished, my friend.'

Filindrin shook his head.

'We must go now,' he said, and turned away.

Talarnidh made all the necessary arrangements with Tor. He paid him well for the men who would row them, and for the use of the boat. He also made sure that Talak would be cared for. The boy was nowhere to be seen. Nor would Filindrin say more about him.

The boat they were to sail in was the largest of those in Melurin. It took a crew of ten men to sail and to row if the wind fell. There was a cabin, and a spacious hold for the fish. Talarnidh eyed the boat gladly for he was prince of the sailor folk of Alban, and now he was glad to put out to sea again. As he climbed aboard to join the other men of the Quest he looked back towards the mountains of Aldel Morn and the high Adanyeth that hemmed in the lake where lay Enchanter's Isle. He remembered those who already lay dead. He wondered if he and those with him would come alone of all of them to the meeting place at Belengar.

Inside those grim mountains Selenthoril sat in fear. He now knew the depths of the malignity that had awoken. He knew that the men he had sent out had been attacked. He knew Ral had set her snares on Anrith. He knew that the old curse had awoken in Wirdrilded. Above all he knew that something unnameable had come out of Aldel Morn. Even with the Sceptre Spiritual he could only begin to guess at its true nature.

In Melurin the unnameable had begun to work its way. As Talarnidh looked down from the boat to bid farewell to Tor, he saw the old man's glance move to the waters by the boat's prow, and his face blanch. Talarnidh quickly looked there.

'What is it?' asked Tor fearfully.

'I saw something moving there, sinking into the water,' answered Talarnidh. 'Did you see the same. Tor? — A skull of a man, that floated on the waves?'

'I saw an omen,' answered Tor. 'Broken bones on the water, and armour hung on them. I tell you, O great one, I am glad you sail from this land, and I am glad you have left the boy Talak behind.'

'Farewell, Tor,' Talarnidh answered. 'I do not know if we will ever come here again.'

'Farewell,' answered Tor. 'Perhaps you will escape your curse.'

As he spoke Talarnidh felt the truth of the old man's fears. He wondered again how many would meet in Belengar. He turned to the man Grel, and ordered:

'Let us cast off! We would be away!'

The coast and the hills shrank behind them. The oars were shipped and they hoisted the sail in the cold north wind. The mountains faded and dropped away below the horizon. The ship's head caught the ocean waves and rose and fell in the long swells. They left Misen Taïrail behind to sail for Belengar.

CHAPTER 9

BELENGAR

From Misen Taïrail to Belengar is nigh on eighty leagues. The first night they made landfall, and put into a bay in the desolate land of Sart Emig. The air was chill, and in the night came flurries of snow from the Empty Lands, though it was still only autumn. They kept watches, and the bleak land reflected their mood. Half of their number had already been destroyed, and they feared for the other men of the Quest, — for Melandir, Erathrir, Karandar and Relnar, who had gone to the pass of Anrith. Also one of their number, Filindrin, still seemed ill and stricken from what had happened to him in Aldel Morn. They slept badly, and when the next day dawned they hastened to depart. Before they could, one of the seamen from Melurin approached Talarnidh as he stood with the other men of the Quest.

'The man of you who has a son, the boy from my land — which is he?' he asked.

Talarnidh looked towards Filindrin, but Filindrin said nothing.

'Why do you want him?' the Prince asked.

'The man's son has been found, hidden in the boat. We do not know what to do with him.'

'We will go to the boat,' said Talarnidh.

'You will need to serve the brat the same fare as I did,' said the man Grel.

'He may be right,' said Yeselwir. 'What will you do, Filindrin?'

'I will not let him come,' was Filindrin's only answer.

When they were aboard the boat he would say nothing more than this to Talak also:

'You will not come. You will return to Melurin. I cannot let you come.'

'You must obey the word of the Lord Filindrin,' said Talarnidh. 'Learn that now, or the learning will be harder.'

'How can I obey if I am sent away?' answered Talak.

The wind was strong and the sky menacing. The great swells

of the wide ocean to westward tossed the boat as they sailed on towards Belengar. All through the chill northern day they sailed, and on till they put in at midnight, cautiously on the treacherous shores. They were near Belengar but they would not go on to the castle. It was not safe to walk freely in Sart Emig by night. They made camp, and the watch fell to Grel of Melurin. He and one or two of his men still eyed the men of the Quest with some bitterness. Talarnidh noticed his sullen look, for he too lay awake and restless, watching the man who kept watch. He also noticed that Talak was still awake, and Filindrin, sitting alone on the edge of the group. Filindrin seemed not to have slept at all since his second return from Aldel Morn.

The night was dark beneath the scudding clouds. The only light came from the faint phosphorescence of the sea. It dimly outlined Grel's hunched form as he sat farther down the beach near to the boat. Out of the choppy waves that slapped against the boat's hull a dim shape rose. Higher above the water, it now moved landwards. It reached the edge of the ocean and stood, a gaunt skeleton with armour hanging on it, and the water ran down from its bones, and seaweed hung from an empty eye socket.

Sightless it surveyed the beach and then with slow purposeful steps moved forward. Its bony joints creaked very slightly and it swayed as it walked. This was one of the apparitions that Talak, son of Filindrin, had seen in Aldel Morn. It was the same shape they had seen for a moment on the waves when they left Melurin.

It passed Grel and, hearing the faint clack of the bone feet on the shingle, he turned and gasped in horror. But even in his fear he stifled the scream that came to his throat. He rose and stumbled backwards. The monster swayed on its way, clawed hands groping, towards the place where Talarnidh lay. Not waiting to see his revenge on the Prince accomplished for him, Grel turned and ran, clattering down the beach.

Talak heard the sound and turned over. It was opposite him and he saw it against the sky, skull and jaw bone clear beneath the helmet, the bony legs slow and angular in their movements. He recognised it from the Black Land, and utter fear choked him. Two and three more steps, and then it was past him and almost over Talarnidh, before the cry could break from his numbed lips. Then he shrieked in the night, a wordless cry.

Talarnidh, unsleeping, rolled over at once. He saw a shape out of a nightmare loom over him. He sprang aside as groping hands brushed his cloak with a touch of undead bone. All the camp was awake now, loud with shouting and alarm. The thing lunged at Talarnidh again with stretched and clawing fingers. The Prince drew his sword, crying aloud in the confusion:

'Bring a light!'

He saw Fandorel's form in the press of men. The Elf Lord bore a blazing torch, but Talarnidh saw the flames through the gaping ribs. The skeleton clawed again, and now he sprang full upon it. His sword hilt smashed upon the shoulder, cracking its bones. As he struck he gazed into the creature's face. He saw no life in the yawning sockets. He did not guess that Turnalordath's soul was trapped within the dripping skull.

Then Talarnidh turned the blade upwards, striking into the staring death's head. Teeth and jaw shattered, and the steel passed out through the skull. Turnalordath, all unknown to them, died a second time. But the power out of the Black Land that controlled him was also banished. The bones rattled down. As Fandorel brought the torch, Talarnidh looked at the ruined helm.

'It was Turnalordath's,' he said.

'So the powers of Aldel Morn could not even leave his corpse,' said Yeselwir.

'I hope it was only his corpse they took,' said Fandorel, and he turned away as Talarnidh let fall the helm amid the broken bones.

The rest of the night brought little sleep. The men of the Quest wondered what they had stirred in Aldel Morn. Filindrin sat alone and bemused, and from a distance Talak of Melurin eyed him doubtfully. He wondered what manner of man his father really was and was afraid, for he had seen him stand in the valley by Aldel Morn, where the undead skeleton and the other horrors had stood. Before the dawn and the departure of the men of Melurin he went quietly into the caves that lined the cliff face. The fishermen would not delay to search for him, and Talak watched while the boat sailed off without him. Then he went down to the men of the Quest. He knelt before Filindrin.

'I could not obey you, my lord. Whip me, as hard as Grel did. That is only right. But do not make me son of no-one again.'

'Stay away from me,' answered Filindrin. 'It is my right to prevent you dying as I must die.'

'We will speak more of this when we reach the castle,' said Talarnidh. 'You forget what your father suffered in the Black Land. You do not begin to know the paths we tread.'

None of them said more to Talak, who followed at a little distance as they turned south along the beach, where the great cliffs that guard all of Sart Emig reared above the very edge of the waters. They waded through the shallows and sharp rocks at their base and rounded the headland to gaze on the tower of Belengar.

Its outer rampart rose on the very cliff edge, its blocks huge beyond the works of that age, seeming about to plunge into the void below. The sheer walls were grey and unadorned, broken only by one vast gateway, barred with iron. Inside the breastwork a perfectly regular mound was built, and on its summit stood the square dark tower. It was as if it was carved of one immense impossible stone, two hundred feet high. Two rings of windows were set in it, so tall that they might have been built for giants, but there was only one door, so small that no more than two men might enter abreast. A ray of sun caught the top of the tower, and the grim slab gleamed like a sword for a moment, massive in its power.

'Is this the fort of Ral?' asked Talak.

'He has heard more of our purpose than you thought, my Prince,' said Yeselwir. '— What do you know of Ral, boy?'

'No, it is not the fortress of Ral,' interrupted Talarnidh, turning to Talak. 'It is Belengar of the High Race, whose name means "Guardian of the North". Once we could survey the whole of these lands from its tower. But now . . . I have not been here since after the War of the Sceptres. — You had best be quiet now, Talak.' Talarnidh said no more, but gazed at the great tower of his people.

'I think the men of the Reavelaw still stop here,' said Fandorel. 'And perhaps the fishermen. There may even be traders from the east who risk the northern passage.'

'Yes, it is true,' said Filindrin. 'There was a battle here between the Reavers and two long ships from Amray. We may find a ship puts in here. It may take my son for us . . .'

'Come!' said Talarnidh. 'I will lead you up the high path to the keep. I described the way to Melandir and Karandar.'

'I hope they are here,' said Yeselwir.

Talarnidh led them up the beach and soon they made out a

stony winding path up the cliff face, perilously narrow. But before they reached it, where the shingle of the beach gave way to a bar of sand, they began to find disturbing signs. In the sand were the marks of many footprints scuffed hither and thither, and on a gorse bush nearby a scrap of cloth. The weave was of Wenyaltrir and matched that of the robe Talarnidh wore. They knew that only Melandir had another such robe. Also in the sand they found a footprint, partly human, partly ape-like, its toes unnaturally long. But the print measured a yard in length. By it lay a mess of blood and bones. A body had been smashed out of all recognition against the rocks. And as they began up the path they found Erathrir's sword.

'They are in the castle or they are dead,' said Talarnidh as they stood before the iron-bound gate of Belengar.

'I know the sort of creature that might have taken them,' said Fandorel. 'There have been Giants in the Empty Lands since the days of Ral. It is likely that they have made the keep one of their haunts.'

'They are here. I saw them that time before,' said Filindrin. 'Only a few escaped from them then.'

His voice was clear but still wavered, and the fear always remained in his eyes. Talak looked at him, and felt the fear, but forced himself to speak.

'How do Giants live in the Empty Lands?' he asked.

'On the flesh of men, my son,' came the answer at once. 'But at least not on their souls . . .'

Talarnidh and Fandorel looked at each other. They knew that what Filindrin said was true, though they wondered at his manner of saying it. Both wondered if the great sword would have sufficed to save Melandir and his companions. Both thought of Selenthoril's plight on far-off Misen Taïrail where four more of the Quest already lay dead.

'I do not think the gate will bar us long,' said Yeselwir, examining the ancient portcullis. 'It is almost rusted away.'

'It has been guardian of nothing for many years now,' said Fandorel. '— But quickly, Yeselwir, set to it now! There is something moving in the great court.'

As Yeselwir and then Talarnidh drew their swords to try to break through the iron, Fandorel's winged form rose in a beat of air, carrying up above the wall in a single leap, and then down in a long swoop like a bird of prey, towards the small creature that scurried away. It was dwarvish, but misshapen and twisted. Its slow ungainly run was further hampered by the folds of a rich long sable cloak hung about it. It was making its stumbling way not towards the great tower but in the direction of a low, half-ruined building, its roof partly open to the sky. As Fandorel descended he half-caught a glimpse of movement deep within the ruins. Then he landed at the door of the building in front of the creature. It twisted, attempted to turn, changed its mind as the sound of running feet came from behind, and then fell in the folds of its black cloak.

'The gate was no problem,' shouted Talak. 'The swords cut right through it!'

'Quiet!' said Fandorel. He pointed at the dwarvish thing. 'It is wearing Erathrir's cloak.'

Sword still in hand, Yeselwir stepped forward and took the creature by the hair. His sword pointed at its throat.

'Tell us where they are, Goblin!'

He shook it angrily when no answer came, and pressed with the sword point. A thin red mark of blood appeared on the Goblin's throat.

'All the prisoners are in the dungeon.' It spoke at once, gabbling shrilly so that they could scarcely make out the words.

'There were no dungeons,' said Talarnidh.

The Goblin turned and pointed into the door of the ruined building behind them. They entered through another barred doorway, though this time the iron had already been broken away. Littered everywhere were smashed weapons and armour, piles of rags and tatters, and bones of men. Smears of blood shewed on the floor and walls. At the far end the roof had been broken through or had collapsed and its remnants overhung a deep pit where the floor also had given way. The men of the Quest looked over into what had been deep cellars, now open to the sky.

Well below, amongst the rubble and more filth and decay, were the forms of men. One of them rose to his feet and chanced to look upwards. His eyes met Talarnidh's. He gasped, and then gave a great shout, crying out the Prince's name. It was Melandir. In a short time ropes were found, and Melandir, Erathrir, Relnar and Karandar, followed by the other prisoners, had been hauled out of the pit.

'These are men of Amray for the most part,' said Melandir,

'taken like us when they put in at the bay. There are also a few Reavers and one or two folk from further afield. We will need the help of all of them. Now the monsters do not have surprise we may be able to defeat them. — But first I must find something.'

Melandir turned and began to search through the wreckage in the room. Talarnidh followed him.

'What do you mean, "the monsters"?' he asked.

Melandir looked up. In his hand he held a sword. A smile crossed his face as he weighed Wenyorel in his hand again.

'Then you have not seen them?'

'I have seen a footprint,' Talarnidh answered.

Melandir nodded:

'You cannot imagine them from that alone, — the Giants of Belengar! They have made the place their home. You will know more about their kind than I. For I think they are survivors of the old wars. More like apes than men, — and huge. But their master is more truly evil than they. They have no real mind, but he has. Nagurad — a dwarvish Goblin. He leads them to their prey and feeds on their leavings. They eat men of course.'

'How did you lose the Sword?' Talarnidh asked.

'They came on us in the night,' Melandir answered. 'The Sword was taken from me by stealth while I slept, before I could use it. I am not sure how it all befell. I took little part after the first blow.' He laughed ruefully. 'But you have not heard of how we came to Belengar. And you must tell us what has befallen you and the others. I doubt you had a worse path than we.'

In a few short sentences Talarnidh revealed the depth of the horror that had befallen the men of the Quest in Wirdrilded and Aldel Morn. As those of the Quest who had survived gathered together, Melandir passed on to his companions what Talarnidh had told him. The rejoicing of the men who had been freed became cold. Karandar and Melandir especially could not believe that four of the great ones of the olden days had perished so suddenly. Karandar had been dear to all of them, and they to him, for years beyond counting. He sat grim and unspeaking amidst the ruined hall of the Giants, and remembered Fermilondath and Turnalordath of the High Race, and Tasarnil from the bright pastures of the East of East, and also Wondrith, one of the last of the Old Elves, come from the Time Before Time, now dead and in the darkness, a thousand thousand years of life come to nothing.

'What then have you to tell?' Talarnidh asked Melandir, and Melandir told of what had happened to them on Anrith and in the Ruby Caverns.

'In Sarmish, a town of the country of Lothchen where we emerged from the caverns, we found the ships of Amray,' he concluded, then turned to the other group of men. '— My lord Admiral Andrai, I bid you to welcome Talarnidh, Prince of Wenyaltrir.'

A tall bearded man came forward and took Talarnidh's hand, smiling wryly.

'I bid you welcome,' he said. 'We had hoped for no rescue in such a place as this, — least of all from the Prince of the High Race.'

'We are well met, for I once expected to see you in far-off Alban where I dwell,' answered Talarnidh.

'The Goblin! Quickly!' Yeselwir's voice suddenly called.

They saw Yeselwir run towards the shattered doorway, and for a moment the form of Nagurad, the servant or master of the Giants, was framed in the doorway. Yeselwir reached the door in time to see Nagurad disappear behind a mound of fallen masonry. But when he reached there he saw no sign of the Goblin. The men of the Quest and the others began to spread out searching, but Talarnidh and Andrai called them back.

'There must be a tunnel,' said Talarnidh. 'There is little chance of us catching the Goblin now.' The Admiral nodded his agreement.

'He will return with the Giants,' he said. 'We must prepare for an attack.'

'Then we had best go into the keep,' said Karandar.

He led them up the narrow staircase which rose steeply from the small doorway. The entrance to the keep of Belengar was designed to hamper attackers, and had once been held by ten men against an army. The first of the great windowed chambers was very high in the tower. Westward, hundreds of feet below, was the grey-green sea, and east the desolation of Sart Emig. The floor was littered with the dirt and rubbish of centuries. Talarnidh looked round at the faces of his own men and of the many others. He saw that everyone had brought weapons from the hoard below.

'Who will help in the fight?' he asked. 'My people will, — but there are many others here.'

'The men of Amray give you obedience for this purpose,' said Andrai.

But some of the Reavers muttered amongst themselves, saying that it was no fight of theirs and the best course was to flee. One from the rear ranks called out:

'Who are you to command us?'

Talarnidh drew his sword and held it stretched out at arm's length before him.

'Anyone may dispute the place with me,' he said.

He turned full circle so that the sword pointed to each in turn. There was silence. Then one of the men of the Reavelaw stood forward and said:

'These men here have saved us from death. That was their affair. But we are of the Reavelaw. What of our revenge? Are they to take it for us? We fight the creatures also. Atreng says so. Who disputes that?'

He too drew his sword. This time there was laughter and cheering from the Reavers, and the men of Amray joined in. Few remained silent, and no-one questioned Talarnidh as he gave swift orders. Those who had found bows were sent to the windows of the keep. The others were to be hidden all around the great court. Before they went, Talarnidh said:

'My plan is simple. Arrows from the keep will serve to blind or at least enrage them. They may not notice the enemy at their feet. Attack the tendons in their legs. All attack at once. Some of us will reach them. Some will not.'

The men began to file down the steps. Talarnidh saw Talak amongst them armed with a sword. At the same moment Filindrin also saw the boy.

'Talarnidh! Give the boy a bow,' he said, pulling Talak over to the Prince.

'I am best with a sword,' cried Talak.

'You will stay in the tower,' snapped Filindrin, more life in his eyes now than for days. Then he turned and went down the stairs.

'I will help you with the art of the bow,' said Fandorel to Talak. Then, as the Elf Lord turned to look out of the window, he cried aloud:

'The Giants! They come!'

In the distance he saw the three strange shapes move towards the castle across the Empty Lands. Talarnidh and the few swordsmen still in the tower hastened down to take cover in the ruins of the courtyard. Above, the Elf watched their enemies approach, the boy Talak at his left, and on his right the only other with the power of flight. This was Celemendil, one of the people of the Fays, who had journeyed with Andrai as ambassador to the Western Lands. As the Giants approached, their very hugeness came as a surprise to Fandorel and Talak, and a sickening memory to those who had seen the Giants before and remembered their own recent captivity. For, though they were thirty feet or more in height, their form was that of hideous apes, walking now upright, now loping on all fours, their dull eyes gazing about. A tiny shape clung to the matted hair of the first of them and whispered in its ear, the Goblin Nagurad.

The men in the courtyard saw nothing of their approach. They waited and shivered in the northern cold. The first of the creatures heaved itself through the great gateway, stooping under the massive lintel then rearing to its full height. The others followed, and all three stood for a while by the gate. All the men had time to remember their fear, to be sickened by the stink and filth that clung to the unclothed bodies, and to choke back the terror in their throats at the sight of the rotten teeth and bone-ridged animal eyes, the curved claws and tree-like arms.

Slowly the foul beings began to move across the court towards the tower. The men below in their weak hiding places looked up at the bulks of flesh above, and cursed the bowmen for their delay. It seemed an age before the flashing rustling flight of arrows sprang from the windows of the keep and gouged into Giants' flesh. A screaming and bellowing, strangely keen and high-pitched from those massive throats, arose. Their great arms went up to protect their eyes. They staggered backwards, twisting as they hooted and shrieked.

Erathrir and Karandar, with two men of Amray, were the first to rush out upon the nearest Giant. One of its eyes was already blinded, three shafts in it, the other also streamed with blood. Its screams became more hideous as Erathrir and Karandar together hacked at the tendons behind the huge ankle. A sweeping blow from the great fist scraped past Karandar, its touch enough to hurl him across the ground like a thing of rags. It struck again, and this time one of the men of Amray screamed as his legs were broken, and his comrade made no sound, but died at once beneath the hammer blow. Then Erathrir, the red jewel of the

King of the Rethrind flashing on his helm, struck again. His sword cut the tendon. The Giant staggered a step, a new note in its howling. When it fell on the shaking earth it was already dying. Erathrir ran over to the unconscious form of Karandar and began to drag him towards the tower.

Of the men who had attacked the second of the Giants, five were already dead, their bodies unrecognisable. None of the arrows had found the creature's eyes. Now it made great sweeps towards the ring of figures about it, and none could reach its legs. Intent upon the men beneath, it did not see the two winged figures launch themselves from the tower — not until the agony of Celemendil's sword hacking at the sinews in its throat made it scream and clutch at the small winged form. But the Fays of Oucidhaloë once were hunted by the great bats of Ral, and they could move more swiftly than the eye. At every clumsy reach of the Giant, Celemendil darted back and then struck again. Already he was streaming with hot blood, but he had not yet cut the jugular. His wings clogged with gore, he began to tire. It was then that Fandorel fired.

The mighty bowman of the Elves, born before time, had awaited his moment. The Giant concentrated on Celemendil so much that he did not see Fandorel hovering only yards away, his arm and bow still as a rock. Then the string twanged and the polished steel head of the arrow cut through the Giant's eye and the bone of its skull. It made no sound at all, but stood for a full minute with the arrow lodged in its brain. Only then did it fall backwards, still silent, already dead.

One Giant alone stood, but Nagurad was its master. It had retreated towards the gate at the first flight of arrows. It bled from many small wounds but its might was unimpaired. Suddenly it rushed forward. The men before it fell to their death one after the other, for the iron-hard fists swung like flails. Five more were already dead, men of the Reavelaw and of Amray. Filindrin and Melandir momentarily reached the great form. Filindrin cut across the front of its foot before a glancing blow spun him away dazed and sick. The fist clamped round the body of Melandir. Any other man must have died swiftly in torment, but Melandir was unharmed for in his hand was the Fate Sword. The massive fingers carried him towards the cavernous mouth, but Wenyorel slashed left and right and the Giant's grin became wider and ragged with blood.

But while its attention was on its prey, Talarnidh had reached the Giant's leg, and with him the Reaver, Atreng, who had spoken in the tower. The Reaver roared with battle fury. He and the Prince cut together. The leg gave way, and the creature crashed forward onto its knees. The form of Melandir was flung from its hand with horrifying force to smash against the stones of the keep. Talarnidh gasped in horror, and the thought flashed across his mind that he had not seen the Sword in Melandir's hand.

In the moment that Talarnidh stood by nerveless, the giant fist of the kneeling monster was raised above him, too late for him to deflect or escape it. This time the arrow was Relnar's, sped from the window in the tower straight to the throat, its whole length buried in the flesh. The upraised hand grasped at the great neck. It half rose to standing again, and then, as its ruined leg gave way, twisted and rolled in its blood in the dust. Talarnidh ran round the massive bulk. By the wall of the keep stood Melandir. He had never released the Sword.

As the Giant fell for the last time, Nagurad leapt from its shoulder and ran, scrambling and limping, towards the ruins nearby. Out from them stepped Filindrin, his sword sheathed. He had fallen there amidst the rubble when the Giant struck him. He had seen the blow fall, and thought himself dead. But he had survived, and now he watched while Nagurad drew a dagger and hurled his misshapen form at his throat. He still did not draw his sword. Only a racing spring from Yeselwir saved him. As the Man and the Goblin fought for the dagger, it fell to the ground and Filindrin kicked it away. Finally Yeselwir held Nagurad, still biting and writhing.

'Kill him now, Filindrin!' he cried.

'He can do no more harm. Take him prisoner. I will have no more blood on my hands, no, not even Goblin blood, — not while I still can choose,' said Filindrin.

Far away, in Thulgarn, Pit of the Werebats, Ral wondered how many of her enemies Nagurad and the Giants had taken, and thought what other servants she might send northwards to destroy the men of the Quest. She trusted that the Giants would not fail her, but somehow her heart was cold with fear, though she knew not why. She gazed north and saw nothing, as the red sun of autumn sank over Belengar.

CHAPTER 10

THE EMPTY LANDS

On the morning after the battle with the Giants, though it was only autumn, snow fell heavily on the castle of Belengar. Only the great tower stood grey amidst the white wastes around. A bitter wind blew the snow in the faces of the men of the Reavelaw as they built a cairn over the bodies of their fallen people. The bodies of the Giants remained, grotesque beneath their shroud of snow. In a high room in the keep the men of the Quest gathered. The shadow of the future and of the evil that had dogged their footsteps was over them. It was a grim meeting, for in everything they seemed to see the hand of Ral. As they spoke there came a disturbance outside the room and Admiral Andrai entered. With him came two of the men of Amray dragging Nagurad. His was a misshapen form, spawned in hideous parody from the Elves, its back hunched where wings might have been, a creature of the tribe of Blundaga, who bore on his forehead the mark of his evil. The men flung the Goblin to the floor, saluted their leader, and went out.

'Here is the prisoner, Prince Talarnidh,' said Andrai. 'I would like to hear what he has to say.'

Talarnidh looked uncertainly at Andrai, unsure of how much he should be allowed to hear.

'We have told the Admiral something of our story, Talarnidh,' said Melandir. 'He knows that Ral is involved.'

'You can trust me, Talarnidh,' said Andrai. 'I am sent out as an ambassador. I know when to keep silent.'

Talarnidh turned to Nagurad.

'Whom do you serve, Goblin?'

Nagurad spat on the floor at the Prince's feet.

'If you do not speak we will kill you,' said Yeselwir.

The Goblin spat again and said nothing. Yeselwir drew his sword now and raised it above Nagurad's head.

'No!' said Talarnidh. 'I will not have even a Goblin slain in cold blood, — but it were better that you answer now, Nagurad.'

'Set me free!' answered the Goblin. 'Set me free! You do not know who my mistress is. She will kill you all. You do not know . . . But now you will be afraid. Now you will set me free. I will tell you. My mistress is the Witch Queen. The Witch Queen!'

'Her name is Ral,' answered Talarnidh coldly. 'It was she who ordered you to attack us.'

' "Take the strangers who come from the north",' said Nagurad. 'That is what she said. The Witch Queen, she ordered it. But my Giants kill everyone, everyone.'

'Are we the strangers from the north?' asked Fandorel.

'You are the ones. The ones who try to kill the Witch Queen. She knows you. The Witch Queen knows you. But you will never reach the Forest. Men cannot kill her. She is the Goddess. All must serve her. These are her lands here. She knows everything you do. She told me you would all come. She told Nagurad. My Giants kill everyone.'

'But your Giants did not kill us,' said Erathrir.

'We would have killed you,' hissed Nagurad. 'But the Goddess, she wants you. You will never reach her in the Forest. She will take you. She will find you. Then you will see the Witch Queen. And only then.'

His voice was slurred and difficult to understand, though he spoke in Northspeech, the common tongue of the Northlands, but they all understood the import of what he had said.

'So Ral has known about us from the start,' said Yeselwir. 'She has watched us, and then destroyed us one by one.'

'Take the creature away,' said Talarnidh. Yeselwir seized Nagurad, and pulled him to the door where the men of Amray took him once again.

'I understand little of what I have heard, O Prince,' said Andrai. 'To us Ral is a name out of legends.'

'I have decided that we must include you in our counsels, my lord,' replied Talarnidh. 'So now you will hear more of Ral, and none of it legends.'

He looked round at the men of the Quest. They all gave their assent. Then Talarnidh told Andrai of the return of Ral and of the terror that brooded once again in the dark forests and reached out its fingers to the far north where Selenthoril dwelt, last of the High Magicians, who alone in the world could check the power of the Great Goddess.

'Then why does this Selenthoril, whose name I have only heard in tales, send you south to fight the Witch Queen for him?' asked Andrai.

'We do not go to fight Ral,' said Karandar, 'but only to seek the means for Selenthoril to fight her.'

'The thing we seek lies in the ruined city of Kruakh,' said Talarnidh. 'We cannot tell you what it is. But the future not only of Selenthoril but of all the Northlands depends upon it.'

'Then you intend to journey through the Empty Lands of Sart Emig?' asked Andrai.

'Yes, we go south along the road,' Talarnidh answered.

'And Ral will watch our every movement, and Ral will follow us to Kruakh. We had not counted on that, Talarnidh. We will have to think again,' said Melandir.

'You are right,' said Talarnidh. He paused, and began to pace the length of the room, his brow furrowed.

'I will take you to Kruakh by sea,' said Andrai.

'You do us good service,' said Talarnidh. '— Is this our answer?' He looked round at the men of the Quest.

'You may be sure that Ral will know when we leave here,' answered Karandar. 'We need hardly doubt that this tower is watched at this moment. If we put to sea every harbour and inlet in the Empty Lands will be watched.'

'And Kruakh is the best anchorage in all these lands,' Fandorel added. 'We do not want to draw any attention there.'

'You have a plan, Karandar?' Talarnidh asked, looking at the Dwarf Lord with half a smile.

'I would not have spoken if I did not,' replied Karandar. 'It is a simple one, — but such I find to be the best. — Ral believes that we have been sent south to attack her. Let us encourage her in that belief. Some of us will go south, along the Nowhere Road towards the Forest. She will focus all her attention on those. She will expect them to march straight into the Forest and seek her out. All her spies will have their eyes on them.'

'— While the rest of us go secretly by sea,' laughed Fandorel. 'It is simple but sure. The Dwarves were ever a cunning people.'

'But will Ral not realise there are too few people travelling along the road?' asked Relnar.

'Our young prince has a good point,' said Talarnidh.

Karandar shook his head and smiled.

'Ral does not know how many were slain by the Giants. Her expectations are probably high. I do not think she will even know quite for certain how many fell victim on Misen Taïrail. Remember, she has exerted all her great power against us.'

'Then all that remains is how we are to meet together again,' said Melandir.

'My ships can wait in the great harbour at Kruakh,' said Andrai, 'if those who go by land can get to the city.'

'There is an ancient way from Kruakh through the Forest of Sorcery and down across the mountains to Chamalat,' said Talarnidh. 'It crosses the Nowhere Road just south of the city. That crossroads is called the Crossroads of Takunan. When the men of the Quest reach there, they will wait until nightfall, and then hasten secretly to Kruakh. — Ral will suspect nothing. She will be waiting for us to turn south down the road into the Forest towards Thulgarn.'

'The journey will take much longer by land,' said Fandorel.

'By the time we all meet again in Kruakh, those of us who go with Andrai should have found the thing we all seek.'

'Whither do you wish to go after Kruakh?' asked Andrai. 'For, if I can, I will take you there.'

'I do not think that you will wish to, Andrai, though you do us still greater service. We must go back to Misen Taïrail, and to Selenthoril on Enchanter's Isle.'

'It is no more than I had expected, Prince Talarnidh,' answered Andrai. 'If this matter is so great, I will do it even so.'

'My thanks to you, and the ships of Amray,' said Talarnidh and clasped his arm.

'Those who are to sail must join the ships tonight,' said the Admiral. 'The longer they remain here, the more likely that prying eyes will see them.'

'Who are they to be, Talarnidh?' asked Erathrir.

'For myself, I will go on the Nowhere Road,' Talarnidh answered. 'It will aid our deception if I am seen there. And my fate is bound too tightly with that of Ral . . . Melandir, will you go by sea? I do not know if we have anything to fear in Kruakh, but I think we may. The Sword may be needed there.'

'Yes,' answered Melandir, '— and let those who were with me in Emrurl Arnag accompany me again, if you will.'

'It is a good choice,' said Talarnidh. '— Karandar, you knew the city of old.' Karandar indicated his agreement.

'Then the rest of us will go with you, Talarnidh,' said Fandorel. 'But what of Filindrin? He is still sick from the things in the Black Land. Do you think he can make the long journey through Sart Emig on foot?'

Till then Filindrin had said nothing, sitting silently beyond their circle. Now suddenly he stood up and said:

'I will go with you, Talarnidh. You need not fear for me on the journey. I will make it well enough . . . It is better if I do not see the thing that is in Kruakh. It is better if I am not there when it is found . . .' His voice trailed off.

'You are not yet well, Filindrin,' said Talarnidh slowly. 'I would rather you went with Andrai. You need never leave the ships at Kruakh. Also there is Talak. The journey would be a hard one for him in the Empty Lands.'

'I will tell you my decision about my son,' answered Filindrin. 'He is of an age to be made an esquire. I give him to serve the Lord Melandir. This is my will.'

'Why is this, Filindrin?' asked Melandir in surprise, and Talarnidh said:

'It would mean that Talak must go with Melandir by sea. If this is your wish, surely you also will now go by sea.'

'You do not understand,' said Filindrin. Then he turned to Melandir. 'It is better this way,' he said. 'You must protect the boy. Train him hard, train him well, — but protect him, Melandir!'

'I will train him. And I will protect him,' said Melandir, his voice puzzled. 'But protect him from what, Filindrin? — Is there something in Kruakh you fear for him?'

Filindrin did not answer. Instead he turned back to Talarnidh.

'I am going with you, Prince Talarnidh. Do not bid me otherwise. The Lord Melandir has taken my son as esquire. He now has all my rights over the boy. The boy will go with his lord.'

Talarnidh looked grimly at Filindrin.

'What now of Talak's future?' he asked. 'Do you still demand that he be taken back to Melurin?'

'You do not understand. I have made him esquire, to serve his lord, to obey him, and be brought up by him. Let him do that. Let him go with Melandir. — But keep him away from me. Keep him away from me!'

He stared fiercely at the Prince. For a long while Talarnidh met his stare, then, shaking his head, turned to Melandir.

'Do you agree to this, Melandir?' he asked.

'He is of an age, as Filindrin says,' answered Melandir. 'And it is his father's wish. And come with us now, by sea or land, the boy must. For he cannot go back to Melurin. — I accept.'

'Very well,' said Talarnidh. 'It is settled. — Melandir shall sail to Kruakh, and with him Erathrir, Relnar, and Karandar, and also Talak as his squire. Filindrin, Fandorel, and Yeselwir shall come with me on the Nowhere Road. The journey by sea will be swifter. So you must need wait a week or more in Kruakh, Melandir. I do not doubt, from all that Selenthoril told us, that you will find It soon. But the dangerous time is while you wait. Let us hope that the deception works, and all Ral's attention is on us on the road.'

'The only thing that may delay us is the sea, Prince Talarnidh,' interrupted Andrai. 'Do not forget the sea. It is a strange coast, and given to great storms.'

'Then I hope we do not see any of them,' said Karandar. 'For the Dwarves do not love the sea.'

'What of the Goblin, Nagurad?' asked Yeselwir. 'He is a servant of Ral and he knows too much. It would be best to kill him now.'

'If he is a servant of Ral, he will also know the Empty Lands,' said Fandorel. 'We are not even sure if the course of the Nowhere Road can still be found. He may be needed as a guide.'

'Perhaps that is so,' said Talarnidh. 'For we will not kill a prisoner.'

'Then we should at least keep him well tied,' muttered Yeselwir.

Andrai turned towards the door.

'My men and the Reavers will make ready the ships,' he said.

'Filindrin, will you tell your son that you have given him as Melandir's squire?' asked Talarnidh as Andrai went out.

'Let Melandir tell him,' Filindrin replied. 'And, — Melandir, tell him he is not to speak to me again . . .' Then he turned and followed the Admiral from the room.

'That is hard on the boy,' said Melandir, and Filindrin half-turned and said:

'I do not know when it will happen.'

'Do you know what he means?' Melandir asked Talarnidh.

'I think he means his death,' said the Prince bleakly. 'I think he believes that he is dying from some foul thing out of Aldel Morn. He wants to spare his son.'

'You think he is right, my Prince?' said Karandar quietly.

'I think I am watching another friend die,' replied Talarnidh.

Melandir shook his head, and then went out to find Talak. The men of the Quest prepared for their departure, and the second parting of their ways. During the night Melandir, Erathrir, Karandar, Relnar, and also Talak made their farewells and boarded the ships of Amray. At daybreak they sailed for Kruakh.

It was before the dawn that Filindrin rose and walked out from the castle. He went as one reluctant to go, his feet dragging on the ground and a listless expression in his eyes. Up into the pitch black valleys he went between grey hills, till at last he halted in a secret place where the rocks stood in craggy pinnacles like a vast grotesque army frozen as they marched. He held his left hand before him, and pain burned in it. He could not run, he could not move. He could only wait, beyond fear, and half-crazed.

The first light of dawn streaked the eastern sky. Expectancy stifled the cold air and the first wisps of a late autumnal mist drifted down from the hilltops over melting snow. Stillness and silence was all around, but now there came one sound only in it, the sound of Filindrin weeping the abandoned tears of despair.

'I have come!' Filindrin cried suddenly aloud, in a voice that wailed with cold desolation.

He raised his face to the sky. Over one of the stone pillars, with its strange contours, a cloud of mist gathered.

'What do you want?' he shouted into the emptiness. And the hills cried back:

'Want!' and were silent.

The cloud of mist stretched over Filindrin. Thin wings spread, delicate as a dragonfly, from a slender body, and streamers of cloud trailed about it. Colours flickered, blue and red and silver upon it as it descended and wrapped Filindrin in itself. Only for a moment did he see the two piercing eyes in the insubstantial form.

'No!' screamed Filindrin. The mist pressed in upon him. His body shook. And then the mist had vanished. A long thin sigh came from Filindrin's mouth. He turned and, slowly, very uncertainly, as if learning to walk, started back towards the castle of Belengar.

★

Filindrin entered the room in the great tower and looked about him. By the window he saw Talarnidh and Fandorel gazing seaward.

'Where is my son?' he asked. His voice was thick and slurred, and at first he had some difficulty in speaking.

'Filindrin!' exclaimed Talarnidh. 'We were about to start searching for you. Are you well?'

'Where is the boy?' demanded Filindrin.

'But you sent him on the ship with Melandir, my friend,' said Fandorel.

'Fetch him back! I have changed my mind. He must stay with me,' snapped Filindrin.

'They have sailed,' said Talarnidh. 'We are watching the ships now.'

Filindrin ran to the window. He looked out, and then turned on Talarnidh. For a moment his face twisted into a mask of fury. With difficulty he seemed to control himself, turning away, bowing his head, and almost choking. Then he looked up again.

'I did not want him to go,' he said slowly. 'I wanted him to know me better. I wanted him to forget what he had seen of me before.'

'We thought you were being drawn down into the darkness, Filindrin,' said Talarnidh, speaking carefully and looking full at Filindrin. 'The darkness out of Aldel Morn.'

Filindrin's whole body shivered for the briefest moment, and a tiny flicker of horror passed into his eyes.

'The darkness came and called me,' he said, still slowly, like a child. Then suddenly he smiled. 'But I am not dead yet.'

'My friend, my friend! You are well! It has passed!' said Talarnidh, and clasped Filindrin to him, laughing in joy.

'Yes, it is over now,' said Filindrin, and he laughed with the Prince.

The door opened, and once again Nagurad was brought in, dragged protesting by Yeselwir. The Goblin suddenly stopped his struggles and seemed to sniff the air in the room. He looked round at each of them in turn. Then, suddenly, for no clear reason, he began to struggle more violently than ever. He was out of Yeselwir's grasp and making for the door in seconds.

'The creature of Ral escapes!' came Filindrin's voice. Then a streak of metal across the room. With unerring skill and aim

Filindrin had flung his sword. The metal stood two hands breadth out from the Goblin's back. Nagurad fell dead instantly.

'We could not risk it escaping again,' said Filindrin. He drew his blade from the body, and dragged the dead Goblin out.

'It was a remarkable throw to make with a broadsword,' said Fandorel. 'But I would rather he had not killed the Goblin.'

'I do not like seeing any prisoner killed,' Talarnidh answered.

'But it was escaping,' said Yeselwir.

'We had better prepare to depart. We are without any guide now, even an evil one. I hope the old road still can be found,' said Fandorel.

The sun was rising in the sky as the four men of the Quest left the castle at Belengar and started out along the Nowhere Road. At first their path was a grassy way heading east, but as the sun passed its zenith the road curved south and the grass now was thin and coarse with cold air whistling in its tufts. Soon nothing grew anywhere and the path became strewn with stones. They did not need a guide, for the old road could still be seen, a lighter grey in the dimness of the land of rocks all around. They saw burnt shapes like broken bones near and far, and sometimes great mounded cliffs hunched over them, pocked with black caves. The land bore streaks of snow, half-melted at first then freezing again as the day wore to a close.

Each walked in silence with his own thoughts in the still landscape. They stopped briefly to eat a meagre meal, but hastened on soon, not wishing to tarry too long in the cold winds. When dusk was falling they seemed to sense movement near them in the dark rocks. They stopped but saw and heard nothing. They made camp in that place under a looming pinnacle of basalt. There was no wood for a fire and the night was chill. Early, and hungry, they tried to sleep. But one of them always kept watch.

It was before dawn when the bitter chill awoke them all. The wind had strengthened in the night, and now it drove hard flurries of snow into their faces. The day grew a little lighter, but they could not see the sun, and dark clouds scudding in the sky soon brought more snow. The wind was fiercer and fiercer, howling through the wide wastes of rock and burning ice-cold on their faces. The snow buffeted them hither and thither. They went on southward as long as they could walk, though all sign of the road was lost. The way seemed to lie through a vast desolate valley, where the whistling of the gale rose to an uncanny constant scream.

Finally they had to take shelter, under the lee of a sheer cliff, its grey slate the only landmark left. Even there they had little enough protection against the raging of the storm. They could see little through the whirling snow — a few broken bushes and trees tossing in the wind, and the white slabs of the hills around. Only in the afternoon when the storm began to abate did they try to go on. They all thought of Ral, and wondered if this blizzard was her doing, — for they remembered Melandir's tale of the pass of Anrith.

When they set off again Yeselwir thought he saw something else move in the great desolation. They all looked, but there was nothing. Their garments were soaked through and freezing. For most of the time Filindrin led the way. He shewed no sign of his sickness, and Talarnidh remembered once again that he had visited these lands before as he watched him stride on ahead.

As they wearily made camp at the end of the second day, Yeselwir again saw the movement amidst the rocks. Though he could not make it out he was sure that it was the same thing. He pointed it out to the others, and this time they were all sure that they too saw something. But it was too fleeting and far away for any of them to guess what it might be.

Another day went by, and increasingly they perceived the thing moving with them, away to the east where the low hills marched with the road. They came to realise that it was the form of a man, but its shape seemed strangely indistinct, as if ragged at the edges. Against the snow they could hardly see the thing at all, which was strange in itself unless the phantom shape was completely white. But all the while they travelled on in the wide open emptiness the sense of its half-seen presence haunted them. They constantly looked back along their tracks in the flat snow plain that hid the Nowhere Road, or gazed to the eastward where they might see the pale form suddenly outlined against the jutting darkness of a boulder or the drab sunless sky. By night their sleep was troubled. They kept even more constant watch, and shivered in the wan heat of a little fire.

Another day of endless trudging through the thick drifts came and went, and always the thing was there. They knew they were watched, and tried in vain to perceive the watcher that hid in the vast trackless wastes all around. By the time the grey evening had closed in all around them they knew at last that it was a tall man who ran forever beside them, all swathed in white rags and tatters. On the fifth night, as the men of the Quest slept under a hillside craggy with slopes of fire-cracked shale, from the rocks above a shrouded head looked down on Filindrin as he stood watch. He looked up, then looked away.

The sixth day brought more flurries of snow, and a greater certainty of the relentlessness of pursuit. All day the elusive thing that dogged them was there, distant glimpses of dirty white, lost in the snow. It had the shape perhaps of a man of the High Race, but on it they now did not mistake the hanging shreds of an earth-stained shroud. It never came near enough to catch or chase, but once, as night was coming on, it ran for a full minute in their sight on a hilltop, stark and macabre against the glooms of the sky. Several times Fandorel had flown up and towards it, but each time he found nothing save footprints in the snow, leading nowhere.

In the inky blackness of the night the shrouded corpse entered their camp. The light of the sparse fire had dulled to flickering embers. Fandorel only saw the muddy grey of the winding sheet when the thing was almost upon him. He was on watch and had kept his sword drawn. Between the cloths that bound the creature's head he saw the eyes of fire. He stabbed blindly beneath them, but the sword caught in the thick funereal robe. A sickly-sweet smell filled his nostrils, the scent of unguents that embalm the dead. Then the thing was gone. Fandorel kicked the fire into life and called the others, but their sleepless watchful night was not disturbed again.

When they set off at daybreak the snow had at last begun to melt, but the slush and mud made no better going. They saw no further sign of the creature that had pursued them, but the sense remained of a lurking watcher out beyond their sight in the lonely places of the bleak land. At last they saw a dark line on the horizon before them, and soon they were walking beside an endless host of trees, the northern edge of the Forest of Sorcery. They camped beneath the dark eaves of the dripping pines. Filindrin took first watch.

In the grey light before the night became total, on a grim hillside near their camp, the shrouded thing stood silent and hideous, listening while a dark form spoke to it. Darkness spread. Though the touch was ever so light on his shoulder, Fandorel still woke at once, woke to stare into the eyes of a corpse. He opened his mouth to shout, and in that moment breathed in the breath of the dead thing as its lips touched his own. He fell back choking.

From the edge of the camp came a sudden cry of fury. It awoke Talarnidh and Yeselwir. Like Fandorel the Prince stared up into undead eyes. He twisted away, resisting the cloying stench of the Ghost Breath already in his lungs. His sword cut at the creature's face as the two hands like claws seized his throat. There was a brittle crack as if its skull had broken, and more of the foetid sweetness. The white material was torn from the face by the sword's slashing cut, and for a moment Talarnidh looked again on the dead shrunken face of Fermilondath. Then the second thrust he had dealt struck home, and Talarnidh saw his own sword in the skull of his lost friend. The Prince fell back, gasping from the deadly exhalation, the same Ghost Breath that had killed Fermilondath in Aldel Morn and now breathed from his corpse to poison his comrades.

There came a rush of figures into the camp. Nearly twenty men, fur-clad and armed with axes and swords, swept into the circle of firelight. Two of them dragged the already-bound form of Filindrin. They had captured him on the edge of the camp. Swiftly they seized Fandorel and Talarnidh, kicking aside the ruined corpse that had been Fermilondath.

'These two are alive,' one of them called out.

'There's a body here too,' another shouted.

'The Witch Queen said there should be four of them,' came an answer.

'Aye, but she never said that one would be a thing such as this.' The man who spoke now swung up his axe, and sent the head flying from the body of Fermilondath.

'The other one's over here!' came a cry, soon taken up by others.

Backed up against a tree, Yeselwir stood sword in hand facing the servants of Ral. They approached him cautiously, then two made a dash. Yeselwir twisted away from the thrust of one, and cut into the sword arm of the other.

'Take him alive, you fools!' shouted one of the attackers. 'The Witch Queen wanted them all alive!'

'Bring him in alive!' another one called, clearly an order from their chief.

They moved round cautiously now, outside the range of Yeselwir's moving blade. Another rush failed, and this time one of the men lay dead at Yeselwir's feet and two others bled from the cuts of his sword. But the men were on him again at once, and he saw the raised axes glinting in the light of the fire. An axe bit into the tree near his head. Again the shout to take him alive, but the axeman was already dead, falling backwards as his throat pumped blood from the single sweep of Yeselwir's sword. And soon two more still of Ral's men were dead at his feet. His arm tired. The attackers came again and again. Once more, finally, the sword stabbed, and then, twisting, cut in another direction. Two fell back bleeding, but Yeselwir had not seen the third come upon him from behind the tree. A club rose and fell, and Yeselwir slumped down, his right hand still clasping his sword.

The dying fire still flickered in the empty camp. From afar came the noise of the servants of Ral carrying their prisoners through the forest. Only their dead remained, their dead and the twice-dead corpse of Fermilondath, once a mighty lord and warrior.

CHAPTER 11

THE SCEPTRE MORTAL

From the deck of the leading ship Melandir gazed up past the billowing sail as the first light of dawn streaked the night-time sky.

'Do you think that the wind will remain against us?' he asked.

'It may do,' answered the Admiral. 'The prevailing winds are south westerlies. But they would help us even less. It is a bad coast, and autumn is its season of storms. Normally I would sail a hundred leagues further out in open waters.'

As he spoke, seamen ran across the deck and clambered up the rigging. The yard swung round, and for a moment the sail flapped lifelessly. Then it caught the wind again as the ship came about on the new tack. The land fell away behind, and the vessel began to pitch with the rise and fall of ocean waves. When the sun came up Andrai assembled all of his men on deck. Along the rail lay the bodies of the men of Amray who had died. One by one, sewn in winding sheets and weighted with lead, they were consigned to the dark waves of the ocean. All the while a single drum was beaten, according to the custom of Amray.

Throughout that day the ships beat to the southward, making fair progress despite the contrary winds, as they followed the line of the coast just beyond their horizon.

Melandir awoke during the following night. The sounds from the timbers of the ship were different. He went up on deck. It was already about first light. He felt the wind stronger and gustier on his face. One by one the other men of the Quest joined him. Soon even Relnar and Karandar who knew nothing of the sea could perceive that the waves were becoming steadily rougher and higher. The seamen had already taken in most of the sails, and now even the mainsail was reefed.

'I know this sort of wind,' said Talak. 'We're in for a storm.'

'Be quiet!' said Karandar. '— I am going below.'

'Dwarves do not like the sea,' laughed Melandir.

Talak smiled, and, for the first time since they had left Belengar, seemed to forget that Filindrin had sent him away.

Before another hour had passed the wind had become a furious gale, full of driving sleet and flurries of snow. The ships of Amray ran before the wind, all sails taken in, and their masts bending and groaning as if the storm would rip them out. For nearly a whole day they were driven far out to sea, away from their destination, the hatches battened down, and the wheel lashed fast. At every plunge the bows of the wind-tossed ships drove into the waves, and green seas swept over their forecastles and washed across the decks, tearing loose anything that was not tied.

The storm only died away towards the evening. The ship of Andrai had not suffered too badly, and the men were set at once to repairing the rigging. Of the other ship there was no sign. They only saw her just before nightfall, far away and wallowing in heavy seas, with the mainmast snapped off at half its height. A line was finally passed, and the two ships drifted, tied together, through the night. All the following day passed in rigging a jury mast, and only then could the two ships begin the journey back towards Kruakh from the middle of the ocean where the storm had left them.

They sighted land on the afternoon of the seventh day since they had left Belengar. At dusk the two ships sailed into the great harbour of the ancient city of Kruakh. In the half-light they could only make out dim shapes, ruins of the once-mighty palaces of the city, their domes and turrets broken and strange against the sky. Closer to them the dark sea lapped at the pale lines of ruined quays and forgotten breakwaters.

The next morning Relnar and Talak were the first on deck. Neither of them had seen the like of the city before. To Talak the very extent of the ruins was beyond his comprehension, while Relnar could not imagine how a city even greater than his own of Chamalat could have become such a desolation. The countless streets and squares and broad avenues had become groves of pine trees. The rubble of endless rows of ruined houses was a flourishing wilderness of thorn and bramble thickets, while broken walls of roofless dwellings sheltered only the grass and nettles. In places even the ruins had fallen down and the lines of the streets were indistinguishable among the undergrowth-cloaked mounds.

Even so, above the long-forgotten emptiness, the remains of the great palaces of the High Race still revealed the majesty of Kruakh of old, though the cupolas and spires were broken, and the colonades cracked and fallen. And in the middle of the city, built of blue-grey granite and seemingly undamaged, rose the vast strangely-shaped dome of the Citadel of Kruakh, its panels of crystal glinting in the sunlight.

'We will return to the ship at evening,' said Melandir. It was soon after, and the men of the Quest were preparing to row over to the city.

'I will be sending my men out to find water,' Andrai answered. 'I will post guards on the quayside. — I hope you may find whatever you seek.'

He watched until the five travellers had stepped ashore in the city of Kruakh.

'Selenthoril told us that the Sceptre lay in the Citadel, Karandar. How do we reach it from here?' asked Erathrir.

Karandar looked up towards the great dome dominating the city.

'It was once the palace and fortress of one of the Nine Kings of Wenyaltrir,' he said. 'This city flourished then, as did all the Northlands. I dwelt here once in the time of Kivandoril, King of Boragalif.'

'You can lead us there then?' interrupted Erathrir.

'I could have done so with ease once,' Karandar answered. 'But you can see as well as I what the city has become now. The place was sacked by the Black Lords, and fought over again in the War of the Sceptres. The High Race reoccupied it for a few years, but that could not last. By then they were so few.'

'Was it ever a city of the Black Lords?' asked Relnar.

'No,' replied Karandar. 'They held Belengar for a while and dwelt there, but never in Kruakh. Now it has been utterly deserted for a thousand years.'

'But can you not find a way to the Citadel?' said Melandir.

'We will find a way in time. Some of my knowledge may still be of use,' said Karandar. 'We are on the Quay of the Spice Merchants now. If we make our way along the harbourside to the tall building you see there . . .' He pointed, and his voice tailed off. 'I think it is one of the grain stores,' he muttered. 'The road to the Citadel . . . well, it should be just beyond there.'

Following Karandar they set off across the huge rock slabs of the quayside. There at least little could grow and, though the slabs were sometimes cracked and broken and slimy with seaweed, they soon reached the ruined building to which Karandar had pointed. They were almost on the edge of the city, and, northward, beyond the ancient canal, rose the cliffs called Kamathanlar. As Karandar had said, a broad thoroughfare once led back to the Citadel from there. It had been lined with tall buildings and most of these had crashed into the roadway long ago. Trees and a tangle of undergrowth hid their rubble and threatened to engulf the remains of those buildings still standing. Everywhere was slippery with mud and melted snow.

With swords and bare hands they began to hack their way forward. It took almost half the day to reach the great gate of the Citadel, and at the gate came another check. Part of the lintel had fallen and there was no way through. They spent a fruitless afternoon, first searching for another way in, and then attempting to dig through the fallen masonry of the gate. By the end of the day the great circular building remained as impregnable as ever. They looked up at the massive unbroken walls and the windows in the great curve of the dome, beyond any means of reach. Wearily they made their way back to the ship.

In the morning of the next day when they returned they brought from the ship with them ten of the men of Amray, bearing a spar from Andrai's vessel. One by one the great fallen stones were levered away from the door, until finally there was a gap large enough for them to crawl through. The sailors returned to their ship, the men of the Quest entered the Citadel of Kruakh.

A bright light ahead of them lit the way, shining onto the blue-grey walls of giant stones. They found themselves in a passageway leading into the heart of the Citadel. Outlined against the light at its end was a dark figure unmoving in the stillness. They walked towards it without speaking, all aware of the eerie and utter quiet that hung in the air of that place. They came near the end of the immense passage, and saw there a statue of burnished bronze. Behind it was the vastness of the central hall of the Citadel. Talak pointed at the statue.

'What is that thing?' he asked.

No-one answered. All now moved slowly and with caution, though none was sure why.

'It moved! I saw it move!' cried Relnar.

'Stand still!' said Karandar. 'I think I know what we are faced with here. It is the Guardian of the Gate, — a statue that walks and speaks. The High Race made them once. This was put here for a purpose. It is very dangerous.'

'How shall we deal with it?' Melandir asked.

'I will see how closely it can be approached,' Karandar replied. 'No-one else is to move. Such things respond to every movement.'

Slowly Karandar approached the statue. The bronze limbs moved slowly and jerkily. The sword it held at rest was brought up to the ready. But the bronze features of the bearded warrior did not change at all.

'We wish to pass,' said Karandar to the thing that barred their way.

'You must answer or fight,' said the statue. Its voice was utterly unlike any human voice, but it spoke, as Karandar had, in the High Speech of Wenyaltrir.

'What is the question?' asked Karandar, and he motioned to the others to come forward.

The brazen lips of the statue moved, and it spoke again:

'Lives on the first,
Dies on the second,
Moves on the third,
Waits on the fourth,
Burns and burrows and swims and flies on the fifth,
Knows on the sixth,
Changes on the seventh,
Is born on the eighth,
Does not die on the ninth,
Does all things again on the tenth.'

'What do the words mean?' whispered Talak to Relnar.

'They are in Peirian, the High Speech,' answered Relnar. 'I have learnt something of it, but for the most part only in books at school. I cannot really understand the words it said.'

'Then you are little worse off than us,' said Erathrir. 'It is a riddle. I for one do not know any answer.'

'The riddle is an ancient one,' said Karandar. 'It was known to the great ones of Wenyaltrir, and was sometimes used as a password. It refers to the powers of the Sceptres of Wenylatrir.'

He looked towards the statue.

'Man of Bronze,' he said, 'your answer is this: — "The Sceptres of Wenyaltrir." '

He began to walk forward again. The sword arm of the statue

fell lifeless to its side. No further movement or sound came from it.

'Do you think that the use of this riddle here is linked with the Sceptre we seek?' asked Melandir.

'I doubt it,' Karandar answered. 'It has been used many times, and, from what Selenthoril told us, the Sceptre only came here many years after the High Race abandoned the Citadel.'

'What does the Sceptre look like?' asked Talak. They had agreed that Melandir should tell him the thing they were seeking when they were all aboard ship, and also explain what such a thing was.

'This Sceptre is dark,' answered Karandar. 'You, and anyone, would know it if you saw it.'

They walked forward past the motionless statue into the central hall of the Citadel. Clear frosty sunlight shone through the solid crystal set in the immeasurable dome. A palace of lambent colours lay before them. All around it was the blue-grey of the granite walls, and throughout the hall were many things of carven stone, each different thing of a different coloured rock. There were tables and chairs, high seats and couches, and other artefacts of unknown use. The soft light seemed to shine out of the muted colours, and here and there bright jewels flashed sudden liquid fire. Under the very peak of the dome stood a round table of white marble, very wide, and at the centre of it lay a fine opal, as large as the head of a man and full of red sparks like a myriad eyes.

'Here the High Race came from all parts of the kingdom,' said Karandar. 'In the long years of peace before the Black Lords came it was a place of rest and contentment. When the Peiri returned after the War of the Sceptres, this they rebuilt above all. New crystal was set in the great dome, and the shapes and colours were restored, but once there were many more. Too few of the High Race returned here then, and now they are all departed.'

They walked through the hall, and the power of it could still work on them, as it had been intended to so many years before. They said nothing, but were full of sudden joy.

'I think this may be yet the greatest of the remaining works of the High Race in all the ancient realm of Boragalif,' said Karandar at last. '— But now the day draws on.'

'Yes, we cannot remain,' said Melandir. 'We must find the Sceptre, and that soon.'

'It must have been easy to stay here for days and years,' said Erathrir. 'There was no haste then, and time did not pass. — Selenthoril said that the Sceptre lay beneath the Citadel, in the Caverns of the Merpeople. — Do you still know a way to those caverns, Karandar?'

'I do,' Karandar answered. 'Come!'

He led them out of the hall into a side passage. Here they lit torches, and followed the passageway as it curved to the left and the light from the crystal dome became faint. Before them was a steep flight of steps leading down into darkness.

For a long time they descended the arched stairway, and then there were many dark corridors with storerooms and other unknown ways leading from them, and other stairs into untold depths. Everything remained as it had been in the last days of the High Race. The rooms they saw near the central passage were still furnished. There was no decay and no ruin. Then they found themselves in a place where, though the floor was still paved, the long passage gave way to caverns of natural rock.

Light from their torches now reflected from the still blackness of subterranean sheets of water that lay beside their path. Suddenly there was water on both sides, and the path had become a narrow causeway between two lakes that stretched into the inky distance. They trod carefully, following Karandar, as they moved in a circle of pale yellow light amidst the utter gloom. The lake ended abruptly at a wall of rock, but the paved way went on into a tunnel through the stone. The tunnel continued for almost as great a distance as had the causeway, and by now they were no longer beneath the city. They came to a metal gate set in the rock.

'Of old this was where the domain of the Peiri ended,' said Karandar. 'Beyond lies the home of the Merpeople and the deep sea-caverns. This gate was fashioned in ancient times by the magic of the Merpeople to protect their realm. Even now the spell of binding remains, written on it long ago in their script. It was here that the Black Lords were held after the sack of Kruakh when they came to plunder the water-caverns where the Merpeople live. But in time of peace this way was always left open. For the people of the seas always welcomed any who came in friendship.'

As he spoke Karandar pushed open the gate of unrusting iron. It gleamed in the light of the torches and swung open at once on silent hinges. When they closed it behind them they saw two steel bolts, massive and burnished, with more words carved beside them in the flowing cursive script of the Merpeople.

Ahead of them lay a wide quay, gently lapped by dark blue waters and lit by a dim glow which seemed to come from the walls of the cavern itself. There was no causeway across this lake and it was far wider than the lake they had already crossed. Drawn up on the quay was a long graceful wooden boat. Its timbers were sound and it shewed no sign of age.

'It was once the custom of the Merpeople always to leave a boat here for their guests of the High Race who came from Kruakh above,' said Karandar.

'How is this ship sailed?' Relnar asked.

'There is a current. It will carry us across,' Karandar answered. 'Come, this is our way to the deep caverns.'

As Karandar had said an unseen current bore them swiftly to the opposite side. They pulled up the boat on the farther quay. Nearby was an arched door leading to a long spiral staircase which the Merpeople had placed there for land dwellers who might come that way. They descended for a long space of time, down the steep winding steps in the pallid glow from the rock walls on either side. At last they saw a brighter light in the distance, growing in intensity as they went on downwards. Soon it had become as bright as daylight, blinding their eyes which had grown accustomed to the gloom.

They stood on a wide waterfront looking out across a bright subterranean sea. The domed roof of the cavern shone with glittering light, reflecting from the changing planes and surfaces of the crystalline rock. In the clear water before them they saw flurries of movement, flecking the sea with white foam. Here and there they caught glimpses of lithe shapes, gliding and diving in the water.

'I think it is here that the Sceptre waits,' said Karandar.

As he spoke the waters near the quay parted and they saw below them a Mermaid. The scales of her tail glinted in the bright light of the cavern, but the tail grew from the body of a perfectly formed woman. Lustrous green hair hung in waves over the brown skin of her body. Between her round breasts hung a single silver pendant, her only decoration.

'Who are you that come to this country?' she said, and her voice made the Peirian speech of Wenyaltrir sound like waves on a far-off shore.

'We have been sent by the Lord Selenthoril,' said Melandir. 'We have come to seek for him Arnorin, the Sceptre Mortal of Wenyaltrir. It was he who told us to find the land of the Merpeople, for they are the guardians of the Sceptre now.' His voice was loud in the quiet of the glittering cave.

'Hearken, man of dust,' said the Mermaid. 'Here is my realm of the muted light and moving silence, of the drifting weeds and flickering fishes. Why should I who am Queen show you, the leaden ones, to the secret places, to the deep sea-caves beneath the rocks where the horns of the triton sound?'

'You have in these caverns a jewel that does not belong to the sea,' Melandir replied.

'Long ago he brought it,' answered the Merqueen. 'It rests among the pearls and the sapphires, hung like a jewel in the Crystal Cavern. It was a dark thing of the Upper Earth, and he who brought it was dying. He bade us keep the bitter jewel, and round it we have woven the Gem of Gems of the Merpeople to mute its fiery light.'

'The time has come for the Sceptre to return to the Upper Earth,' said Karandar.

'It may not be given,' said the Merqueen. 'For these are his words, the words of Imaholin, dead Guardian of the Sceptre Mortal:

"Talmond the Emperor gave me the Sceptre.
I give it to guard to the Merpeople.
Surrender it only to the servants of Talmond.
By these signs shall ye know them:
The Standard of Wenyaltrir,
The Ring of the Emperor,
The Sword of Fate." '

Melandir drew the Sword of Fate, and held the hilt out towards the Merqueen.

'This is the Sword of Fate,' he said. 'The other tokens, the Ring and the Standard, await with Selenthoril. He is the lord we serve.'

The Queen reached out her hand and touched the glittering sapphire which burnt uppermost in the hilt.

'It is one of the Star Sapphires,' she said, 'that was brought from Heaven long ago. Great is our lore of jewels in these halls and many we have woven, but none like the jewels of Heaven. I acknowledge the token, and now I know our guardianship has ended. — Walk along the waterside until I tell you to halt.'

They did as she commanded.

'Now step forward into the water.'

All hesitated for a moment, then Erathrir stepped forward. He seemed to stand on the calm surface of the water. He walked a step or two forward, then knelt down and ran his hands across the surface. He turned to the other men of the Quest.

'There is a bridge through the water. It is made of rock crystal, and very hard to see. Its top is level with the surface. You will have to watch where you step.'

Slowly they began to cross the hidden bridge, the Merqueen swimming beside and just ahead of them. All around, the smooth brown bodies of the Merpeople broke surface, then twisted away and vanished in sudden movements deep into the water, laughing and shouting as they disappeared. They seemed to delight in diving under the arches of the wide crystal bridge and then appearing again near the men on the other side, reaching out to touch them with half-webbed fingers. Everywhere on the water were the ever-young faces of Mermaids, or the graver features of the Mermen, their sea-green beards spreading out on the lapping swell.

The bridge ended beside the entrance to a natural rock tunnel. They followed a twisting narrow path along its wall beside the still water. Only the Merqueen now swam on with them as they entered the small and secret cavern. No light came from the walls of this cave, but it was full of light. For in its midst, suspended in the air, hung a great gem. It had been fashioned by the Merpeople, strange and many-faceted, to shine with a light of its own, silver and brilliant. They had woven it in the deep sea-caves for a purpose. In its heart shone a different flame, a deep and pulsing crimson fire, so that the water beneath and the lesser gems piled round the cavern's edge flickered to the interchanging lights, white of the Merstone, and red of the Sceptre Mortal that lay within its heart.

'You must break the gem,' said the Queen's still voice. 'There is no other way.'

Melandir drew Wenyorel again. He reached out across the

water and swung the blade in a wide arc. The tip of the sword struck the great crystal, and it smashed with starry brightness into falling diamonds. A single perfect clear note filled the cavern for a moment and was gone. For that moment the Sceptre pulsed vermilion, then fell a dying flame into the hand of the Merqueen below. Its translucent shape became opaque, then inky dark. The flame of its jewel dulled to polished rock. From the path around the chamber and from beneath the waters a thousand new pale lights lit the cavern, the broken diamonds from the last and greatest of the gems of the Merpeople. The Merqueen handed the lifeless rod to Melandir.

'You must guard the Sceptre now. But beware, for only the strong may claim it.'

'It is not mine to claim,' answered Melandir.

'It will be claimed now,' said the Merqueen. 'In the Upper Earth it is a dread thing. But go quickly away. Do not give me any thanks. Our task is done.'

CHAPTER 12

THE GREAT GODDESS RAL

In the Forest of Sorcery Talarnidh and those with him tasted the full fruits of their plan to deceive Ral by advancing to her own realm. The men of the Quest and their captors had been marching for four hours or more. The inert form of Fandorel was tied across two poles dragged by the servants of Ral. His face was white and twisted from the Ghost Breath and he seemed only just alive. Talarnidh also was pale and sickened, stumbling as he walked and often falling against Yeselwir and Filindrin to whom he was tied. Yeselwir's face and arms were bloody where the men his sword had injured had struck him again and again in their fury. Only Filindrin still struggled against his ropes, though he too bore the marks of their enemies' anger. Often they crashed against the trees or tripped on their roots, only to be kicked and dragged upright again by the men of Ral.

These men seemed to know unerringly the winding paths in the pitch black of the forest night. Only their leader carried a torch, and it cast flickering and fitful shadows, made strange by the serried ranks of gloomy pines that pressed in on them from either side and vanished into the limitless darks beyond. All the while the fur-clad men talked to each other or jeered at their prisoners in a slurred form of the Northspeech. But their pace never slowed, though those of them who had been wounded cursed their companions and begged for a rest.

The march continued till dawn. To the men of the Quest each step had become an effort, their eyes open but unseeing and their thinking blurred by utter exhaustion, until only the blows and taunts of their captors were real to them as they stumbled onwards. Fandorel now had awoken from his unnatural sleep, but his face was still twisted and contorted as if in the pain of a wracking fever. The men still dragged him along on the rough stretcher. All the men of the Quest now knew that they were in the hands of the servants of Ral, and were on their way to the presence of the Witch Queen.

In the darkest hour before first light they came to a clearing in the forest, overshadowed by the huge trunk and boughs of a strange and ancient fir tree, faintly seen and menacing in the smoke and blown flames of the torchlight. The leader of the men of Ral went to the great tree and pressed his palms against the gnarled bark. He looked up into the shadows. All saw the tiny shapes that were moving there, and heard the high-pitched whispers.

'What are they?' Yeselwir hissed to Filindrin.

'Perhaps the bats of Ral,' came the reply.

The noises stopped, and the man stood back from the tree. At its base the needle-clad ground shook. Black lines appeared across the earth. A hidden door groaned upwards on wooden ratchets, and earth and pine needles fell into the pit of darkness below. More torches were lit, and the prisoners were bundled underground. They went down steps formed from tree roots and along sloping tunnels with nets of roots for roof and walls, through arches of living roots, massive as stone, guiding them ever downwards. Light shewed ahead, but before they reached it Yeselwir, Filindrin and Fandorel were pushed aside into a blind alley. A solid wooden door slid across its entrance and bolts slammed home behind them. The last remaining light, gleaming through chinks in the wood, grew fainter and the noise receded. The men stood alone and imprisoned. Fandorel leaned against the door, hardly able to stand upright since he had been taken from his makeshift stretcher.

'Why have they taken the Prince?' he asked, his voice breaking in renewed pain.

'Because he is the Prince, Elf Lord. They will question him, and when they have learnt of the Sceptre they will kill him,' said Filindrin. Yeselwir looked up, startled.

'He will tell them nothing,' he said.

Surrounded by his enemies Talarnidh stood at the door of a wide underground hall, its roof beams roots of vast size forming a vaulted dome high above. Shafts of the earliest light of dawn cut down from slits round the roof, below which, in that strange cavern, young pine trees grew like offspring of the huge tree above. And around the pines, as if guardians of the trees, with tiny spears, and helmets fashioned like pine cones, were the Pine Sprites. They stood like perfect miniature imitations of men, fierce-faced, their weapons pointing at Talarnidh, a secret people of the deep forest, in the red of the smoky torches and the wan light of the early morning. Their skins were brown, covered with many minute pointed hairs like pine needles, their faces bearded in the same way. They wore only stiff green cloaks woven of pine needles. Behind them, in the shadows of the cavern, larger but stealthy grey forms moved, and there came the low growling of wolves. Amidst the wolves Talarnidh thought he half made out a tall man-like shape.

But Talarnidh did not look long at the hidden beings of the deep pine halls. For in the centre of the cavern was a high seat, part of an ancient trunk weathered and hollowed to make a throne and stood upon a mound. Around it, cloud-like, hovering almost motionless but twittering, a fearful shapeless mass, were the black bats. Through the darkness of the centuries many of their kind had been bred into huge half-knowing things in the Pit of the Werebats, deep in the forest. Ral had made them her most dreaded messengers. Ral it was who sat on the throne.

A robe like a bridal gown hung about her, more silver than white, with flickers of pale green in the shimmering folds that spread about her feet. On her head was a tall crown spiked with silver and brilliant with diamonds. But her face was paler than all, bloodless and with skin drawn tight, all white as a fair still corpse, save for the faintest red of drawn lips, and the utter black of her eyes.

Her eyes held those of Talarnidh, as he looked on his sister. He perceived that the guards had backed away into the passage. Alone, watched only by wolves and Pine Sprites and dwellers in the forest, he walked towards the Great Goddess, for so she had chosen now to appear. Ripples of movement and unseen sounds ran through the evil crowd above her. He could not look away, but approached her throne, sick and stumbling, a ragged wayfarer before the Queen of Queens.

Suddenly the fetor and nearness of the Ghost Breath had returned to him. He could hardly stand. The wan lips of the Witch Queen parted in a smile. The great chamber was full of the twanging music of a harp, yet he could not be sure if it was Ral who held it. He knew that the sweet scents which swirled and rippled and the cloying thickness of the air emanated from her. There was no warmth in the room, but a cold icy glow. He felt himself held and checked in a snow-cloak, his senses subdued in a frozen sweetness. At the foot of the high mound, gazing up into her face, Talarnidh fell to his knees, unable to advance any farther, unable even to move.

'Welcome, Talarnidh, my brother.'

Her voice was cold and sharp in the High Speech. Every word she spoke, though it be ever so quiet, seemed to pierce him. He was aware more fully of every aspect of her, but the great cavern around had become vague and indistinct. He tried to speak and could not. There were unreal shapes about the Witch Queen, fauns and satyrs and stranger half-formed things out of memories and dreams.

'You know who I am,' said Ral.

'You are the traitor,' said Talarnidh, his voice a whisper, hardly spoken, 'my sister . . .'

Her laugh came like an ice sword.

'You know what I truly am. I am Moon Queen, White Queen, great Queen of the Night and the Darkness. I move amidst stars. Listen! Think! Remember!'

Suddenly, clearly, Talarnidh saw pale frozen plains stretching away into distant mountains, barren against a black sky. A ring of fires burnt with upright flames that gave off no heat, and in their midst were two thrones on a high hill, for the Goddess and her consort. Unearthly servants waited to attend him to his high place amid the pastures of the Moon.

'Welcome, Talarnidh, my brother, my lover,' said the voice of the Great Goddess. He tried to move, but his body was like a corpse.

'Not yet! You cannot come to me yet. Lovers have no secrets. Tell me Talarnidh, tell me. Then you may enter the circle. Tell me!'

He opened dry leaden lips and tried to speak. At last the words came, harsh and croaking in a white light.

'No secrets . . . no secrets . . ,'

'What were you seeking before you found your Queen?'

The cold vivid scent became cruel in his nostrils.

'The Sceptre . . . The Sceptre Mortal . . .'

A sigh, half a hiss, came in answer. The balefires suddenly vanished.

'Where is it?'

Somewhere Talarnidh half remembered another world, but the effort of memory had become too much.

'The Sceptre . . . The Sceptre, it is in Kruakh . . . beneath the Citadel.'

'With the Merpeople,' sighed the answering voice. 'And now I see it all . . .'

'Melandir is seeking it now . . .'

The halting voice of Talarnidh stopped suddenly at the cry which broke from the lips of Ral.

'Selenthoril has deceived me! You have deceived me! Now! Now! They are in Kruakh now! I see all the plan unfold . . . And it is my death! — Come, fool, cross into my circle!'

She screamed at Talarnidh, her voice become so high and screeching that he only half understood.

Slowly with infinite effort he rose to his feet. Crouching and shielding his eyes from the light of the unearthly places he saw, he stepped onto the mound where the thrones were placed. The fierce scent suddenly became acrid, the music a jangling discord, then silence and the growling of wolves in an empty cavern. In the light of dawn and dying torches, with the stench of Ghost Breath in his nostrils, Talarnidh saw the single throne of Ral. He fell, and tried to drag himself upwards, but could only raise his head.

Ral was standing before the throne, her arms outstretched. Across her robe colours now flowed, turning it from white into a progression of dull reds and livid blues. It seemed the cloak had become part of her, flowing into her body, the flickering colours suffusing her face and arms, all the while darker. Her face changed, the features flattened. Her cloaked arms had become wings, her form utterly black. Misshapen and parodied, her body was become that of a huge and hideous bat. Talarnidh fell senseless at last as Ral and her rushing flock rose up and streamed through the windows above, away into the morning light, towards the ruins of far-off Kruakh. Her last words echoed through the hall.

'Kill him! Kill them all! None must live!'

Though the grey skies of morning, like a flapping cloud, the thousands of black shapes flew purposeful behind the one great form, the shape into which Ral had changed herself. And always, as she flew, in her mind came the grim final thought that in the Citadel of Kruakh her death might already be assured.

Ever faster she urged on the twittering host. Long she had watched Selenthoril in his island refuge. She had known of the

Quest and watched its coming. She had stirred up the Rethrind in Emrurl Arnag, and made a storm on the Pass of Anrith. She had called up again the ancient curse in Wirdrilded, and laid it upon Tasarnil. Her Giants had waited in Belengar. And always the lurking things of the Empty Lands and the ever-present bats by night had watched the Quest and told her.

But always there had been something awry in all her devising. The Rethrind had been broken and the Ruby Caverns had released their prey. Her storm magic had been overmatched and subdued on Anrith, and she knew of few save the great ones of the world who had that power. Her Giants had been slain. But what befell in Aldel Morn had frightened her most. Her servants had told her of the things that emerged from the Black Land. She could not tell how such as they had come to be. They were not of her making. And then at the last she had been deceived about the true purpose of the Quest. She sensed dangers that came from out of immemorial years and beyond the world, but above all she smelt her own death, for she knew well what the Sceptre Mortal was.

Ral came to the Citadel of Kruakh. Rubble lay across the gate, but also signs of clearing and a tunnel leading inside. Points of fire gleamed fearfully in her black bat eyes. She and her flock passed into the Citadel. Ral, born of the High Race, was not to be delayed by the questions of the Man of Bronze. She passed beneath the crystal dome down into the deep caverns, and with the witch sense she knew even then that her danger was overwhelming.

Melandir, Erathrir and Karandar, with Relnar and Talak behind them bearing torches, paused on the causeway in the middle of the lake. Their eyes strained to see the shapeless thing rising up like a shadow in the darkness over the still, underground waters. The light of the high-held torches glinted on black leathery wings and a thousand bright eye-points, a mass of moving shapes in the air, but one great shape over all. Melandir, Erathrir and Karandar drew their swords as that shape fluttered and flapped down onto the causeway a hundred feet from them, and stood there, half human, half a winged and swollen bat. Its eyes did not shine in the torchlight, but were pits of night in a shadow face, its skin and bones stretched and distorted.

'It is Ral,' said Karandar.

'She is hideous,' said Relnar.

The form of Ral shook momentarily as if she heard. Then she spoke, the pure and sweet voice of a young maiden.

'Now you must give me the Sceptre.'

'Go away, Witch!' shouted Talak's voice.

'Silence, boy!' snapped Melandir. 'Do not even try to speak to such as her. — But hearken to me, Witch. Go away! There is nothing for you here.'

'I have Talarnidh. I have your friends. And now I will have the Sceptre Mortal. I have power over you. For I am the Great Goddess.' Ral began to walk forward.

'The tunnel! Run!' cried Karandar, and suddenly he had thrown his sword full at the bat-thing. In the darkness Ral only saw the glint on its blade. She moved, and it sliced into the membrane of her spread wings. She screeched, high-pitched and full of malice, twisting as she rose into the air. The men of the Quest had already reached the tunnel and plunged back into its darkness. In its narrow confines Ral could not fly, but soon it was full with the rush of her bats behind her. Swords and torches struck out at the wheeling shapes, but already claws and teeth had fastened in the flesh of the running men. Talak screamed in terror and stumbled, bats all around him. Melandir dragged him to his feet, striking out at the creatures.

Karandar, Erathrir and Relnar were already dragging shut the great iron gate of the Merpeople as Melandir and Talak raced through. In the tunnel came the rush of a great shape, but the door was shut and the unrusting steel of the bolts drawn across. The bats that had followed them through seemed to lose their purpose, and fluttered up to the distant roof.

'It will not hold the Witch long. She will catch us on the lake,' said Relnar.

'It will hold her a while,' answered Karandar. 'It is the protection of the Mererealm. Even Ral will not break it so easily. You forget, young prince, that there are other sorceries than those of the enemy.'

The boat swept them back across the waters, their eyes fixed on the shining door, expecting any moment that it would crumble away. But no sign or sound of Ral came from the door. They left the boat and came down the winding stairway again to the lighted halls of the Merpeople. Ahead of them came the sound of the blowing of conch horns and the beating of a mighty gong far away in yet deeper watery chambers.

The waters before them were full of the Merpeople, but in their hands now glittered tridents, and spears of narwhal horn, and their flowing hair was hidden by strangely-shaped helmets rising in fish-fin crests. On rocks in the midst of the great lake the Merqueen sat. Now a crowned helmet was on her head, vivid with blue jewels. In her hand was a slender rod of spiralled coral.

'The ancient gate is shut,' she said. At her voice the uproar became instantly silent. '— What have you done?' She looked at the men of the Quest.

'O Queen, enemies are upon us!' cried Erathrir.

'What are your enemies to me?' answered the steady voice. The waters shimmered with shaken weapons.

'It is the enemy of the Peiri and the enemy of the Sceptre,' answered Melandir.

'We have laid down that trust,' said the Merqueen.

'Lady, Ral herself is at your gate,' Melandir answered.

A ringing sound as of a great bell filled the hall, welling down from the caverns above until it had flooded all the deep world. The note became higher and turned into a weird and shrilling scream, drawn out and wailing, until it had become a piercing shriek. Then there was silence.

'The door is broken,' said the Merqueen. Weapons clashed among the growing host of Merpeople. 'We will fight our enemy. — You men will go from here with the Sceptre Mortal.'

'How?' asked Erathrir.

'Enter the lake. Swim towards the wall there. There is another way.'

'Quickly!' ordered Melandir. 'Into the water!'

Talak and Relnar looked blankly. They had understood nothing of the things spoken in the High Speech. They obeyed Melandir. As the men of the Quest lowered themselves into the dark lake, the hands of Mermen and Mermaids seized their packs.

'I hope they know I cannot swim,' Karandar muttered, but the green-bearded warriors had already taken his arms and struck out swiftly to the far walls of the cavern. Beside the grey rock one of the Mermen spoke to them again.

'You must dive down here. There is a way through the wall

to another place. It is below the water, but less than a minute is the dive. We will guide you through. Be swift!'

Melandir turned to Talak and Relnar.

'You two first! Hold your noses and dive down. The Merfolk will be with you.'

Talak looked uncertain, then nodded and ducked beneath the water. When Ral, attended by her dark flock, entered the hall of the Mererealm, only Melandir remained.

'You will go no further,' said the Merqueen.

Ral stood black and terrible beside the water.

'I am the Witch Queen,' came her bitter voice.

'I am Queen here!'

The lips of the bat face drew back at the answer. Ral stretched out a clawed wing. The pointing talon moved slowly round the great cavern. Everywhere the white light dulled and lost its lustre in a gloom that deepened every second. The darkness reached Melandir, and Ral stared straight at him.

'I see my enemy better now,' she said.

'All are your enemies here,' came the Merqueen's answer at once.

She glanced at Melandir as he dived down towards the underwater passage. Then she looked back to Ral. The coral rod in her hand began to shine, brighter and brighter, until the light in the cavern was greater than before, and the surface of the waters blazed with reflected light, more brilliant than a sheet of silver in the sun.

'Though the sun and moon die there will be light in the deep caverns and the dark places of ocean,' said the Merqueen.

'If light you wish, I will shew you a different light,' came the woman's voice from the bat shape again.

Tinges of colour whispered across the blazing sheen of the water, and flickers of flame ran through the air. There was no change in the intensity of the light, but it had become green and fearful. And it was concentrated more and more on the rocky wall where the men of the Quest had vanished. A keening note echoed from the high roofs, the same note that had sounded when the gate of the realm was broken. Higher and more dissonant it grew.

A shower of weapons flashed towards the Witch Queen, but she had already turned, anticipating the attack. For a few moments the piercing wail died away, replaced by shattering cracks as ivory and metal smashed into flying shards almost before they had left the hands of the Merpeople. The rushing mass of bats fell like a storm on the people of the Mererealm. Knives slashed upwards at the clawed biting throng, but the shouts of the battle were lost in the renewed crescendo of foul sound and broken ugly light. The wall cracked apart in a thunder and ruin of huge boulders and rock splinters, crashing into the waters among the Mermen and Mermaids, and their cries became shouts of terror and pain.

Beyond lay a chamber with a pool into which rose the underwater tunnel from the great cavern. Around the walls of the cave were the dark openings of many passages. But the chamber was empty and no sign remained of the men of the Quest. Ral rose on wide wings and crossed into the cave of many ways. The bats at once followed. Slowly she looked round at the many entrances. Then she pointed to one of them.

'Are you not a witch too?' She spoke to the Merqueen. 'Have you not the witch sense to sniff out your foe? — But no, — you have no power. Who is queen here now?'

'I am no witch, but I am still Queen. You have chosen the right passage, Ral the Fair.'

For a moment, hatred in her unnatural eyes, Ral moved back towards the Merqueen. Then she turned and rushed into the dark tunnel, her bats streaming before.

'Open the Sea Gate!' came the Queen's voice. 'Let the oceans reclaim the caverns!'

As the men of the Quest ran up the steep tunnel into ever-darkening gloom a trickle of cold water came down to meet them. The trickle increased second by second until it covered the floor of the passage. Already their footing was slippery, and Relnar tripped and fell. He rose at once, his face surprised.

'The water is salt! It is the sea!'

'All the water in the caverns was fresh,' said Karandar. 'I wonder if this is Ral's work. — But I do not think so . . . There is something entering the tunnel now, far behind us. — There are many sounds, but confused —.'

'How can you hear them?' Talak asked. 'The water is so loud.'

'I am a Dwarf Lord,' Karandar answered, 'and this is a cave. — Faster! . . . Less talk!'

The floor of the tunnel was a rushing stream, and they had to force their way against the flood.

'The Merqueen has allowed us enough time. There is a fork in the tunnel ahead. I can see steps going upwards,' cried Melandir above the sound of the water.

'I am less sure,' Karandar answered.

The water surged round his chest. Talak also was gasping and struggling. He too had been swept over in the torrent, and Erathrir had only just been able to save him. Every step had become a fight, and their hands clawing at the jagged rock were cut and bruised as they dragged themselves forward against the pressure of water. Fear added frenzy to their movements. Melandir was the first to reach the fork in the tunnel. From the steep flight of steps in the new cave he dragged Karandar and then the others up into safety. The Dwarf and Talak were gasping and choking, almost drowned. All were chilled to the bone by the bite of the icy sea-water. Two of their packs were lost, but Melandir still held that which contained the Sceptre. Numbed and shivering they began to mount the rocky steps before them. Already Melandir had to support Talak, and Relnar's face was drawn with exhaustion.

The flood swept Ral and her black brood back into the deep caverns. Everywhere came surges and torrents of sea-water, down tunnels and from fountains gushing out of the lake's floor with such force that they struck the roof and fell back in cold spray. Already the level of waters had risen by a yard or more, and in the swirling sea were the forms of the Merpeople. Ral looked and saw the crown of the Merqueen vanish in foam and tumult, but she could not delay. The spiral stair to the Citadel above was already surrounded by water. As Ral in her fury escaped the flood, the one sure defence of the Merpeople was completed. The great cavern lay drowned in the sea, and the chamber where once the Sceptre Mortal stayed guarded near a thousand years was now forever beyond the reach of the Men of Dust.

Far above, the men of the Quest carried the Sceptre by torch-light up the long steps of darkness. The way was long and difficult, a single passage of slopes and jagged stairways in the rock, away from the deep halls of the Merpeople, out beyond the city and ever upward beneath the cliffs of Kamathanlar to the north of Kruakh. Only at the very end of their journey did the path deteriorate into climbs over slate and shale unshaped by any hand, until they emerged through a narrow cleft.

It was night, and the wind that flapped their cloaks for the first time since the morning blew clouds across the starlit sky. In bright moonlight they saw a rocky landscape, slabs of cracked slate breaking through the patches of grass. None of them could guess where they were after the winding ways underground. Karandar gazed at the stars through the scudding clouds. Relnar and Talak collapsed onto the ground exhausted.

'I cannot say for certain where we are,' said the Dwarf. 'I think it must be on the Plateau of Kamath, north of the city. There are low hills all around the high plain there. Those hills behind us to the south there could be part of them. — It was once a hunting park of the High Race.'

'We will climb the hills,' said Melandir. 'If you are right, Karandar, we may see the city, or at least a light from the ships in the harbour. — Come, Talak, come on! Here, lean on me, boy.'

Talak leaned on Melandir as he was bidden, shaking and half-unconscious. Erathrir gave his hand to Relnar, who pulled himself up, then smiled.

'I can walk, Lord Erathrir. — I am a Prince of Chamley.'

In the air a sound rose slowly from far away beyond the hills and froze them as they stood. A distant and monstrous baying, as of some huge vast hound, echoed across the deserted landscape.

CHAPTER 13

LORD OF THE PINES

At the noon of the day on which the Sceptre was found in Kruakh, Iroi Girindhouz, greatest of the Pine Lords, stood in the secret hall beneath the tree in the Forest of Sorcery. Talarnidh stood before him, empty-eyed and stricken, and with him were the other prisoners. Filindrin had managed to break the door of their prison, but wolves stood guard on it. Now he stood bound and suffused with fury. Fandorel was pale and weak. Only Yeselwir stood still and on his guard. It was to him that the Pine Lord finally spoke.

'You are the chieftain of these?'

Yeselwir looked at the Pine Lord. He was head and shoulders taller than a man, his brown face and body almost covered with spike-like black hairs. He wore coarse green britches bound round with thongs and a long cloak flung across his shoulder. On his head was a conical helmet, the same as those worn by the Pine Sprites. The Sprites now thronged the hall and grey wolves attended the Pine Lord; one greater than the others stood before him. On his shoulder sat a raven. In his hand he held a wooden spear, iron shod with many barbs like arrow heads. His language was the Northspeech, but clipped and harsh.

'I am not the leader. That is the man,' Yeselwir answered, and pointed to Talarnidh.

'He is the one who could not withstand the pale magic. I watched him betray his friends. He is weak. I will have him killed.'

'We are no enemies of yours,' shouted Yeselwir. 'Free us, and let us fight!'

'You are my enemies. You are the enemies of the White Witch, so you are my enemies.'

'The White Witch is Ral,' snarled Filindrin. Then he turned to the Prince. 'Ral, Talarnidh! She who is now on her way to take the Sceptre Mortal in Kruakh!'

Talarnidh's body shook visibly, but he still said nothing. He seemed to gasp for breath and his eyes were unfocussed. Yeselwir pointed at Iroi Girindhouz and, turning to Filindrin, said:

'He knows well enough the name of whom he serves. He is the servant of Ral.'

'I am Iroi Girindhouz,' roared the Pine Lord. 'I serve no-one. This is my house.'

'Then how was it that Ral was here to enchant the Prince?' cried Yeselwir. 'You say you watched her sorceries. Who do you think she was then? Who do you think this guest in your house was?'

'Stop asking these things,' cut in the voice of Iroi Girindhouz. 'The White Witch is welcome in my house. She is a great one of the woods. But so am I. I do not serve her. I do not serve the Wizard of the South. — See, his people are here also.'

He pointed towards a blue-grey mist-like figure nearby. Yeselwir looked and gasped. Dimly through the shimmering figure, winged but man-like, he could see the young pine trees beyond.

'It is a Sylph, — a wind creature,' said Filindrin, with a snarl. Then, with a sharper tone: 'Who is this Wizard of the South that is served by Sylphs, Pine Lord?'

'Beware, man!' the Pine Lord answered. 'You may ask me nothing. I am Iroi Girindhouz.'

'You are of her party, this one you call the White Witch,' said Yeselwir.

'She is welcome here. I have helped her before. She has helped me. She has left word that you are to be killed.'

'So you will kill us,' said Filindrin.

'The Witch does not order me. I do not choose to obey her. This is my house. But I will kill your leader. He is of no worth. He betrayed you. You do not want him.'

'He was under an enchantment,' said Yeselwir, stepping forward.

'I would not speak for a traitor. If I betrayed my people, I would rather they killed me. I would wish it. — The wolf will have him. — Or will you die in his place?'

'Yes! I will die in his place,' answered Yeselwir.

'Bind that one!' said Iroi Girindhouz quietly, pointing at Yeselwir. 'I will let him live, and he will serve me.'

Nooses like cotton threads but strong as rope fell over Yeselwir. He fought against the tiny cords but strands caught round his legs and he fell, surrounded by the Pine Sprites armed with bright spears. Fandorel tried to move to his aid, but staggered and nearly fell.

'Is the Elf also under a spell?' asked Iroi Girindhouz. '— And what of you?' He looked long at Filindrin.

'There is nothing I can do,' answered Filindrin. 'If you are going to kill our leader you will kill him.'

A single guttural cry broke from the Pine Lord's throat, and the greatest of the grey wolves leapt full upon Talarnidh. Talarnidh fell beneath it, and the men of the Quest saw the teeth snap at his throat. The crash of his fall shook the enchantment out of Talarnidh's spirit. He stared into the animal eyes and saw the teeth about to close. His forearm thrust between the jaws and the grim teeth closed in his flesh. In the shock of pain, Talarnidh's senses became utterly clear and certain. Ignoring the claws cutting his chest, his free hand seized the upper jaw of the wolf. With all his power he pushed upwards. The head jerked back and the wolf fell backwards, off balance, releasing Talarnidh's wounded arm. Swifter even than the wolf could twist free Talarnidh fell upon it with his full weight. The wolf howled and snapped, but Talarnidh's hands were into its throat strangling its breath. The animal thrashed about in the dust, but the man was the stronger. Its struggles lessened.

'Do not kill it!'

Talarnidh looked up at Iroi Girindhouz who had stepped forward.

'Why?' He released his hold a little, and the wolf writhed, trying to breathe.

'Because I told it to attack. You have beaten the strongest of my wolves. You have won. I will let you also go now.'

Talarnidh stood up. The wolf wriggled to its feet snarling until another animal-like cry from the Pine Lord called it back to his feet.

'You may let us go if you will,' said Filindrin, 'What does it matter? You have let Ral, your mistress, steal our great secret from this prince. You have served Ral well, slave of Ral!'

'Be still! You have fought no wolf! You have no right to life! If you did not speak like a child you would already be dead now. — I have heard you say this word, "Ral", and "Ral" again. I know this name. I am an old one of this world. There was a Ral who ruled here once. A cruel queen. She is dead. The woodmen call her name to frighten bad children. Why does the name frighten you, man? Even the guardian kings of Chamley far southward do not watch for Ral now. I am not a fool for you to mock. I am a Pine Wose. I am Iroi Girindhouz, Lord of the Pines.'

'Iroi Girindhouz, the man does not mock you,' said Talarnidh quietly. His wounded arm hung loosely at his side and he was still gasping from the fight. 'More than children fear the name of Ral,' he went on. 'She is not dead, she did not die. Her power was broken and she long lay hidden — here in the Forest of Sorcery. The White Witch you welcomed here, — she is Ral! The same Ral that you knew of long ago . . . And know this. Your name is remembered also.'

The Pine Lord looked long and hard at Talarnidh beneath dark brows, his face frowning, his whole body still. There was a long silence throughout the hall.

'I have heard the name one of these men called you. Perhaps we have spoken once before, you and I.'

'There was a message sent to you. It begged for your help when the Ghost Trees stood about Mindrim with Thunalt the Black Lord in their midst.'

'It was long ago.'

'Over a thousand years ago.'

'The message came from the last of the Princes of Telmirandor,' said the Pine Wose slowly. 'His name was Talarnidh then.'

'My name is Talarnidh still. Why did you not come?'

A long sigh broke from Iroi Girindhouz's lips.

'It would have been better if the wolf had slain you,' he said.

'You can still slay us.'

'You know I cannot. Now you have asked me why I did not come. Now all is changed.'

'I could not order you to come,' said Talarnidh.

'No, for I was never the servant of any creature. I have no master. I am master.'

'The battle was far from your halls.'

'So far that my tall warriors would not have come in time.'

'You were not pledged to the war.'

'It was never my battle, nor my peoples's battle. What are these things to us in the deep wood?'

'And for all this you did not come,' said Talarnidh.

'Perhaps.'

Again a long silence. Yeselwir looked from Talarnidh to the Pine Lord, not understanding the things of which they spoke, but realising that some ancient drama was being played out. On Filindrin's face was a look of intense attention.

'But you have forgotten something,' said Iroi Girindhouz. 'There was a time — it is almost before memory even for me —. The Great Enemy went about in the wood that grew over Tharang. I have not forgotten the Fire Demons. They took me to the land of Aldel Morn. That was before ever Ral came into the world. That was when the Great Enemy delved deeper pits there than ever did Ral. He built more terribly than she has imaginings to build. You do not remember when Sagoth ruled in Aldel Morn.'

Yeselwir gasped, and again looked round at the others. His gaze fixed on Filindrin. The words he might have said died on his lips. Filindrin's eyes were wide and staring, and a long whistling sigh came from between his lips. He seemed to be remembering the things out of those vastly ancient times, and his body quivered in the force of the memory.

'How did you come to escape from Sagoth and his hell?' snapped Talarnidh at the Pine Lord.

'I was brought from there by a man named Talmond,' said the grim voice of the Pine Lord in reply.

'I am his son,' said Talarnidh.

'I know.'

'You were once the Lord of all the Pine Woses. All the folk of the great woodland of the north were yours.'

'I have given no rule and made no laws since the day in the war against Ral. I have sat in my halls in my own place, dark in the forest. I have watched and let be. — I am still the Lord of the Pine Lords.'

'Our comrades are in great danger in the city of Kruakh. Ral may have taken from them a thing of great power.'

'Is it the thing you told her of?'

'You heard me.'

'I heard you.'

'I told her of it,' said Talarnidh bleakly.

'Is there to be the war again?'

'It may be. — It may be too late already.'

'You had best hear the words of the Sylph called Whirrirrish,' said Iroi Girindhouz. 'He also comes here to speak of ancient wars.'

The Sylph that they had seen before came up to Talarnidh. He did not walk, but flew above the ground. His body was made of blue-grey moving cloud, and his eyes were like blue glass. Cloud wings rose above him.

'Whom do you serve?' asked Filindrin abruptly.

'The one who is here called the Wizard of the South.' The voice was full of sighs and rustlings, seeming to come to them clearly over great distance, soft and very fair.

'What name do you call him?'

'The Lord of the Winds.'

'That is a great lordship,' mocked Filindrin.

'It is not his only lordship,' came the answer. '— I am come from my master to say this to the Lord of the Pines: "The time is gone for waiting in the deep woods. The time is gone for those who serve neither good nor evil. The time is come for war. The war will be against the White Witch. Her name is Ral." '

'Iroi Girindhouz has heard this name twice now. From me and from the Sylph, Whirrirrish,' said Talarnidh looking straight at the Pine Lord. 'What now does he say?'

'I say this,' answered Iroi Girindhouz. 'The one whom I named the White Witch is named Ral. It is the same one returned from long ago.'

Then he turned and climbed the mound to the tall wooden throne. He gazed around the underground hall at the young pines, the Pine Sprites, the wolves, and the woodmen who stood behind the men of the Quest to guard them. Then he sat on the throne. From all around came the tinkling clash as the Pine Sprites joined to strike their spears together.

'This is the throne of the Lord of the Pines,' came his voice, louder than before.

'It was Ral who sat there last to enchant the Prince Talarnidh,' said Filindrin. 'Ask her whose throne it is.'

'I have not taken my throne for a thousand years,' answered the deep voice, steady and unangered. 'But now I take back my throne. I am the Pine Lord, Lord of the Lords of the Pines.'

As the Pine Lord spoke, Fandorel, who had stood pale and unspeaking with the men of the Quest, fell to the ground.

'Take up the Elf Lord,' commanded Iroi Girindhouz, and the

woodmen came forward. 'Take him to the Room of the Fountain. Let him be cured.'

'He is dying from the Ghost Breath,' shouted Filindrin. 'Can you cure the death of the undead?'

'I am Lord here,' came the answer, firm and sure, untroubled by Filindrin's angry contempt. 'I have bidden the Fountain flow again. It was made by the Mendoral. In it is the Blood of the World Tree. It would even cure you, if you will.'

'Speak no more, Filindrin,' said Talarnidh. 'Your tongue is become too ready. We are no longer among enemies. We are no longer prisoners.'

'In this forest,' said Iroi Girindhouz, 'there are many powers. Many have grown great while I have sat in the silence. The White Witch came very long ago. For long years her power was slight. But it has always grown. All the northern edge of the forest is in her power, and much of the western stand. This, my hall, is almost surrounded by her people. She is mighty in the wood, and in the Empty Lands beyond. The Wizard also came at that time. His power also grew slowly. He has built a great palace to the southward. I know less of him than of the Witch Queen. But it seems I knew her not at all. The Witch and the Wizard, the men of Amray on the further shore, the Reavers, — all are nothing to me.'

'All except Ral,' said Talarnidh.

'I have never served Ral,' came the answer. 'I am the Pine Lord, and here I rule.'

'What of the coming war?' said the voice of the Sylph.

'It may be that I will fight if a war comes,' answered Iroi Girindhouz.

'It may be that we will speak again, Iroi Girindhouz,' said Talarnidh.

'It may be that I will hearken to you — this time,' said the Pine Wose.

'We must go now. Five of our comrades are in Kruakh. There lies a secret without price. — You heard me name it. I have told Ral where it lies, and where she may find our friends. Perhaps she has not found them yet.'

'She has not found them. — Or at least she has not taken it from them,' said Filindrin. '— We will know when she does.'

'How?' asked Yeselwir.

'Fool! — On the instant Ral has it in her hand each of you

will be dead. On the instant! Have you forgotten what it is? — Dead, Yeselwir!'

'Then we can expect to fall dead at any moment,' said Talarnidh. 'You are right, Filindrin. She will use it at once to slay all her enemies.'

'Then let us get out of this pit in the ground and reach Kruakh before Ral follows your careful directions to where our friends are, my Prince.'

Before Talarnidh could answer the angry Filindrin, the Sylph Whirrirrish spoke again:

'I will help you on the way to Kruakh. My master bade me seek allies who will fight Ral. Whatever you seek, I can best serve in the coming war by aiding you now.'

They made their way swiftly along the forest paths. Whirrirrish the Sylph led their way. Fandorel flew down from among the treetops. Now he bore no trace of the Ghost Breath.

'It is gone the first hour after noon, Talarnidh,' he said. '— Did you know that the forest around is full of the Sprites? They are moving with us in the trees and on the ground.'

'There are some of them still ahead with Whirrirrish also,' Talarnidh answered. 'Even a Sylph who travels the winds cannot know all the paths in the forest.'

'We are making south-west. There is a true road through the forest about ten miles away.'

'Yes. The South Road it was called, from Kruakh down into Chamley. Now it passes hard by Thulgarn, Pit of the Werebats, the fortress of Ral.'

'This road goes east to west,' answered Fandorel.

'It is the same one. — It curves to the southward when it is deeper within the forest. — After we strike the road we follow it westwards to the Crossroads of Takunan, south of the city. At this pace we will not gain the road before night. The soonest we can reach the city is the day after tomorrow. By then all will be decided. Perhaps Filindrin is right. The first we will know of Ral's utter triumph is when we feel the cold death from Ral as she wields the Sceptre Mortal.'

'Ral believes we are dead already,' answered Fandorel. 'She left word for us to be slain. We may yet be beyond her accounting. — Also, Talarnidh, do not be so sure in all that Filindrin says. He is not recovered so fully as we thought. He is changed.'

'Do not make light of my betrayal,' answered Talarnidh.

'I only tell true,' said the Elf. 'You have taken the words of Filindrin too much to heart. The blame is not wholly yours. You had not the power to resist her. Only one wizard came on our Quest.'

'And he is dead . . . Your comrade Wondrith that I sent to his death in Aldel Morn,' said Talarnidh. 'Better the Sceptre had remained forever forgotten. There will be no power in Tharang to stand against Ral now. Better if Ral does remember to slay us.'

They went on for about seven miles along the winding paths. Then Whirrirrish halted.

'This is the end of the country of Iroi Girindhouz,' he said. 'The Sprites will come no further, but they have told me the path. We will have to camp before we reach the road. This is Ral's country. We are near the northern edge of the forest. It is her people that use the road and few others. — There have been many more of her servants of late, both on the road and in the wood.'

The tiny forms of the Sprites in their cone-like helmets and with their foot-long spears faded into the surrounding pine woods. The dark of the evening was already drawing on and, led by the Sylph alone, they made little over another mile. Talarnidh, Filindrin and Yeselwir then made camp amidst the trees, while Whirrirrish and Fandorel flew ahead, scouting on as far as the road. They were a long while returning, and the early night of late autumn had closed the darkness around the camp when they did come.

'The road is two miles ahead of us and it is empty,' said Fandorel. 'We have searched it in both directions. There is no-one.'

'Why were you so long returning?' demanded Filindrin.

'It is dark, Filindrin. We could hardly find the path, and this camp is well-hidden,' Fandorel answered. Then he turned to Yeselwir. 'You can safely build up the fire more, Yeselwir.'

Yeselwir smiled, and put more wood on the fire. The men of the Quest sat down to eat their provisions, a good supply given to them by the Pine Lord.

'Ral is already at Kruakh, Talarnidh,' said Fandorel. 'Perhaps she has not found it.'

'Beware how you speak. The Sylph is with us,' said Filindrin.

'Whirrirrish, we may not tell you what we seek,' said Talarnidh. 'This much only can I reveal. It is a thing beyond value, greatly dangerous, — deadly. There is one who has sent us to seek it, an enemy of Ral.'

'Now let the Sylph say what his quest is, Prince. You trust him too easily,' said Filindrin.

'I have no quest. I go about my master's business,' answered Whirrirrish. 'I do not wish to know what you seek. I only know or care that you are Ral's enemies.'

'Like your master,' added Filindrin, still half sneering. 'His name you would not tell me when I asked. Who is he that commands the wind creatures?'

'He is one of the great ones of all the world,' said the Sylph. 'My people name him Shahr. But other races have other names for him.'

'What do the Elves call him?' asked Filindrin.

'I am not an Elf.'

'No you are not,' laughed Fandorel. 'You fly faster and better than even we Elves do. — Let be with your questions, Filindrin.'

'Not yet. I have one more question. — What name do all this great one's servants call him in all tongues?'

'We call him the "Old Wise One",' said Whirrirrish, and for the first time laughed, with a sound like breezes on warm oceans. 'He is a good and a great lord to us all. You need not fear him or distrust him, O man.' Yeselwir and Fandorel had joined in the Sylph's laughter.

'That name will not help your investigations anyway, Filindrin,' said Yeselwir.

'But it does,' answered Filindrin, and his voice had become as bitter as cold iron. 'For I think that I know of a "wise old one", whose power is to rule over the winds.' He stood up. 'I will walk in the dark woods awhile.' His face was a white mask as he strode between the trees.

'Though I cannot understand his moods, I follow his meaning well enough, Talarnidh,' said Fandorel after a while, quietly.

'The man he thinks of is dead. He died in Werendilren in the Tower of the Crown,' answered Talarnidh.

'I know, my Prince. But I speak for this reason. I do not understand what has happened to Filindrin. Why should he hate and fear that one man, who was good and mighty, your friend and mine?'

'He is still under the curse of Aldel Morn,' Talarnidh answered in a cold voice. 'We hoped too soon. He did not recover. It has burnt into him and blighted him, Fandorel. He is full of hate and fear of all the world, even of us his friends. I cannot blame him. It is the same curse . . . and it is on all of us, old friend, on all of us.'

'Lie down to sleep, Talarnidh,' replied the Elf Lord. 'There is no curse on us. And if you do not blame Filindrin, — you must also cease to blame Talarnidh! Perhaps the old Filindrin is still not lost. Perhaps he will return one day.'

Talarnidh slept, wrapped in his cloak. After a long while, as they sat beside the fire, Fandorel said to Yeselwir:

'Filindrin was the closest friend of Talarnidh once.'

From far away to the westward as he spoke came the distant but huge sound of a creature that bayed in the night. The Man and the Elf Lord stood and listened. Walking in the blackness beneath the trees, Filindrin stood suddenly still and heard the sounds. Again and again the wolf-like cry, — but there were other sounds also. If it was a great hound that bayed, it seemed as if other dogs also gave cry, and there were horns on the still air. All far away to the westward came the sounds, and it seemed that they were very far off. The silence that followed was the more oppressive.

Filindrin returned unerring to the camp, and without a word lay down to sleep. Fandorel and Yeselwir lay awake listening to the keening, soughing wind that had sprung up out of the mist. Fandorel turned and looked up into the ice-like eyes of Whirrirrish, burning blue in the dark as he stood guard.

'It is no wind of this world,' said the creature of the wind. 'It is a wind out of Hell.'

Yeselwir heard, and coldness trickled through his body. None of them slept well in a long cold night. Talarnidh and Yeselwir, while they did sleep, dreamt of monstrous things that rode the sky.

They awoke soon after dawn, shivering from the thick frost the night had brought, unnerved and tired after a fitful sleep. They spoke little of the noises that they had all heard, made a meagre breakfast, and set off again as quickly as they might. They all knew that the sounds had come from the westward where Kruakh lay.

An hour or a little more brought them to the road. It lay under inches of hard snow. In the deeps of the pines almost no snow had penetrated, and their way had been soft and muddy underfoot. The frost of the night, and now the firm way of the old road, speeded their journey. It was a wide path, cutting a swathe through the great trees. For long stretches it ran straight. Throughout it was uncluttered by any undergrowth, though none had cared for it, years without number. Pausing only long enough for a meal at noon they journeyed on all day, led by the Elf and the Sylph who flew ahead in turn.

Fandorel espied the Goblin band that ran at speed along the way behind them, and he gave them good warning. Hidden in the trees at Talarnidh's bidding, the men of the Quest watched the loping ungainly forms go by, a military formation armoured and bearing weapons.

'They are Goblins of Ral,' said the Sylph. 'The war is very near now.'

'Perhaps it means that Ral has found It,' said Talarnidh.

'Why should it?' Filindrin answered. 'As the Sylph says, war is near. — And we have merely seen a war band.'

'We should have fought them,' said Yeselwir.

'We would have been destroyed swiftly. Do not be foolish. Also, try to remember that we have another purpose but to fight Goblins,' snapped Filindrin. 'Let us get on. They are well ahead now.'

'I will go ahead and search the road again,' said Whirrirrish. 'There is still just enough light. We may make another three miles or so today.'

They set off again, but Whirrirrish's return was swift.

'There are others ahead.'

'Goblins!' said Yeselwir.

'On the road?' Filindrin asked.

'They are on the road now, though they were not. They are coming down it, travelling towards us. There are many Goblins, but they are not marching. They run and scatter, and they are evidently very afraid. Something has happened, and it is to do with the House in the Forest.'

'What house is there in the middle of an unpeopled place like this?' asked Yeselwir.

'It was not all so unpeopled once,' Fandorel answered.

'Yes, — and there are still beings that dwell here now,' went on Whirrirrish. 'There were bodies of Goblins on the road also, and I think some men going into the house itself.'

'Whirrirrish,' said Talarnidh, 'how well did you see them?'

'Not well. I did not wish to be seen myself. Two of them seemed to be too small to be true men. They might have been of the tribes of lesser Goblins. At least one of them was wearing armour. He certainly did not have the look of a Goblin . . . I am not sure.'

'Do you know exactly how many there were?' Talarnidh asked.

'That I know well enough, — or I should know it. Their tracks were clear on the path to the house, and there were five. But I am sure that there were six figures who went into the house.'

'Melandir, Erathrir, Karandar, Relnar, and Talak,' said Talarnidh. 'Five! — Could it be them?'

'There were six, not five. It could not be them,' said Filindrin. 'Why should they be here in the forest . . .? — O, but we will look, my Prince. We must look now. — This house, Sylph, what do you know of it?'

'It is ancient. It was there in the days before Ral. Of that I know little though. In these days it is a strange and haunted place. It is no place of any goodness.'

'Do you mean it is held for Ral?' asked Filindrin.

'We are not sure. — It is known only as the House in the Forest. It has no other name. Lights always burn there . . . in the house, and in the old gardens about it . . .'

'Filindrin is right. — We will have to look,' said Fandorel. '— And we must hurry. I do not believe that our friends could have come here, but if by chance they have, in search of us, then they are in great danger.'

'Why did you not look more closely at these six, or five, or however many, who entered the house?' demanded Filindrin of the Sylph.

'Because there are Goblins on the road. They are coming this way. They will meet the Goblins who marched past us. Though they are fleeing now, who knows what they might have done if you had come upon them unawares. So I returned to warn you.'

'You did right,' said Talarnidh.

'If they are on the road between us and the house, I do not perceive how we may reach it,' said Filindrin.

'We will merely have to go cautiously,' Fandorel answered.

'Whirrirrish and I will watch ahead. We will avoid the Goblins when we come upon them by using the woods.'

The fleeing Goblins had met the marching band. When the men of the Quest came upon them, they had all made camp, lit with many fires in the middle of the road. The men of the Quest passed them easily enough in the shadows of the great trees.

Darkness had fallen as they turned into the pathway that led to the house. The snow glistened in the intermittent moonlight, and on it were five sets of tracks. In the darkness of the trees and the tangled undergrowth were lights, candlelights or corpse lights, flickering and moving to and fro, and a muttering or singing of tuneless songs, quietly and secretly in time to the moving of the lights. Ahead, but to their right, a single light came into view. It did not move when they looked at it.

'It must be the house,' said Yeselwir.

'I had thought it was that way,' said Whirrirrish, pointing to the left away from the constant light. 'But you are right. It is the only one unmoving.'

'Hurry!' ordered Talarnidh.

As they made towards the light, the twitterings in the woods died away. All the other dancing lights in the trees were behind them now. They began to mount a snow slope.

'The house was on a rise,' said Whirrirrish.

They went on, dark stands of trees and thick overgrown hollows looming out of the night around them. The Sylph halted again.

'This is too far,' he said. 'The house should not be more than a quarter of a mile from the road.' The men looked at each other in the darkness.

'Watch the light!' said Filindrin after a moment.

As he spoke he drew his sword and pointed at the single fixed light they had been following. The moon came from behind a cloud for a moment and shone on the blade, then vanished again. But as they watched in those seconds of moonlight, the light moved, imperceptibly unless they were concentrating on it, away from the line of the blade.

'It is also growing ever fainter to draw us on,' said Filindrin. 'It was simply a deception.'

'A will-o'-the-wisp,' said Fandorel. 'We must go back.'

'Which way?' asked Filindrin. '— I do not know. — And look up there, Fandorel. Look there, Yeselwir! See!' He pointed with his sword, and they saw that other lights had appeared, some moving, some still, some clear, some hazy.

'We have to find the five tracks again,' said Talarnidh.

'I doubt that we could even find our own,' Filindrin answered.

The whispers in the wood and the bushes returned, and now they were unmistakably summoning.

'Whirrirrish spoke truly,' said Yeselwir. 'This is a place full of ghosts.'

'Pray that it was not Melandir and the others who left those tracks,' said Fandorel.

CHAPTER 14

THE WILD HUNT

Ral had swept away from the house of Iroi Girindhouz to seek the Sceptre Mortal in Kruakh. She had left Talarnidh in the hands of the Pine Lord, whom she believed was her servant, and had bidden him slay the Prince. Though she did not know it, Talarnidh and his companions were already free. Had she known, she would have cared nothing, for Ral stood in the ruins of Kruakh and she had lost the Sceptre in the deep caverns of the Merpeople.

Now, pale in her fury, she stood, the Great Goddess, in a grim robe. She spoke in a cruel and sibilant voice, swift and high-pitched, to the black flapping flock around her. She bade them search the empty streets and the broken buildings. For Ral had expected to die as soon as her enemies found the Sceptre. Now a new perception dawned on her. She knew the mind of Selen-thoril well, and she guessed that he would let no servant or dupe of his claim the Sceptre. And again she doubted that any save the great ones of the world could claim any Sceptre and live. She knew little of the man called Melandir that Talarnidh had named. So now, somewhere in Kruakh, a mere mortal carried that great prize and had not claimed it. Somewhere they would have to emerge, and everywhere would be waiting the bats of Ral. She herself would go to the ships she had seen in the harbour. Even if the men escaped the bats, they would assuredly come to the ships finally.

Thus she planned in the dusk when the sound came to her, echoing through the deserted places of the ruined city. A long and deep note it was, very distant, but full of suggestions of power. It seemed to come from impossible depths far beneath the world in caverns beyond imagining. She thought of the Merpeople in their water caves. But then came the sound again, and it was much nearer, full of animal notes, deep-throated, hoarse and malevolent. Still, inexplicably, it came from out of the earth. Suddenly Ral was afraid. For something was coming towards her, something that passed through earth and stone and that walked in the half light of the underworlds. Somehow that thing had been released from where it dwelt at the Gate of Hell. For now the sounds were clearer and unmistakable. They were the growling snarls of an immense dog.

Ral stood, immovable, the cloud of bats spread like a dark protective hand above her. A rumbling growl, no longer muffled, came from nearby, and the crash of falling ruins broken by a huge force. Then was the sound of slow, thunderously heavy footfalls, unnatural for they were the imprint of the immaterial on the world. Round the corner of that forgotten road came the form of it, and Ral's power and Ral's evil became as the playthings of children beside its utter horror. She looked on the Hound of Hell.

Its shape was of a great dog, formed of half-real changing substance which seemed to spread about it and cover the ground in foul pools. Its mouth opened and closed, and the head moved, huge nostrils dilating. Ral saw that it perceived her by senses beyond those of the world. Red and white fluid coursed across its flickering lidless eyes. The thing moved towards her, and its tongue lolled out of the seeking jaws.

She was able to move again. Her hands stretched above her, then flung forward. The bats rushed upon the monster, hurled into its eyes by their mistress. The thousands of tiny black creatures enveloped the red liquid pits, and the claws entered into the pulsing fluid. The great dog shook its head from side to side, slowly, almost leisurely, and suddenly the crimson of the awful eyes shone through the bats. Numberless tiny voices rose then died away. The charred bats fell in their hundreds down from the eyes that had burnt them.

Already the hands of the Witch Queen were moving in long-remembered passes in front of her face, and her countenance twisted as she muttered the words. Out of her body grey smokes rushed, flooding the air and building a barrier between her and the Hound. In seconds it had become a solid wall of grey stone, growing as new smokes became part of it, and the whole gave off an unearthly reek. For this was no illusion but a real thing, made from the heart of the mighty sorceries of Ral. The Hound moved towards it. For a moment the two substances mingled, the smoking stone and the fluid flesh of the Hound. Then the creature stood back, and from its mouth came a vast baying roar, waves of sound forcing through the air with a fury that caught the sorcerous wall in their shock. The stones melted into each other and crumbled, became smoke again, fell away and disappeared.

In front of Ral rose a silver sheet, glass-like and shimmering, her final defence, the Witch's Mirror. In the mirror, facing the creature, stood its own reflection, real and solid by the sorcerous art. But the eyes of the Hound did not see with any natural sense. It perceived only the flicker of weak magic before it. The two things, reflection and foul reality, met, and the Witch's Mirror vanished with a soft crack.

Ral's shape changed. Her cloak became part of her, spread wide like dark wings. Her face distorted, and she was the great bat again, rising on her wings upwards across the face of the Hound as it came on, up past the tongue and the bitter eyes, and away into the sky to the southward, fast and direct, no thought left to her but fear.

The Hound stood a while, the head moving round, the nostrils flaring. Then it rose into the air, for earth and air alike were unreal to the being out of Hell. It did not rise up to follow Ral. The thought of its master had commanded it in Aldel Morn, had bidden it wait in Sart Emig, had told it to seek for one who bore a Sword, and one who bore a Sceptre. The dark thought of its master had taught it of those things, and its tortuous mind had understood how to perceive those things, the Sword and the Sceptre. And now it perceived them both.

On the plateau of Kamath, high above the city, five small figures stood in the darkness and heard the unearthly sound. For the great Hound bayed as it rose up, bayed as it came towards the plateau, and let the voice of Hell ring among the cold rocks. They saw it, dark on the scudding clouds of night, rising above the ring of hills around, a cloud itself, but unmistakable in its shape, clearer every moment, its eyes a vision of the great abyss, and its mouth as cruel as the mouth of Hell. It stood above them, a mile away but huge in its foulness, silhouetted against the moon, high on a hill. And then it was running towards them, loping over the ground, long muzzle thrust out, jaws gaping, and the howling of its endless cry beating out ahead of it.

'This is a matter for you alone, Melandir,' said Karandar quietly, and even the voice of the Dwarf Lord shook.

Melandir had already drawn the Sword of Fate.

'What is it?' he asked.

'It is a thing known as the Hound of Hell,' Karandar replied. 'I have never seen it. Few have. It is hardly even spoken of. It was banished out of the world long ago.'

'Then how can it have returned?' asked Melandir. His eyes were fixed in mounting horror on the loping monstrosity, now terribly near.

'Only its master could call it.'

Melandir looked round at the Dwarf.

'Its master is Sagoth, the Devil,' said Karandar.

'Stand back, Karandar,' said Melandir. 'Get the others out of here.'

Blade held out in front of him, Melandir stood facing the onslaught, the four others close together but behind him and edging backwards. The creature was upon him. The blade entered it, cutting into the jaw, vanishing into its oily substance up to the hilt. Still the Hound came on, and Melandir realised in a moment of sickness that his arm had also entered the creature. Only then did the Hound raise its head. The Sword cut deep all along its throat as it rose in a leap over the heads of the men. And the howl that broke from its mouth was full of pain and rage, pain more bitter than anything it had ever known. But the substance of its flesh closed over the ragged cut and it was not injured.

The creature turned and found the dull sword facing it again. It lunged at the small group clustered behind the blade. The jaws reached for Talak and Relnar. Erathrir's sword was also drawn and it entered the flesh of the monster. He felt it burn and saw the blade twist then crumble. He cried out as the hilt became too hot to touch. Unarmed he looked up into the great jaws above him, outlined against the light of the flaming eyes. At that moment Melandir had run beneath the Hound and plunged the Fate Sword into its heaving chest. The beast gave cry, roaring and bellowing, but Melandir stabbed again and again, and the Sword went to its unknown heart. It pierced and burnt and tortured, but did not kill the thing out of Hell.

The Hound rolled over onto its back to twist away, scattering parts of its substance over the ground and leaving a track of slime where it had passed. And where the mark of the creature was, the grass burnt and withered in the instant, nor would it grow again. The Hound stood again, huge in the shadows, with its fetor hung about it.

'Why can the Sword not kill it?' cried Melandir, white-faced and gasping for air amidst the stink of Hell. Karandar shook his head.

'I do not know. I do not know. Its power is unknowable. Sagoth is its master, but he did not make it.'

'So it is not part of him,' gasped Melandir. 'The Sword is the bane of Sagoth . . . only. — Karandar, Erathrir, run. Run! Take the others and get out of here. Go to the ships. There is nothing I can do except delay it. I cannot protect you . . . I do not even know if I can protect myself much longer. Run!'

'We will fight! We are warriors!' said Relnar. But he and Talak both could hardly stand up, so broken were they by the toils of the caverns and the unutterable horror of the thing they now saw.

'We are in the way here and can do nothing,' Karandar told him. 'Now is no time for us. — Come!'

As the Hound moved slowly towards him again, Melandir heard Erathrir call as he backed away:

'The Sceptre, Melandir! Remember the Sceptre!'

The Hound leapt at the man. The Fate Sword cut down and Melandir sprang aside. The Sword cut through the monstrous paw and part of the flesh fell away. As it twisted and roared in unthought-of agony, Melandir rushed in close upon it, hacking in fury at its flanks, his gouging Sword scattering gobbets of foul flesh from side to side. Everywhere they fell the ground was seared. Only Melandir, safe in the Sword's protection, was not burnt.

But the Sword could not kill the monster. Again Melandir found that his thrusts entered deep into the swirling fluid of its flesh. His arm was drawn in and half his body. The miasma of its foulness filled his lungs and his whole being. Even as he cut at it, the unnatural substance closed about him, and though the Hound suffered there was no fatal hurt to it. Melandir felt the fear and loathing that filled his being take on a new quality, a strangeness full of unknowable dreams, all hideous, but strange beyond any mortal's understanding. In a haze of terror, Melandir realised that as he was being drawn into the substance of the creature *it* was entering into *his* being and making him part of it.

Shouting soundlessly, for the vile fluid filled his mouth, his movements like those of a swimmer as the substance closed about him, Melandir tried to turn and cut himself free. He tried to reach for the Sceptre slung at his back. Everywhere that the Sword drove the flesh separated. Suddenly his body was free again, and his ears full of the snarling fury of the creature. Stumbling he ran a few steps, but the tincture of Hell pervaded his mind. He felt the Pit yawn beneath him and the insensate voice of the great Hound commanding him. He fell to the ground, writhing and crawling. Though the slime fell away from him, the breath of the monster was in his being. He heard the command in the baying, and now the Hound was his master. He obeyed it and dropped Wenyorel. The Hound of Hell looked warily on its prey, and then gave voice to great rolling howls of triumph.

The ring of a horn that was wound in the distance cut through the baying with a high note, singing and clear though far away. Over the grey mists of the shadowy forest its notes rung, a hunting horn blown in the darkness, a call to the chase. And the huge beast paused in its bellowing, and the great vile head looked round from side to side, and the steaming muzzle was raised. For the Hound sensed something blown on the air in the notes of the horn. Into its half-animal, half-demon soul came sensations new to it, stirrings of fear and memories of a life beyond life and beyond the count of years, where it fled through the ages amidst great woods from the Huntsman who wound that Horn.

Deep in the Forest of Sorcery, long grown over by generation on generation of trees that had reached maturity and fallen into the loam, were the long homes of those who had ridden the skies in the youth of the world when the Spirit of the Green first banished the dark gods to the depths. In mounds long levelled down to the ground, unknown memories stirred. The earth shook about the bases of the tall pines. The pine needles and fir cones stirred. The foxes and squirrels watched, as green hands broke through the heaving soil and twisted in the air. Then the little animals ran as the fearsome heads and bodies shook off the earth of untold centuries. The Green Riders stood again in the world, and heard the Horn notes that called them.

They were taller than men, with strong sinews not of flesh, but in the shapes of men. Their faces shone vivid green. Their earth-flecked tunics were soil-brown, their rustling cloaks were crimson. Their black hair was tangled with soil and roots. Their eyes were dark and frightening. In their hands were wooden spears with iron barbs. Each of them stood in his own place, above his long and silent home in the rich earth, and the Horn rang again in the sky. Each of the Green Riders whistled shrill in the night, and out of the surrounding woods stepped a lean horse, red-maned and raw-boned, its eyes green in the darkness. The horses threw back their heads and whinnied in answer for the Horn was ringing again. In a moment the riders had sprung to their mounts. The horses reared up, kicking at the air, and then leapt from the ground, no leap of a natural horse, but up, pawing the air, between the trees, past the treetops into the night sky, whinnying and snapping at the clouds.

And down from among the clouds came the Hunting Dogs, palest grey so that they shone with unearthly light, red-eyed, red-eared, and red-tongued, giving cry as they raced and jumped about the iron-shod hooves of the horses that rode the sky. The Wild Hunt in its fury and tumult wheeled and cavorted high above the forest, and the long tongues of the lean dogs lolled out as they gazed southwards, and the spears of the Horsemen pointed away there into the distance.

From far away came a dim light that grew rapidly nearer until it had resolved itself into the shape of a mighty figure mounted on a red horse, more wild-eyed than all the others, stronger and leaner, galloping across the sky, swifter than an eagle in flight. On it sat the Huntsman.

He was clad in cloak and tunic, that crackled with yellows and whites like the flames of a fierce pale fire. His face shone vivid green like those of the others, surrounded by the dark circle of his matted hair. But his eyes were white and unblinking, fixed on the uttermost distance. And above his head rose the huge-tined antlers of an ancient stag.

The Riders shouted in joy as they saw the sheen of the fearsome face, and the Huntsman laughed and raised the Ram Horn to his laughing lips, and wound and wound it till the skies and the forest were echoing. The spear he bore was all of ancient iron, dull brown in his hand. He pointed to the northward, then leaning forward whispered into the thrown-back ear of his steed. The horse sprang forward and he lay stretched along its back as it flew. The Hunting Dogs gave tongue and followed, the Riders cried out their hunting calls and followed. The Wild Hunt rode again in the world, and it hunted the Beast.

The Hound of Hell stared, unseeing but sensing many things, to the southward. It forgot the man who lay defenceless nearby. It remembered the time out of mind when it had walked in a dark dread world. From that place it knew the clear call of the Horn, as now it came nearer and nearer, till it filled all the air with its fierce notes.

Erathrir and Karandar ran forward to Melandir, and began to drag him back away from the Hound. Erathrir took the Sword, and thrust it into Melandir's hand. Melandir stirred, clasped the hilt of Wenyorel, and looked up.

'A something is coming, something in the sky,' he said.

A long moment passed and then the Huntsman stood out over the low hills, tall on his rearing horse, his face green fire, with flames like leaves tumbling down from him, dark hair like smoke and the monstrous antlers above. Suddenly the throng of the Hunt surrounded him, the snapping dogs rushing round the flinging hooves. The Riders reined in their steeds beside him, rearing and snorting. Shouting of Riders and neighing of the horses and cries of the dogs blended together, the sound of joy of the Wild Hunt. One note only rang on the Horn. The Huntsman's spear pointed at the Hound. The great Beast lay, its belly and snout to the ground. Its hackles rose and it waited, a half-shaped mound; then it sprang.

Up into the sky it sprang, full towards the Hunt; and the Hunting Dogs leapt up to meet it. Three of them leapt full into its maw, and it bayed its pleasure. The others seized at the flanks of the Hound, snapping and biting, and they were of the same substance beyond nature as was their prey. They found a hold in its skin, they tore at its flesh, and their teeth were bitter ice in the burning fluid that made up the great Hound. Round and round it swept in the sky, and all the while the Hunting Dogs tormented it. Many of them perished in its jaws, but there were hundreds and more in the pack, and now the Riders had come. Round and about the Hound they rode, and gazed on the monster, and laughed their defiance.

The first of the spears flashed towards the Hound. In the air its tip became a red flame. Scattering fire, it plunged deep into the creature. The other spears followed, and as they sped through the air, new spears were in the hands of the Riders, come from nowhere. Spear after spear plunged into the Hound. Whenever it lunged at the Riders they twisted away, shouting and laughing, only to return at once to the attack, unscathed by the giant ungainly creature.

At last the Hound descended to the ground, its foul breathing forced out in great gasps, its pulsing flanks still hung about with dogs that tore it, its whole body embedded with the hafts of the long spears. Inside its form the spearheads still burnt, and the monster howled its rage and pain. It lay on the ground, massive and snarling, its body drawn together, ready for any new attack.

The Riders drew back, calling the Hunting Dogs to them. Through their ranks rode the Huntsman, his horse stepping slowly down the sky till it stood on the ground. The tall-antlered shape of the Huntsman faced the humped black mass of the Hound. Again the Horn was placed to his lips, and three short notes sounded, keener than any yet. The Hound stirred and snarled as the burning spears inside it flamed again. Then the Huntsman spurred full into the face of the Hound. The mouth gaped, and dark fires rolled out of it, full of the stench of Hell. Through them the Huntsman rode, body flat, clutching the horse's mane. Then he sat upright, arm stretched back and the ancient spear brittle with rust in his hand. Right to the lips of the jaws he raced, and then the spear flew.

Down into the throat of the Hound it flashed and it too kindled in the air, its whole length become blazing and white, too bright to look at. Deep into the Hound it went slicing through flesh and burying itself in the pulsing mass that was the heart of the creature. The heart burnt and dissolved in a flame so fierce it had become like the ice that was before the worlds were.

The Hound lifted up its head and bayed a single long cry at the stars. The ground shook beneath it. The earth stirred and low rumblings arose out of the hills around. Cracks ran across the soil and the trembling ground welled up round the sides of the Hound. The earth where it lay crumbled and dissolved. The Hound began to sink down into the earth. Deeper and deeper its baying form descended, until only the monstrous snout rose above the rim of the crater. Then the soil from the sides collapsed in upon it, and only the echo of the baying remained. For the Hound of Hell had been banished back to the depths of the Pit, and for it there would be no returning again until the end of all things.

The Huntsman dismounted and looked down into the pit for a long while, with the last sounds of the Hound still echoing from the deeps. Only when there was silence did he turn from the burnt soil of the crater. He walked slowly towards the place where the men of the Quest stood. Ten paces from them he stopped and, one after another, fixed his white and dreadful eyes on them. His face was as green as the forest. Then he spoke, with a voice like the crackling of fires and the blowing of leaves, like waves on the coast and the voice of birds afar off. It was a voice from beyond human knowing. All understood him, though none knew his language.

'I am come out of the earth and out of the trees, the Unborn One. I am outside of time and alive without life, the Forgotten One. I walk the wild ways and the streets of midnight, the Haunted One. I ride the sky and rush through the grass, my steed is a flame through the treetops, I am the Huntsman.'

None of the men could answer. Their tongues clove to their mouths. They could not look away. They could do nothing, unless He chose.

'I am the Master. Speak, Man with the Sword!'

The words came choking to Melandir's frozen lips.

'Where is the Hound?'

'I have sent it to Hell.'

'What was it?'

'It was the Hound of Hell.'

'Who are you? Why did you do it?'

'I am the Huntsman. I hunt for the Beasts of the Night. For days now I have heard it, the call of the Beast through the deep earth and the silence. Slow I was to waken, for long was my sleep. But I heard and the Horn leapt in my hand. Tonight I stood up out of the darkness. I called to my Dogs and my Riders, the Wild Hunt, to ride again.'

He looked at the man and laughed, like showers in the forest and waters on stones. His steed had come up and nuzzled his shoulder. He turned and sprang onto the lean red horse, and the mighty antlers shook on his head like a spiky crown.

'My Sword could not hurt the Hound,' said Melandir.

'It is blunt, mortal. It is blunt! You must seek out the Grindstone of Time and sharpen it. Sharpen it! It is good for nothing without.'

He laughed again and turned the horse, rearing and neighing

as it leapt into the sky. Higher and higher he rose and the Wild Hunt closed around him. Round and about in the air they rode, spears glowing, wide cloaks flown back. Then away to the south they were rushing, and the Horn of the Huntsman who led them sounded its call that the Hunt had killed.

And the rumour of it passed throughout the Northlands. Ral heard it as she fled from the Hound. It came to the other men of the Quest in the Forest of Sorcery, and there also to the hidden one who was the master of the Hound. It came to Selenthoril and troubled his dreams. It came to the Wise Old One in the forest, who sent out his winds to search for what it might foretell. For the Wild Hunt rode in the skies again and the Horn of the Huntsman rang.

CHAPTER 15

THE HOUSE IN THE FOREST

'What will you do now?' asked Admiral Andrai.

Melandir, Erathrir, Karandar, Relnar and Talak sat around the captain's table aboard Andrai's ship as she lay anchored in the harbour at Kruakh. It was the morning after they had fought the Hound and seen it vanquished by the Huntsman.

'I do not know,' said Karandar. 'Talarnidh and our companions are probably in the hands of Ral somewhere in the forest. We have to try to save them, but we owe it to the Lord Selenthoril to return to Nyaroth Khrathril, — now that we have the thing he sent us for.'

'Is the great Hound really gone?' asked Talak.

'I believe it has vanished out of the world,' said Karandar.

'Which does not tell us why it came,' said Erathrir.

'It has not been in the world since the days of the old High King. It was the Hound that slew the High King, and in the wars that followed the Mendoral came to Tharang and made the Sceptres, though it was not the Sceptres that banished it.'

'But what manner of the thing is the Hound?' Relnar asked.

'This thing you speak of is not a creature known to mortal men,' added Andrai.

'It is known well enough in the lore of the Peiri, the High Race,' Melandir replied. 'It is that which guards the Gate of Nether Hell, one of the greatest of the powers of darkness. It obeys only Sagoth himself.'

'Are you sure of this?' asked Erathrir. 'Do you think it could have been Ral who summoned it?'

'While I dwelt at the court of Talarnidh on Alban I studied much of the lore of the High Race. In particular I studied concerning Sagoth, because of the Sword.'

The men at the table stared silently at Melandir. Talak, Relnar, and even the Admiral shewed fear in their faces unmistakably. For few men speak of Sagoth, and fewer name him.

'I know that the Hound serves Sagoth, the Devil, in some way. Ral has no power over it. She could not have. It is from what is called the Time Before Time. I had not known that it still existed. I had not wildly imagined what it would have been like. — I do not wish to say more of it . . .'

Melandir stood and, walking over to the stern gallery, looked out across the sea. The fullness of dawn was now broken. Melandir seemed to be still in pain from the happenings of the evening before.

'My own knowledge of the creature confirms what Melandir has said,' said Karandar. 'Also I have spoken with one or two of those who had seen the Hound in former times. .There is no doubt that it was the same being.'

'Why has the Lord Melandir sought out the secrets of the Dark One?' asked Relnar, a tiny note of hesitancy, even fear, in his voice. Melandir turned from the window.

'It is my concern because of this Sword. It is the Fate Sword. It is known as "Sagoth's Bane".'

'It alone has power over Sagoth,' said Karandar.

'Yet it did not kill the Hound,' replied Melandir. 'And the Hound is merely Sagoth's servant.'

'I do not understand it,' said Karandar, 'unless it is that the Hound is not made by Sagoth, but is older than he.'

'Or perhaps it is because the Sword is blunt,' said Melandir. 'Remember what the Huntsman said: — "the Grindstone of Time . . ." '

'That I do not understand either,' said Karandar. 'I tell you this Melandir, I have seen many things and learnt much of all the lore of Tharang. I did not believe I would ever see the like of these things though, — neither the Hound, nor the Wild Hunt.'

'But who are they?' Talak asked. 'Where did they come from? I think they were terrible.'

'They are terrible,' said Karandar, 'but not how you mean it. They are said to be the Guardians of the World. They once hunted the beings from outside that roamed unlawfully in Tharang.'

'Then the Hound was one of those creatures?' asked Erathrir.

'Yes — The tale is that it was the Wild Hunt which banished it that time before, after the death of the High King. — I can think of no other reason why it should have appeared again in the world now,' replied Melandir, 'save to hunt the Hound. — I can think of no reason for the coming of the Hound. Unless its master called it, — unless Sagoth, the Devil, is loose in the world.'

'If I had known only a part of all this at Belengar, I do not think I would have come this far with you,' said Andrai.

'Then you will not take us back to Misen Taïrail?' said Talak angrily.

'You insult the Admiral,' said Melandir, rounding on him. 'Do not forget that by your father's word you are an esquire. Be silent! I will tell you when it is your place to speak.' Talak's face reddened, and he looked down.

'I will not break my word,' said the Admiral. 'But I fear and more than fear the things you have spoken of here.'

'I do not think we will keep you to your promise,' said Erathrir. 'I think we have no choice but to go into the forest and look for our comrades.'

'If they are still alive,' said Melandir. '— All we know is that Ral claimed to have captured them. If she has, she has likely enough killed them already.'

'But so long as there is any doubt we must go and look for them,' replied Erathrir.

'What of Selenthoril?' asked Karandar.

'Selenthoril sent us on this Quest to help him fight Ral,' replied Erathrir. 'That is the whole purpose of the thing we found in Kruakh. He needs it to kill her.'

'The Lord Selenthoril would not wish us to abandon Prince Talarnidh and the others to Ral,' said Relnar.

'You are right,' said Melandir. 'But we do not know where they were captured, nor where Ral might have taken them.'

'Then you do not think they are alive, my lord,' said Relnar.

'We can only hope,' replied Erathrir. '— And as for where we must search, — we all saw the fortress of Ral, Thulgarn, Pit of the Werebats, marked on the map Selenthoril shewed us before we set off from Nyaroth Khrathril. It is the centre of all her power. There the Sword of Doom lies hidden. The place is south-east of Kruakh, on the "Road of Ral". If Ral has them prisoner at all, that is where she will keep them.'

'I know the road you mean,' said Karandar. 'It is the road we spoke of in Belengar, called correctly the South Road. It is the road from Kruakh that goes down through the Crossroads of Takunan. In ancient times it went on to Dorangad, where Chamalat now lies, and thence to Sarras, greatest of all the cities of the High Race in the Northlands. — But I do not know the state of the road now. It has probably been little used since the time of the Black Lords.'

'We have little choice,' said Melandir. 'We must take the old South Road to Thulgarn.'

'I will await your return,' said Andrai.

'No,' said Melandir. 'Wait for one week only. If we have not returned by then, I doubt we will ever return.'

'Very well, I will sail in a week for Azantul, but I sail with a heavy heart.'

Noontide found the men of the Quest standing at the Crossroads of Takunan. The sailors of Amray had brought them there in a small sailing boat across the Bay of Kruakh and up the River Galmin, that the Reavers now called Blackroot. They had landed where the South Road crossed the river on a tall bridge, still standing, just north of the crossroads.

'We should try to make a dozen miles or more before sunset,' said Karandar.

'The road looks clear enough,' said Erathrir.

They all looked to the south where the edge of the forest lay nearby. They ate a hasty meal as they walked towards it, and soon they were amidst the crowded host of pines. All the land south of Kruakh still lay under a carpet of snow, though little had fallen in Kruakh to the seaward or even on the hills of Kamath. The road itself was a broad white track through the dark shadows of the snow-cloaked pines. Beneath the snow the smooth stone surface of the road was as regular and as unbroken as it had been in the days Karandar had remembered. No trees or undergrowth intruded onto its path, though the pines seemed to mark its edge with exact rows.

As they journeyed deeper into the forest, the trees became taller and darker, casting ever-longer shadows on the road as the sun slowly fell towards the west. The pines were pressed close together, tall and thin, each one fighting the other for the meagre sunlight. The floor of the forest was a deep green carpet of rotting pine needles sprinkled here and there with snow, and even this was grey in the stifling gloom. They saw few birds and no other living creatures. Yet now and again there were strange tracks in the snow on the road and beside it, and rustlings from amidst the pines.

'There is an unhealthy feeling about this place,' said Erathrir.

Talak looked at Melandir who walked beside him.

'May I ask you something, sir?' asked Talak. Melandir smiled and nodded.

'You may speak freely amongst us. But you must remember you are no longer in the place of your birth or among your people. You must behave differently now. More is expected of you.'

'I understand,' said Talak. '— I would like to know why it is called the Forest of Sorcery.'

'It has an evil name among the people of Chamley,' said Relnar. 'We have guarded our borders against its denizens for a thousand years. The tale amongst us is that a wicked witch and a dread wizard war forever beneath the gloomy pines. That is why all the peoples of the Northlands call it the Forest of Sorcery.' He smiled at Talak in sudden friendship, for there were not many years between them.

'The witch must be Ral,' said Talak, looking more seriously at the young prince.

'Ah, but the people of Chamley did not know that,' Relnar answered.

'I wish I could speak so lightly of such things,' said Erathrir to Melandir.

'Talak is a child and Relnar little more,' answered Melandir.

'Whoever lives in this place now, — they are watching us for certain, Melandir. Have you thought of the only real means we have to fight Ral, if we find her?'

'You mean by claiming the Sceptre. — Oh, I have thought of it. To do so might seem to be to betray Selenthoril's trust.'

'If the Sword has no power over Ral, as it did not over the Hound, then only the Sceptre may be able to defeat Ral and save our friends,' said Karandar. 'If you claimed it, you would still free Selenthoril from Ral's power. — You will have to be prepared to do so, Melandir . . .'

'Why can you not claim it Karandar?' asked Relnar.

'If it were necessary for our safety, or the safety of the Prince of the High Race, I might have to try to do so. But it is one of the Sceptres of Power, and I am not one of the great ones of the world. It is at least likely that the attempt would be the death of me. — Do not forget that the Sword of Fate protects Melandir.'

The Dwarf Lord looked at Melandir.

'I know this, Karandar,' he said. 'I will remember what you have said if need be. But it is not yet. — I know the lore of the Sceptres. I studied much in Alban of these things. Once claimed the Sceptre would be mine forever, and I its Guardian.'

They went on farther into the realm of the trees. Afternoon had passed and evening drew on. The men closed together in a tighter group, but they were unprepared for the attack when it came. Out of the shadow of the trees on both sides of the road came a screaming band of Goblins. They were of the Goblin tribe called Grintunt, one of the Thirteen Tribes of Goblins, now in the service of Ral but spawned by Sagoth long before. The head of the tallest of them came only to the shoulders of a full grown man. Unlike many Goblins their heads and bodies were hairless, but their grey-brown skins were thick and leathery like those of reptiles and they wore no clothes despite the Northland cold. Their legs and arms were short for their barrel-like torsos, and their great round heads lolled from side to side as they ran. On their foreheads was the mark of their evil birth. As they came upon the men of the Quest they cried out in the Black Speech, and the name of Ral was on their lips.

The men of the Quest easily resisted the wild swings of the curved swords. The Goblins were many but unskilled. When they drew back in disorder from their first charge five of their number lay dead. Following Melandir's shouted orders the men of the Quest moved back towards a great pine on the northern edge of the road. Here they stood, around the tree, their backs to it, and waited for the Goblins to attack again. The Goblin band spread out warily across the road. Some moved into the forest behind the men.

'I am glad they have no bowmen,' said Karandar.

'Yes, but I think they will wait for dark now,' replied Melandir.

'Or keep us here until Ral is informed,' said Erathrir.

A light flitted through the trees opposite the men and behind the Goblins.

'What is that?' asked Talak.

More lights appeared in the darkness of the trees, at first only on the farther side of the road, then on their side as well. Sometimes they seemed to move, sometimes to stand still, pale globes that would suddenly be extinguished. The Goblins stood in the roadway. They had moved closer together, and their shouts and taunts had become muted. They muttered amongst themselves and looked round doubtfully at the flickering lights.

'I fear these things more than I fear the Goblins,' said Talak. 'I think that they are ghosts. We should run from here.'

'We do not run,' said Relnar sternly, but there was a tremor in his voice too.

'We might run if it served any purpose,' said Erathrir. 'But I am not so sure about these lights. If you look, Talak, you will see that the Goblins are more afraid of them than we are.'

Talak looked uncertainly at the Goblins, then back at the flickering moving lights, a host of tiny moons in the darks of the woods. Every moment there seemed to be more of them. And now they were coalescing into softly luminous shapes, suggestions of figures that seemed to move from tree to tree, never fully seen. The Goblins now were utterly silent, their swords lowered, held lifelessly at their sides.

'They *are* ghosts!' said Talak. 'This is a haunted wood. We must go back at once.'

He took two steps away from the tree back onto the road, his face as pale as the flickering lights.

'Talak! Get back!' shouted Melandir. But Talak went on, into the middle of the snow-clad road, nearer to the Goblins. One of them lifted his sword and approached the boy cautiously.

'Run, Talak!' cried Melandir again, but the boy seemed to have eyes only for the dancing lights. There was fear in his face.

Melandir reached Talak just before the Goblin did. He struck its sword away, and thrust once with Wenyorel. The Goblin screamed and fell dead in its blood in the snow. At that moment, as Melandir roughly caught hold of Talak, he saw the pale figure beyond any doubt. It fluttered like a white cloth blown in the wind, a robe with arms stretched out, but a dark and hollow-eyed face above it. It glowed with an unearthly phosphorescence, and the solid trunks of the trees shewed dimly through it. It was as all mortals imagine a ghost to be. Talak screamed, and only the strength of Melandir's grip held him. The Goblins broke and ran, fleeing wildly down the road to the south east. Their swords lay behind them in the snow. The ghostly shape came out to the edge of the road. Melandir pointed the Sword at it.

'Stand still, Talak! Do as you are told this time, and do not move!' he ordered grimly. Then he stepped towards the figure.

As he approached, he saw it dissolve, separating into spinning globes of light, which themselves scattered into stardust of swiftly vanishing phosphorescence. From out of the forest, behind where the thing had been, stepped the form of a man. He was clad in a rich red cloak, ornately patterned with gold threads and clasped with a golden belt. Round his neck hung a jeweled chain. He was a heavy figure, with a fleshy face, darkly bearded.

'Stand and answer,' said Melandir. 'Who are you and what are you doing here?'

'My name is Shajal, — and as you see I have stood still. Nor do I carry any weapon.' His voice was deep and firm, his eyes looked steadily at Melandir. 'As for what I am doing here, — my house is nearby.'

'Are you the friend of Goblins or the friend of ghosts?' Melandir asked. 'Who is your master?'

'I am not the friend of Goblins, and, as for ghosts, I do not believe they are real. — See!'

He turned to the forest and stretched out his hand. Wherever he pointed one or another of the pale lights appeared or vanished. He moved his hand round, and the lights followed it.

'Do you wish me to make the shapes into a ghost again?' he said. '— These lights are my protection. You have seen how the Goblins fear them. They enable me to live here in the Forest of Sorcery despite my neighbours.'

'Perhaps he is the wizard that the old stories in Chamley told of,' said Relnar.

The other men of the Quest had come and stood beside Melandir.

'So it was you who saved us from the Goblins,' said Karandar. 'We thank you for that, but we would know more of your purpose in doing so.'

'My reasons are simple. I do not yet allow the creatures of Ral to do as they will in my land. — No, you need not start; the name of Ral is real enough. I who live in the forest know who my enemy is. — I can only guess, from the ambush laid for you here, that she is also your enemy. — But perhaps you have never even heard her name?'

'We have heard it,' said Erathrir.

'You will have to trust me now, my friends,' said the one called Shajal. 'There is another Goblin band on the road, and those I scared off will return when they have the courage of greater numbers. You cannot stay here, nor can you go on by night. My house is nearby, as I told you, and it is safe. I merely offer you my hospitality.'

'We will go with you,' said Melandir.

The man, Shajal, led them swiftly along the road, and then turned to the left up a long and curving path through the wood, almost as wide as the road itself. Though the moon was not up, as dusk deepened into night the way was lit by the phantom lights in the trees and all around them in the forest were flickering and flashing phantasms. There seemed to be many paths leading off their way.

'You see how I deceive unwelcome visitors by night,' said Shajal.

'I do not see how they are deceived by day,' Karandar answered.

'There is a mist about my house when needs be,' answered the level voice immediately.

They rounded a corner in the drive and saw amidst the darkness a mansion of many rooms, most of them unlit, but some shining with the glow of candles. A great door stood half ajar in the centre of the long front of the house. And from the crack a stream of light fell across the snow of a wide courtyard. Around the house there seemed to be shadowy gardens in the midst of the forest. They climbed the stone steps up to the entrance.

The door opened onto a large hallway panelled with dark wood. Weapons were hung on the wall. There were many of them from all parts of the world, curved swords and barbed maces of steel and long black spears. There was also heavy armour. Shajal led the men of the Quest through the hall and opened double doors hidden with carvings. They went before him into a long room also dark with wood panels and hung with tapestries and paintings. In the centre of the room was an oak table laid with places for six to eat. On the table stood silver platters, heaped high with food.

'Your house is like that I dwelt in not long ago. It was amid the forests of an island far in the Western Ocean,' said Melandir.

'You honour me in the comparison,' said Shajal. 'Please share my table, my friends. My servants have set places for you.'

'It is truly as fine as many of the great halls in Chamalat,' said Relnar. 'But how did you know we would be coming to your house? How did you know how many of us there were?'

'Few now journey on the road save the servants of Ral. I have my spies, of course, and they told me of your coming. You are strange travellers in a hostile land. I knew you must come to me.'

'Our thanks are certainly due for your hospitality,' said Karandar as he sat down at the table.

Melandir sat next to him, and Talak by Melandir. Erathrir and Relnar faced them, their backs to a fire which blazed high and crimson. Above Karandar hung a huge picture painted in colours of red and gold. It shewed a man wrestling with a long, scaled worm. The worm's coils were twisted round the man, but his hands clasped its throat, and his arms glistened with sweat in sunlight. The flames glinted on the scales of the worm, and they glowed redly in the firelight.

Shajal sat down at the head of the table. He motioned his guests to eat. The table was laden with heaped plates of aromatic food-stuffs. Slices of dark meat swam in oils and glazed fowls and hare stewed in blood and wine lay on silver dishes. There were sweet sauces and pungent spice in everything, and the red wine was thick and perfumed. The men of the Quest ate little of the banquet set before them. Though they were hungry, they found it too rich and cloying. But Shajal drank and ate freely, and pressed the heavy wine on his guests, so that they found its taste more pleasing. Talak alone did not taste the wine. He was unused to any save simple food and drink, and little enough of that. When Shajal gave him the cup Melandir said:

'Let him be! He is only a boy and the wine is too strong for him!'

And even if Talak would have accepted, he dare not disobey Melandir's command. He drank water from the skins of it they had.

As Shajal ate he spoke of himself and his house. The men of the Quest questioned him closely about strangers like themselves in the forest, but he could tell them nothing. They asked him of his own doings and of what he knew of Ral. He spoke freely and told them much, though little of it unknown to them. They asked where the deep-delven fortress of Ral lay, and of its strength and the creatures that lurked there. But Shajal told them only that it lay far to the south, nigh to the road, and that he had never ventured there. And through all the evening they learnt nothing that they wished to know. Then Relnar asked him if he was indeed the wizard in the forest of whom the legends of Chamley spoke.

'There is no wizard,' he answered. 'I have heard the tales of course. Perhaps once a Goblin king or such as that dwelt in the ice caves and made some weak magic there, but that is all. Do not bother to look for any wizard.'

As he spoke his cloak shone brighter red in the light of the fire, and the golden threads seemed to ripple and twine in the fine fabric. His guests now only half attended to his words. They had become more tired than they thought. Erathrir looked at the painting on the wall opposite to him, and in the flickering light thought that he saw movement there. Shajal spoke on, softly and level-voiced. His words were only a pattern without meaning to Erathrir's dulled sense. On the wall, in the painting, the worm moved, twisting round and round, and the man moved with it. In the swirl of changing colours, one flowed into the other and then back, as if worm and man were but shifting shapes of each other. Erathrir stood up abruptly.

'I am falling asleep, and already half dreaming. I thank you for the food you have given us, Shajal,' he said.

Melandir too stood.

'Our journey was long and tiring. We have suffered some evil things. All of us would sleep now, with your leave.' Melandir's words were spoken with something of an effort. He found it hard to remain awake.

'There are rooms prepared for you, friends. Let me show you to them,' said Shajal. 'Forgive me that I have kept you up . . . My guests are so few. — We will talk more tomorrow, and I will do what I can to help you on your way.'

He rose and the men of the Quest followed him wearily from the room.

'Did you see the thing in the picture?' Talak hissed to Relnar, as they went up the broad stairway. 'It was behind where I sat. I am sure that the Lord Erathrir was looking at it.'

'Saw what?' Relnar yawned.

'The shapes in the picture. They moved! That man, — he saw it also, and he was smiling when it happened.'

'You are dreaming, Talak,' said Relnar, and yawned again. 'We are all so tired it is no surprise . . .'

'I am not so tired as all that,' answered Talak angrily. 'And I know what I saw.'

'Then you had best ask the Lord Erathrir if he did see it. Or perhaps you should tell the Lord Melandir who is your master. — But I would not speak out of turn again too quickly, Talak, especially with this foolishness. — You are asking for a beating.' Relnar stumbled on the stair as he spoke. 'I am so tired,' he said.

'I have two chambers prepared for you,' said Shajal, as they came to the top of the thickly-carpeted stairway and stood on a wide landing lit by guttering candles, their light reflected in mirror upon mirror that lined the walls.

In one room three beds had been prepared, and here Erathrir, Karandar and Relnar would sleep, while Melandir with Talak his esquire were put in another chamber, on the farther side of the gallery that overlooked the hall beneath. Shajal bade the men of the Quest a soft goodnight and went silently away.

'My lord, may I speak?' said Talak.

'Yes, of course, but I am tired, Talak . . . Can it wait till morning?' Melandir answered.

Talak shook his head, and then told Melandir of the thing he had seen in the painting.

'So there is something strange about this place . . . That much I knew already, my watchful squire. Our host is a magician of some sort I think. He turned and piled the pillows at the head of the bed, then leaned back.

'I will sit up and watch. Then you will have to stand your turn. I have bidden Erathrir do the same. — But I am tired though . . .'

Melandir lay the Fate Sword in its sheath at his side. The Sceptre, wrapped in cloth, was beneath the pillows.

'You were right to tell me what you feared,' said Melandir.

'There is something else,' said Talak. 'I should have told it before, but I dared not. It is about my father, Filindrin . . . I think he is in great danger. It is all to do with the great Hound, and the skeleton-man. They came out of the Black Land.'

'I know,' said Melandir, 'and you are right to fear them. They are part of something even more terrible than our enemy Ral. I do not know what they mean. But why do you fear for your father?'

Talak opened his mouth to speak, but before his eyes he seemed to see Filindrin's face, and he heard Filindrin's voice, far away in Melurin: 'Never tell, never speak of it. It will want you too!' He heard himself promising never to tell, never to tell. He shivered.

'I do not know,' he said. 'But I am afraid for him. Where is he now? Has Ral got him?'

'Filindrin, your father, would probably have more fear about you if he knew I had brought you here into the forest with me,' said Melandir. '— Go to sleep now, Talak. We will find your father.'

Talak lay down and slept, moving as he dreamt of the changing picture, or of the dark vale by Aldel Morn where his father had stood with the things from Hell. Erathrir had fallen asleep as he sat watching, his eyes too heavy to remain open, his senses overpowered by an unbearable weariness. He and Karandar and Relnar slept soundly, but Melandir only dozed fitfully, his hand on the hilt of Wenyorel.

In the great kitchen, built in the cellars under the House in the Forest, Shajal stood, a tall heavy man in red and gold robes. The round brick arches of smoke-stained ovens shewed in the light from the candlestick he carried. The vats and the spits over the hearth threw strange shadows across the wall. Black cooking pots glinted dully.

'You have them, Witchweird?' said a woman's voice from out of the blackest corner.

Shajal started, and looked around, his formerly steady eyes blinking and furtive. Out of the blackness came a form all in black. Only her face was not black, and that was unhumanly pale, thin lips drawn back in an eternal sneer, eyes cruel and vivid. The leathery cloak clung to her body, and snapped and creaked at her jerky steps. She stood close enough to the man to touch him.

'You are welcome here to my house, O mighty one, O Queen, O Great Goddess, O Ral!'

'Still! Be still! Shajal the Shapeshifter, weak little Witchweird! I am welcome because you fear me, and are sold to my power. — Now answer my question. — Do you have them?'

'They sleep like hogs in my fine rooms, O my Goddess.'

'They are all drugged then?'

'I put the magic potion you gave me into the wine. Its power is subtle but undoubted. They did not even know they had been drugged. They are asleep now and they will not awaken.'

'You are sure that they all drank the wine?'

Shajal, the Shapeshifter, in his man shape, twisted his body as if tortured by the glance of his mistress.

'The men all drank of it.'

'What do you mean?'

'There is a boy with them, a thing of no matter, a mere child. They would not let him drink.'

'I know of the one. — There are five of them, three Mannish, though one of those is young, the Dwarf, and this child. — It is of no matter to me, save that I will remember how on this detail you failed, Witchweird. — Come! Show me where the one I spoke of lies! This time there will be no mistake. This time It will be mine!'

'Why do you not let me kill them for you, mistress? I will bring what you seek.'

'I bade you keep them for me. You will not go near them! Stay away!' cried Ral, and her eyes burnt and her voice was fury. The Witchweird cringed away.

Ral entered the room where Melandir lay. She glanced at his form, hunched and facing the wall on a pile of pillows. His bed stood at the far end of the long chamber. She looked more closely at where Talak lay but he seemed to be sleeping soundly. She crossed to where the packs were on the floor and began to search swiftly and methodically through their possessions.

A groan halted her. She swung round, teeth bared in anger, to see Melandir sat on the bed staring at her, eyes half-glazed, but not sleeping. In his right hand he held the Sword of Fate, and it was the power of the Sword that had delayed the effect of the sorcerous drug. But it was not this that made her hiss in an icy agony of sudden utter fear. In Melandir's left hand she saw the Sceptre Mortal, that had lain with him as he lay half-drugged but still just awake. She knew that if he claimed it as his own now, then she might die within seconds. She had never seen death so near, nor so clearly.

'Ral! Ral!' gasped Melandir.

He stood up, staggering, hardly able to lift the Sword. The movement sent waves of nausea through him and let the drug take firmer hold.

'What is it?' Talak sleepily pushed back the thick coverlet on his bed. He saw Melandir first, puzzlement in his eyes, — then he saw Ral. 'Help! Help! She is here! Ral is here! Help! Ral!'

His shouts rang through the house, full of frenzied terror. Ral had reached him in a moment. Her open hand went back then swept forward. Talak ducked, and only the very fingertips caught his head. But the blow of the Witch flung him spinning and crashing backwards against the wall. Had she struck as she had intended, his neck would have snapped like a stick. Then she sprang at Melandir, fixing the last of her hopes of life on speed. She must take the Sceptre before he claimed it.

In her rush, she discounted the Sword, for her body was well guarded against death from earthly weapons. Of Wenyorel she knew nothing, until its blade cut her, tearing a shallow gash through her robe in the flesh of her side. Her scream was as shrill as the cry of her bats. The pain was like a flame. For a moment half of her body was stiff and immovable as if she had been poisoned. Then, when she could move again, she leapt away, shouting and hissing, clutching at the wound from which no blood came. Melandir swayed on his feet, too weak to follow up his advantage, able only to follow her movements with his eyes and the sagging blade, as she cautiously went to and fro before him. Then he saw her lips moving in words mumbled too swift and quietly to hear, and saw her hand make unknown signs. A scent like that of the wine he had drunk began to fill his nostrils. He lurched and fell onto one knee, resting on his Sword. His clasp on the Sceptre began to relax.

CHAPTER 16

THE LOSS OF THE SCEPTRE

'I will lead now, Talarnidh,' said Filindrin.

The Prince stared coldly and angrily at him in the night.

'Do you know the way then?'

'You will find out soon enough if you follow me. — Or you can stay here and give up the search.'

He turned and strode into the darkness.

'Follow him,' said Talarnidh bitterly.

Filindrin led them between the lights and the ghost shapes that suddenly formed, ignoring them all. From time to time he paused and looked around, seeming to sniff the air, then continued at once on his way. Soon they could all see that the lights he was making for were definitely fixed and unmoving. They came out into the courtyard in front of the House in the Forest. The door stood a little open, and without pausing Filindrin climbed the steps, pushed the door wide and went in. Before them, as they blinked in the candlelight, stood a man in red and gold, strong and bearded, and with anger in his eyes.

'What do you want in my house?' demanded Shajal.

Yet in his heart he was afraid, for Ral had spoken of no other strangers, and Ral was a cruel mistress. He had obeyed her perfectly. He had rescued the strangers from the band of Goblins that she had set to ambush them. He had brought them to the house and drugged them. Now she would have the thing she sought. But Ral had spoken of no others. He looked uncertainly from one to another. He saw the Sylph and the drawn swords of the grim figures. He guessed that they came from the enemy of his mistress, the enemy in the south against whom war was preparing. How else had they passed his defence if they did not come from the wizard?

'Your voice is not real,' said Filindrin. 'Everything about you is as false as your phantom lights. — You are not even a true man.'

The feigned anger in Shajal's eyes turned for a moment to real terror, for somehow this stranger could see past all his appearances. Then he sprang, full at Filindrin's throat, a white, clawed and spitting form, sword-like fangs bared, a snow-tiger out of the Northern Wastes.

Filindrin fell, twisting beneath it, shouting in rage. The two forms rolled over again and again before the tiger gave a snarl of pain, and leapt away. Down the side of its head and across one eye was a vivid red gash like the mark of one of its own claws. Yet Filindrin, as he struggled to his feet, had no weapon. Only as he stood, blood streaming from the clawed and ragged wounds in his own face, did he draw his sword. Yeselwir ran to him and took his arm.

'Filindrin! You are hurt! — What is it? I have never seen a creature like it?'

'It is a Shape Shifter, one of the Weirds,' snapped Filindrin, holding his cloak to his injured face.

'What does that mean?' Yeselwir asked.

'It means that this creature can change its form as it wishes,' said Fandorel. 'It is no illusion. It becomes a different creature each time it changes, and each one is quite real and very deadly.'

From his back he had swiftly unslung the great bow. One eye fixed warily on the tiger as it prowled to and fro at the end of the hallway, he bent the bow and strung it. Talarnidh moved toward the creature, sword held at arm's length in front of him.

'When it leaps at me I will dive under it. Take the arrow to its throat, Fandorel,' he commanded.

Slowly he approached the tiger, saw its muscles bunch, and then, as it came, dived for the floor. The arrow of Fandorel and the blue wind spear of Whirrirrish flew at the same moment straight for the throat of the leaping beast.

Before they reached it, in the middle of its spring, the creature changed. It became a leaping man, clad in full armour, black and heavy steel. On its arm it bore a tall shield, and a straight sword was in its hand. The shield took the wind spear which smashed into blue fragments that disappeared. The arrow hit the helmet and spun away to embed itself in the wood of the lofty staircase. The Shape Shifter had changed in less than the blink of an eye, while the weapons were in flight towards it.

The armoured knight was upon them before they could even realise what had happened. The swing of its sword turned Talarnidh's blade, and its shield struck out flat into Yeselwir's face. Yeselwir fell, and Filindrin with him, still clutching the cloth to his bloody scars. Yeselwir managed to parry the downward sweep of the sword upon him, and Filindrin rolled aside to the foot of the stairs, dragging himself upright by the banister.

The black-armoured knight turned slowly a full circle where it stood. Its enemies were now all about it, Fandorel and Wirrirrish before, Talarnidh to the left, Yeselwir to the right, and Filindrin behind. Its shield took Talarnidh's thrust, and then, heavy iron that it was, had disappeared. Where the knight had been, a tiny bird fluttered up into the roof, and Fandorel's second arrow flashed past to sink up to the feather in the pinewood panels. There was a sudden silence in the house. Then, through it, faintly, came a muffled cry from one of the rooms above.

'Help! Help! She is here! Ral is here! Help! Ral!'

Filindrin knew the voice at once, — his son, Talak, — and he understood well what it meant if Talak was there in the house and Ral with him. It was not for his son he thought, but for Melandir, and for the Sceptre Mortal. He raced up the stairs, following the faint sound of the shouts. Round the gallery, mirror-lined, above the hallway he ran, ignoring the piercing scream that came suddenly from below.

He pushed open the door, and stood gazing at Ral and Melandir. His eyes took in the Sceptre, still in Melandir's grasp. He also saw the Sword, and shuddered briefly at the memory of long ago. Slowly, sword dangling loosely in his hand, he walked into the room. Ral and Melandir watched him, his face a mask of blood. Suddenly his right hand went up and in that second all the panes of glass in the full-length window smashed into fragments, and even the window frames broke and splintered to the ground beneath. A gust of wind rushed into the room and dispelled the scent created by Ral's spell.

'Stay awake, Melandir! Just a while longer!' shouted Filindrin.

His head cleared by the cold air, Melandir struggled to his feet again.

'I am drugged by her potion, Filindrin,' he gasped. 'I can only last a few minutes more.'

'That will be enough. It will serve me well,' said Filindrin.

He looked away from Melandir; first at Talak who lay wide-eyed where Ral had flung him against the wall.

'Father . . . you have come . . !' He began to speak, but Filindrin spared only a glance for him. Then he advanced on Ral.

'So you have failed to claim the Sceptre, Witch Queen. What befell at Kruakh? Perhaps the Dog that guards the Threshold was there.'

'What manner of sorcerer are you?' came the cold voice of Ral. 'You have no business here! Go, or I will kill you!'

'I doubt that your powers are great enough to kill me any more,' answered Filindrin. 'And I have business here. Nor will I leave without what is rightfully mine.'

Ral glanced quickly at Talak.

'So, he is your son. — Take him! For that I care nothing.'

'Nor do I, Witch Queen. — O how little you know of me. — What do I want with a puling brat, I who have many slaves?'

'Father!' cried Talak, his face white and suddenly tear-stained.

'Filindrin, what is the matter with you?' said Melandir, his voice choking.

'What manner of man are you?' said Ral, clearly and quietly.

Her face betrayed nothing but she looked full into Filindrin's eyes for a time that stretched into minutes, but seemed hours long. Then her eyes grew wider. She opened her mouth to speak, but no word was uttered. Filindrin smiled, a slow sardonic grin, his teeth and eyes glinting amidst the blood on his face.

Through the open door came a crescendo of new screams from the hallway below. They seemed to jerk Ral back to reality. She said three words only, short and harsh, spoken in the Black Speech, and her finger pointed at Filindrin's head, then moved slowly down his body. Filindrin gave a great cry. His hands went to his bloodstained face, his head jerked and twisted. Then his hands came away slowly, and Talak cried out in repeated shouts of:

'No! No!' his voice frozen into a single word of horror.

For the skin and flesh on Filindrin's face was wriggling and twitching, and where he had touched it the flesh had fallen away. The white cheek-bones shewed through. Drops of something fell from Filindrin's fingers, and again white bones appeared through the crawling flesh of those fingers. Swiftly and inexorably Filindrin's flesh was rotting away from his bones, and as it rotted it gave off a stench like that of a corpse decaying.

'I believe now that you are only a man after all,' said Ral, and she laughed. 'Perhaps you have heard tell of the Rotting Spell long since. When all the skin and flesh have turned to foulness, when the organs of the body and the brain have dissolved, when only the naked bones stand up, then, man, you will be dead, and all your powers become a pile of dry bones.'

Filindrin said nothing. He stretched out his right hand and Melandir and Talak saw that it was the hand of a skeleton. Filindrin fixed his eyes upon the dead hand. Slowly, as his eyes burnt with concentration, the flesh reappeared on the bones. The hand reformed, flesh, blood and sinew, as it had been before. But his face was almost a skull already, and the stench of rotting was overpowering.

'That is a fine sorcery, mortal man,' said Ral. 'But it is too slow. First the extremities of the body will rot. Then the rest. You cannot restore it all in time. Do you not feel it inside you now?'

Her hand had remained pointed at his heart, as it had been all the while.

'Die, Ral!' screamed Filindrin. 'Let her die! Let her die!' And again and again and again he snarled a word — unknown to Melandir, unknown even to Ral.

A ripple of flame ran suddenly across the floor from the smashed window to Ral's foot. Then it sprang up, a swift thin single flame in front of her face. Her hand dropped and she backed away. The spell was no longer fixed on Filindrin. All her thought was for the thing that took shape before her. The flame expanded into a sheet of fire, grew denser, and a column of fire formed in the midst of it. Ral shouted her spells that ward off burning, but she shouted in vain. Filindrin held his face in his hands, and the flesh grew back where bone had been.

The pillar of flame became a blazing orange body streaked with many flames of lesser colours, and at its side spread out wide wings of blue and yellow leaping flames, many-feathered with fire. Clawed hands formed out of the wings, crimson and violet, and a huge head blossomed in fire out of the flame body. Green and yellow fire-eyes shone in it, and a mouth that gushed fire, — flashing tongues of it leaping out towards Ral as the wings beat and the claws clutched at the air. The being of fire became clearer and more distinct. The lapping flames at its extremities drew in, the fires coalesced, and the light of the flames grew darker. No smoke rose from them, for nothing was burnt, but the flames themselves turned from vivid scarlet to a dull and murky crimson. Only the eyes remained brilliant orange, while the blue of the wings was darker than the ocean. A deep and continuous roar as of a furnace came out of it, and sparks and flickers fell from it, to burn momentarily on the floor.

'Take her!' shouted Filindrin. 'Take her! I command you!'

The Demon stretched out arms of flame to surround Ral, and renewed torrents of flame rushed out of its mouth upon her. She had run back across the room into the corner. The thing was between her and the door or the window, flames cutting off her hope of escape. Already her face and hands bore the livid marks of burning, but of Ral's strong magic the body of Filindrin now bore no sign.

'Shout your spells, Witch! All your little powers are drunk from my great power. You feed from my Sword,' cried Filindrin. 'They will avail you nothing against my creature of Hell.'

He turned and saw that Melandir had fallen back onto the bed, still moving feebly but hardly conscious. Filindrin was edging cautiously, with care, towards the Sword and the Sceptre that he sought as a rush of flame went up from the Fire Demon. So fierce it was that it burnt up and through the roof of the house into the sky. Ral's last spell had been spoken, and it had been ice-like pain in the molten heart of the thing of fire. Even that spell had no power to quench it, but it turned the Demon's might into rage.

Crouched against the wall, Talak saw the sorcery of Ral work on Filindrin. But when, at his father's bidding, the Fire-Beast formed, he had crawled and squirmed along the side of the room to the door, weeping in fear and horror and disbelief. From the doorway he saw the room become a sheet of flame, and he fell back from the great heat. For a second he saw Ral through the orange glow; then, as it died away, he saw the bat form she had become again sweep past the Demon, twittering its agony as the leather wings touched the fire wings.

The Demon turned and, as Ral reached the window, a rolling ball of flame gushed out of its being towards her. The heat of it scorched Talak's face, and sent him reeling back towards the banisters around the gallery. Filindrin half turned from the two things he sought, saw the flame come upon him, and felt the cry choked and burnt in his throat by the rush of fire. Though the centre of the fireball did not touch him, its nearness was enough. The mortal body of Filindrin fell, suffocated in flame. Ral fled safe through the window, and the heart of the fire enveloped Melandir.

The rhythmic roaring growl of the Demon became louder, angry, and then suddenly irregular. The guiding force had gone out of it. Again the column of fire rushed upwards, and now the Demon seemed to be climbing up the fiery pillar of its own body, rising upwards on a sheet of furnace light till it roared and bellowed and snapped its wings on the roof above in the ruin of charring rafters and smoking beams.

Talak went back into the room. Fire had taken hold of the panelling around the walls, and now for the first time there was thick acrid smoke. Flames flicked amidst the floorboards, and a rich wall-hanging blazed above the burning bed where Talak himself had lain. Both the farther ends of the long room seemed to be full of fire. A gaping hole up into the roof burnt crimson above the charred and crackling circle of flame where the Demon had stood. The bed on which, somewhere, Melandir lay blazed in a mass of burning. But Filindrin could still be reached. He lay, face down, a silent huddled form beside a crackling smoking chair, the corner of his cloak charring in the flames.

Hand over his mouth, yet trying to shout to Melandir or Filindrin, Talak went back into the room, though he was sure that both men were dead. Choking in the thickening smoke he reached the body of Filindrin. His hands reached out for the still form of his father and he cried out in pain and despair when the very rings of the mail that Filindrin wore burnt his hands. Staring involuntarily at the surges of flame where he knew that Melandir's body lay on its pyre, he painfully dragged Filindrin across the floor while the flames spread about him, enveloping furniture and walls, outlining the doorposts through which he finally pulled the leaden body.

Weeping silently above the hallway on the smoke-filled gallery, ignoring the battle beneath and the fire above, he sat on the floor and turned the body of his father over. He looked into a face charred black, lips and eyelids and hair burnt away. His hand brushed the cheek, and burnt flakes of skin fell away from the bone. He might have screamed and screamed again at that sight alone, but the burnt-blind and useless eyes of Filindrin moved in their sockets, and the blackened thing in his arms said:

'Talak! Talak! Go back and get the Sceptre!'

In the hallway, Talarnidh had backed against the panelled wall. His sword swept, and where there had been a flapping bird a serpent's head darted forward, fangs bared, tongue flickering. The sword swung again, and the head fell, rolling upon the floor, and it screamed as it fell. Six other heads of the monster twisted and turned, and they all screamed out again and again in high-pitched anguish. Filindrin had not even paused on the gallery above to look at the newest form of the monster.

Fandorel raised his bow and an arrow whistled through the air, burying itself in the floor where the hydra had been. The creature was slithering like quicksilver towards Yeselwir, still slumped and dazed from the assault of the armoured knight. But Talarnidh was there, and with one cut of his sword hacked into the base of the deadly heads. Three of the necks were severed, and they fell to the ground writhing while the heads on them screamed and hissed. Whirrirrish leapt at the bloated body behind the remaining heads. His wings flashed as he twisted away from the darting tongues and then his blue bright dagger was falling once and again, and two more of the heads were rolling and snapping on the floor. Blood spurted from the ruined serpent as it slid away, its one remaining head low on the ground amidst the blood.

As it writhed across the ground the body of the creature seemed to expand, filling out its neck, the whole of it growing broader and longer, huge and coiling. And as its shape shifted, the men heard a sudden roar and crackle of fire from above. Faint streamers of smoke came out from an open door, and dancing flames reflected on the mirrors above and threw strange shadows down the stair-well. In the light of the fires overhead, the red scales of the worm glistened all along its snake-like body. Its mouth was open wide, and a red tongue flashed between rows of sharp curved teeth set in a great serpent head.

The worm's tail whipped round and struck Fandorel, flinging him against Yeselwir. Again the tail flicked towards the two men of the Quest, and suddenly the coils of it had taken Fandorel, twisting about him in a scaly embrace, and the worm still grew, and its coils writhed crimson about the hall. With lithe sinuous motions it drew Fandorel towards its open mouth. Talarnidh leapt upon it, and his hands were clasped round the massive throat. The worm's round eyes bulged as Talarnidh's grip grew tighter. Its body twisted and wriggled, and the tail thrashed about, releasing Fandorel and flinging him against the stairs. But

Talarnidh did not release his grip. Always, wherever the worm flung itself, he kept hold.

Above, a new roar of fire rose up, and there seemed to be flames everywhere. On the gallery the mirrors cracked and the whole house was shaking as if in a monstrous spasm. A gust of smoke burst out and filled the air. But the worm fought on. With a last effort it twisted its scaly tail round so that the tip wound about Talarnidh's body. But the grip on its throat only tightened. The worm issued a deep unnatural groan, unlike its earlier sibilant cries, more like the dying groan of a man. Then its shape changed again, became half man, half worm, then worm again, but always Talarnidh gripped its throat. Half-formed creatures shifted beneath his hands, but he squeezed ever tighter. There was a last serpentine writhing and thrashing, and then stillness. The crimson worm that was the Witchweird lay dead at Talarnidh's feet.

As he stood above it, gasping for breath, Talarnidh heard Talak's voice screaming and shouting above him, incoherent in terror. He looked up and saw the boy silhouetted against a flaming doorway, a hunched form at his feet. Talak had dropped Filindrin when his father, that he knew had to be dead, had spoken from his blackened lips. Now he stood in the red glare and swirling smoke and wept and screamed he knew not what. Talarnidh sprang up the stairway to where he stood. Yeselwir and Whirrirrish followed, but Fandorel still lay hurt and gasping where the coils of the creature had let him fall. The gallery was strewn with the shards of the broken mirrors. The men were half blinded by smoke. A gout of flame came from the open door, and Talak ran forward away from it yelling, to be caught by Talarnidh. He screamed in unseeing terror, and Talarnidh struck him across the face.

'Talak! Where are the others?' he demanded.

Still the boy could hardly speak, and looked about him in horror. Talarnidh shook him.

'Answer, Talak! Where are they?'

'There! In there!'

He pointed to the door at their right. Talarnidh turned to it.

'But Melandir is in the room with the fire!' Talak screamed suddenly. 'And my father Filindrin . . . He is a ghost now. He is dead, but a ghost. A ghost!'

'Take the boy, and try to save your friends,' said Whirrirrish.

'I will go into the fire to look for the one he speaks of. Fire has less power over me.'

Like a gust of wind the Sylph rushed towards the doorway of fire, for a moment blue-grey against the redness. Then fire seemed to stream behind him as he passed into the crimson flames and the darkness of smoke.

'Try to get your father out of the house,' Talarnidh ordered Talak. He shook the boy once again. 'Do you understand?' Talak nodded dumbly in anguish, and stumbled towards the form of Filindrin.

Talarnidh and Yeselwir ran towards the room Talak had pointed out. Fandorel joined them as they flung open the door. Inside they saw Karandar, Erathrir, and Relnar lying, still sleeping under the rich coverlets, their heads on the silken pillows. The room was already filled with smoke. Talarnidh attempted to pull Karandar to his feet, but the Dwarf Lord did not awake.

'They are poisoned,' said Fandorel. 'But they are still alive.'

'Then let us get them out of this monstrous place,' said Talarnidh.

Each lifted one of their sleeping comrades in his arms and went out onto the gallery. The fire now licked along the walls. The wooden banister rail was half burnt away, and the carpet on the stairs was burning in patches of flame. The noise of the conflagration was all around — the crashing of timbers and the roaring of fire as it consumed the house. And with every second that passed the roar became louder and more like a great thing breathing, deep-throated and full of rage. They ran down the stairs, and flames caught at their clothes as they went, their companions in their arms. The door was open before them and they rushed out into the night.

All around the snow was lurid red, and even the dark trees of the forest seemed to dance in the fiery light of the burning house. They carried their burdens a safe distance from the house and then lay them down. Talarnidh ran back into the smoke to help the weeping Talak drag Filindrin's body from the doorway. Then, in the ancient gardens, they turned to gaze on the house as a sound of tearing and breaking came from it, drowning the incessant roaring for a brief moment. They saw the roof collapse inwards upon itself and great bursts of flame leap crackling into the sky. But in all the ruin and destruction they saw no sign of

Whirrirrish the Sylph, and flames poured like a torrent from out of the window where Melandir had lain with the Sceptre Mortal and the Sword of Fate.

Within the flames above the roof there was a great shape formed, dark crimson against the leaping orange of the fire. Its wings spread out beside it, blue and livid, flecked with darting feathers of ochre. Orange eyes burnt in its burning head, brighter than all other flames, and from its mouth came the roaring breath of a thousand furnaces of Hell. As they watched, it grew, rising upwards from the roof of the house. Its wings reached out across the night and its form was mighty above. Huge against the sky, it loomed over the tiny figures far below, and its redness lit up the black of the sky, while yellow flashes of flame rippled over its body, and gouts of crimson fell from it, spreading fire in the forest. Ral saw it as she fled to her lair in the Pit of the Werebats, and she feared for its coming. The Goblins on the road saw, and fled in uttermost terror. The Wizard afar off saw what it was, and his mind bent to the messengers he had already sent when he had heard of the great Hound's coming.

'It is one of the Demons from Hell,' said Fandorel.

'And within it are Melandir and the Sword and the Sceptre. All our hopes are ended now. The greatest of our fellowship is dead,' said Talarnidh. 'Something has come into the world, greater the Ral, greater by far. This Demon is just a part of it.'

From the north west, a wind blew up. At first it was no more than a cooling breeze on the faces of the men, as they awaited death in the shadow of Hell. But it grew stronger with every second, and now it was a gale rushing through the forest and bending the trees in its path. They saw vast clouds scudding low towards them, grey on the night sky, blown by the storm wind. When the clouds came over the house, they stopped still and seemed to hang in the air next to the monstrous shape of the Fire Demon, though all around them the gale still blew. More clouds and more were blown by the raging winds to the blaze of the house until they all gathered around and above it.

Then, as the men watched, they saw the clouds shifting and coalescing, their great white billows being shaped by the very wind that blew them. Now they had become like white spears pointing at the very heart of the fire. Dancing particles streamed behind them like the tails of comets. All around, the men of the

Quest saw the nebulous forms of many Sylphs darting among the cloud shapes and prodding them with blue goads. Then the clouds flew forward. Ridden by the dancing Sylphs they sped into the heart of the fiery being.

The fire leapt up anew as if fanned by the winds. The hands of the Demon reached out to clasp at the huge cloud forms. The flames passed through the immaterial shapes, and flared and crackled in dampened violence. Then the rents came in the fabric of the Fire-Beast. The white dew-laden cloud spears transfixed it, and the flame was torn to tatters and did not mend. A vast gust caught the Demon, and the lurid column twisted on itself. The head swirled and bent downwards. The wings flew apart in rags of crackling blue light that showered into sparks throughout the sky. The Demon withdrew into itself, becoming smaller and more concentrated, hunched and dark gloomy red on the smashed roof of the blazing mansion.

From down in the fire-shadowed darkness of the ruined gardens, red around the mansion, came a great cry. The men of the Quest heard its shrill unnatural words, and it seemed to come from near them or amongst them, as they stood or lay, scattered and choking and gasping, watching the battle in the sky. Crackling from the Demon came an echo of the same words, words made out of the roaring and moaning of mighty flames. Then, in a moment, the grim shape had vanished. The Demon had gone, sent back to Hell by a word spoken in the Speech of Hell. In the house was fire, and the mighty winds swept over it to fan the destruction of the House in the Forest and all the hopes that seemed to lay ruined within.

Down they swept, cloud giants with Sylph riders, crying out in voices of wind. Upon the men of the Quest they came. Huge immaterial hands seized the men and somehow lifted them up from the ground, away into the sky. All of them were suddenly in a different world, full of moving formless shapes and bright-winged Sylphs, carried up into impossible heights where the flame of the burning house became only a ruined star below.

CHAPTER 17

THE ICE CASTLE

The clouds were silver-grey in the cool clear starlight. Their giant shapes turned and twisted in the air as they rushed across the sky. All around, the Sylphs danced, Elementals of the air who laughed and sang as they goaded the cloud giants onwards and upwards to meet the waning moon.

Erathrir awoke from troubled sleep and nightmares to the sound of their songs, now like the breeze of autumn in fallen leaves, now loud as the wild wind in a mountain pass. He lay, wrapped in cloud, the other men of the Quest all around him. But Melandir, his companion from the Outer Worlds, was not there. He looked at Fandorel beside him, and the wings of the Elf Lord spread back, gossameres glistening in the starlight, while his eyes burnt with the fire of his youth before time as he gazed on the flight of the Sylphs. For around him Sylph maidens swam in the air, blue tresses swept back, and Sylph lords with crowns of azure light above them. Their eyes were blue with distance, and their forms though manlike sped in the air and were part of its substance. The prongs of their blue and quicksilver goads flickered and flashed as they spurred the wandering clouds through the reaches of night.

Time passed and the men of the Quest slept or rested and dreamt on vast cloud beds amidst the air and motion and darkness. All fear left them, blown in the wind and haunting song, and only the eyes of Filindrin were dark with horror. Night became day and the forms of the Sylphs were less clear as the light glanced from them and their wings of wind flickered in the clear crisp air. Bathed in cold light beneath was the green vastness that was the Forest of Sorcery. But ahead to the south tall mountains rose from the trees, snow glinting from their summits and a white fire that flashed somewhere amidst them. Other mountains and far hills lay westward, fading into a distance of sea and sky, while east all lay hidden in the brilliance of the sun. They did not look back to the northward.

Before them the mountains grew swiftly as they raced on in

their cushion of cloud. Now they saw the meaning of the flare of white they had seen at the dawn. For standing alone from the other peaks was a solitary mountain, steep and craggy. On its summit was a castle of sheer ice that flamed white in the sunlight. The wind ceased and its captive clouds fell like feathers from the sky to settle gently on a snow-clad plateau. Before them rose the Ice Castle.

A wide road, polished like glass, cut through the fresh snow plain before them, and crystal fountains poured water that froze in patterns of ice all around. A few paces behind, the plateau fell away in jagged cliffs to the green of the forest far below, half-hidden by the drifting insubstantial clouds that had carried them so far. For a moment the Sylphs were still there, whirling above and below, and then in a rush of wings and wind were gone, fled upwards like blue darts to the castle above with only the notes of their songs left to fade in the air.

'This must be the dwelling of the one that the Sylph, Whirrirrish, served,' said Talarnidh. 'He wished us to come here, and now we have been brought. We will go into the sorcerous castle, and we will see the "Old Wise One" of whom he spoke.'

Talarnidh's voice had become firm again, and harder.

'Talarnidh is right,' said Karandar. 'But I wish I knew who this "Old Wise One" might be.'

'That is a puzzle too great for the Lord Talarnidh,' said Filindrin.

'If you know any more than we do, you had best say it now, Filindrin,' answered Talarnidh. 'You are speaking too much in this manner. You speak little like the Filindrin I once knew.'

'You will all learn soon enough who this man really is,' answered Filindrin, and his voice had become soft, where the Prince's had been sharp. 'Come, Talarnidh, let us visit this mighty aeromancer in his windy halls.'

Talarnidh stared straight at him, then nodded his agreement to the others, and the men of the Quest turned onto the ice road that led up to the great door. Filindrin stood still and, as Talarnidh passed him, he caught the Prince by the sleeve.

'How well do you think you knew Filindrin then?' he said, and his mouth smiled. Talarnidh brushed off the hand and replied:

'That I cannot answer. But now I know him not at all.'

Filindrin stood back and said no more, but again he put his

hand to rest on the arm of one who tried to pass him. This time his grip was like a talon. He held Talak and looked into the boy's pale and fearful face, while the others walked on.

'Why are you frightened, boy?' he said, and his voice was still soft, but his eyes were not. 'Why do you look at me in that way? Why do you stand near the others and hide from me and say no word?'

'Father? . . . I saw your face . . . Your face, it was all burnt. It was black, black and burnt.'

'You are mistaken, boy. My face was black with soot and grime. — And it was scarred. Can you not see the dried blood and claw marks here on me now? Understand that, Talak! My face was cut and blackened only, — nothing else. Do you think I could have remade my face — and even remade the scars on it? Do not forget it! Get it clear in your mind! Do not be mistaken about it ever again!'

The grip on Talak's arm tightened, so that he gasped with pain, and the face of Filindrin close to his own was a grim mask.

'I do not understand!' cried Talak.

'What do I care what you understand, — so long as you obey? And you will obey me . . . Now, come! And stay close by me! Do not wait with these others you like so much. Come!'

In the brightness of the air the castle had seemed nearer than it was. They walked along the glass-like road, on which it seemed no snow had fallen, and, though the surface was wholly smooth, they found that their feet did not slip. The water in the fountains glittered like rainbows, already part crystal as it fell. On the wide plain were other crystalline shapes, trees and flowers of glass or diamond, full of colours and lights, vivid amid the brilliant snow.

At the roadway's end was a sweeping frozen staircase leading to the glittering gates of the Ice Castle. In the sunlight the castle seemed to be made of silver; domes, towers and steeples lost in the brilliance, and soaring heights bridged with iridescent ice. It was as if a great fortress of the Peiri had become a thing of glass and light. Yet the ice of that castle was as hard as granite, and the edges of its walls as bitter as adamant.

Slowly the men of the Quest ascended the stairway, and the rainbow light of countless ice prisms flashed on their faces. They reached the shining doors, and looked through them into a palace of mirrors full of unending reflections and lit by cold inner fires.

Talarnidh struck with his gloved fist upon the great doors, and a peal of shivering sound rang up through the heights, echoing away from tower to tower. The doors swung silently open and the men crossed the rime-crusted threshold into the halls of crystal. They walked in silence and, in the heart of the ice, felt no cold. They were almost blinded by the depth of light.

At the end of the great hall were two smaller doors that also opened before them. The light in the room beyond took on a paler, more milky, glow, and in it moved strange shapes. They were living beings, man-like, but less than a man's height, thin and slender. They gleamed and glistened as they moved like quicksilver in the ice-light. Their arms ended in spiky fingers, all of equal length. Their toes were the same. Their hair stood up from their heads like a jagged crown. They wore no garments, but their bodies were cloaked in frost. Their eyes were like pearls, and their faces carven like stone. They were all of blue bright ice.

'Be welcome in the Ice Castle, O travellers! Be of good cheer in the halls of the Wizard!'

One of the creatures of ice had spoken, moving before them in a way unlike any other living thing, as if the water that made it became liquid again for the briefest moment. Its voice was brittle and sharp, each word clear, and yet with the notes of running water hidden in it.

'I come to speak to the Wizard,' said Talarnidh.

'We know how you came here,' answered the voice of frost. 'You are weary. Here in the warm heart of the ice there will be rest and healing. Then you will speak to the great one, our master.'

'I do not trust this, Talarnidh,' said Filindrin. 'You may not like what I say, but it would be best for you if you listened. Have you forgotten the house of the Shape Shifter? This place has the same feeling about it.'

'Filindrin believes it is an illusion,' said Fandorel.

'I know full well that it is no illusion,' Filindrin answered.

'Then you think it is the house of Ral?' said Erathrir.

'I do not even think that. — Tell me, Talarnidh, — who commands the beings of air and of ice? You know as well as I what these creatures are. They are Elementals. — Come, Karandar, you tell me who rules the Elementals?'

'You asked these questions before when we were in the forest,' said Talarnidh. 'Most of us here know who you mean. But he is dead. He fell out of history when Telmirandor the Golden was broken.'

'Tell me this also, Filindrin,' snapped Karandar. 'If the one you name has built this castle, and rules over these beings, why should you be so afraid of it? For, I tell you this, he could only be a friend and ally to us . . . Even our lord.'

'If the Old Wizard dwells here,' said Filindrin, 'it is the end of our Quest. That much I tell you, Dwarf Lord.' Then he strode forward so that he stood over the being of ice. 'Where is your master?' he cried. 'Why have we been brought here, Ice Undine? Where is the aeromancer, the Old Wizard?'

'My lord is a great one of the world,' came the answer. 'He will come when he comes.'

'Filindrin, stop this!' came Talarnidh's order. 'We will wait here and we will see.'

'Always this same counsel,' replied Filindrin, and his voice was angry and uncontrolled. 'If you are a Prince of Wenyaltrir, be a leader! If you are our leader, show us some sign of it!'

'Filindrin! You follow me as far as you choose,' answered Talarnidh, quiet and grim. 'You may obey me, if you wish, or you may turn now, and leave these halls and leave the Quest, — and there will be the end of your bitterness. You have changed since you came through Aldel Morn. You have changed since your son was found. And there has been no cure to it. For, whatever you do now, go or stay, there will be no end to this sorrow of yours.'

For seconds on end Filindrin stared into the steeled eyes of the Prince, and his face contorted, and many expressions fled across his features, hate and fear and loathing, until his eyes widened and despair was written across his whole body. He cried out one awful shriek and fell as one dead to the ground.

'He should have stayed in Melurin,' said Relnar, 'and cared for his son there. He is broken and will never be a whole man again.'

'He was bad when I last saw him, in Belengar,' said Karandar. 'Now he is worse. How long has he treated you in this way, Talarnidh?'

'Let it be, Karandar. He cannot help it,' sighed Talarnidh.

'Bear him up and lay him on the couches here. — Lie here all of you. My lord commands it,' said the Elemental. 'Here there is healing that comes from the fire of the ice and the song of many waters.'

'There is no healing for Filindrin,' said Talarnidh. '— We will lie here and await your master. Do for us what you may. We have come far, through so much evil . . .'

From tall windows light streamed into the high-domed room. The Wizard sat on a royal throne. A blue robe was over his shoulders. Under grey eyebrows his dark eyes glinted and gleamed as he listened to the Sylphs before him. One, called in the Sylph tongue from the Time Before Time Safaarasaa, who had led the Sylph company that came to the burning of the House in the Forest, spoke to the Wizard. She told him of what events had brought them to that place.

The Sylphs had gone to Kruakh as their lord had bidden them when the first rumours of the strange sounds and stranger apparitions hard by the ruined city had reached the castle. Faster than the wind they had sped to ancient Kruakh. They reached the city when the sun was low and searched until darkness, but found no living thing. They saw where the undergrowth had been newly cut and the place outside the Citadel where the rubble had been cleared. Flying over the plateau of Kamath, they had found a blackened pit among the tumbled rocks. It was scorched black all about, and heat lingered in it still. The Wizard heard and was troubled. He guessed much but not all. He nodded and said nothing. The Sylph spoke on.

Only in the harbour had they seen any real sign. A ship was anchored there. They read its flag, the towers and the ship, as that of Amray. There were men on the ship. After nightfall the Sylphs listened to their talk, but though they stayed long they learnt nothing more of what had befallen. But the sailors were concerned for certain men, perhaps their men, who had gone into the forest. They also spoke of a journey back to Misen Taïrail whence they had come. The Wizard heard each word and then bade the Sylph relate it again. For here were parts in another puzzle that he was piecing together.

The captain of the Sylphs then told how they had at last left Kruakh, flying low over the forest to avoid the bats of Ral. They had seen the glow of fire above the treetops. They had found the House in the Forest, where the Witchweird dwelt, all aflame. But above and within the fire was a monstrous form, as if made of flame. Here the Sylph looked up at her lord, for she knew him as Lord of the Fire also. But the Wizard made no sign. Seeing the dark fire of the Demon towering above the forest, the Sylphs had gathered together what winds they could and shaped the clouds into spears. These had rent the wings of the fire creature, and smothered it, so that it withdrew into itself, a humped, dark-flamed form. They had been prepared to assault even this, when out of the night came a weird and hideous cry, not from the creature, though that had echoed it. And as the creature had echoed it, it had itself vanished away.

In the melting snow of the gardens by the blazing house the Sylphs had found people who had escaped from the fire. Some were still in a swoon, some bore marks of flame and of fighting. All these men they had swept up and borne back to the Ice Castle. For the thing of fire in the house and the marks of fire near Kruakh were of the same sort, and in them was the scent of the Pit.

'Tell me of those you have brought here from the house of Shajal,' said the Wizard when the Sylph had finished her tale.

'They are Men, and an Elf and a Dwarf. Their arms and their clothes are like those of the High Race who are gone. They are nothing like the people of Ral. There are no Goblins among them. One is young and black-skinned like the men of Chamley. One is younger still, and very small, and he is like the people of the North, with yellow hair and eyes like the Sylphs. The others are such as once I saw when I served thee, Lord, in Telmirandor long ago. But one of them has a scent of strangeness about him. All the earth-bound are strange to me, Lord, but this one bears the scent of fear.'

'Have you spoken with these strangers, Safaarasaa?'

'We have given them rest and healing where we may. We have told them nothing of ourselves or our lord. They are watched now. We thought it strange that men should walk alone in the Forest of Sorcery when all prepare for war. We saw them where the Fire Demon was, in the house of the Witchweird. We think they had come from Kruakh, where strange things have befallen.'

'But you do not think they are the folk of Ral?' said the Wizard quietly. 'No, Safaarasaa, — you are right. Nor do I think the Fire Demon is anything to do with Ral. I have seen the like of the thing you describe. The memory is as bitter as their dwelling place. — All is not clear. Some things seem good, some ill.'

'My Lord, we must go to prepare against Ral.'

'Go, Safaarasaa. You have served me very well in this as in all things. I have not forgotten the coming war. Return to your task. I will go to see the strangers.'

The Wizard stood on a glass-like balcony, and looked down on the men of the Quest in the room below. Twice during the day he had come and looked long at them and thought, while they slept and grew strong again. Now evening drew on once more. All of them had awakened and were eating the food the Ice Undines had brought them. Talarnidh sat alone and ate little. He had heard from Erathrir and Karandar of all that had befallen in Kruakh. Of the Hound and of the Wild Hunt he knew enough for a single overmastering fear to enter his mind. He wondered how great the power of Ral might truly have grown, or who had come to her aid, if now she could give command to the Hound of Hell. But this was not his only trouble. For Melandir was lost out of the House in the Forest, and with him the Sword and the Sceptre. He sat in the ice halls, a guest or a prisoner, and bleakly surveyed the downfall of his Quest, the ultimate death of Selenthoril, and the utter triumph of the giant of evil that he now saw in his sister Ral the Fair.

'The halls of Eldhoril bid welcome to the Lords of Lost Wenyaltrir!'

Talarnidh's face jerked upwards to the balcony above. For a long time he looked at the figure of the Wizard. One by one the other men of the Quest joined him, their faces different pictures, some doubt, some disbelief, some uncertainty. Slowly Talarnidh knelt on one knee. Karandar looked at him for a fleeting moment, then followed suit, as did Fandorel.

'Do not kneel to me, Talarnidh, Prince of Wenyaltrir! Do not kneel to me, noble lords! Let us look on each other and be glad.'

'It is the one I spoke of,' said Filindrin bitterly. 'Out of the forgotten time and the betrayal of the High Race to Ral he has come back.'

'Who is it?' asked Yeselwir.

'It is Eldhoril, Wizard of Wenyaltrir,' said Talarnidh. 'O, how I greet you and greet you, great one. I had no hope for such a meeting as this.'

'Nor had I half such a good hope. You have come in my time of trouble, and I have found you in yours. Greeting and greeting again, Talarnidh. I will say it a thousand times over. And greetings Karandar, and Fandorel, — and to all you bring with you.'

The Wizard of Wenyaltrir descended the ice staircase and embraced Talarnidh, and then Karandar and Fandorel. Questions, parts of stories, things seen and befallen, passed between them in those few moments. One after another the Wizard greeted those of the Quest who had not known him of old. And though they spoke together of war, of the Witch Queen, and of long years of sorrow and sadness and downfall, they laughed with joy, Talarnidh and Eldhoril, for they spoke together again. Only after a long while the Wizard raised his hands.

'Talarnidh, have your company yet rested well enough? For if they have we must talk more seriously now. Come into my counsels! All that each of us know or guess must be made clear. For there is little enough time left for talk. You know already that I am in the midst of preparing for war. You know whom the war is against. — Come, we will go down into the mountain. You will see my fortress and know all my designs.'

Down stairs and glittering passages of crystal he led them and then out of the ice into the rock of the mountain. Through level after level they passed, with glimpses of carven chambers and spacious halls with rich hangings and blazing hearths. Then the rock-cut stairway brought them through armouries and forges, storehouses and barrack rooms. All around were the half-real forms of the Elementals, male and female, and all were preparing for war. At length they came to the lower levels of the mountain. They saw other darker passages sloping down into the earth beneath, and black stairways from which came the echoes of hammering and strange cries. They entered a wide room, the first they had seen for a long time which had any windows, — slits cut through the thickness of rock. They looked out over a clearing in the forest. Below them was the Mountain Gate, a vast doorway cut into the rock and barred with immense gates of steel. In the room there was a long table with many chairs round it.

'This is my room of counsel now,' said Eldhoril. 'I have to come down out of the Ice Castle all too often if I am to watch over the readying of war. — But counsel I have found little. Be seated! There is wine for you. I wish to be told all of your story now. For all the news that ever reached me, Talarnidh, was that you dwelt in Alban and the past was forgotten forever.'

'The past was never forgotten, great one,' said Talarnidh. 'You were remembered, though all believed you dead six thousand years and more.'

'But the Sceptre, Talarnidh? How is it that the Sceptre Mortal is suddenly remembered again? Of all the snatches and parts of tales you have already told me, that is most important. I must know more of it now.'

'It was to find the Sceptre Mortal that we came from Alban,' said Talarnidh. 'We sought it in our own war against Ral. — But do not question me more, Eldhoril. I will tell all the story from the start.'

'On Alban it was the Festival of the Lamps, for that is also not forgotten. Karandar and Fandorel had come there, sent by Parvaloril who is still King in Morena. Wondrith was also with them. Many other folk came. One was Relnar, whom you see here. He is King's son of Chamley. My own people were also there, Filindrin who sits yonder, Tasarnil the One-eyed, Fermilondath, Turnalordath and Melandir. It was from the Festival that Selenthoril called us.'

Eldhoril started suddenly, and a breath that was a sigh of anguish escaped his lips. Talarnidh's voice faltered, and he looked at the Wizard.

'Tell on, Prince of Wenyaltrir,' said Eldhoril, but now his voice was hard and heavy, and a lingering pain remained in his eyes. His face grew darker as Talarnidh spoke.

Talarnidh told how Melandir had come to Alban bearing the long-lost Sword, Wenyorel, called the Sword of Fate; of how he had slain the Fire Dragon, and been welcomed into the high councils of the island. Then he turned to Erathrir and bade him relate the story of their coming from the Outer Worlds to Tharang the Midworld, and of the parting of their ways at the Island of the Stars. In silence Eldhoril heard how Erathrir and Yeselwir had come to the Castle of Selenthoril on Nyaroth Khrathril, Enchanter's Isle.

Talarnidh then continued the story of the visions of Selenthoril they had seen on Alban and the sorcerous journey from there to Nyaroth Khrathril, to help Selenthoril find the Sceptre Mortal, the Sceptre he must have to slay Ral before her net was closed around him. He related the death of Tasarnil in Wirdrilded, and of Fermilondath, Turnalordath, and Wondrith in Aldel Morn, and the Wizard wept for the fallen of the Sacred Band. He told how Filindrin alone came out of the Black Land, and of the dark power the men of the Quest had encountered within that place. He told how they all met again at Belengar, and all that befell there.

Karandar took up the story of the journey by sea to Kruakh and the finding of the Sceptre Mortal in the caverns of the Merpeople. He related how they had been attacked by Ral, and again by the Hound of Hell, come back into the world from the deeps of the abyss. Stranger still, he spoke of their rescue by the Wild Hunt, and then their journey through the forest to the house of Shajal, where they had been tricked and drugged by sorcery.

Last of all Talarnidh took up the tale again. He told of how he and his companions had journeyed through the Empty Lands, and all that happened there, and of their capture by the servants of Ral. He told them that Ral had bewitched him and that he had betrayed the great secret of Kruakh to her. He told how Iroi Girindhouz, the Pine Lord, had set them free to rejoin their comrades, and how they had chanced to find them again in the House in the Forest where the Witchweird dwelt.

The story was long in the telling, and when all was told and a silence had fallen on the room, Eldhoril slowly stood up. His movements had taken on a new weariness, and he seemed loath to speak.

'There is more evil by far in this than you know of, men of the Quest,' he said, finally. 'Talarnidh, I must question you closely. Answer with care, for much depends on it. I ask about Selenthoril. Tell me who he claims to be.'

'His name is Selenthoril,' said Talarnidh, puzzlement on his face. 'It was a name given to him by the Guardians of the Sceptres. Before, men named him Banatem. He was the last of the High Magicians. He is the same one who gathered the hosts of the High Race in the War of the Sceptres, and broke the power of Ral.'

'Yes, — he is the same one,' answered Eldhoril. 'But *what* is Selenthoril?'

'He was one of the High Magicians, one of the Order of the Wise. They worked great things in Telmirandor, but they were mortal.'

'He is the last of these,' said Yeselwir.

Eldhoril smiled wearily.

'Yes, yes . . . He would need to be a mortal . . . That is why he would need to dwell in the Timeless Zone you spoke of.'

'So he told us,' answered Talarnidh. 'The timeless place was made for him by the Lord of the Sceptre Temporal before the Guardians of the Sceptres were slain and the Sceptres vanished.'

'He had no story of how that happened?' asked Eldhoril. '— No, and nor have I for sure. But all the rest I know well enough. I heard it all, a thousand years ago . . . And what of Selenthoril now? — He sits, trapped in his halls far away, and Ral has learnt of him. Despite her long struggle with me, Selenthoril is more important to her. She stretched out her hand north again, and in the nick of time Selenthoril found help. He had learnt of one of the lost Sceptres, and the means to find it came to his doorstep. — I wonder if he offered a prayer of thanks to his Goddess.' The Wizard gave a short bleak laugh.

'What does all this mean, Wizard of Wenyaltrir?' said Filindrin. 'Why this riddling talk? If you have something to tell us, then tell it and have done.'

Filindrin had not spoken before, and Eldhoril looked up at him.

'There are many riddles about your Quest, man of Alban. Some I have yet to pose to you. One I have solved. I am sure now, and I will tell you. It is not a good tale or a happy one. It is the grimmest you have heard for many years. I know of this Selenthoril. I know him well. I met him long ago. I know all about him. His true name is Niaherz, the Hooded One. He is the last of the Black Lords.'

'But he is the bearer of the Sceptre Spiritual!' cried Talarnidh. 'Eldhoril, great one, you are wrong. I have seen him!'

The Prince stood, fists clenched on the tabletop, his face twisted with anguish, his eyes fixed on Eldhoril.

'You must listen, Talarnidh. You must hear it all,' said Eldhoril. 'He does carry the Sceptre Spiritual, and he has the power to use it. He has used it to deceive you. He can give himself what shape he chooses. — Now listen, all of you.'

'You know that when Telmirandor was overthrown by Ral and the Black Lords the Sceptres were given to Guardians. The Guardian of the Sixth Sceptre, Spiritual, came down into the Underworld. With him were a good company of the High Race and Delwen, your mother, Talarnidh, and Elandril, your sister. They dwelt there long years. I do not know all that happened there, but the Guardian of the Sceptre and all his followers died. It was there that Selenthoril took the Sceptre, — and also Delwen and Elandril.'

'But if he is a Black Lord, why should he fear Ral?' cried Talarnidh. 'It cannot be, Eldhoril!'

'Selenthoril, the Hooded One, was the greatest of the Black Lords. He rebelled against his Queen and Goddess, and fled away into the Underworld. There he found the Sceptre, and also Delwen . . . Talarnidh, — you must know this . . . In his way he loved Delwen, your mother. He dwelt there with her. No, do not speak! There is nothing now to say. I searched for Delwen and Elandril, and found them. I too was deceived by Selenthoril's appearance. It was then that the Black Lords — other Black Lords — attacked and seized the Empress. They taunted Selenthoril as they held her, and named him as the Hooded One. In his rage Selenthoril put forth all the power of the Sceptre. He made Monsters of the Mind. The Black Lords died of sheer terror, — but so also died Delwen. I saw all this. And while all his power flowed into the Monsters, there was no disguise. I saw Selenthoril as the Hooded One. It was the Hooded One who knelt and wept over Delwen. I challenged him, and in his fury — for I was weak — I was defeated. I barely escaped alive. It was from his grief for Delwen that his fear of Ral turned into hatred. He blamed her for Delwen's death. Because of that was the War of the Sceptres.'

All eyes were on Talarnidh. Slowly he sat down, head bowed into his hands. At last he spoke, almost a whisper.

'I thank you that you searched for her . . . I am glad she died then, rather than return to him. — I think I believe it now. All of it . . . It is so cruel. The evil is so much, so much of it . . .'

'Hear the end of the story, Talarnidh. The bitterest is done. — The false Selenthoril spoke truly about the War of the Sceptres. He appeared to the High Race in fair form. He rallied them, and in the War of the Sceptres he had all his revenge on Ral, his mistress of old. He defeated Ral, and he and the Sceptre Bearers set up their court on Enchanter's Isle near the ancient heart of the realms of Ral, and hard by the Black Land. He prepared to restore the power of Wenyaltrir. Messengers went forth and the ancient strongholds were reoccupied.'

'Yes,' said Fandorel. 'I was with the hosts of the High Race on Misen Taïrail, I and Wondrith and Tasarnil who lie now in that island. I was sent away by the Lords of the Sceptres to Talarnidh and those who came from the West.'

'While all this was happening, I lay in the darkness beneath the world. At length the people of my Sceptre cared for me, Gnomes and stranger creatures still. Finally I was able to set off in pursuit of the false Selenthoril. I learnt much as I returned to the Midworld of how he had deceived the Peiri and the allies of the High Race. I went on the wings of the wind to Nyaroth Khrathril. The Sylphs bore me through the mist barriers along the secret way into Selenthoril's castle. Before the Lords of the High Race I named him Niaherz, the Hooded One. But he bore the Sceptre Spiritual, and was great in its power. The Sceptre Bearers saw the Hooded One, — but they saw him as Me, — not as Selenthoril. Once again the Sceptre deceived them. They bound me in bands of gold and cast me into the dungeons.'

'But I had set the suspicion, and Selenthoril was no longer sure of himself. He resolved that he must kill the Sceptre Bearers, and again the Monsters of the Mind stalked in the night. I alone was prepared for the attack; only I did not die that night, out of all the host of the High Race on the island. But the following day Selenthoril came to me, screaming his rage. For though all the Sceptre Bearers lay dead, their Sceptres were gone. He blamed me, and tried to find the truth of how I had done this deed.'

'I yet had some sorcery left. I broke the chains, and called the Sylphs and wind giants to me. There was a great battle fought in the sky by the unreal creatures of Selenthoril's making and the forces of the Elements. Even wind giants were maddened by the Sceptre Spiritual. My power over my Sceptre was weakened. For never before had Sceptre fought Sceptre. — I believe Selenthoril's hold over Spiritual was also damaged. At the last my forces fled in confusion southwards. Finally broken, I fell into the Forest of Sorcery and lay long as one dead.'

'But Selenthoril too was trapped in the timeless place, lost in mists. Though he sought for the Sceptres that had vanished away, he never found them. Nor did any who searched for him and the lost hosts of the High Race find any but the dead and terrible tales. Years went by and the lands of the North were peopled again. Even in the far north the frightened remnants came out of their hiding places. Only Sart Emig remained desolate, and only in the Forest of Sorcery did the old fear linger. Here in that forest I made my dwelling, and watched and waited, and slowly let my strength grow again.'

'I thought little about Selenthoril in all those years. I had pieced together most of his story, as I have now told it to you. I guessed that he was trapped forever on his island. Meanwhile, near to me in the forest grew a shadow. I have said that the old fear lingered. It also grew and spread itself. I began to fight against it. Years, then hundreds of years, went by, and I knew that Ral had not died. I knew that she was here in the forest. Her power increased slowly, but still swifter than mine. Of late I have only waited for the time she might choose to come against me. It would have come already had she not found Selenthoril again. She had turned her eyes away from me and towards him. Now all her thoughts are focussed here in the forest once again. The Sceptre Mortal is loose in the world. She must attack at once.'

'I do not know what is more bitter evil,' said Talarnidh, 'the tale of my mother's death and desolation a thousand years and more gone by, — or the tale of my own wrong now. I have been the servant of the Hooded One, O Eldhoril.'

'You fought against Ral. Does it matter who it was that you fought for?' asked Eldhoril.

'I betrayed the Sceptre to her. I have not forgotten that, though no-one will speak of it to me. Does it matter that I thought I had condemned Selenthoril to death, and now I find that I have condemned Eldhoril? The doom is the same.'

'The doom is not sure. It may yet be the doom of Ral,' answered the Wizard.

'There is this, Talarnidh,' cut in Filindrin. 'Had your Quest not failed, you would have set up Selenthoril in the place of Ral. We may be thankful it did fail.'

'It was your Quest also, Filindrin,' snapped Karandar.

'No, Karandar, Filindrin is right. He has always been right. I have listened to him too little. I have been a fool and a dupe and a traitor. I have led many of my friends to foul and monstrous deaths. — And all this for what? — To try and set up a Dark Lord in the place of the White Goddess. The last of the Black Lords, — that is my master.'

'The same that defiled your mother, and still holds your sister,' said the inexorable grim and level voice of Filindrin.

Karandar sprang to his feet.

'Now you do go too far!' he shouted. 'Beware, or there will come a time for a reckoning between us, Filindrin!'

'Karandar, leave him! He is sick in his soul,' cried Fandorel.

'Elf Lord, be assured my soul thrives and grows strong. — If the Dwarf Lord were to come and fight me now, his life would be short. I have said nothing that is not true, and if I alone have the courage to say it aloud, that is my strength. Is that not so, Talarnidh?'

'Filindrin, I do not know where our friendship has gone. I wish you had chosen to go away from this castle earlier today. I wish you had not told me the truth all along our way, — as you tell me the truth now. Yes, he has Elandril my sister. I will go back to Misen Taïrail, — to kill the false Selenthoril or be killed by him.'

'When will you go?' asked Filindrin, a cold smile on his mouth. 'Have you forgotten about Ral, your other sister?'

'You let me forget nothing,' said Talarnidh.

'Your family has been cursed since Sagoth came to your sister,' said Filindrin. And he spoke with the coldness of utter uncaring, and when he said the name 'Sagoth' his voice was the hiss of a serpent. 'Sagoth came to Lidhelm at the moment of her womanhood; he raped and defiled her. She bore his child, the child of the Devil. They took the child from her, and she hated them for it. Her name became Ral, the word for Witch in the Old High Speech. She killed her brother Talmoran. In the end she was the instrument of the destruction of her people, and the death of her father, Talmond. The curse of Sagoth lies on your whole family, Talarnidh, your father who is lost, your mother who bore you and loved a Black Lord, your sister Ral, your sister Elandril, and now you who are broken. Now is not the time for any choice or decision on your part. There is no revenge for you, not on Ral, and not on Selenthoril.'

'Then you tell me, Filindrin! You tell me what I am to do!' said Talarnidh, but he seemed to stare straight through him, and his words, though clear, had no expression.

'You have done your work, Filindrin,' said Eldhoril, 'though I do not know why you have done it. It is not your place to tell the Prince Talarnidh anything. — Talarnidh! You are in my house, and you are a lord of my people. I ask for your aid in the battle that will come. Stay here and fight against Ral, Talarnidh!'

'I will do what you bid me, Eldhoril. I will serve you as you wish and command,' Talarnidh answered, speaking slowly and with a long sigh.

'And the company you command will obey you,' said Eldhoril. 'For you are the Prince of Wenyaltrir. — Even Filindrin will obey you.'

'I have no right to ask them,' said Talarnidh.

'There is no asking needed,' answered Eldhoril. '— Is there, Filindrin?'

Filindrin looked up from the council table and smiled.

'You were never a fool, Wizard of Wenyaltrir,' answered Filindrin. 'Yes, we will stay here and fight. I will fight Ral, for Ral is my enemy too. But it will be a short fight and a poor one, and the long darkness for many, if Ral has in her hands the Sceptre Mortal when she comes to your fortress, Eldhoril.'

'That is the next matter, Filindrin. — You are right that I am not a fool. I have thought long of Ral and of the Sceptre since I first heard word of it today. But now I wish to hear all that the men of the Quest know of the Sceptre, all that any of you have heard of it. But above all I must know every last detail that each of you can remember of when and where and how he last saw the Sceptre and the man who has it.'

'Filindrin and Talak were the last to see Melandir,' said Yeselwir, 'in the house of the Witchweird. But Filindrin was unconscious. It was Talak who brought him out of the house.'

'Then we will hear from Talak,' said Eldhoril. 'Stand up, child. Speak out and tell us exactly what you saw. Do not leave anything out.'

Talak stood hesitantly. All the others except Filindrin had sat down again round the table. Filindrin alone stood at one of the windows, behind Talak.

'I was in the room with my master, Lord Melandir,' said Talak. 'I woke up and saw that Ral was there. She was trying to get the Sceptre. Then my father came in. He broke the windows and let the air in. That broke the spell. But she turned on my father. She said another spell. And I saw his hands . . .'

'The spell failed,' said Filindrin from the window.

'What manner of spell was it?' asked Erathrir.

'It was an illusion,' said Filindrin. 'She and her kind seek to frighten their enemies by changing the seeming of things. But I have grown strong against such things since I passed through the land of Aldel Morn.'

'Where all the pity was taken out of you,' said Karandar quietly.

'What did you see, Talak?' asked Eldhoril sharply.

'My father's hands, and his face. The flesh . . . I saw the flesh rot away . . .'

Talak looked at Filindrin, wide-eyed and unsure, but his glance was met by the broad bland empty smile.

'An unpleasant deception. My son is a child though, and has not the will to withstand. Is that not so, boy?'

'Yes . . .' said Talak hesitantly, shaking his head. 'I do not understand . . .'

'Tell the rest of your story, Talak,' said Eldhoril.

Talak looked from Filindrin to Eldhoril, then back to his father.

'I do not understand,' he said again. 'There was a monster made out of fire.'

'How was it called up?' asked Karandar.

Talak's eyes were held by those of Filindrin.

'It was summoned by Ral,' said Filindrin.

'Can she call Demons out of Hell?' asked Eldhoril.

'I am not acquainted with the extent of her powers,' answered Filindrin. 'You will have to ask my son, as he saw it all. — Didn't you, boy?'

'What was it like, Talak?' asked Relnar in a gentle voice. But Talak's voice now shook with fear.

'I do not know . . . It was like my father said.'

'You saw Ral call up the Fire Demon from Hell itself?' said Filindrin, a voice like ice.

'Yes,' said Talak, and now he spoke in the merest whisper.

'It is the same as the great Hound,' said Relnar again.

Filindrin laughed suddenly, seemingly for no reason.

'Yes, we had forgotten the Hound of Hell. — It seems that Ral is already greater now than she ever was before.'

'I had not forgotten the Hound,' said Eldhoril.

'And I do not know why Ral and this mighty Fire Demon did not take the Sceptre,' said Karandar. 'You are too eager to magnify her powers, Filindrin.'

'I do not magnify them, Dwarf. Few who call on the powers of Hell have real mastery over them. I saw it all. She could not hold the Demon. It overmastered her. She fled screaming. That is why she did not take the Sceptre.'

'Did you see that, Talak?' asked Erathrir.

'She flew past it like a bat,' answered Talak. 'She was screaming from the fire.'

'Did she take the Sceptre from Melandir?' said Erathrir. Talak looked round helplessly.

'Well, answer,' snapped Filindrin. 'What are you afraid of?'

'No, no, she did not take it,' said Talak. 'She did not go near Melandir. She flew through the window. But there were flames. Fire everywhere! It went over my father too. It went over both of them. I could not see where my father lay. My Lord Melandir was in the centre of the fire. It was everywhere. Oh, leave me, leave me alone! I do not know anything!'

He collapsed suddenly into the chair, his face buried in his arms, his body shaken by sobs. Relnar went swiftly and knelt beside him, putting his hand on his head.

'Do not ask him anything else,' he said.

'Talak, go out now with Relnar,' said Eldhoril softly. 'The Sylphs will take you to the room they have prepared for you. Rest there. Come back when you feel better. We will not ask you anything else.'

Talak stood up and turned to go, but even then he had to look swiftly at Filindrin. Filindrin said nothing. His lip curled, and he looked away. Talak sobbed again.

'Talak,' said Erathrir suddenly. 'Was Melandir holding the Sword?'

'Yes, yes. My master was holding the Sword,' answered Talak, his whole body shaking as Relnar held him.

'I am sorry,' said Erathrir when the two had gone out, 'but that question had to be asked.'

'I understand the meaning of the Sword well enough,' said Eldhoril. 'I knew much of its history. Today I have learnt a little more. It is clear that the fire of the Demon filled the room. It should have killed any mortal man. But the man, Melandir, was the bearer of Wenyorel. If he was holding the Sword in his hand when the fire came over him, then I do not believe he can have died.'

'Then where is he?' asked Filindrin. 'I saw the room full of fire, — just as you heard from my weakling of a son, and Melandir was in the very midst of it.'

'Your son was weakling enough to rescue you from the fire,'

said Karandar. 'He has told us that you too were there in the midst of the fire.'

'I dived beneath it,' answered Filindrin. 'I was overcome by the smoke, while trying to rescue Melandir. — Hardly hurt at all . . . The boy helped me to get out, in between his screaming and terror. You need not pay too close heed to everything he says.'

'Except that Melandir was in the midst of the fire,' said Erathrir.

'The Sylph Whirrirrish went in to find him,' said Fandorel.

'My people the Sylphs are not easily subdued by fire,' responded Eldhoril.

'Then where are the Sylph and Melandir now?' asked Filindrin.

'We have seen nothing at all of them since then,' agreed Yeselwir.

'But in the forest, when we searched for Melandir,' said Fandorel, '— do you not remember, Filindrin, how often you told Talarnidh: "If Ral has the Sceptre, we are as good as dead already"? Filindrin, you have lost hope as well as pity.'

'I have my hopes,' answered Filindrin. '— So tell me, Elf Lord Fandorel, where is the Sceptre now? For it is plain that you do not think Ral has it.'

'I do not know where it is. I believe Melandir and Whirrirrish may well have escaped into the forest. Both may be sorely hurt. No, I do not think Ral has it, Filindrin. — Do you think she has?'

'No,' Filindrin answered.

'Perhaps the Sceptre was destroyed,' said Yeselwir. 'Or it might still be in the ruins of the house. We could search the ruins of the house.'

Filindrin laughed.

'Do you think Ral has not sifted through its ashes time and again by now?' he said. 'No, the Sceptre was not destroyed, nor has Melandir inadvertently dropped it. Not if he held the Sword.'

'This time I believe Filindrin is right,' said Erathrir. 'Melandir may be hurt or under a spell. But he did not drop the Sword. He did not die. He still has the Sceptre.'

CHAPTER 18

SAGOTH SON OF THE MORNING

As dawn broke dull and icy over the Northlands, a messenger came to Eldhoril, flying weary and hurt from the north. He was the first of the Sylphs that the Lord of the Sceptre Elemental had set to watch the lands of Ral. Others came as the grey and sunless morning wore on. They all told the same. The armies of Ral were on the move. By the time a cold and watery sun had come up over the tree-tops Eldhoril knew that Ral herself had come out of Thulgarn, her great fortress. With her was the full strength of the Goblin army.

One by one the men of the Quest-that-was-broken came into the room of counsel, and were told of the coming of Ral. All of them were refreshed in body. All now knew that their former purpose was ended. They heard the news of the coming war silent and grim-faced for the most part. Only when all were assembled did Eldhoril sit down with them at the great table.

'Why has it come now?' asked Talarnidh, before Eldhoril could speak.

'Because Ral knows you are here,' Eldhoril answered. 'Perhaps she may fear that if she does not attack now, we may, be it in days or in weeks, have the Sceptre. She must even fear that we already have it.'

'She would know that if we had it, it would have been claimed and we would have killed her,' said Filindrin. 'The reasoning we have applied to her must also apply to us.'

'What are her forces?' Talarnidh asked.

'She has to collect them from far afield. Unless she intends a siege she will only be able to bring her immediate strength. There are Goblin bands near us, not only northwards, but east and west as well. Then there is the main strength of her army at Thulgarn. That has always been the heart of her power. I believe that the Sword of Doom is undoubtedly there, and from it she can drink in power as she did of old. Her forces there may be seven thousand — perhaps even more — mostly Goblins but some Trolls, and Giants also. And the great Werebats from the pit. So much my spies have been able to tell me. I believe she will gather another three thousand on the march. I doubt it will be many more.'

'How many do you have?' asked Talarnidh.

'I have my Elementals. They could fight in a battle. But for the most part they live far away in the places of their own elements. I have my servants who dwell here, and those that I can easily call for. There are perhaps a few hundred Gnomes, some of them Deep Gnomes, a thousand Sylphs, a very few Ice Undines and Salamanders.'

'Is that all?' said Relnar.

'You cannot bring the army of Chamley here, Relnar,' said Yeselwir.

'I wish I could,' the young prince answered.

'There are the Woodmen who live in the southern part of the forest,' said Eldhoril. 'Many of them are under my protection and will come if I call them. I have already sent messengers throughout the forest. There are also Elves. They will certainly come. They give allegiance to Ciranouth.'

'I know him,' said Fandorel. 'We met once, but that was in the days of Wenyaltrir. He was a mighty lord then.'

'He commands maybe a thousand warriors of the Elves, no more,' said Eldhoril.

'How many in the whole army?' asked Talarnidh.

'Three thousand, perhaps,' said Eldhoril. 'Decide now, Talarnidh. I know what is in your mind. Will you lead my little army?'

Talarnidh sat a long time, then rose and strode to look out of the window onto the treeless plain amid the forest.

'Can we retire into the castle and hold it against siege?'

'The mountain is full of passages. There are many ways up to the castle. I did not at first build it for defence. — We might hold it, but we have not enough people to do the job properly.'

'And we will decline while the forces of Ral grow greater every day,' said Talarnidh. 'We will go out and fight them, — there on the plain below. Yes, I will lead your little army, Lord Eldhoril. How can I do otherwise? My men will fight with me.'

'So you give command again,' said Filindrin.

'Yes, I give command, Filindrin. Obey me, or go at once.'

'Go? Where, Talarnidh? You brought us here . . . And I would not miss the fight now.'

'Then you are good for war, if nothing else,' snapped Talarnidh.

'I hope you are as good at generalship,' answered Filindrin. But Talarnidh only turned away from him, and spoke to Eldhoril:

'You must send at once to the halls of Iroi Girindhouz, the Pine Lord. He may come to our aid.'

'The lands of the Pine Woses are well to the north. The power of Ral is near around them. If they serve anyone, it will be her.'

'Not so,' answered Talarnidh. 'Send him this message: "Talarnidh, son of Talmond, summons Iroi Girindhouz, Lord of the Lords of the Pines, to come to the Ice Castle of Eldhoril with all his host, and mend the broken promise of a thousand years." '

Eldhoril looked long at Talarnidh, but the Prince said nothing more.

'The Sylphs will take the message,' said Eldhoril.

'What of Melandir?' asked Erathrir.

'My Sylphs have reached the ruins of the House in the Forest. It is thick with Goblins searching.'

'So we now know for certain that she does not have the Sceptre,' said Filindrin.

'And that Melandir is free,' said Erathrir.

'My people have hiding places deep in the heartlands of Ral's domain,' said Eldhoril. 'If Whirrirrish brought him out of the house he may have taken him to one of them. But little news comes to us now from beyond my frontiers.'

'Will the message reach the Pine Lord?' asked Talarnidh.

'It may,' was all Eldhoril would answer.

'Why are the woods so dangerous for your spies?' asked Yeselwir. 'The Goblins should all be with Ral's army.'

'They are searching the forest for the Sceptre, are they not Eldhoril?' said Filindrin.

'So it would seem', said the Wizard. 'But she has not let that delay her advance.'

'How long do we have?' asked Talarnidh.

'A week, I judge,' said Eldhoril. 'I have not sent to any of my allies that dwell more than four days' march away.'

The day passed in talk and plans, fruitless hopes, and the coming of messengers from the north. They weighed their chances in the coming battle and counted them little. Night came, and away to the northward the forest was alive with the fires of the camp of Ral, a dark flock of bats like a cloud above it.

On the following day Erathrir looked out of the window in the mountain.

'There is something in the sky!' he called. 'Far away to the north.'

They all looked out.

'It is a Dragon,' said Talarnidh. 'We did not count any such in Ral's forces. If she has Dragons we cannot fight on the plain.'

'They can be killed by sorcery,' said Filindrin.

'Ral is unwise to call on the Dragons,' answered Eldhoril. 'I command more Dragons here than Ral can summon.'

Talarnidh looked sharply toward the Wizard.

'You did not speak of them.'

'I did not intend to wake them. I do not wish to wake them. But now we must.'

'Do Dragons sleep in the winter?' asked Relnar.

'They have slept for more than a thousand years,' replied Eldhoril. 'Once awakened those that survive will not sleep for another ten centuries.'

'I had heard that all Dragons were evil,' said Erathrir.

'Many are greedy for gold,' answered Karandar. 'Those, once their treasure is won by wrong, sit guarding it forever. Others are born with evil souls. Some have come out of the Underworld. — But there were Dragons who served the High Race and were friends of Wenyaltrir.'

'Those that remain of them are here,' said Eldhoril. 'They are Ice Dragons for the most part.'

'Where did the Dragons come from?' Talak asked hesitantly.

'Some came from the Time Before Time,' Eldhoril answered. 'Some were born into the world. Of that first kind I know of only one. — They were never mindless creatures like the great lizards that linger yet in the world.'

'There are such lizards in the marsh of Nyaroth Khrathril,' said Erathrir.

'Can you rouse the Dragons now, Lord Eldhoril?' asked Fandorel.

'I can wake them. The Silver Horn must sound. I will go now. I have had it in my keeping these many years. But know this, it will rouse all the Dragons in the Northlands. All those who hear it will wake wherever they sleep. Some may come from afar to our aid. Some may go loose in the world.'

'And there will be no man with a magic sword to rid the people of them, Talarnidh,' said Filindrin. 'Remember the Dragon that came to your land of Alban!'

'Yes, Filindrin, I remember,' Talarnidh answered. 'But you have no choice to offer us other than waking the Dragons. You are only taunting me . . . Have done with it. — Go, Eldhoril, waken your Dragons!'

Eldhoril passed swiftly through the ways in the mountain to the Ice Castle above. From a chest of crystal figured with runes he took out the horn, a thin curved shape of silver, beaten so fine that it seemed almost as if the light passed through it, so old that the shapes of Dragons carved on it were almost worn away. With the horn he went on up into the heights of the castle till he stood on the pinnacle. He put the horn to his lips and blew a long note upon it. The sound rang in the ice and filled the air, and drifted into vast distances of space. Far below him in dark caves he sensed a slow movement.

He blew a second note, higher and more shrill, and huge shapes moved in their mountain halls. Bright eyes winked red in the darkness, and vast slow breaths beat in the echoing caves. A third time he sounded the horn and all the forest seemed to quiver at the note, while ripples of wind ran all about the castle. In the rock beneath, the Dragons awakened, and great wings crackled and stretched.

Eldhoril sensed the scaly forms moving, but when he looked away to the north he saw other things. With more than mortal sight he saw the movement in the forest and on the road. It was the host of Ral. The war came nearer. He went down again into the mountain and came to the counsel chamber. Talarnidh, Erathrir, Karandar, and Fandorel were there.

'I am going to the Dragon Caves,' he said. 'Come with me.'

They went down into the utter darkness beneath the mountain, where the Gnomes had cut and burrowed over the ages through the regions of solid granite. Dark passages branched off from the way they took and ever and again they heard distant hammering, often so far beneath them that the sounds were the faintest echoes. Eldhoril lit their way as they passed out from under the mountain into an endless network of natural caves, more immense than any hall of man. These were the Dragon Caves.

They stood in a chamber so vast that its end could not be seen. From it many high tunnels led away. A faint hint of a cold breeze on their faces told them that somewhere was a way to the air outside. They stood silent, and slowly the many sounds that filled the cave became apparent to them. In all the tunnels were the faint echoings of mighty breaths, like gusts of gale afar off.

Eldhoril began to speak, a strange sibilant chant in a tongue unknown to all of them. It was the Dragon Speech. Long he spoke, his voice rising to a great sound, then dying away in whispers. It was like a voice from another world, remote and unhuman. The four of them shivered at the sound of it. At length he stopped, and when he turned to them they saw that there were beads of sweat on his brow despite the chill of the air.

'Now we must wait a moment or two. Then you will hear a Dragon speak again, Talarnidh.'

'Do they speak then?' Erathrir asked.

'O, they speak, and none who have heard them forget the sound of that speech,' said Karandar. 'I have heard it a few times, long ago. — I did not think I would ever hear it again.'

There was a silence, and then the voice of the Dragon.

'Hail, Eldhoril the Wizard!'

It was a sudden snake-like hissing voice from one of the caverns behind them. They swung round sharply. Though the words were in the Northspeech, it was altered so that the sound was unearthly and the words subtly changed to the same cadences they had heard when Eldhoril spoke the tongue of Dragons.

'I have not been asleep. I have heard much. I have heard near and far. I know who has come here. I know who is coming here. She is not far now.'

'I welcome you and greet you, Dagdaloun the Old,' answered Eldhoril.

'They are all awake, Wizard. Speak to them. They hear you.'

Again Eldhoril's voice took on the haunting nature of the Dragon Speech as he spoke it to the silent listeners.

'What have you told them?' asked Fandorel.

It was the voice of the Dragon that answered.

'That Ral comes. That war is near. The horn has called us. We have heard it. We are called to the war. As of old we are called. We wake. We will come.'

'What have you heard, Dagdaloun the Old?' said Eldhoril. 'Tell me of the one who is coming.'

'Ral is coming from Thulgarn. Ral the Fair. Ral the Witch Queen. Ral the Great Goddess.'

'Is that all you know of Ral? That much I know.'

'I know this. The trees quiver as many Goblins pass.'

'How many?'

'I hear ten thousand. And more perhaps —.'

'How can he know this?' asked Erathrir.

'They hear and scent things over hundreds of miles,' answered Eldhoril. 'Their senses are not mortal. They come from before time, some of them, and do not obey the laws of this world.'

'I scent something in your castle, Wizard. I scent strangeness. It has the smell of night. It is old, but I am older. Its shape is hideous and always changes. It flies in the storm. It speaks fire.'

'What does this mean?' asked Erathrir.

'It is riddling talk, the talk of Dragons,' Karandar answered.

'Then what might be the answer to the riddle?' asked Eldhoril.

'I do not know,' came the answer of the Dragon.

'I do not understand this at all,' said Erathrir.

'It may be important,' responded Eldhoril. 'The Dragon would not speak without reason. Dagdaloun, what does the riddle mean?'

'I will tell to you the puzzle, Wizard, but I cannot tell you the answer. There are strangers here, and I know their names. I heard. I was listening all the while when they told. I know all the tale of their journey.'

'We came to fight Ral for the false Selenthoril,' replied Talarnidh. 'All our way she has pursued us. We have suffered grievously through my fault and in ill cause.'

'And there is the riddle,' answered the Dragon voice. 'I will tell you again some of your story, as I heard you tell it. But I have put the pieces together. They are the riddle. First this. Four went in to Aldel Morn. How many came out? One came out as a skeleton. That was Turnalordath. One came out as a living corpse. That was Fermilondath. One did not come out. But the Hound of Hell came in his place. That was Wondrith. Where did the Hound come from? What made the dead walk?'

'Then there is this. The fourth man did come out of Aldel Morn. That is Filindrin. He is here. Before he went in he was your friend. Now he comes out, he hates you. What happened to him in Aldel Morn? Then there is this. In the House in the Forest, the Demon of Fire came out of Hell. Hell is where the Hound of Hell dwells. What made two of the dwellers in Hell come up to the earth? That is the riddle.'

'But many other things happened to us,' said Karandar. 'There were the Rethrind in Emrurl Arnag. There was the Sentinel in Wirdrilded that killed Tasarnil.'

'There were the Giants in Belengar,' added Fandorel.

'Ral has ruled the Giants of Belengar for many years,' said the Dragon. 'Ral put the Sentinel in Wirdrilded to do her will. Ral was worshipped by the Rethrind in the days of her power. There is no riddle. Ral was your enemy.'

'Aldel Morn was once the dwelling place of Ral also,' said Talarnidh. 'Do you not think that all the evil which befell our company there also came from Ral?'

'The Black Lords of Ral built in Grathgel. That only. It is a land from before Ral. It was evil when Ral was not even in the world. It was made by Sagoth.'

There was silence at the name.

'Dagdaloun is saying that there is some evil at work among us other than Ral,' said Fandorel.

'The riddle is this,' said the Dragon. 'Evils of evils have come upon you. Ral is not so strong as that. Does Ral command Demons? Does Ral command the great Hound? — Ral is on her way here. Ral has ten thousand Goblins. Ral is not the answer to the riddle.'

'Filindrin saw Ral call up the Fire Demon,' said Talarnidh. 'So did Talak.'

'They say they saw it. They may think they saw it. Did each see the same? What did they see?' asked the Dragon.

'What about the Wild Hunt?' asked Erathrir.

'The Huntsman comes when the Beasts of Hell walk. The Huntsman comes when the Beasts of Heaven walk. The Huntsman guards the boundaries of the world. He hunts the beasts of the earth and the sky down the tunnels of ages. He does not hunt Ral. That is the riddle.'

'What else is there?' asked Eldhoril.

'I sense something strange in your castle, Wizard. I will say what I scent. I scent fear. I scent despair. I scent death. I scent doom. That is the riddle I scent. I say no more. I puzzle the puzzle. I wait and I watch and I puzzle the puzzle. — We will come when the Wizard calls. Soon there will be other pieces of the riddle. The riddle will grow when the war comes here.' The echoes of the voice died into eerie silence.

'I do not like this, Eldhoril,' said Talarnidh. 'I do not understand it. Is there something in the Dragon's talk, or is there nothing?'

'Dragons make riddles from a wisp of straw,' said Eldhoril. 'All their talk is so. But Dagdaloun the Old is different. He is the last of the Dragons that came from the Uttermost Beginning. I had known that all was not well. The Dragon is right. There is a riddle. And the more I think of the riddle the less I understand its meaning.'

'It means evil if it means anything,' said Talarnidh. 'It changes nothing in the war to come though. If it means that Ral has great power, we must fight her the same. If it means that there is some other evil in the world, that we knew already.'

'Talarnidh has lost hope since the end of the Quest,' said Fandorel to Karandar as they followed the Wizard out of the Dragon Caves.

'He has become grim and harder,' answered the Dwarf. 'He will be more deadly a foe to Ral when the battle comes though.'

And so the second day of their waiting passed, and like it the third day. Evening drew on when the first of their allies arrived at the foot of the mountain. Flying through the darkening sky they came with the beat of gossamere wings, hundred upon hundred of them, and the last afterglow of the sun caught like flecks of silver in their flight. They were the Wood Elves of Ciranouth, and in their hands they bore the great bows that the Elves had always used in their wars. Fandorel went down with Eldhoril, and greeted the Elf Lord. The two of the Elvenkind clasped hands and embraced, for many years had separated them. The Elven host did not enter the mountain, but made camp in the forest on its eastern slopes. The night became cheery with their singing. And the morning came of the fourth day.

Through the fourth and fifth days, with the cold flurries of snow, the little armies of the remaining allies arrived. Four bands of Woodmen came in, all from the south, perhaps six hundred in all, axemen and spearmen. They had sent their families to hide in the deep forest and the hills, and now they came to Eldhoril's call. Their leaders were mounted on mighty stags.

Unexpected allies were the Dwarves, three hundred strong, from the hills to the east. Eldhoril had sent to them, but had had little hope of their coming. They had not served him before, but hatred of Ral had brought them, forcing their way through the bands of Goblins already foraging in the forest between their own hills and the Ice Castle. When they saw Karandar they rejoiced that they had come, for he was accounted the greatest of the Dwarves that yet lived, and many tales were told of him.

On the afternoon of the sixth day, Eldhoril entered the room of counsel to find Talarnidh and all the company with the leaders of the Elves and Dwarves and Woodmen. All were armed, many wore their armour.

'Then you have seen it also,' said the Wizard. 'They have come.'

Out on the treeless plain a great army spread itself, rank upon rank of Goblin soldiers, and the flash of waving spears and iron helmets. More and more they came, along the road, and then marched into the plain, some to the right, some to the left, but most forming a great mass in the centre. It was as if the company watched for hours while their enemy occupied the farther part of the plain. Above the Goblins wheeled flocks of bats, so many that they hid the forest behind.

'They are better disciplined than I had expected,' said Karandar. 'She has drilled them well.'

'And there are many more of them,' said Talarnidh. 'Three or four thousand more than we had guessed.'

'Can we expect any more help?' asked Relnar.

'None,' answered Eldhoril.

'And there is no news of Melandir,' said Erathrir. 'And no word from the Pine Lord.'

'We will fight with what we have here,' answered Talarnidh.

'We could have attacked them as they marched, or ambushed them as they came into the plain,' said Yeselwir.

'We have no forces to waste. We will not divide the army.'

As Talarnidh spoke, there came a great braying of horns from the enemy host. They looked out again and saw that they had halted. Slowly the ranks broke up and spread out. Tents began to be set up on the plain. The Goblin army made camp in sight of their foe.

'They are contemptuous of us,' said Fandorel.

'I am glad they have chosen to delay,' Talarnidh answered. '— Relnar, spread out on the table the map I have made. We will set out our array for the last time.'

'We know it well enough already,' said Filindrin. 'We should instead be preparing a night attack on their camp.'

'They will be prepared for that,' Talarnidh answered. 'They will fight better at night than our people. Have you forgotten, — they are born of night. Nor will I waste our forces. We do not have enough.'

He pointed to the drawing of the mountain on the parchment.

'Eldhoril will be here at the gate. He has the Sceptre Elemental if need be. He has the horn that will summon the Dragons. Before him will be most of our strength: Ciranouth and all the Elves, and the Sylphs with their commander, Safaarasaa. On our right will be the Dwarves, and they have accepted Karandar as their captain. Erathrir will stay with him, and keep contact between the Dwarves and our centre. The Earth Elementals, the Gnomes, will be with the Dwarves. On the left will be all the Woodmen. Ganakhrin here is their leader. Yeselwir will go with him, and his post also will be to keep contact with me and the centre. Fandorel will stay with Ciranouth and his own people. Relnar and Talak will stay with me to be my messengers.'

'You have not named me,' said Filindrin.

'Where do you wish to take your stand?' asked Talarnidh.

'Why, with my Prince and with my son,' answered Filindrin. 'Here, in the very centre.'

His finger pressed hard on the map.

'Beside me,' said Talarnidh.

'What now?' asked Erathrir. 'We know all we need to know. We know what we have to do.'

'Now, you go to sleep. — The Sylphs are keeping watch on the enemy camp. The Elves lie in wait in the forests beside the mountain. We are prepared against a surprise attack. Tomorrow we wake early for war.'

The first light of the earliest dawn fell through the window in Filindrin's chambers. Talak stood silently looking out. Below there were Elven soldiers and blue Sylph warriors moving out from the woods and the mountain. Further away was the haze of smoke from many fires, and a distant clatter and shouting. Talak shivered. Since they had come to the Ice Castle he had slept in this room next to where Filindrin slept. In that time the man who was his father had added to the fear. His every word made Talak more fearful and more alone.

A sudden sound came from the next room. Talak started, then walked to the door and listened. Filindrin expected Talak to attend him each morning when he rose. Quietly the boy now opened the door. The sound he had heard became clearer, a whispering, whistling sighing that filled the room, a sound sick with anguish. Talak saw the dark silhouette of his father against the window.

Around the dark shape of the man a mist hovered, full of changing colours, shaping itself into vivid wings, ever more solid as Talak watched. The man-shape became less clear, hunched and shadowy, and a heart of blackness was in it, unnaturally dark. The air seemed full of murk, and the substance of the great awful wings flowed into space and flowed back. The air reeked with a scent now sweet and decaying, now sulphurous and bitter. Then came the voice from the figure that had been Filindrin. It was no voice of the world, too chillingly sweet, softer than a woman's voice. And as the words were spoken, the huge wings became black and solid, and the reek in the air became a foul cloud.

'The Sun of Victory dawns for Sagoth Son of the Morning.'

So spoke the sweet dead voice from the dark shape that Filindrin had become.

Talak choked on the fumes, and the shape shook before his eyes. The wings seemed to fade and become only uplifted arms robed in black and silver. Slowly the figure turned and Talak looked into a smile carven on Filindrin's face, looked into the empty eyes of a corpse. Smokes fled away from the figure of his father through the window, and the hideous sighing of dead souls faded into the most complete silence.

'No! . . . No! . . .' said Talak, shaking his head as if to shake the vision out of his mind.

In a second Filindrin's hand had fastened on his arm, and the grim face was pressed close up to Talak's. The boy tried to cover his eyes with his other hand, but Filindrin struck it away.

'Look at me! Look well! Look closely!' he commanded. And Talak could not but obey. 'Now tell me! Tell me who I am!'

'I do not know,' answered Talak, writhing in the grasp, his face pale and frightened.

Filindrin struck him with all his might across his face. Talak's head snapped to one side. Blood ran from the corner of his mouth and from his cheek. He fell back through the doorway into his own room. Filindrin followed him.

'What did you hear? What name? What name?'

Talak said nothing, and again his head jerked across at Filindrin's blow. More blood ran from his torn lips.

'Sagoth!' said Filindrin. 'Do you remember the name?'

Talak nodded wordless.

'What is Sagoth?' asked Filindrin, and now he held both of the boy's arms, and had lifted Talak like a doll off the ground.

'The Devil,' came the answer, the faintest of whispers.

'Then who am I?' asked Filindrin.

Talak's head shook again, his eyes wide, his mouth open and gasping, blood on his face.

'You know! You know, boy! Is it not true? — Do you know who I am?'

'Yes,' whispered Talak.

Suddenly Filindrin flung the boy from him, hurling him against the wall. Talak's body twisted in the air, and crashed into a corner of the room. The boy screamed aloud and clasped at his side. The cracking of his ribs left him sick and fainting.

'Who is your father, boy?' asked Filindrin.

'No . . . no . . .' whispered Talak.

Groaning and stricken he reached out a hand towards Filindrin. The dark figure looked down on him, and the smile which had never left his face grew wider. Sunlight glinted from his breastplate.

'The Sun of Victory dawns,' he said, 'for Sagoth Son of the Morning. — Your father is Sagoth, child, — the Devil.'

And as he spoke he brought the heel of his boot down onto Talak's outstretched pleading hand. The bones of the wrist snapped aloud. Talak fainted.

Still smiling, the body of Filindrin went out to war, and in it was Sagoth, Son of the Morning.

CHAPTER 19

BATTLE OF THE TREELESS PLAIN

With the beating of many deep drums the army of Ral moved down the treeless plain towards the door of the mountain before which stood the little army of Eldhoril. The Goblin centre was a vast close-packed mass, many and many ranks deep. All of them bore long spears, many were armoured. In the very centre of them were huge forms of Stone Trolls, taller than the tallest man. In places stood Giants, twenty or thirty feet high. Of the Goblins, each of the tribes was there. Some were almost elf-like, one or two of them with gleaming wings, while others were like great shambling apes. Some wore armour or the trappings of battle, others went naked, — but all were armed. Amidst the bristling spears there were also many that bore curved swords and long two-edged straight blades or heavy axes. Separate from the main body of the Goblins were two other bands, one on each flank, both nearly two thousand strong. Behind the army was another band of a thousand. Over that force hovered all of the bat flock, for there in their midst stood the silver standard of Ral, dazzling in the early sunlight.

Before the mountain gate was the army of Talarnidh and Eldhoril, like the greater host of its enemies drawn up in three squadrons. Talarnidh and the host of Elves and Sylphs in the centre were flanked by Dwarves and Gnomes to their right and Woodmen to their left. All the soldiers save the Elementals of the air were armoured, and their swords and spears were strong and new-forged. The forges of the mountain had worked long at the task. The Elves all bore their tall bows, and each of them had three quivers of arrows slung under his rustling wings.

From out of the forest behind the army of Ral rose two Dragons with a vast snap of wings, so strong that the gust of air shook the standard of the Witch Queen. Great reddish-gold serpents with scaly bodies and wings of leather thicker than a man's arm, they rose slowly and jerkily, gaining height in impossible upward leaps until they soared on wind currents high above the mountain. Then both fell like monstrous darts out of the clouds down towards the Elves and Sylphs around Talarnidh.

Talarnidh turned and spoke to the Elf at his side, and three clear shrill notes rang out on the Elven horn he bore, repeated again and again. In a moment the Elves and Sylphs had scattered in all directions, back and forward, swirling upwards and outwards, for the Elves and the Sylphs have the power of flight. From the mouths of the plunging Dragons came long spurts of fluid venom. Where it struck the ground, where Talarnidh's army had stood a moment before, the ground caught fire. Rushes of red and green flame shot up into the air, rebounding from the burnt earth beneath the Dragons, as they swooped on over the heads of Ral's Golbins.

Two or three Elves fell out of the sky screaming. One was no more than a blackened cinder, already dead where the venom had burnt deep into his body. Others cried in despair for their wings were burnt. Where the venom had touched the Sylphs they vanished away as if they had never been. Again the Elven horn sounded, now four notes repeated again and again. The scattering swirling flying forms sped back to the blackened smouldering ground where they had stood before. They had lost hardly any. From the Goblins went up a shout of rage, and their spears shook, and their line surged.

No sooner had the Elven horn died away than its notes were taken up by a higher keener sound. The Silver Horn, thin and ancient, gave cry again across the plain and forest. Eldhoril wound it three times from the height of the castle above, and the waking Dragons in caves far beneath heard clearly. Before the keening notes from the Time Before Time had died in the air the huge forms were moving with swift angular movements along dark passages.

At the foot of her standard Ral cried out in rage, and now the Dragons in the sky were five, beating the wind above her lines. It was in these five great beasts of ancient evil that Ral had set the greatest store of all her host. There were none that she knew of like them left in the world. Their help had cost her much in magic and service and gold. She cried out to them in the Black Speech, and the Dragons, who know all speech, rose up again and scattered across the sky. Now they would come from all directions.

But now Ral spied the sixth Dragon. Slowly and ponderously

it rose from behind the mountain, glittering and mighty, upward and upward. Her voice faltered. She stared at the Dragon and concentrated her will on it, but her sorcery met with an impenetrable wall. All she saw was that the Dragon was huge, twice or three times bigger than her own creatures, and the scales on its back glittered blue like ice, not fire-red as did all her Dragons. Her mind and attention became fixed on the immense beast, still vast though it was now higher than her own Dragons. The cries and shouts of her army came to her faintly, and suddenly she realised that the spell of the Dragon had caught her. She wrenched her eyes away, and saw with horror eight other Dragons high above the army of her enemy, and her own Dragons circling aimlessly below them. Again the commands sprang to her lips, but high above, Dagdaloun the Old was already dropping like a stone.

Below, along Talarnidh's army rang the signal for the advance. Slowly Elves and Sylphs walked forward, nearer and nearer to the huge band of Goblins before them, four times as many. Then they were running. Arrows and spears came out to meet them, but few seemed to find their mark, for now they were flying, sweeping through the air like a cloud of the storm. Out of the cloud came the rain of arrows. Each of the Elves drew his bow at once. Each put the arrow to it and let fly. Hardly a Goblin in the front rank was not struck. Through cloth and flesh and armour the Elven arrows fled, and the screaming and shouting became an uproar. Swords and spears swung hopelessly upwards, but their enemy was already gone.

Leaving the Goblin centre to rage and scream in confusion, the Elves and Sylphs had swung to their left. There stood the Goblin right, a wedge-shaped mass of foeman. The Sylphs came upon it from the side. They dived with spears of frozen cloud, and they pierced through the Goblins as if they were made of water. The cloud spears were still being pulled from the wailing Goblins when the second flight of Elven shafts struck upon them. Hundreds and further hundreds had already fallen. The Goblin force tried to turn to face its assailants. They milled in confusion and trampled the dead and the dying. No help came from the great army of the centre, still uncertain and without orders, injured by the first blow of the attack.

Everywhere the Goblins struck, their sweeps and thrusts fell upon air, for the nimble Elves and the wind-beings had leapt away skyward. They could not fight their flying foemen. They turned and twisted in their fury, and the hands of Trolls and Giants grasped nothing as they bellowed their monstrous rage. No more than a spear or two of the Goblins found a mark. Only once did the hand of a Giant crush an Elf. At once the Elves and Sylphs were all around it. Arrows flashed into its eyes. Spears bristled from its throat. Already slain, but slow to die it leapt and danced in its torment, and more Goblins died beneath its feet, or ran scattering from it. Then it fell, full on the Goblins below. The uproar and tumult grew greater. Everwhere were the hunched dead and the screaming and horror of the wounded.

Then the whole of the Goblin right was broken and fleeing. Those furthest from the bitter bows of the Elves were running for the forest, those nearer had dived to the ground, or ran wherever they could. The standards went down, and the captains stopped roaring their hopeless commands and fled. Everywhere the arrows followed them relentlessly. Across the whole plain between the lines the Goblins scattered, and where they came near the Elves that Talarnidh had kept with him to guard the Mountain Gate, or the Dwarves, or the Woodmen, they were slain. And when they ran to their own ranks, they found that Ral in her fury had also ordered them to be slain. Fifteen hundred Goblins lay dead on the field when the Elves and the Sylphs flew down to land all about Talarnidh.

In the sky above, one of Ral's Dragons was flapping, a broken immensity, helplessly towards the forest behind the Goblin ranks, the leather of one wing burnt away by the only Fire Dragon in Eldhoril's halls. Another Dragon lay dead where it had fallen, smashed and ruined where the plunge of Dagdaloun had caught it full in a flood of ice venom. For Dagdaloun was an Ice Dragon, and his breath froze the life out of any it touched, turning flesh and skin in an instant to bitter crystal, so utterly chill it was.

'We have destroyed the Goblin right,' cried Fandorel as he landed beside Talarnidh's horse. 'The plan has succeeded to the full. They are broken and fleeing.'

'It is as I thought,' answered Talarnidh. 'They have not prepared for our sort of war. They do not know what to do when attacked from above. But Ral will be prepared for such an attack again.'

'Their centre is moving forward,' said Filindrin.

'And there is movement far over on the right,' said Relnar. 'Our Dwarves and Gnomes have moved a long way over.'

'Yes, there is fighting there also,' answered Talarnidh. 'Where is Talak? He must ride over to Karandar and discover what is happening.'

'Talak would not come out,' said Filindrin. 'He was too afraid.'

Talarnidh shook his head angrily, then turned to Relnar.

'You will have to go, Relnar,' he said.

'It will not be needed,' interrupted Filindrin. 'Someone is coming to us.'

From the right of the army a rider was spurring across Talarnidh's front. Only the men of the company and messengers had horses, and it soon became clear that the rider was Erathrir. He reined in before the Prince.

'What is it?' demanded Talarnidh from the gasping rider.

'Goblins! . . . Goblins have moved up beyond our right. They are on the spur of the mountain. Karandar has moved out with the Dwarves and Gnomes to try to hold them off, but they are already above us in many places.'

'What are our losses?' asked Talarnidh.

'Many. Well over a hundred, possibly two hundred. The fighting is fierce, and it is still going on.'

'They are outnumbered and the enemy have the high ground,' said Talarnidh. 'We will have to go to their aid.'

'Have you forgotten that Ral is moving towards our centre?' asked Filindrin. 'Send the Dragons to the mountain spur. They are above us, while the Dragons of Ral have now all fled behind her lines. You cannot weaken the centre now.'

'I cannot summon the Dragons at my will,' Talarnidh answered. 'The Sylphs will go to the right flank, the Elves will stay with me here.'

'I will go back to Karandar,' called Erathrir, and spurred away.

'Safaarasaa! Take the Sylphs now!' ordered Talarnidh.

With a whirring of blue wings the cloud of a thousand Sylphs rose into the air. They swept away to the eastward slopes of the mountain, from which came the distant din of fighting. They swooped low over Erathrir as he rode, and then soared high above. The Dwarves and Gnomes shouted and cried out as they saw them in the sky. Then the cloud-spears were plunging into the Goblins from above and behind. Those who a moment before had stood on commanding ridges found themselves the easiest prey. Down they fell before the flashing spears. In a moment the ridge was clear, but now from the forest Goblin arrows began to fall amidst the Sylphs and those Dwarves who had climbed up to take the place of the fallen Goblins on the heights. Where the trees covered the mountain slopes the Goblins still continued their advance, and now the Sylphs could not use their power of flight to such effect. They and the Dwarves and Gnomes began to seek out their enemies amid the trees. In the chaos of the woods the fight grew fiercer and, though as many Goblins fell, the forces of Eldhoril could bear the loss less well.

'It was not the quick victory you had expected on the right,' said Filindrin to Talarnidh. 'The Sylphs do not return, and Ral's whole army moves forward.'

'They have not yet found a way to fight our Elves,' answered Talarnidh. 'Ciranouth! Fandorel! We go to meet them. Keep pace with me as I ride. Then, when I turn, let fly, and turn with me. — Come!'

Slowly at first, he began to ride forward towards the immense mass of the Goblin armies. Behind him the Elves rose into the air, and with slow beats of their gossamere wings kept pace. Steadily Talarnidh rode faster until, only a few hundred yards from the enemy front, he reined in suddenly. A shout went up from the Goblins. At first it was laughter as they saw the Elves turn away. Then it was fear and anger and pain, for as the Elves turned, the flight of arrows flew. Hundreds of Goblins went down in the tight-pressed ranks. The army swayed as those in the rear pressed forward over their fallen brothers. The Elves had already sped back beyond the range of the Goblin spears and arrows that followed them.

'Again!' cried Talarnidh. 'Forward with me, and then the turn!'

Again the Elves swept forward behind the single horseman.

'We should ride with the Prince,' cried Relnar, and started to spur his horse forward too.

'Fool!' said Filindrin, and sat unmoving at the Mountain Gate.

From the Goblin host came the braying of signal horns. From the rear of their army rose the mass of bats, up into the darkening air, Werebats among them come from their hideous pit in Thulgarn, as large as men, with black wings spread. Countless thousands of the bats swirled in a whirlwind round and round, then swept towards the advancing Elves.

'Shoot at the bats! Shoot at the bats!' cried Talarnidh, pulling his horse to a sudden halt.

The Elves needed no bidding, and the whole flight of their shafts sped into the bat flock. Hundred upon hundred black forms fell pierced through. There was no way they could avoid the arrows, but the number of bats was countless, and before a second flight could reach them, they had fallen upon the Elves. Now in the air a swirling battle came about. Elven hands and narrow Elven daggers tore at the black cloud which enveloped each of the flying warriors, and the teeth and claws of the bats rent the wings and flesh of the Elves. Suddenly above the shouting and the screeching came the cry of Ciranouth.

Their wings beating fiercely the Elves rose up, swift and twisting, rising higher and higher, up towards the mountain. Some of the bats stayed with them. Some Elves, surrounded by too many of their black assailants, fell groundward, screaming as the bats tore at their eyes and throats. As they gained height, the Elves put new arrows to their bows. Few bats remained with them now, save the giant Werebats, and these fell easy marks to the arrows. One by one, as they could, the Elves flew back down to the Mountain Gate. There Talarnidh awaited them with Filindrin and Relnar. In front, the Goblin army with the black flock above it marched slowly forward, with the great drums beating steadily to its advance.

'The Dragons again!' cried Relnar.

Ponderously through the top of the wheeling cloud of bats came the three remaining Fire Dragons of Ral. In the heights above, Dagdaloun and the Dragons of Eldhoril were already dropping through the ragged clouds. The red-scaled beasts below heard their roaring cries, and attempted to rise to meet them, wheeling and twisting as sheets of venom rushed down about them. Gouts of fire rose from their own snouts, cascaded into a myriad droplets of flame, and then fell onto the Goblins below. One of the Ice Dragons was suddenly caught in a gout of flame, roaring and orange. Flames rushed out to the leathery wingtips and wrapped the vast blue body in a cocoon of fire. The trumpeting cries tore the air and drowned all other sounds of battle. Then they were joined by the hideous tormented screams of other Dragons. Two were surrounded by the gushing brilliant fluid that was the ice venom. Their flesh froze and bones snapped as the crackling wings tried to beat. In mighty death agonies they twisted and writhed, shooting upwards in the sky and spouting the dying remnants of their ancient fires. Then both had fallen to the ground, one full on the fleeing terrified Goblins beneath it, one into the trees of the forest making a wide clearing of broken trunks and branches where the huge corpse lay. Further away in the sky one burning sheet of flame still flew, its wings fanning its own fires. Dagdaloun dived towards it, and the ice breath quenched the flame and ended the agonies of his brother, as that Dragon too fell into the woods. The last remaining one of the Dragons of Ral was already high and far to the eastward, returning to its secret home.

'It is as Eldhoril said,' said Talarnidh. 'Ral should not have called up the Dragons. She has destroyed herself.'

'Ral is a sorceress,' answered Filindrin. 'She has not yet used her powers.'

'But their army has halted!' cried Relnar.

'Listen!' answered Filindrin.

The Goblin horns sounded again, and then a single trumpet shriller than the others. Through the midst of the enemy ranks came the Witch Queen Ral herself. She stood before her army, white clad, tall and fair, her hair blown back. Above her the bats whirled and raced. Behind her the Goblins and Trolls and Giants roared their exultation. Then out of the sky came Dagdaloun and another of the Ice Dragons. Low and level with the ground the vast shapes moved, coming in from the west, so that their wing-tips touched the treetops. The venom came from their gaping jaws like sheets of slow running water spreading out above the bat flock and then showering down upon them. Everywhere it cut through them like a knife. Down they fell like an unholy rain until a great mound of them lay in front of the Goblin army. Droplets of venom began to fall on the Goblins also, and they fell dead in the instant it touched them.

Ral looked up into the sky, her face twisted with rage. Dagdaloun and the other Dragons were far away now, rising in their slow flight towards the mountain. But she saw yet more Dragons coming down towards her army. Her hands went up and moved in the air, and language flowed like a solid stream from her lips, unknown and hideous even to the Goblins, who stopped their ears and cried out. Now she stood silent and her palms were upraised towards the three Dragons as they bore down upon the Goblin Host.

'She has not the power!' said Filindrin, his face a paler mask of fury than that of Ral.

'What do you mean?' asked Talarnidh.

'It is the rotting spell, — a great thing of witches. But she cannot do it to Dragons in the sky, — to three Dragons. She cannot have the power!'

'How do you know what the spell is?' demanded Talarnidh.

'I know!' answered Filindrin. '— Look up! She *is* doing it, Talarnidh! Curse her! Look at the Dragons!'

As the Elven host watched from around the Mountain Gate a cloud of darkness flowed ever-thicker from Ral's outstretched palms. It had already enveloped the Dragons. At first they seemed to come on through it. Then the leading Dragon trumpeted, a weird cry of pain and fear and horror. Its cries became louder and its wing beats failed. It tried to rise, and for a moment they saw it come out of the cloud. Scales and flesh were dropping from it. They saw the side of the skull glistening bare and white. They saw the fierce blue eyeball fall inward. The flesh of the Dragon was rotting and falling to the ground as the living beast decayed in the grasp of the spell of the Witch Queen.

Three more Dragons now lay dead on the ground. One of them was no more than a heap of clean bones. The others were half-rotted carrion. For all of them the head was but a bare skull, eyeless and mindless, for the spell had eaten away the ancient brains within. Scales and smashed wings made strange sails in the gusting wind, and already wolves that ran with the army of Ral were sniffing about the great carcases. Of the nine Dragons that had slept long in the caves beneath the mountain, only four remained. High beyond the reach of any spell they circled and wheeled. The voice of Dagdaloun spoke among them. They circled and waited. Dagdaloun looked north, and saw the forest moving. Then he looked back to the battle below.

'So she does have the power,' said Filindrin to Talarnidh. 'Curse her, and curse her again!'

'You said she was a sorceress,' Talarnidh answered grimly. 'Now we have seen you spoke the truth. She will use the spell next on us.'

'I think not,' Filindrin answered. 'See! She is gone from the forefront. She had been ready to lead them to victory, but she must be weakened after that. She is resting.'

Again the drums beat and horns sounded.

'Her Goblins do not rest,' answered Talarnidh. Before them the Goblin army began its measured advance again. 'She will buy her victory with her dead. What are they to her?'

'There are few of the bats left,' said Relnar.

'Will you not attack now?' demanded Filindrin. 'What other plans do you have left?'

'Relnar, ride to our left wing. Order the Woodmen to attack,' said Talarnidh to the Prince of Chamley. Then he turned to Ciranouth and Fandorel. 'Into the air, my friends, wait till I ride! Then fly with me! This time there must be no turn! When we come to their line fly straight over them. Shoot until your arrows are gone. All we can do now is fight and fight till the end. We may still defeat them before Ral returns.'

'Where is Eldhoril?' asked Fandorel as the Elves arose on their spread wings. 'Only he can fight Ral. He must come soon.'

'I do not know,' answered Talarnidh.

From their left came a great shout. They saw the charge of the Woodmen. The antlered stags of their leaders raced before, and the men charged close behind, a line that spread out thinly, but a line of swords and swung axes. The ground between them and the Goblins was covered, and the Goblin ranks strove to turn to present their lances to the new enemy. But they could not halt the measured advance.

'Now!' cried Talarnidh, when the Woodmen were no more than a hundred yards from the Goblins.

Forward his tall horse leapt, and beside him rode Relnar. He looked to his left, and saw Filindrin also, his face a smiling mask. Talarnidh raced towards the left where the Woodmen and Goblins had met. Relnar followed, but Filindrin's horse passed behind them. They saw Filindrin alone, sword in hand, strike the Goblin centre where the Stone Trolls stood. He was lost for a moment in hundreds of enemies. Then Talarnidh saw him for a last time, swinging his sword wildly about him, still mounted, the smile still fixed on his face.

Then Talarnidh, and Relnar too, were in the Goblin lines. Staring faces shewed up at him. His sword cut and he saw red gashes appear. An arrow struck across his breastplate, and sparks flew up from it. A sword gashed the side of his horse, and it screamed its pain and reared up. Everywhere there were swords and spears. Somewhere in the air above him he heard the rush of a thousand arrows sped at once, clear even above the cries and tumult. He fought for a time that seemed an age but was a few minutes. Then his horse was free of the mass of the Goblins. Everywhere there seemed to be Woodmen fighting. He looked around trying to regain his bearings. He knew he was on the Goblin right. He looked up to the mountain. Between him and the Mountain Gate was the great part of the Goblin army. He had passed through the thin ranks on the right flank of the enemy. He saw the Elves in the sky above the Goblins. But they were no longer a line. Each Elf still shot arrow upon arrow. But the Goblin ranks had not been broken. They were still advancing slowly to the drumbeat. And now only yards were between them and the Gate. Talarnidh was behind the Goblin army. Now he spurred towards their rear — alone.

While the armies fought below, in a room in the grey mountain a small form stirred. Slowly Talak lifted his head. He swam in waves of nausea. Every movement was agony in his ribs, and his right hand hung a useless torment at his side. Somehow with his left hand he dragged himself upright against the wall, then pulled himself along it to reach the door to the passageway. It was locked fast. A long while he leaned against it, sobbing with the effort and the pain and the utter anguish of what he knew.

Then he began to make his way round the room. Through the door into the room where Filindrin had stood by the window he went, and now he was crawling, one-armed, spears of agony cutting through him at every movement. Gradually, gasping and weeping, he pulled himself up onto the window-ledge and looked down. Directly below him was the window of the counsel chamber. He looked at the rocky slope, so steep in its seeming, and the distant forest seemed to flow before his eyes. He wiped the caked blood from his face and, weeping in fear as he did it, lowered himself with his one good hand, down over the edge onto the face of the mountain.

For a moment his feet groped for a hold, and the pain in his side almost made him faint. Then he was clinging hard to the rock, balanced on a ledge. Cautiously he explored it with his feet, his face still pressed close to the rock. It was broad and smooth. He crouched down on it gasping out his pain. For a long time he nursed the broken hand. Then he knew the time had come again. Trying not to think about it, he began once more to lower himself over the edge.

His feet sought for a hold and found nothing. Suddenly his sweat-soaked hand was slipping. He gripped with his other, ruined, hand, and screamed at the agony. He let go, and found himself sliding down the slope. His hand caught at a tree and held it with a jerk that almost tore out his arm. He felt the tree pulling loose, and struggled for a foothold, but his legs and half his body seemed to hang out beyond an overhang. His feet found only space. Again his hand slipped. Desperately, shouting out in pain and despair, he twisted his body into the space beneath the overhang as he fell from the tree.

His body struck the ledge of the open window of the counsel chamber, and lay broken and still across it. The Sylphs who had been standing there with Eldhoril pulled him inside, and laid him on the stone floor. The Wizard saw the injuries, and his face became drawn with a sudden fear. He remembered the riddle the Dragon had told, and into his mind, as he saw how Talak had been broken, came a monstrous and impossible solution to it.

The Sylphs he had sent returned swiftly with salves and wood for a splint. They also brought a certain cordial. Eldhoril placed the flask to Talak's lips. The boy swallowed, and his body stirred suddenly. He groaned, then, as he became more conscious, screamed in pain. But still he struggled to sit up. Eldhoril knelt down beside and helped him. Already one of the Sylphs was binding up Talak's arm.

'You must try to speak, Talak,' said Eldhoril gently.

'I can speak,' answered Talak, his face twisted awry, his body shaking.

'Who did it to you?'

'Filindrin,' came the answer.

'Why?'

'Because I know who he is,' Talak's answer was fainter.

Even with the Wizard's cordial he could hardly fight the pain that wracked him. Somehow he stopped himself sliding backwards and collapsing onto the ground into welcome oblivion. His left hand grasped the Wizard's robe.

'Who is he?' asked Eldhoril.

'I heard it all,' said Talak, his voice grief-ridden and tormented. 'He called himself this: "Sagoth Son of the Morning" . . . It is his day of victory.'

He fell back at the effort into the cradling arms of the Sylph.

Slowly, grey-faced and drawn, Eldhoril stood up. As the blackness closed in on him, Talak reached out towards the Wizard.

'It is the Devil,' he whispered.

And then he was silent. His eyes closed, his body broken by Sagoth, he lay unconscious.

CHAPTER 20

WIZARDRIES OF WAR

In the midst of all the armies and warfare no Goblin sword cut Filindrin, no spear so much as tore his cloak. He rode through them, and they fell to his slicing blade. War axes flashed at his horse but were somehow turned away. Suddenly he was through the front line of the Goblins, on open ground littered with corpses. Before him he saw another mass of Goblins, among them three of the mighty Giants such as had been at Belengar, and many Trolls with them. He saw also all that remained of the bats and the hideous Werebats. He saw the Man-Wolves. But he had eyes for none of Ral's creatures. For he saw Ral herself among them. He rode his horse full at her, sword outstretched, lips screaming a war-cry of death.

The Witch Queen saw him, and her black bat-eyes widened. She stood, and stretched out her hands again. Again the smokes rushed out of them, coalesced in an instant, built themselves into blocks of crystal, a solid wall sprung out of nowhere glinting and massive. Through the ice-like blocks Filindrin saw the hazy shape of Ral, and she was laughing at him, as his horse reared and bucked. In a moment he had slid down from the saddle, and faced her through the wall of transparent rock. He heard her voice, strangely clear above the din and through the wall, for she spoke in the Sorcerers' Speech, and any sorcerer nearby could not but hear.

'You cannot come nigh me, mortal.'

Filindrin walked up towards the wall. He drew air into his lungs, then breathed out a great gust, more than he had taken in, more than any mortal man could hold in his lungs. A great gale rushed out of Filindrin's mouth and crashed against the wall. The wall swayed and rocked. Cracks ran through it, and then the magic blocks were falling to the ground. As they struck the earth, the ruins of the wall of massive crystal crumbled into dust that blew on the gust of Filindrin's breath full in the face of Ral.

'I am no longer a mortal,' said Filindrin, in the Sorcerers'

Speech. On his face was the fixed smile of death. His voice was softer and fairer even than Ral's.

'I will make your flesh rot from you,' cried Ral.

'As you did in the house of the Witchweird. But then I was weak. Now I have this body fully. I can grow from it. I am established in earthly form. I am Sagoth.'

'Also you are drained, O Ral,' said Filindrin that was possessed by Sagoth. 'The power went out of you when you slew three mighty Dragons of Eldhoril. It is a great spell you used. Even Ral the Fair could not use it without being weakened. Only Sagoth could do that.'

'I am not so weak,' answered Ral.

'Then why did you build the wall against me. That is a little spell to me. Tell me, Ral, did the spell of the wall stop my Hound when he walked upon earth. My Hound, the Hound of Hell, is but a shadow and a servant of me. For I am Sagoth, Ral. I it was who made you what you are. What little power you have you drink from the Sword of Doom. Yet though you have my Sword, you have not the power to draw it. I am Sagoth, that made you into the Witch Queen, Ral. Worship me, Ral! I am your master!'

'You raped and cursed me,' answered Ral. 'Now I will return the curse. Sagoth, go back into the darkness, curse you and curse you forever!'

Filindrin, the body, with the smile of Sagoth on his dead face, stood, and slowly the air around him took on a strange new light. A green glow spread over the face of the Son of the Morning, making the features shine and glisten. Everything in front of Ral took on the same vivid greenness as of the lush grass in the middle of the morass. Beyond that light, the great Goblin army and the remaining Elves under the very Mountain Gate became things of another flimsy unreal world.

The light grew and became more fierce. The green took on streaks of yellow, like grass that has rotted away. Streaks of blackness and ash ran across it, like grass that has burnt in vitriol. Yet brighter still burnt the greenness, as the streaks of ruin flowed across it. The Goblins and the great bulks of the Giants groaned at the seeing of that light. Patterns ran through it like a thousand thousand different faces, painted on the verdant life of it with muddy reds and dull flame colours. The light became yet more intense, and the face of the figure in its heart was revealed as the face of a corpse cloaked in the false green of life.

Viewed from outside the circle of curse, the light had become the flowing together of shades of darkness. The vivid greens had all dulled into grim red and grey, had become a sphere of blackness through which colours ran and flickered, a darkness that swirled and gave off some unknown opposite of light, more than any darkness of the world. Ral's outstretched arms encompassed the sphere of the dark light. In it, utterly lost to sight, swallowed in its darkness, was Filindrin. And out of the darkness came the voice:

'You have learnt well, my little accurst one. You have made the light of hell upon earth, that men name Evernight. You have poured the colours of midnight upon me. Any other than me would scream in their torments and die. But I am made of the colours of midnight. My heart is of black great stone, my eyes are the fire. My wings are the colours of dawn that breaks lightless in Nether Hell where Dahak stands alone. I drink in the darkness. I drink and grow greater.'

Suddenly the cloud of darkness drew inwards, was sucked into itself, became part of a man-shape, — but a man with wings of flowing colours, black like changing oils, a man with a form of darkness, and eyes like coals in the furnace. The shape of Sagoth stood before Ral, and it was built on the ruined body of the man that had been Filindrin, the man it had claimed in Aldel Morn, the man it had entered at Belengar, the man it now at last possessed utterly. Ral felt the power pour out of it like a torrent.

'Ral who holds the army of evil, I take it from you, the Prince of Evil! I am Lord here! Here Hell is come into the world! I call the creatures of Hell to me!'

The voice like a woman's voice, sweeter than Ral's voice, spoke again. Everywhere the Goblin armies wavered at its words. In the minds of Goblins and Trolls, of bats and Giants, came the image of Sagoth, and the name of Ral sounded faint. The spirit of Sagoth, grown great in the world, began to take over the army of Ral. The Goblin spears swayed, were half lowered, half raised again in a new allegiance. Ral knew what was happening, for the force of it flowed over her, and she realised that she too was Sagoth's creature. She sensed the beginning of her end, and cried out against it in the midst of her army's triumph.

★

From the room where Talak lay in the arms of the Sylphs, Eldhoril went down to the Mountain Gate. In its way stood thirty creatures of fire. These Salamanders he had bidden wait inside the mountain until the enemy came near to the gate. Now, made of fire, their very being kindled in flame, and armed with swords of flame, they barred the way to the screaming Goblin army. Elves there still were, fighting in the sky, but so few compared with the enemy in front.

In the hand of the Wizard there was suddenly a wand of thin fire blazing brighter red than the Salamanders in front of him. He said no word, but pointed with the rod of fire that was the Sceptre Elemental. Across the whole front of the mountain a sudden curtain of fire went upwards, leaned over, and gushed upon the Goblins. They fell back, shouting in fury. Eldhoril waited. Then the fire advanced and split into two curtains of leaping flame. With the flashing fire he cut a passage through the heart of the Goblin army.

For Eldhoril no longer thought of his defeat and ruin by Ral. He thought only of the dark presence which he sensed in the middle of the field of war. Suddenly his corridor of flame was clear into the open beyond the Goblins. He was aware how much of the Sceptre's power he must conserve. The flames were the least thing he could call up. At the end of the path between the fires, he saw the wings and the blackness, the colours of Hell. He recognised the shape of Sagoth, built upon the shell of the man, Filindrin.

He sensed with wizard's sight the immensity of strength that went out of the thing of midnight. He felt the surge of magic that threatened to take over the army of Ral and turn it into the army of Sagoth. He knew that Sagoth's guard was down now, all his will concentrated on the subduing of Ral, even Ral, to his own purpose. Eldhoril held up the Sceptre that he had not dared to use to the full since his contest with the false Selenthoril. All his might and command and wizardry went into it.

Sagoth did not see the fireball that fell out of the sky upon him. His eyes did not perceive the intensity of the light that made Elves and Goblins, Woodmen and Trolls, drop their weapons and shield their eyes, or hide on the ground in terror. He did not feel the heat that scorched the wings of the Dragons, not until the fire took him into it. Then he felt it burn. Every inch of the flesh of Filindrin burnt to nothing. The bones began to melt and crumble to dust. The armour became liquid.

And the will of Sagoth screamed out in its anguish and rage. All the will of Sagoth turned in upon the vessel that contained him. Desperately he remade the body about him, and remade it again and again as the fire made it ashes and ashes. He had grown so great that the power in him could do even that. In the heart of the fire he built the shell of a man long-lost and damned. He built and rebuilt that shell, and ever and again it was consumed in the fierce intensity of fires hotter than any furnace ever made in the world. The power was used. It drained from him in rushes and gusts, more of it and more of it as he continually remade himself, for without the body of Filindrin, the spirit of Sagoth had no home in the world.

Eldhoril fell back, gasping and reeling against the Mountain Gate. The fireball burnt into nothing. He looked down the tunnel of flickering flames before it too faded. He saw the charred ruined crumbling body fall down to the ground and lie still. He saw the face of Ral, white and afraid beyond. But he had no more strength to attack her. The fires faded. Hesitantly the Goblins closed in where the passage of flame had been. Now they were all across the front of the mountain.

The last of the Elves, perhaps three or four hundred, had reached the mountain above the great gate. Far to the left the Woodmen were backed hard against the rock cliffs. Over half of them were dead, and the survivors were pressed by ever greater numbers of Goblins. On the right, the Dwarves and Gnomes were falling back up the steep slopes, as great Stone Trolls aided the Goblins in their advance out of the woods. The Sylph host of the Wizard could not halt such as these. Their cloud spears broke on the stone of the bodies. Yet the Trolls bore immense clubs and hammers of iron and granite that smashed the rocky bodies of the Gnomes to fragments and set their heads rolling into the forest. At the Mountain Gate only a handful of Salamanders, their fires bright, barred the way within against the army of Ral. It was through these that Talarnidh now came back, fighting aside the surprised Goblins as he came from behind them. He slid from his horse and looked at Eldhoril.

'I was behind the Goblin lines. I got back through them, but I do not know how. I saw it all . . . Was it you that burnt Filindrin?'

'It was I, — but it was not Filindrin.'

'I saw what it was,' Talarnidh answered. 'How did you know?'

'Talak told me. If he had not, it would be Sagoth's army that overwhelms us now.'

'Have you no more fire sorcery?'

'Not now, not any more. Not yet. I am too weak. Weaker than I have been in a thousand years . . .'

'So is Ral,' said Talarnidh. 'She tried to fight him, — and lost.'

'What of our army?'

'I do not know for sure. Everywhere we are hard back against the mountain. We have lost very many.'

'The Salamanders will hold the gate until their Trolls come,' said Eldhoril. 'I hear the thought of Dagdaloun. He is returning. — They are our only hope now, Talarnidh, — the Dragons.'

'Your fire magic could have destroyed Ral,' said Talarnidh.

'I did not think I would have to choose which to slay, — Ral or Sagoth,' Eldhoril answered.

Full on the Stone Trolls, massive bestriding the flank of the mountain, Dagdaloun and the other Dragons fell. In the ice-breath the creatures that had withstood stone and iron and cloud-spears cracked into the clay they were come from, and fell dead at once. On the press of the Goblins too the cold breath sprayed, and more of them died than had died on the axes of the Dwarves or the hammers of the Gnomes or the spears of the Sylphs. In a few moments the Goblins were everywhere broken and fleeing down the steep mountain sides. A few of them ran for the high windows in the mountain behind the Dwarf lines as they fled. But there, there were the Ice Undines who guarded the upper fortress, their spears of ice frozen so hard that they could pierce any armour. No Goblins remained alive on the western spur of the mountain.

Dagdaloun stood amidst the heaps of splintered frozen Goblin dead, a huge bulk on the side of the mountain, and watched as the Dwarves pursued the remains of the fleeing enemy army. He saw as they spread out at the foot of the slopes. Then came the braying of the horns of Ral again. The Dragon saw new Goblins run to the aid of the defeated. In the centre of the Dwarves he saw the taller figure of a man. Then the man had fallen. In the thought of Dagdaloun came the notion that one of the three last of the First Race of Men should not perish. The figures were too close and small for him to breath icy death over them. He leapt down the mountain side with one beat of his wings, and landed in the battle. Goblins screamed and fled. Dagdaloun reached down a great clawed hand, and lifted up Erathrir into a crevice in his scaly armour on the shoulder.

'Clutch tight!' came the voice from before time was, speaking the speech of men, but in the way of Dragons.

Erathrir, his armour cracked, his face bleeding from a thin cut on the cheek, and the blood of Goblins all over him, clutched at the great blue scales, and gasped in shock at the force of the huge wing beats that carried the beast and its tiny passenger high up into the air.

Erathrir clutched tight. Beside them he saw another Dragon, its wings stretched to their full extent as it floated on the wind, the long tongue hanging down from the patterned blue of the snout, the lidless eyes glinting. Then, of a sudden, along the line of the head, a streak of white appeared. At first the man could not understand it. Then the line of whiteness spread out into a patch. Erathrir saw with sickening horror that it was bone shewing through. Scales flaked and twisted away and fell to the ground. Ragged holes shewed through the thick leather.

'It is the rotting spell again. Ral has recovered that much of her power.'

The Dragon voice spoke, almost in Erathrir's ear. Then with a jerk they were racing skywards, upwards amidst the echoing crash of the wings and the flow of air. Erathrir clung on for his life. Clouds passed them, and the mountain dwindled beneath. He saw other Dragons with them, but far away.

'Are the Dragons leaving the battle?' asked Erathrir shouting at the top of his voice.

'They will wait here in the heights. — I am going over there.'

The arm of the Dragon stretched out and the clawed finger pointed. Erathrir saw the forest to the north, and it was moving. Ripples seemed to pass through whole stands of trees. Then the trees themselves were drawing back, making a wide road, hundreds of yards across. Where dense forest had been was now an open path. Erathrir gaped. Into the gap moved other trees, taller trees, immense impossible ones. As the Dragon spiralled down towards the new road in the forest, Erathrir saw it all clearly. The trees were moving in the ground, their roots dragging great furrows through the thick earth, drawing aside to allow the column of new and greater trees into their place. On these he saw roots thicker than the body of a man drawn from the ground and crashed back into hard soil. Each step of the tree giants was thirty paces of a man.

Dagdaloun landed at the point where the clearing was being formed. His wings folded back behind his body. In the widening glade was an eerie silence, broken only by the scraping churning sound as the trees drew back farther and farther. From the end of the long path cut through the ancient forest, a wall of dark massive green advanced to fill the newly-empty spaces. As they drew nearer the grinding roar of their advance increased until it filled the air. Erathrir shivered. Rocking treetops, giant above him, swayed and shook at the monstrous movement of the immense trunks and gnarled deep roots below.

It was only as the trees drew close that Erathrir noticed the two figures riding on swift horses in front of the lurching advance of the trees. One was too tall for an ordinary man. He was clad in green and wore a pointed cone helmet. Erathrir knew at once the blue-robed figure mounted on the other steed. It was Melandir. The mounted figures halted before the Dragon and Erathrir, but the trees did not. Round each side of the small group they surged, leaving an island of heaving broken ground amidst their earth-ripping strides. All around there flowed a monstrous sea of green and brown, its wave-tops higher than towers. And under the sweeping boughs of the moving pines was darkness and a long murmuring of aroused and ancient power. The noise of their passing was too great for any speech to be heard. The brown figure clad in green stretched out his arms but said nothing. The gap between the moving trees, the island where they stood, became wider, and beyond the moving giants the trees of the forest receded farther to let their sentient brothers pass.

'My name is Iroi Girindhouz. I am the Pine Lord,' said the tall figure. 'I come to pay my debt. I owe it to Talarnidh.'

'My name is Dagdaloun the Old,' said the Dragon. 'The one you seek awaits on the battlefield beyond.'

'Melandir, were you hurt? What has happened to you? Where have you been?' cried Erathrir. 'How did you get out of the house?'

Melandir leapt down from his horse and clasped Erathrir's arm.

'Whirrirrish brought me out of the house,' answered Melandir. He carried me through the forest to the house of Iroi Girindhouz. — I have the Sword, and I have the Sceptre. I am almost well now. The Pine Lord did not wish me to come when he first received Talarnidh's message. But, Erathrir, I saw something in that house that cannot wait. It concerns Filindrin.'

'Be still now! Listen!' said the Dragon voice of Dagdaloun suddenly. 'I will tell you both all that there is to hear of the one called Filindrin. I have watched from above. Many things have befallen on this field today. The least of them concerns Ral. I will tell you of the dealings of Eldhoril this day. His dealings with Sagoth!'

The Goblins had failed to take the Mountain Gate in their first attack. Now, as they drew back, all the forces of Eldhoril gathered before it. The flanks of the line were abandoned. Woodmen stood bunched together to the left of the gate, Dwarves and Gnomes, grim and battle-scarred to the right. In front of the gate itself were the Elves and Sylphs. Talarnidh and the remaining men of the old company stood together again in the centre, above the line of the Sylphs, while the Elves rested on the ground behind. Relnar had been injured in the attack, and brought back safe by the Woodmen. Now he lay inside the mountain next to Talak. Eldhoril came out between the Salamanders to join his army.

'This will be their last attack!' he said. 'They are three to our one.'

Wearily they all looked out towards the Goblin army as it massed now, full of bristling spears. The beat of war drums rolled all along it behind the ranks, and the Goblins stamped and shouted.

'The ground is shaking beneath them,' said Yeselwir hopelessly.

Talarnidh looked at Eldhoril, his face bemused.

'What he says is right!' he said. 'That is no Goblin dance causing it though. — Ral has some more sorcery in store for us.'

The drum rolls seemed to take on a more discordant note, deeper and louder, louder still every second and with strange sounds mingled in them.

'You will have to do the fighting, Eldhoril,' said Talarnidh quietly. 'Even if it drains your power to the last.'

'I am ready,' said the Wizard. Again the Sceptre appeared in his hand, and now it had the appearance of a rod of ice.

'Look there!' cried Karandar. 'Above the Goblins! — It is like nothing I have ever seen!'

'The tops of trees,' said Fandorel. '— But there were no trees on the plain . . .'

As they watched, there seemed to be more and more pine trees behind the Goblins. It was as if a magic forest was growing up there as the seconds passed. Ever bigger the trees appeared, dark green branches spread. The grinding and tearing sound that they had thought part of the Goblin drum call now drowned out the drums completely.

'They are not growing there at all . . . They are getting nearer! They are moving towards us!' cried Talarnidh, and his voice rose in renewed hope.

'What do you mean?' asked Yeselwir.

'Do you not see?' shouted Talarnidh, clasping Yeselwir's arms. 'The Pines have come! He has answered my call! It is the pines of Iroi Girindhouz. The Walking Trees out of the legends! They have come to fulfil the promise.'

The vast earth-laden roots fell upon the rear of the Goblin army amidst their beating war drums and their shouts of triumph. The shouts became screams and cries. The very ground they stood on shivered, and suddenly all of the Goblins could hear the great crashing and rending behind them. All turned, and above them towered a vast and growing forest where none had been before.

The forest swayed, though the wind had died to nothing, and thick branches moved as if of their own will. Sweeping arms of wood smashed against the close press of the Goblins. The ground collapsed beneath their feet and, as they slid down into sudden holes, their last sight of the world was the twisted roots raised high above them. Wood fastened on the stone-like bodies of Trolls, and branches of many trees twined and wrapped about the Giants they dwarfed. The bodies of the Trolls smashed in the rock-rending roots. The Giants fell to the ground and were trampled into the earth beneath the weight of the moving forest. For the Goblins there was no refuge.

Their front ranks charged in panic towards the Mountain Gate to be met by showers of arrows. They turned and fled where they could. Those few hundred on the far right of the Goblin line could scatter across the plain, but everywhere else that the fleeing Goblins turned lurching swaying monstrous shapes of green came through the erupting earth, a moving wall that crashed itself down on the tiny forms beneath. Flailing branches smashed bone, and crushing weight lay low the struggling press of yelling helpless foemen. The trees moved inexorably forward, so close to the army before the mountain that the people of Eldhoril might have touched the raging branches. Beneath them the Goblins died. At last the trees were moving away, leaving the ground as if an earthquake had torn it apart, everywhere strewn with the mangled wrecks and ruins of bodies. No Goblins remained alive on the battlefield.

When the trees had come Ral had been unprepared. The rotting spell she spoke, that could eat away the flesh of Dragons, had no power over the bark and wood of trees. It was the last of her strength. Her sorcery was drained. Her army was falling beneath the utter horror and carnage of the monstrous forest. She raised her arms and black membrane spread between them. Her features changed. A black Werebat, she rose amidst the last few bats that remained. Above the grasping branches she rose, then low to the eastward, and at last away to the north, with all her warfare broken and downthrown.

Through the death and destruction Melandir and Iroi Girindhouz rode on their war-horses. Slowly they came up to the gate in the mountain where Eldhoril and his captains awaited. From amidst the dark groves of the Walking Trees three other Pine Lords came out, the Sylph, Whirrirrish, with one of them.

'I have paid my debt,' said Iroi Girindhouz to Talarnidh.

They looked out across the torn ground and the many many dead. All was still, only a few groans sounding distantly from the dying. A wind blew out of nowhere in the centre of the field. It swirled and eddied round a pile of broken cinders, black with only a stump or two of bone still white in them. The wind twisted round and about the consumed corpse, and dust blew up around it. Then the wind bored down into the crumbling ashes of what had been a man. From the ground beneath those relics of life came writhings and stirrings, and the strange wind was full of sighing. One of the broken bones jerked and half moved. Slowly the corpse changed. The body became less a pile of embers. it took on more of the shape of a man. Bone extended, became more whole, and bone grew from it. Out of the ashes a human skeleton formed, and now charred flesh that clung to it spread out, wrapped round, and became whole flesh. Tatters of cloak billowed about it. It raised itself with a new-made arm, and lifted itself off the blackened ground. Pink flesh and skin grew out of the patches of ash that were all that remained of its former flesh. The thing rose up on legs re-formed out of cinders and shards, and onto their cracked bones grew new muscle and sinew.

Upright, the body of Filindrin shambled towards the mountain, and its strength grew in it. None of the captains knew who was first to see it. But one by one as they looked out over their victory they realised that a single thing still moved in the desolation. Across the blackened land it came. The resting army became aware of it. Warriors stood and shaded their eyes to look. They saw a burnt rib cage through rags of flesh. They saw an empty face where the eyes had long burnt away and the cheekbones gleamed white. But as they watched they saw the ribs grow flesh. They saw new blood pump so that it spilled from the wrecked face. They saw blackened muscle grow red again, raw meat of a corpse in the sunlight.

'It is the last part of the riddle now,' said Eldhoril. 'It is the part Dagdaloun never told and never knew. Why did the Men of the First Race come out of the Stars? Why did they see the Allfather? Why was one of them given the Sword? That is the last part of the Dragon's riddle.'

Eldhoril looked at Melandir.

'The Dragon told me what he saw on the battlefield, and what he heard,' said Melandir. 'I know who was here, and how you fought him.'

'I did not kill the body, though I thought I had,' answered Eldhoril. 'It walks again. It still has the shape of Filindrin. But in it is Sagoth.'

They looked at the monster that staggered towards them.

'You know the meaning of your Sword,' said Eldhoril.

'It was told to me by Ask the Allfather,' answered Melandir. 'It is the Sword of Fate. It is the power whereby Sagoth may be slain.'

'Sagoth is there!' said Eldhoril, and pointed to the walking corpse.

Melandir drew Wenyorel, the Sword of Fate. Turning, he walked slowly out into the treeless plain towards the thing from Hell. As he came nearer he saw its shape grow. He saw the features knit around its skull again. He saw the bones of the hand form from smashed stubs into long fingers. He saw the trail of blood left in its footmarks. Suddenly he ran at it. Wenyorel swung, a blow full of power. It bit the throat and was hardly checked. The head of Filindrin fell with a thud to the ground, rolled over so that the face was down in the dust, and lay still. The body swayed for a moment then fell forward. Melandir stood over it. A sigh went up from the watching army. But they could not see the sight that held Melandir's eyes like a spell. From the severed head came a whisper. The lips pressed hard to the ground moved. The eye turned, white and half-made in its socket.

'Come to me!' said the voice. 'Come to me!'

The headless body of Filindrin twitched. The legs jerked in spasms. The dead body began to writhe and slide along the ground, a headless wriggling maggot thing. From it the arm reached out, feeling towards the head that called it. The fingers crawled across the ground, spider-like and searching. Then they caught in the matted hair of the head. Slowly they dragged it across the dust as the body writhed eagerly towards it. Slowly the hand pushed it towards the red dripping neck. The flesh rejoined where the sword had cut it. The hand pressed, and the skin grew over the cut. The whole body shivered. Then it pushed itself up with both its arms. It stood again, swaying on its legs. The hideous head turned and looked all along the line of the army. Then its eye fastened on Melandir. Uncertain, disbelieving, in a sudden dream of unending horror, Melandir took one step forward. Hesitantly he lifted the Sword again.

'Stand, mortal man! Stand and look on me! My shape is fairer then Ral!' The voice of Sagoth, sweet and clear came from the lips of death. 'The Sword cannot slay me. Though its name is Wenyorel. Though it is Sword of Fate, yet it cannot slay me. Long ago it was blunted. You must sharpen it, mortal man . . . Sharpen it on the Grindstone of Time! Only then will it have power over the Prince of Darkness. It will never be now. I am Sagoth! The body is wholly mine. I have come into my full power in the world. I cannot be banished, for the body cannot die. I am Sagoth, Son of the Morning! Give me the Sword, mortal man! Your hour is come!'

Melandir held the Sword before him, and the laughter of Sagoth rippled like a fair stream flowing.

'I drink power from the Sword. I grow great. Long has the power grown in me. Not the Wizard of Wenyaltrir, nor the bearer of the Sword of Fate can harm me. I am come into my own! — Sagoth Son of the Morning! Your soul is mine now, mortal man.'

Melandir felt the power and life he had always known within the Sword suddenly ebb. He felt a great darkness far away drinking it in. He felt the same darkness fasten upon his soul. And before him, about the body of Filindrin now perfect and fine, the shape of Sagoth grew. The black wings formed and the oils of Hell swam many-coloured upon them. The head of the Devil towered above the mortal form and in it the eyes kindled and grew brighter and brighter till the patches of snow reflected their fire. Greater and greater it became, a giant of ruin, for Hell had come upon the earth.

Melandir felt the smooth rod that he had fastened to his sword-belt long before. He undid the two clasps and held the thing he had brought out of Kruakh. His eyes still held by the eyes of fire above, he sheathed the Sword of Fate. In his right hand he took the Sceptre Mortal.

The rod was short, shorter by a half than the Sword. In the carved mounting at its top was set a stone, dull and lustreless, cut to a roundness but with no life in it, a piece of rock rather than a jewel. The rod was heavy and smooth, its feel unlike stone or metal, yet its weight so great Melandir felt he could hardly lift it. Life seemed to be flooding out of him, and in the eyes above he saw long visions of the final Hell. Slowly, with a last effort of will, he lifted the Sceptre, a dead thing, hopeless, in his hand.

'Die, Sagoth,' he said.

He almost cried out at the pain that shot down his arm. The Sceptre glowed faintly, an inner light inside the jewel, the black shaft glinting with flecks of red. In the Devil above the colours raced in its wings and its body grew darker. Melandir found that he could tear his eyes away from those of Sagoth.

'Die, Sagoth!' he cried.

In the Sceptre the jewel shone out red, and the whole rod pulsed with an awful surge of power. Melandir writhed and shook in its embrace, but he could not die, for at his side Wenyorel hung. But the might of it left him sick and struggling, and still the Prince of Darkness was above him. The red of its eyes shone brighter than the jewel of the Sceptre. Dazed and longing to drop the rod of power that had become a weight beyond bearing, Melandir flung his being into a scream of hate and fear and last doomed hope.

'Die! Sagoth!'

The words echoed from the mountain amidst the plain of silence.

A light burnt out of the Sceptre, so bright that all the watching army shielded their eyes. It bathed Melandir, so that he seemed first molten silver, then made of blood and pouring blood, as the colour changed to a ruby star, brighter and brighter. But Melandir could see in it. He felt the power now, not shocking and destroying but coursing through him, as if his blood had turned to undiluted light in his veins. And he felt the power go out from him in the blessing of death.

In the midst of the monstrous shape of darkness the Sceptre Mortal took the frail body of Filindrin for dead. The man shape swayed. Its head quivered, and then across its neck a gaping cut opened. Blood pumped and the head fell rolling to the ground. The body went down, and, as it fell, flesh peeled from it and bones snapped and crumbled. The ribs and legs and backbone cracked and gave way. The cloak vanished, and the skull of the severed head became a heap of blackened ash. The figure with wings of colour and eyes of flame remained, but in it was a hole in the shape of a man where the body of Filindrin had stood. Through the emptiness in the heart of the form of Sagoth the sun shone faintly. Across the being of darkness thin cracks ran, more and more, gaping wider. The wings fell apart, the body of utter night crumbled and collapsed, the coals that were its eyes fell in, and were the merest ashes before they landed on the ground. A bleak chill wind stirred the dust, and a few multi-coloured motes blew away on its gust. Then there was nothing, only the last remains of the corpse of Filindrin that Sagoth had claimed and from which he was gone. Melandir stood alone. The Sceptre Mortal that he had claimed and taken for his own shone faintly now in his hand. Sagoth was dead and gone.

CHAPTER 21

PIT OF THE WEREBATS

The Dragon rose with snapping wings from the clearing amidst the moving host of trees. From the sky Dagdaloun and the small figure that rode him looked down on the ruin and destruction of the army of the Goblins. And as the Goblins and Trolls died beneath the flailing roots of the tree giants, they saw a small black shape rise out of the broken and doomed army. Desperately it strove to gain height, as immense branches snatched for it. First it flew eastward. Then as smaller flapping figures joined it, it turned north. The last of the bat flock had gathered about their fleeing mistress, while her army died on the field of war.

'It must be Ral,' said Erathrir.

'It is Ral,' came the Dragon's answer.

'What should we do? They will expect us at the Mountain Gate.'

'They will manage without us there. The war is done. We will follow Ral,' answered Dagdaloun. He wheeled his enormous body in the sky, as Erathrir held tight to the glittering scales.

The beating of the Dragon's wings grew swifter as he pursued the bat shapes that flew low over the forest far beneath. Soon they had caught their enemy, and Dagdaloun was diving steeply towards them, ice venom pouring from his jaws. A ruin of bats fell into the forest, their wings cracked and split by the intense cold, the warm blood frozen in their veins. But the venom did not touch Ral. She turned and, staring full towards the Dragon, opened her bat mouth wide. A thin wailing hissing screech tore at the air with sudden relentless intensity. It went on and grew louder till the very motes of the air seemed to dance to its jagged tune. It pierced the ears of the Man and the Dragon. Erathrir clasped his hands over his ears in pain, and swayed on his precarious seat. The noise surged through his whole body. Dagdaloun bellowed a huge trumpeting cry, but even his voice could not mask the shrill cutting sound that tore at the air. His wings jerked in their beat, his rush halted, and the great Dragon turned steeply away. Ral became a black speck against the darkening green of the forest as she flew on. Dagdaloun floated on air currents high above.

'What was it?' asked Erathrir. 'How did she do it?'

'It is the voice of the bat. She is a bat now, and a witch also, — but I think that may be the last of all her magic.'

'Her own voice, come from the bat shape,' mused Erathrir. 'Do you think it could have killed us?'

'It might have killed us,' the Dragon answered. 'It would certainly have killed you.'

'But we must go on following her. We cannot let her escape now. Do you think we are far enough away?'

'You ask many questions, O Man . . . Yes, we are too far away for her spell to reach us. But I can still see her. We will follow her.'

'Do you know where she is going?'

'She flies north,' said Dagdaloun. 'See, there is the road up to Kruakh, not far from the path she flies. She is returning to her fortress. Its name is Thulgarn. That is in the Black Speech of Ral. It means "Pit of the Werebats".'

Time passed. They flew on northwards. Always they kept the shape of Ral in sight, as it sped low over the endless treetops. They could see all the forest spread out below. Dagdaloun's wings were hardly moving as they floated in the windy currents of the heights. Ral did not turn her face to them again. Wearily her bat wings carried her on, slower and slower. Her power ebbed, and she knew the Dragon was following.

It was dusk as they reached the fortress of Ral. A wide empty plateau arose like a pale island amidst the green darkness of the forest. Its surface was strewn with rocks and boulders. Heaps of spoil and wreckage lay amidst stinking middens. Dagdaloun circled above. In the shadowed cliffs of the eastern edge where the plateau rose, they made out a dark cave mouth. Round it black bats circled, and the distant echoes of twittering cries came up to them from the rocky cliffs. Ral passed over the silent forest. She entered the dark mouth and was gone.

Dagdaloun floated down on a long curving glide to land on the clifftop close by the edge of the plateau. In the dying daylight the great tips and rubble threw long shadows across the Dragon and his rider. The stink of decay came to them from the Goblin debris all around.

'She hides deep in her lair,' said the Dragon. 'She must needs repair her power. She is weak. Her hopes are smashed. She knows we follow, — so she hides.'

'We cannot capture a fortress,' said Erathrir. 'The army will have to besiege it.'

'There is nothing to lay siege to,' answered Dagdaloun. 'I can hear all the sounds below. There are some bat sounds. There are a few Goblins. Very few. — We cannot go back to Eldhoril. That would give her her wish. She will see us go, and we will have given her time. When we return, Thulgarn will be empty and bare. Ral will be deep in the forest. It will all begin again.'

'So she must be attacked now,' said Erathrir.

'My ice venom would crack the stones till they crumbled into sand. The caverns would collapse upon her. — But she would escape. I sense many ways, many passages, many entrances. I would not be able to block them all. It is night, and she is a witch.'

'Then it will have to be me,' said Erathrir.

'A Dragon could not get into the caverns,' answered Dagdaloun. 'Yes, you must do it.'

'Where is the entrance?' Erathrir asked.

'You have already seen it. It is where the bats entered, below us. I cannot fly that close to the cliff. So you must climb down to it. I will kill the bats around it and inside first. Then you must enter.'

'How will I find Ral?'

'I do not know, but you will find her. This is the last of the riddle now. You came from the Outer Worlds. You stood on the Island in the Stars. You sailed the endless sea in the Ship of Gold. Why? Why? Why? The answer is here . . . perhaps.'

'What is the answer?'

'I do not know. perhaps you will find it inside. If you need me, call my name. I will try to come to you, through the rock and the darkness.'

'I will go,' said Erathrir.

He lowered himself down from the side of the Dragon. He took off the breastplate he had worn over his surcoat in the battle. He walked to the plateau's edge nearby and looked down to where the bats circled a hundred feet below. Behind him Dragon wings cracked in the air. The wind rushed as Dagdaloun swept over him. The bats died instantly and unknowing, amidst a rain of venom. Then the Dragon was curling round in its flight, and the icy breath poured deep into the cavemouth. Erathrir began to climb down the cliff face as the last daylight faded of the cold northern day.

The tangled rock of the cliff gave many footholds, but the stone was sharp, and soon his hands were cut and bleeding. Slowly he felt his way downwards, searching for cracks and ledges. Twice his foot slipped, and he hung by bloodied hands alone. He swiftly grew weary. He had fought all day long, the climb was hard, and the light was vanishing fast. At last he dropped the final few feet to the ledge before the cave mouth, and lay there panting. Against the sky above was the dark circling shape of the Dragon. Warm foetid air came out of the tunnel to meet him.

He went down into the darkness. Underfoot the rock was slippery with bat droppings. He felt his way by hand along the cold stone walls. He often stumbled, and the going was painfully slow. Frequently he paused to listen. At last ahead he saw a faint yellow glow. He came to a place where three tunnels joined. There was a torch there, burning low, and down one of the tunnels a distant line of torches, faint and widely-spaced. In all the tunnels was the pervasive odour of bats. He took the lighted tunnel. The bat smell decreased, and was replaced by another stink, that of Goblins.

The floor had become smooth, worn by many feet. He went with even more caution, passing from pool of light to pool of light. There were rooms and tunnels to the side, in which he saw piles of food and heaped armour. He was passing through a great jumbled storehouse and, though there was the stink of Goblin nests, he saw none of them until he became aware of the distant sound ahead. He began to edge along the wall, round a curve in the passage and up to a half-open door.

In the room beyond were five Goblins round a rough table strewn with food and spilt drink. Bones and flesh lay amid the rubbish on the floor. One of the Goblins lay slumped over the table. The others ate greedily from the carcase of a deer, or drank from the ever-present wine skins. Erathrir ran forward and killed one on his drawn sword as the Goblin sat. Another turned, shouting out at the monstrous shadow suddenly sprung across the wall. Erathrir tugged loose the dripping sword and cleaved at the second Goblin. It fell, clutching its spilling vitals.

The third of the Goblins had his dagger drawn. The other

scrambled round the floor yelling for his weapons. Erathrir laughed suddenly. He cut over the top of the dagger, slashing the face of the Goblin above its eyes. The creature howled and fell. The other of them had found a spear. Screaming its rage in debased Northspeech, it ran at Erathrir. The man fenced aside the spear blow. For a second, Man and Goblin looked at each other. Then the Goblin turned. Still clutching the spear, it ran, and as it ran its voice yelled and howled for help.

Erathrir chased it. He saw it turn aside down a long flight of stairs. From far beneath he heard voices. He halted at the top of the stairs. His arm went back and he flung the sword. It caught the Goblin in the middle of its back, and it fell on down the stairs. Erathrir could not go down to retrieve his sword. He ran on along the passageway, listening for Goblin voices behind. He came to a place where the way forked. Both tunnels were lit. The one to the right reeked of Goblins, while to the left the stench of the bats was solid. This time he chose the left.

A long while he ran down the tunnel, and it was suddenly that he came out into a great dark cavern. In the centre of it he perceived a chasm. There were more torches hung about the walls, and as he saw more clearly he realised that what he stood on was not the true floor of the cave, but a wide ledge all around it near the roof. The immense pit in the centre contained the true cave. Cautiously he moved towards the edge and looked down. A stench came up to meet him, fouler than any he had experienced yet, the reek of bats and stale blood. For a long time he gazed into the vast emptiness, and slowly became aware of its nature. It was a huge inverted cone, the floor of it very far away and unlit. Its sides sloped gently up to the ledge where he stood, and in the sides were cut many cells or niches, each of them lit with one of the guttering torches. He could half make out a cracked and ruinous pathway spiralling down past each of these holes.

But it was the cells themselves that held his attention. For in each of them was an occupant. He saw the figures of Elves and Men, Dwarves and Goblins. They were all chained to the walls of their tiny dungeons. Some were alive, but very many others dead or nearly dead. Most of them seemed shells of bodies, skin stretched tight over bone, no flesh or blood or muscle left. There was only absolute despair written in the horror-drawn faces of them all. All were terrifyingly pale.

From above in the roof came a sudden flapping. Erathrir looked up, then froze, crouched on the edge of the pit. The black leathery ragged shape of a bat flapped grotesquely down from its perch on the roof. It was one of the giant Werebats, such as those that had fought in the ranks of Ral's army. These were men who could become as bats, or men who had taken on the shape of bats and cast off their human form forever. And in the roof of the cave there were many of them. In a glance Erathrir could make out thirty or forty tiny eye points glowing in the torchlight. In the middle of the roof a dark and narrow tunnel rose straight upwards, the route by which they sought their prey.

The bat-thing flapped down into the pit, hovered for a moment before one of the niches, then landed in front of the chained helpless man in it. Erathrir saw him strain and writhe in his chains. He heard him scream and scream. None of the other listless captives even raised their heads. The bat wings went round the victim. The bat head lowered onto his face, and the long white fangs bared. Erathrir watched as the teeth sank into the cheek of the man, and the bat sucked deep from his flesh. He watched as the teeth were withdrawn and the blood dripped red in the torchlight. Then he saw them sink again into the throat. The man hung silent a long while in the bat's embrace. Then slowly the foul bloated creature lifted into the air. It flew heavily upwards past Erathrir to its perch in the roof. The figure it had left lay back against the rock walls, eyes rolled upwards, all the blood gone out of it. Erathrir saw that the man was dead.

Slowly and with endless caution Erathrir moved from his crouched position. He edged his way back towards the wall. Then he began the slow movement round it, eyes fixed on the silent hanging forms of the Werebats. Though their eyes glinted they gave no sign that they saw him. At last, sickened by the stink, and by the foulness of what he had seen, and by his own helplessness in the face of it, he reached the far side of the place named the Pit of the Werebats. Now he knew to the full what manner of place the fortress of Ral really was.

Back in a wide tunnel with few torches Erathrir went onward again. He ignored every narrow passage that branched from the main way. His path was guided simply by the line of torches. He went on for a long while before he became aware of a sound that followed him. He stopped and listened, heard something that left him with a vague sense of disquiet, then hurried on.

The sound became louder and more distinct, still only a hint of what it might be, but enough to turn the unease in Erathrir's mind to a fearful certainty. For a rustling sniffing and snuffling followed him. Heavy padded footfalls, though they were distant echoes, seemed to ring like bells of fear in his straining ears.

He came to another cone-shaped funnel in the rock. This time he stood on its narrow base. Without pausing he ran to the lowest of the torches that marked the jagged broken path up its sides. Half remembering the pit of the bats, half listening to the sounds that pursued him, he climbed the cavern. Just before he reached the top he saw it. Emerging from the tunnel he had left below was the head and snout of a wolf, a wolf pale and colourless in the half-light, but with wide white eyes, and jaws that gaped open to shew the cruel teeth. As it began to come up the spiral path Erathrir reached the top. He drew his dagger, and regretted the sword he had thrown.

He ran down the only passage, hardly noticing as the lights became many and brighter, then out into a long room. Down its length he raced. There was one door only at the end. He reached it, pushed and dragged at the handle, and then, with the panting of the white wolf echoing in his ears, hacked with the dagger at the wood round the lock. Twice he cut through the panelling. Then the lock fell away, and he swung open the door. Before he was through it the wolf was upon him.

Erathrir fell into the room. It was full of lights, and he had to shield his eyes. The wolf paused and sniffed the air. Erathrir half realised that its eyes were wholly white and sightless. But though the wolf was blind, its sense of smell was unerring. It sprang full at him. Still unable to see clearly, Erathrir went down beneath it. He felt the teeth fasten in the collar of his surcoat, and the claws cut through the tattered cloth to tear at his chest where his mail had been broken in the battle. For a moment the hand that held the dagger was pinned by the weight of the wolf's body. Then with a frantic twist he had it free. The blade hacked into the foreleg of the wolf. It howled, lifting its long snapping head from Erathrir's throat. Erathrir cut again, swinging and stabbing at the leg, the only part of the animal he could properly reach.

The wounded foreleg gave way, bloody and useless. The wolf sprang aside, howling anew. Erathrir rolled over and stood up. The wolf, limping, closed in towards him, low by the ground. The dagger came down full into the front of its head between the two blind eyes. Erathrir felt the skull crack and cave in. The wolf lurched and fell forward, silent already, but still twitching in its death. As he watched, Erathrir saw the shape shift and contort, changing before his eyes. He saw a naked man, completely white, an albino. Across the man's face was the awful wound of the dagger and spilt brains. It had been a Man-Wolf, but one that lived out its existence in the deep caves, and never saw daylight.

Wiping his bloodied dagger, Erathrir looked about the room. It was no chamber rough-hewn into rock, but a place of rich carvings, jewels and crystal lights. He knew the carvings at once. They were the same as he had seen in Selenthoril's castle in far-off Nyaroth Khrathril. But he did not look long at them. His eyes were drawn to the far end of the rich, bare room.

There a cross stood, made of blackened wood. It was taller than a man, and the cross-piece was at head height. Draped over it was a sword belt, held in place with great protruding nails. From the sword belt hung a sword in its sheath. He saw the iron hilt, and the black unfigured scabbard and belt. He went up to them, and lay his hands on the Sword. Both hands rested on the guard of the Sword. He closed his eyes and swayed, suddenly dizzy.

In the darkness of his mind he saw that same room. He saw Ral in it. She stood where he now stood. Her bat wings stretched out and embraced the cross, her head rested against the Sword. She wept as she clasped herself to the iron Sword in the black sheath. Somehow a part of Erathrir's mind, pushed to the back of his consciousness, told him that this was the second time of his gift. For this he had drunk the Drink that Men Desire on the Island of the Stars. He was being granted knowledge of the Sword.

He saw the time long ago when Sagoth came to the Festival of the Lamps and defiled and cursed Lidhelm, daughter of Talmond, and made her into Ral the Witch Queen. He saw the combat then between Talmond and Sagoth. Long days they fought, and Talmond bore the Sword of Fate, and Sagoth bore the Sword of Doom, and they were equally matched. Only when the Nine Kings put forth the power of the Sceptres was Sagoth overmatched. Then he called into himself all the power of the dark God he was, and rose up above Talmond as the Devil incarnate, a tower of darkness and majesty. But it was over the

Avatars of the Gods themselves that the Swords had power. Talmond clove the immortal form with the Sword of Fate. The Sword was blunted, but Sagoth was banished, screaming out into the Outer Darkness. His Sword lay on the ground where he had stood.

Erathrir saw Talmond and the Nine Kings and the Lord of the Mendoral, and the magic they made about that Sword. He understood that they had sealed it in its sheath, but that Ral had stolen it. He understood that, though Ral might drink power from it, she could not draw it forth. He knew that it was a sword of eternal life. He knew that it was the twin of the Sword of Fate that Melandir bore. He knew that it was Sagoth's Sword, the Sword of Doom.

Behind him a sudden hiss made his head turn. With his hands still clasped to the Sword, he saw Ral, a black tattered shape, half human, half bat, face animal and wild, but eyes burning with furious hatred and bitter knowledge. She did not move. Her eyes seemed fixed on the blackened cross and the Sword there.

'Let it go,' came the voice of the Great Goddess Ral.

Erathrir tugged at the Sword fastened tight, and a shiver ran through the body of Ral. He tugged again, and the ancient cross shook. Ral moaned and took one step forward. He pulled hard at the scabbard and the sword belt jerked loose from the wood. The great nails clattered to the ground. He stood back holding the Sword by the hilt in both hands. But it was still sheathed. Ral cried out. Her voice was full of horror turned into rage. Her whole body trembled, her bat face twisted in strange pains. From the holes of the nails in the wood of the cross came two thick gouts of dark fluid that coursed slowly over the grained timbers, and began to drop noiselessly to the ground. Erathrir saw that it was blood.

'Now I will slay you,' said the voice of Ral. 'Your death will be endless, mortal man, for I will hang you there in its place.'

'I have the Sword of Doom,' came Erathrir's answer. And Ral again stood silent and unsure.

'What do you know of it? How did you come here?'

'I know of it, and I have come,' was the only answer.

'Give me the Sword. You cannot use it . . . It has no power for you,' she said at last.

'It is locked in its sheath by ancient magic,' answered Erathrir.

'The Sword was forgotten,' said Ral. 'Who are you, mortal?'

'My name is Erathrir. I am he who has knowledge.'

'And how will knowledge aid you?' said Ral, her voice half sneer but half afraid.

'I am the one who knows how to draw the Sword,' answered Erathrir.

'No!' said Ral. 'No! It cannot be . . .'

'It can be,' said Erathrir.

'All the sorcery of the High Race went into this. There is no spell to break it. I could never find it, never find it. I know! How long have I searched . . . It is sealed there forever. It will never be drawn.'

'It is the source of all your power. The heart of your power is locked in it,' said Erathrir. 'But the Sword is locked no more. This is not a magic of the High Race. You looked in the wrong place, Ral. This is older magic, older than you know. Like the Sword it comes from the Time Before Time. Like all magic it is mere knowledge . . . It will be drawn.'

'Give me the Sword!' screamed Ral.

'Grenyorel, Come Out, the Sword of Doom!' said Erathrir.

The Sword shook in his hands.

'Names!' said Ral. 'The Names of the Sword! . . . You know its Names!'

'Du-Apsu, Come Out, the Brandiron of Chaos!' said Erathrir.

And now the Sword trembled in its scabbard, jerked and came out an inch. Ral hissed her terror, and rushed at Erathrir, clawed wings spread wide.

'Zaroq'ar, Come Out, the God Cleaver!' said Erathrir.

The scabbard crashed to the floor. The dull iron glinted in torchlight. The first time in fifty thousand years. Ral ran full onto the outstretched blade.

Ral fell back from the Sword. Her hands clutched at her breast. No blood flowed. She stood gasping, her whole being held by the Sword in Erathrir's hand. Then the bat-form lurched and staggered. For a moment it seemed two figures, one within the other. Then a white-clad shape slid away from the bat shape. It was the figure of a woman. Pale-faced and holding her heart, the woman fell onto her knees. Her hand held the wound, and blood spread out from it, red blood soaking through the shimmering silk that was as if she wore a bridal gown. Her face was fair, but there was death already in her eyes.

'It has been so long,' she said, her voice soft and sweet. 'I have served It, and I have drunk from It. I could never make It mine . . . So much I remember . . . There were so many, so many who loved me. I was their Goddess, their Goddess . . . All gone, all forgotten. The joy and the splendour. And only a Witch is left. Only the great black bat . . . Once they called me Lidhelm. I was young in my joy, in Temirandor long ago. All lost . . . all forgotten. I am dead, I am dead, Man of the Sword. Dead five hundred centuries . . .'

The voice grew fainter, and through the fair shape Erathrir saw the cavern walls and the glowing torches. She became a ghost, fading away, fading away, a last long sigh on her lips. And then nothing.

With a rustle of wings and a hissing cry the bat shape rose up. Its eyes stared at Erathrir. It tried to speak, but only the same animal hiss, shrill and wild, came from its lips. Spreading its wings about its misshapen form, the last of all Ral's being fled through the door. Then rose on wings of darkness away through the caves. For Ral the Fair was dead and passed away.

CHAPTER 22

THE FESTIVAL OF THE ICE FIRE

'And so I came back to the Pit of the Werebats,' said Erathrir. He stood in the halls of Eldhoril, and with him were all the company of the Quest-that-was and of the battle. 'They were awake now, — all of them — the air full of monstrous shadows and shrilling cries. I think they knew of the doom of Ral. This time I did not succeed in moving round the wall of the pit. They were upon me almost at once. The only Sword I had was this one, Grenyorel. It had remained in my hand. Now I had to use it. For every one that I struck down there seemed to be more in its place. Their claws were in my face. Talons were ripping at me everywhere. I almost went down under the weight of them. But I did not feel anything. There was no mark where they had torn me, no blood, nothing. — But there were so many of them. I knew what was happening. I knew the powers that the Sword has, — but if I were to drop it . . .! I called out: "Dagdaloun! Dagdaloun, help!" '

'He heard me from somewhere far above. There was a crash and uproar from the roof. Sand began to pour down the chimney in the rock, then great boulders, bouncing off the sides of the pit. I heard some of the poor prisoners crying out. Then the whole roof was coming down. The Werebats left me and began to fly back and forth screaming. There was a huge hole through to the sky now, and I saw the Dragon coming down through it. The ice venom began to spray among the Werebats, — those few that remained. Wherever they fell dead, I saw them change into twisted broken man-forms. Soon there were none left.'

'There were few of the prisoners in the pit alive. Most had already died. Their empty shells were awful things. I roped those that were still alive to Dagdaloun's back as best I could. With the Dragon's talons and the Sword we could break their chains easily . . . But so many were already dead.'

'Six of them have awoken. The rest still sleep,' said Eldhoril. 'They are poisoned and no more than half alive. I do not know now if they will ever awake.'

'So that is the end of Ral,' said Karandar. 'You tell your tale well, Erathrir.'

Those that remained of the men of Selenthoril's Quest sat with Eldhoril in the room of the throne in the Ice Castle. Seven remained of the twelve that had set out from Nyaroth Khrathril: Talarnidh, Melandir, Erathrir, Fandorel, Karandar, Yeselwir, and Relnar. Of them only Relnar had been wounded, and even he not badly. Talak still lay broken in mind and body, and the Sylphs tended him. He would be the squire of Melandir again, for that was the last wish of his father before he became wholly the thing and possession of Sagoth. Also seated about the crystal table in the room of ice were Iroi Girindhouz, and Ciranouth, Safaarasaa, and Whirrirrish. It was the day after the Battle of the Treeless Plain.

'I am not sure that it is an end to Ral,' said Eldhoril. 'Erathrir saw her bat form fly off. That is still in the world somewhere. But she is no longer the Witch Queen. She will no longer be able to call herself Goddess.'

'Then she can no longer change back?' said Yeselwir.

'She is trapped in her bat shape,' Eldhoril answered. 'The Sword in the sheath from which her power was drawn is lost to her forever. It was the Sword that slew her fair-seeming.'

'I fear because the Swords are come back into the world,' said Talarnidh. 'We do not yet know what they really mean. I sense evil in this Sword of Doom. It was Ral's Sword, and Sagoth's Sword.'

'The two Swords are bound together,' Eldhoril answered. 'Let us first hear how the Fate Sword served Melandir in the House in the Forest.'

'There is little to tell,' Melandir answered. 'The Witchweird had drugged me with the brew of Ral. Even then the Sword helped me withstand the sorcery of it. I saw Ral and Filindrin fight. Filindrin already by then had the power to call up the Demon. It was he that did it, not Ral. The fire went over him and over me, after Ral had fled. I have heard that it was Talak who rescued him. — You know that it was Whirrirrish who brought me out safe to the house of Iroi Girindhouz. His people tended me when I awoke. It was the sap of the World Tree that restored me. But I had never dropped the Sword, so the fires did not burn me. We would have returned here, had not the message come from Talarnidh. When I knew that Iroi Girindhouz would come and bring the Walking Trees I rode with him.'

'I fulfilled the debt,' said the Pine Lord.

'It is well that you and Melandir came then,' said Eldhoril.

'This tells us no more of the Sword of Sagoth,' said Talarnidh.

'No,' Eldhoril answered. 'It tells us this much, that the Sword of Fate and the Sword of Doom have much the same powers. They protect their bearers from harm and injury, even from death. — I will tell you what I know of Grenyorel, the Sword of Doom.'

'It was once Sagoth's Sword, but it was not made by him. Who made it and how he came by it is not known to me. When Sagoth was banished by Talmond, the Emperor and the Nine Kings — for I was one of them — called on the Lord of the Mendoral to aid us in sealing the sword forever in its sheath. We knew how great a thing it was. Even when locked in its sheath Ral stole it and still drew great power from it as we had feared she might. She kept it hidden, even from her Black Lord lovers in the Love Death. Now Erathrir has drawn it, with knowledge from beyond the world and before time. It is his Sword now.'

'Then it is not evil?' said Erathrir.

'The Elves believed that Sagoth shaped its blade and no more. He did not make its substance,' said Fandorel. 'It was evil when he and Ral bore it, because they were evil. It is not the Sword, it is the one that bears it.'

'It is strange that both the Swords should be seen once again in Tharang,' said Eldhoril. 'Both are borne by Men of the First Race, come from the Outer Worlds. It is all part of a greater story, where all the world is changed. Here in the Midworld the fate of everyone will be shaped.'

'Yet there are things I do not understand about Wenyorel,' said Melandir. 'Ask, the Allfather, told me that it was Sagoth's Bane. Yet it could not kill Sagoth. It may even be that he grew stronger from it. It was the Sceptre that slew him.'

'The reason for that I do not know for sure,' answered the Wizard. '— Consider the whole of the tale. It was you who saw Sagoth flying into the world on wings of midnight when you crossed the Sundering Sea. I think it was then that Sagoth went to Aldel Morn. It was the old heart of his evil before he was banished. There he will have gathered strength, but he had no shape in Tharang, and his forbidden flight from the Outer Darkness must have left him almost helpless. For five years his strength returned and he waited.'

'Then Selenthoril brought the Quest together on Nyaroth Khrathril. He was intent on the destruction of his old mistress Ral, because she had renewed her interest in him. Yet maybe even then Sagoth was working on Selenthoril's mind, and bending it to his purpose. Four of the Quest went into Aldel Morn: Fermilondath, Turnalordath, Wondrith and Filindrin. Three of these he slew, and two of them in turn used for his own purposes. The fourth he took to be his vessel.'

'Here Talak begins to be the heart of our answer to the Dragon's riddle. He was the one who saw, in the valley called Tewfell on the edge of Aldel Morn, the four figures. There was the skeleton of Turnalordath, the corpse of Fermilondath, the Great Hound, which we may be sure was the slayer of Wondrith, and also the man Filindrin. It was to these four that Sagoth himself came.'

'He had trapped the souls of Fermilondath and Turnalordath in their dead bodies, and he used them as his puppets. But Filindrin, in some wise at least, was still his own master at that stage. From what you have said, I do not believe that Sagoth entered him fully till later, — perhaps at Belengar. You remember at Belengar he seemed to have tried to get himself killed in the battle. It might have been to prevent Sagoth from using him. He sent Talak away, deliberately entrusting him to the bearer of the Fate Sword, Sagoth's Bane. He did not want his son to suffer when his father's body was claimed by evil. It was after Belengar that Filindrin became a different man, — not a man at all as we now know.'

'Yet it took a while for Sagoth to obtain complete mastery over the body. A fragment of Filindrin still survived, and Sagoth was not yet grown strong. He was unused, perhaps, to his new shape. So he hoped still to gain part at least of his ends through his servants. First the living corpses of Turnalordath and Fermilondath, then the Hound of Hell. The Hound was beyond the power of Wenyorel, though the Sword did wound it. That much Melandir has made clear. I do not think that Ral either could have availed against the Hound if she had met it. The Beast was banished by the Wild Hunt, as it was before when it slew the old High King. For the Wild Hunt was set in Tharang long ago to guard the confines of the world against the Beasts of Heaven and Hell. It has slept for long ages and is slow to awaken. It may be, from what you have told me of the Hunt and the Hound, that this time the Hound was really slain.'

'So we see that all Sagoth's servants were destroyed, but all the while his own power was growing inside the body of Filindrin. Yet at the House in the Forest he had to face Ral sooner than he wished. Again he had to call on one of his servants. That was the Fire Demon out of Hell which Talak and Melandir saw summoned. His power was not enough to control what he had called on. In the end, after it came near to destroying him, he sent it back to Hell himself. That was the cry which came from the garden of the house.'

'There in the house he failed to gain the Sword or the Sceptre. How he must have feared both! But both at least were lost. Ral knew who he was, but she could do him no harm, for now his power in his stolen body was almost complete. I think perhaps the last vestige of the old Filindrin came here in the Ice Castle, when Sagoth had made all his friends into enemies, and had blighted the life of his son with awful terror. You remember that Filindrin's body collapsed and fainted. After that the body was Sagoth's, — to do with as he wished.'

'It was his arrogance that was his downfall at the last. On the morning of the victory he awaited, he named himself Sagoth, Son of the Morning. Thus he was named at the dawn of the world, when he was the first of the newly-created. Talak heard the name of Sagoth, but Sagoth was sure of his victory, and contemptuously flung the boy aside. He hurt him, but did not kill him. In his arrogance he did not consider us to be a danger when he faced Ral alone on the battlefield.'

'The fire of my Sceptre burnt his body beyond the possibility of survival for a man. But Sagoth possessed the soul of Filindrin within that shell. He would not let the soul die. He remade the body and returned, as it were, from the dead against us. So all came to this point: — that Sagoth faced the Sword of Fate which had banished him from the world before. Yet now the power of the Sword was gone. All of the riddle pointed to the Sword. Yet the answer was different.'

'The riddle is greater than I had thought. Both Swords have come back into the world. The Sword of Doom has been the curse of its former possessor Ral. Yet the Sword of Fate has no power over Sagoth. The tale of the Swords and the Men that bear them is not ended here. This is no more than its beginning.'

'And so at the end it was the Sceptre Mortal, Arnorin, that slew Sagoth. Its gift is final death. It freed the soul of Filindrin at last from Sagoth's thrall. It broke the vessel that Sagoth had stolen. It cracked his image of might and terror and scattered it onto the winds of the world, a thing of dust. If he still lingers, his power will be long in remaking.'

'So it was that the Quest Selenthoril sent you on was not in vain. The Sceptre he bade you seek was the only thing in the world that could slay Sagoth. The man that found the Sceptre was one of the few that could claim it for his own and live. For he bore the Sword of Fate that gave him life. Without Selenthoril, soon Sagoth would have come, mighty and unvanquishable out of the land of Aldel Morn, more terrible by far than ever was Ral.'

'There remains Selenthoril,' said Talarnidh. 'He has Elandril, my sister, and he has the Sceptre Spiritual.'

'And he no longer has Ral to fear,' added Karandar.

'But he is still trapped, and will remain so,' answered Eldhoril. 'He is no danger to us or the world, as he has been no danger for the thousand years gone by.'

'I will return to seek him out,' said Talarnidh.

'Why?' asked Eldhoril.

'Because of my mother,' answered Talarnidh. 'And my sister, whom he still has.'

'Yes, it is enough,' answered the Wizard.

'We will all return,' said Melandir. 'He sent us to seek the Sceptre Mortal. The Sceptre Mortal shall go back to him.'

Eldhoril looked from Melandir to Talarnidh.

'You mean to kill him,' he said.

'Yes,' Talarnidh answered.

'Though you have the Sceptre Mortal, you may find it hard to kill this man, — for reasons you do not dream of,' said Eldhoril. 'But enough now. — I will not riddle, like Dagdaloun. You are right, — you must return to Misen Taïrail. But that is another matter and another Quest. — For now you must stay here with me!'

'For it is the time of the Ice Fire,' said Whirrirrish.

'It is the time when the creatures of ice are loosed from their bondage,' said Safaarasaa.

'Come, we will watch with them and be glad,' said Eldhoril. 'It is their Festival, when they bathe in the Ice Fire, and their limbs are loosed and they become free.'

'I remember another Festival,' answered Talarnidh, 'when I lay in Fire and a voice came to me. It was the voice of Selenthoril. Since then I have never been free.'

High over the plain of crystal, a hawk circled on weary wing. It had watched there a long while now. Before then it had flown from afar through snow and storm from Nyaroth Khrathril in the north. It was one of the Wise Birds, and it had come from Selenthoril. It had seen all the battle and the downfall of Ral. It had seen all that happened on the field of war. 'Bring news of the Sceptre!' Selenthoril had told it. Now it turned north again, with news of the Sceptre for Selenthoril far away.

THE EMPTY LANDS AND PART OF THE FOREST OF SORCERY
The Castle of Selenthoril on Nyaroth Khrāthrīl
The Giant's Sword
MISEN TAÏRAIL
Sagaefan
GAUR IACHAD
The Sea of the Curse
The Empty Lands of SĀRT EMIG
The Everway
Belengār
The Nowhere Road
ITHIĀZ KEIDEN
The Halls of Iroi Girindhouz
The House in the Forest
Kruakh
The Crossroads of Takūnān
Thulgārn, Pit of the Werebats
THE FOREST OF SORCERY
The South Road
The Ice Castle of Eldhoril
Treeless Plain

APPENDIX

THE COUNT OF THE YEARS

The Time Before Time

In the Time Before Time there was Zehrvan, outside of reality and uncreate. It was Zehrvan who made space to be discrete from him and it took the form of the Cosmic Egg. Therein the World Tree stands and on its roots and branches are held up the Seven Worlds. On the worlds dwelt many creatures, and among them were the Elves. Everywhere was Chaos, and there was no Time.

The First Aeon — Aeon of the Timeless Ones

Zehrvan, of a whim, determined to create Balance and Order. So the Wind of Time blew from him, who was himself Boundless Time. All that had been created was blown through the Gateway To Time. Since then all creatures dance to the silent tune of time. It was then that the Mendoral came into the world. They are the mighty twigs of the World Tree snapped off by the Wind of Time and thus granted life of their own. Greatest of them was the Lord Mendra. Many living things were changed by the Wind of Time, and the Fays were sundered from the Elves, and death came into the world.

Zehrvan made the two great Gods. Yazdan and Dahak were these Gods. Each had great power and each was the enemy of the other, but each was naught without the other. In Highest Heaven, crystal and gleaming, Yazdan the God now stood alone, and he is The Rock of Ages. Beneath him lies the world of Heaven, and beneath Heaven is the Overworld. Held by the midmost branches of the World Tree, poised between Yazdan and Dahak, the Midworld lies, the largest of the worlds, that some call Tharang. Beneath lies the Underworld, where the dead dwell, and beneath the Underworld is Hell. Beneath again is Nether Hell where Dahak the God stands alone, a pillar of dark obsidian, and he is The Grindstone of Time.

These then are the Seven Worlds of Faerie, first created of all worlds. But Yazdan and Dahak were bound each into his own world by Zehrvan, for they both had great power. Though they were bound, each into his own world, yet each had an Avatar who trod the soil of the worlds in his stead. The Avatar of Dahak, the first created on the first day of time, was Sagoth Son of the Morning. The Avatar of Yazdan was Tyrvaz. So, out of order, chaos returned, and there was war and destruction. For the Avatars warred throughout the worlds, but most of all in Tharang the Midworld. And blood gleamed newly-spilled in the changeless light of the Cosmic Egg.

The bright morning of creation ended forever when Dahak put forth his power to take the light from the Cosmic Egg. Though he took the light, yet he could not drink it into him, and the light shone on amidst his darkness. For in the balance of all things, light is a thing of Yazdan the Good. And so in Nether Hell Dahak fashioned shells to hold the light, and there were made twenty-seven lesser eggs to contain the light of the Cosmic Egg that he had darkened. For, though he might not leave the Nether Hell, yet Dahak determined that Sagoth, his Avatar, should use the power of the lesser eggs to triumph in Faerie. Like a God Sagoth used the light from the Cosmic Egg to make creatures, thinking beings born of evil, Goblins and Trolls and others that dwelt in the darkness. For the light that went into their making was cursed in its very light.

This then was the long and terrible time called the Great Darkness, when Sagoth grew mighty in the worlds, and evil walked abroad in the shadows. Then it was that the World Tree glowed with the fire of Zehrvan, lest all creation perish in the long cold.

At the last, Tyrvaz, the Avatar of Yazdan, made his quest, through all the darkling worlds alone, and came in stealth to Nether Hell. Dahak sensed him there. But Tyrvaz, mighty in strength, turned the adamantine wheels and from the Grindstone of Time came gouts of flame and fire, and grim light in the utter darkness. Dahak was afraid in the tumult, and so Tyrvaz departed. He bore away with him from Nether Hell those eggs that Dahak made which still remained, and so came back with them to Highest Heaven.

So Yazdan took the greatest of the eggs of light and broke it on the Dome of Heaven. Light and warmth cascaded down the Cosmic Egg. And hope returned. Yet the light was much less than before. The lower worlds were left in darkness, and so in part was the Midworld, save when the God put forth his power and the light pulsed further down the dark shell of the Cosmic Egg. So it was that Yazdan determined to bring warmth and light to Tharang also. With the lesser eggs and the Cosmic light of them he made the suns and the moon to traverse the skies of the worlds. Thereafter there was day and night in Tharang in regular cycle, and this was later taken as a sign of the war between Tyrvaz and Sagoth. But in Hell and Nether Hell there came no sun nor moon. In Hell Sagoth has set eternal fires to burn in flaming pits, and their light alone glares red in evernight.

The Second Aeon — Aeon of Men

Though the Darkness had ended, Faerie was still wracked and despoiled by Sagoth and his minions. So Yazdan bethought himself again, and he determined to make a place free from Evil. With the light from the Cosmic Egg and the demiurgic power that dwelt in him he made the stars and the firmament of space, the Outer Worlds, beyond the Cosmic Egg, where before was the Void. Mightily he wrought and the stars and the planets were countless in his sight and great was their glory and majesty, and the God rejoiced in his creation. But even then beyond the shining nebulae was the Outer Darkness, and there was only Zehrvan.

Now Tyrvaz took the last frail eggs of Cosmic Light. And he came down into the Garden of Eternity that blossoms round the trunk of the World Tree in the Midworld. The two eggs that alone remained he broke together, and light rose from them and fell in dew-bright fountains. From the Light came Ask the Allfather and Embla the Allmother. And from their intertwining came others of their kind, Men and Women in equal numbers. This was the First Race of Men, that sailed in Golden Boats across the Sundering Seas into the Outer Worlds their God had made for them there in the darkness lit by stars, where Time was longer and flowed more slowly.

In those days also the Second Race of Men came into Tharang the Midworld. They were created from the Cosmic Light cast unknown upon the shores. As year followed year they spread over the land and peopled many places in Tharang.

At first these things were not known to Tyrvaz who went to

the Outer Worlds and walked with the First Men. He helped them raise up cities of towers and glittering halls and fruitful gardens. So there on those worlds was indeed paradise and there was no Evil. Many years of slow time Tyrvaz dwelt there in the Outer Worlds, and Sagoth the while was in Hell, far from the light of the suns that Yazdan made and that he hated. But the creatures that Sagoth made still roamed far and wide and there was no ending of the war in the Midworld.

At last Sagoth himself returned to the Midworld in all his panoply. There was fire and slaughter, and many bowed down before him in his power. Long was his triumph until Tyrvaz came back from the Outer Worlds. And then the war between the Gods was renewed, more bitter and ruinous than before. Many of the races of the world were stricken and lost, and over the broken land the Beasts of Heaven and Hell ranged. Even in the Underworld, where the dead dwell, and in the Overworld, there was fear and tumult, and the beasts of light and darkness stalked the worlds.

Only now was it that Zehrvan stepped forth from the shadows of his being and the Gods trembled. The Grindstone of Time that was Dahak groaned in its travail, and the Rock of Ages that was Yazdan shook in the Heavens. And Zehrvan laughed and banished the Gods Tyrvaz and Sagoth into the Outer Worlds that Faerie once more be free, and their power was taken away. This then was the Ban of Zehrvan.

The Third Aeon — Aeon of Zehrvan's Peace

Zehrvan the Unknown called up the Spirit of the Green, and the Riders came and the Huntsman, and this was the Wild Hunt. Zehrvan spoke and it leapt to his command. Thereafter down the ages it hunted the Beasts of Heaven and Hell, and where it rode it beat the bounds of the world of Tharang. When the beasts were hunted from out the Midworld and the Gods were banished away, there was peace of a sort in Faerie. Suffering and strife did not depart. But each man had his own mastery and men were free once more to find their fate. This was called the Peace of Zehrvan.

In the Outer Worlds, that Zehrvan had not made, there was little peace, for in them dwelt Sagoth and Tyrvaz and ever they warred with each other, and Zehrvan gave but little thought to them.

Long, long was the Peace of Zehrvan in Faerie, and long the years of Zehrvan the God. And after long years was the Metamorphosis of Zehrvan, of which the learned speak. So it came to pass that Zehrvan went about in the worlds as a human, and some called her Math, the Wise, and some called him Mat, the Fool. For Zehrvan the God was made flesh and dwelt in the world.

The Fourth Aeon — Aeon of the Mortal Gods

The peace of Zehrvan remained, though Zehrvan now was made flesh. Still Sagoth and Tyrvaz fought in the Outer Worlds and through the vastnesses of the void far away from Faerie. There were those who thought that Zehrvan the God would return in his Godhead, but he did not. And so with the passing of the days and with the passing of the ages, Dahak bestirred himself and thought himself safe. He reached out and took back that part of himself that was Sagoth, and Sagoth came and dwelt in Hell. Thus ended his banishment to the Outer Worlds, for Zehrvan the God was no more. Yet Sagoth could not come into the Midworld, for the Ban of Zehrvan had not changed. The Wild Hunt hunted the bounds of the world, and Sagoth, Avatar of Dahak, might not enter.

Finally a man was brought down into Hell and taken before Sagoth. And Sagoth possessed that man and took his body for his own. Then Sagoth, the Man, went up into Tharang, and the Wild Hunt did not heed his coming. He built there a great power for himself in the cold places of the Northlands. On an island in the Northern Ocean he built mightily in a land called Aldel Morn. From this heart of Evil, Evil spread out, and Evil came again in Tharang, and with it war.

At this Tyrvaz returned into the Highest Heaven where all is bliss and was at one with Yazdan. Now even in Highest Heaven, where Yazdan sits alone, the green shoots of the topmost branches of the World Tree reach upwards to the brightest light of the Cosmic Egg. On their tips are iridescent blooms, the flower-jewels, and there too grow the seeds of life, the winged seeds of the World Tree. Yazdan took the seeds and by his power changed them. He changed the amaranthine flowers so that they became as many-coloured cups of crystal, and light was in them. And in heaven a child was born of a virgin, and the Spirit of Tyrvaz entered into the child, and the child grew into a man, and that was Tyrvaz the Man. The Man Tyrvaz was brought down the stem of the World Tree by Ratatosk to the Garden of Eternity. With him he brought the seeds of the World Tree that bore the breath of Yazdan's thought and the jewelflowers also. Around his head there flew the Birds of Paradise that are solace to the God on High.

Twenty seeds he sowed that came from the highest branches where the Tree and the Cosmic Egg came together. From these were sprung the Kings and Queens of the Peiri, and first of these were the High King and his Queen. To each King and to each Queen were given a thousand more of the Seeds of the World. From these were sprung the sires of all the Peiri, High Race of the Midworld, formed like Men, undying like the Elves, yet neither Men nor Elves. These were the Peiri that were brought forth from the Seeds of the World in the soil of the Garden of Eternity in that First Day long ago, and a new Aeon of the World was born with them.

The Fifth Aeon — Aeon of the Peiri

The First Age — Age of the High Kingdom. On that First Day Tyrvaz gave to each King and to each Queen a jewelflower. The lights of the jewels were intermingled and from them a flame struck up incandescent in the twilight, the light of heaven come down to earth, as a burning silver fountain. And the Peiri called it Royal Fire. The Peiri saved that magic fire and held its undying light in the jewelflowers and they shone as lamps that flashed in the darkness and were not extinguished, and so began the Festival of the Lamps. The High King was crowned with the mystic flame. On his finger Tyrvaz, the Man, placed the ring from his own hand, and this was the Ring of the High King, symbol of the High Kingdom.

Tyrvaz nurtured the Peiri there in the Garden and they grew many and great, until they came out into Tharang and built cities and founded kingdoms. Then Sagoth was wary of their growing power. He courted them with sugared words as he had courted the sires of Men. But the Peiri were born of the power of Yazdan that is Goodness, and they scorned the words of Sagoth Son of the Morning, God of Evil Incarnate. The Goblins came against them, and the High Race broke the Goblin armies and grew stronger thereby. Sagoth was made to retreat ever farther, until at last he withdrew his power into his northern fastnesses. There he watched and waited while the High Kingdom of the Peiri, the Realm of Wenyaltrir, brought peace to many lands far and wide.

This was the first flowering of the Peiri. Newly come into the world, they delighted in the world and in all living things, and there was no evil in them. They talked with the ancient peoples, and taught them and learned from them. Great was their friendship with the Elves, that came from the Time Before Time. Many years of peace went by in wonder and the shadows were lifted from the world.

But Sagoth bided his time though his hatred was strong. He went in a guise into the Great Forest where the High King was hunting the fell beasts of those far-off days. Out of the depths Sagoth called to the Hound of Hell, and out of the depths it came. In engulfed the High King and all his power and glory were as nothing against it and were swallowed up within its foulness. And only his Ring was left to mark where he fell, and great was the triumph and great the rejoicing of Sagoth, Son of the Morning.

The Second Age — Age of the Nine Kings. The coming of the Hound of Hell had woken the Wild Hunt that guarded the bounds of Tharang from the Beasts of Heaven and Hell. The Huntsman and his Hunting Dogs and his Riders pursued the alien Hound, and it fled from them in fear and was gone from the world. But Sagoth, the Man, still grew in strength, for the Peiri, his enemy, were in confusion, and he had long prepared for this moment. So it was that he came against the High Race in great panoply, and there was war, and blood flowed beneath the sun. The Peiri fought bravely and they were strong in this hour. Great too were their losses. Long fought was that war and bloody and the tide of battle ebbed and flowed, but always it seemed that Sagoth grew in his power, and the power of the Peiri was lessened.

At the high tide of Sagoth's power the Peiri called in their desperation on the Mendoral, the mighty scions of the World Tree. From the bright meads and woods of the Overworld they came, and from the Pastures of Heaven, and 'the Lord Mendra was among them. The Lord Mendra received from the Kings the jewelflowers that Tyrvaz gave them at their birth, full of Royal Fire. Then the Mendoral, melding all their power together, fashioned from the jewelflowers the ten Sceptres of Power. To each of the Nine Kings a Sceptre was given. The Tenth Sceptre, made from the jewelflower of the High King, lay in the thought of the Lord Mendra and was not claimed. With these Sceptres, the Sceptres of Wenyaltrir, the power of Sagoth was utterly cast down and the ruin of all his works was as vast as their making. And the Sceptres of Wenyaltrir killed Sagoth the Man, the God Incarnate.

Then the Nine Kings made the Nine Realms of Wenyaltrir and wielded the power of the Sceptres. Many of the Mendoral returned to their far abodes but some remained and dwelt in the garths in the Great Forest and in the western lands, though few men saw them and fewer still know of the spells that their minds wove. Thus came the second flowering of the Peiri, greater than before, and they ruled over the peoples of many lands and the earth was filled with the majesty of their glory.

During the many years and long of the glory and power of the Nine Realms the Spirit of Sagoth fluttered insubstantial in the caverns of Aldel Morn. At last it found what it sought, a man of grime and tatters who cursed goodness in his want, for it had not been good to him. Sagoth entered into him and possessed him, and he was not unwilling. Slowly as the years passed the new man Sagoth gained in strength and the wraith of the great god became one with the flesh of the man. Even so his Goblin armies had been broken and his former power was long gone away. The Peiri ruled in wonder and splendour. Yet by some chance it was at this time that an ancient thing came into the possession of Sagoth. This was the Brandiron of Chaos that Zehrvan carried with him through the Gateway To Time. Now, in the great furnace of Misen Taïrail, Sagoth forged the dull iron into a blade, and the heat of the forging melted the mountain and left a lake where its peak had been. As he held it, newly forged, in his hand, he named it Grenyorel — the Sword of Doom. But even then the voice of Zehrvan said: 'Its name is Zaroq'ar, the God Cleaver.'

Just as the power of the World Tree that lay in the Sceptres of Wenyaltrir gave dominion to the Peiri, so now the ancient mysteries of the Time Before Time were bound into the Sword of Doom and Sagoth drank their sombre power into himself. Armed with the Sword he renewed again the ancient and unending war, and as he grew strong so Wenyaltrir was lessened. The Nine Kings were hard pressed and their Realms reduced and everywhere Sagoth went, the Swordbearer, there was fire and ruin and death. Though the Kings called on the Mendoral, even their thought could not work its way on the Sword.

So the Lord Mendra went up into Heaven. In the midst of that golden land was a cave of crystal, and there asleep on a bed of unfading flowers lay Tyrvaz the Man who once had sown the seeds of the World Tree in the Garden of Eternity. The Lord Mendra called to him and he awoke and rose from his bed and his path was strewn with flowers. Then Tyrvaz heard the cries of the Peiri come up from the stricken earth, but he did not go there at once. Strange ways he trod and little is told of the tale of them. But when he came to Tharang a Sword was in his hand. This was the second of the Brandirons of Chaos. In Heaven he had forged the dull iron, just as Sagoth had forged in Aldel Morn. Of it he had made the Sword of Fate, twin of the Sword of Doom.

To Tharang he came as Talmond — 'Lord of Light' in the tongue of the High Race. He took the Ring of the old High King and he took the Tenth Sceptre of Power from out of the thought of the Lord Mendra. The Peiri hailed him Emperor in panoply and splendour, and on that day of the Empire it was also the Festival of the Lamps, and the Second Coming of Talmond was celebrated with the First.

The Third Age — Age of Empire. With great rejoicing and song the Peiri greeted their new Emperor, come to them from Heaven. Their hosts went forth to war and their lances shook like the waves on the sea and their banners shone in the light. Before them was ever Talmond and in his hand the Sword of Fate, and with him the Kings of Wenyaltrir, and in their hands the Sceptres of Power. Thus began the Hundred Years War which lasted from the one Festival of the Lamps to the next. In that war Sagoth and his creatures were driven inexorably back, for victory was in the hearts of the High Race and none could withstand them. So Sagoth came again to his ancient holds and nothing else of his dominion remained, for everywhere the Lords of Wenyaltrir were triumphant.

At this time Talmond took to wife after the manner of the High Race Delwen, High Queen of the Peiri, that was widowed by the Hound of Hell. Their eldest child was a daughter and they named her Lidhelm. At the time of the next Festival of the Lamps after the coming of Talmond, the child Lidhelm was thirteen. In the darkness of the Festival, after the ceremony of the Royal Fire, a stranger came upon Lidhelm in the woodland outside the new city that Talmond was building. That stranger was Sagoth. There he raped and defiled Lidhelm and cursed her in that act. Her cries came to Talmond, still wreathed in the undying fire of the Lamps, and in the shimmering silver of the light he saw the despoiling of his firstborn child.

Swords unsheathing fought Sagoth and Talmond, blade against blade, Sword of Fate against Sword of Doom. Day followed day as they fought, neither gaining nor losing. Then Eldhoril the Wizard and the other Kings of the Peiri encircled that ruined glade. They put forth together the power of the Sceptres of Wenyaltrir. That power fell upon the man in whom Sagoth's soul now dwelt, — and the power was flung back in the faces of the Kings and was overmastered utterly. The Kings cried out in their torment, and the harmony of the Sceptres was broken, and the Sceptres were changed and lessened. For now before them there stood a Man no more, but Sagoth Himself, Prince of Darkness, Son of the Morning, Avatar of Dahak, God on Earth.

Thus Sagoth broke the Ban of Zehrvan. But there was no time for the Wild Hunt to awake and seek him out. The Sword of Fate swung in the hand of Talmond, and clove Sagoth the God. For Wenyorel too was the God Cleaver. Out of the World, and out of all the worlds, the soul of Sagoth fled screaming, and abode in the Outer Darkness and wailed in the Utter Ice. On the ground where the God had stood lay Grenyorel, the Sword of Doom.

By ritual and magic, in secrecy and stealth, the Sword of Doom was sheathed that none might draw it again. Lidhelm bore the child of Sagoth, and that was also kept secret. The child was taken from her, and few know the tale of that child's sorrow. And Lidhelm grieved bitterly and was not consoled. To her hatred of Sagoth that had raped her was added a new hatred — a hatred of Talmond her own father, and a hatred of all the Race of the Peiri, her own people. Thus the seed of doom was sown even as the Great Years of Empire began. Werendilren the

Golden was built and became the capital of the Peiri, that was Sarras before. The Empire grew greater than ever the Kingdoms were, and it was named Telmirandor, and that also was the Golden. There was peace in the world and the Goblins and the other brood of Sagoth were weak. They hid away in dark woods and forgotten hills and shivered at the call of the trumpets of Telmirandor. Even the fastnesses of Sagoth were scoured and cleansed. Many many years of goodness and splendour passed, and it seemed that the balance was weighed forever towards the side of good.

Through those years Lidhelm grew in bitterness. She learnt of the Sword of Doom, the sword of her defiler. She found its hiding place and learnt how to draw power from it. The ritual was foul, and she sank deeper into the evil of Sagoth. But she did not learn how to draw the sword from its sheath. Talmoran, a son, was born to Talmond and Delwen. Lidhelm his sister hated him from birth. Secretly she contrived his death. A new sadness came to Talmond and his wife. And the insidious evil began to grow and spread.

Lidhelm's voice was now great in the counsels of the Peiri, and she was fair and majestic as a queen, mighty in lore and wisdom. But always her counsel brought dissent and strife. In the very heart of Telmirandor the worm gnawed unceasing. The gold faded and shadows lengthened. The High Race began to wane though few perceived it amidst the splendours. The endless centuries wore on, and always fewer children were born. Some of the Peiri and many Men became followers of Lidhelm, and even the greatest and the most noble were deceived as to the evil in her heart.

Finally she threw off her guise. She named herself Great Goddess and Moon Queen, and her people bowed down and worshipped her, for she was become as Sagoth had been. Her rebellion smote the soul of Telmirandor. She seized the Moon that Yazdan made, and twisted its light and marred its form so that from that day it took on strange shapes that haunted the night of Faerie. Also she seized into her power the dwellers of the Moon. By blasphemous devices she created the Black Lords. These were to be her lovers, who must join with her in the Love Death to renew their accursed immortality. The Peiri named her Ral, which means Witch, and Ral she became, Ral the Witch Queen.

But her power was not yet great enough. She came to Tharang bearing the sheathed sword, and she was broken by the power of the Sceptres. The Black Lords fled away to the Underworld and grew great there, though a few still lingered in the white plains of the Moon and in the ancient haunts of Sagoth in the Northlands. Ral herself was captured and imprisoned in the Tower of the Sword in Werendilren. Time passed. Another son, Talarnidh, and a daughter, Elandril, were borne by Delwen to the Emperor. Every hundred years, at the Festival of the Lamps, Ral was brought forth before Talmond, and he begged her to repent. Twelve times she cursed him and spat upon him, but on the thirteenth she wept and knelt for his forgiveness. Gladly he gave it, and Ral was named Lidhelm again.

As a token of her repentance, Lidhelm promised to restore the Sceptres of Wenyaltrir to their harmony of power, that was broken when Sagoth the God came to Faerie. This she would do by the greatness of the wizardry she had learnt, and thus would all her wrongs be undone. Sweet was her voice and she was full of beauty when she told of the days that would come when all ills would be washed away. The Lords of Wenyaltrir hearkened to her. What she bade them do was to build the Sceptres into a great crown, set above a throne in a mighty tower. There he that sat upon the throne would hold the Sceptres in his thought and their power would be as one again, united in the Crown of Telmirandor. And so in the midst of Werendilren the Fair there began the making of the Tower of the Crown, and many rare and precious things were brought to the city for its building.

But the repentance of Ral was utterly false. There was no Lidhelm born anew. There was only Ral. Ral it would be who would sit in the tower on the throne, and Ral would wield the Sceptres and Ral would wear the Crown. Secretly she summoned back the Black Lords, and her strongholds were rebuilt. Black Lords reigned again in Aldel Morn. Secretly she went to them, and they were united with her in the Love Death, lest they die, for their immortality was already waning. The great Crown itself was nearly complete when Eldhoril discovered Ral in hideous embrace with the sheathed sword of Sagoth, drawing its force into her. Eldhoril had always doubted her. Now he knew the truth, she fled from him. But it was to the Throne Room, the Room of the Crown, that she fled. There, Ral the Witch Queen sat upon the throne of Talmond and claimed the Crown for her own.

Talmond and Eldhoril came into that place in pursuit of Ral, and there they beheld her in majesty and glory seated upon the throne. And in her thought she held the power of the Sceptres, united in the Crown. Talmond, the Emperor, drew the Sword of Fate and struck at Ral. The Great Goddess put forth the power of the Sceptres. Mighty was that power, restored again and united. Mighty was the ruin that came from that power. In the moment of her wrath all Ral's hatred flowed out upon Talmond and upon the city of the Peiri and all its people. Werendilren the Fair and the Golden was lain low. In their thousands the Peiri were slain, smitten by a thousand forms of death. And all their Kings died with them save Eldhoril alone. Though the power of the Sceptres and the awful wrath of Ral lay upon all the land, yet in the eye of the storm the Tower of the Crown and the Throne Room still stood. And there in the dust lay the Sceptres of Wenyaltrir, lifeless where they had fallen from the Crown, broken above. There in the dust lay Eldhoril the King, and there lay Talmond the Emperor. There in the dust lay Ral, for she had not the strength to wield the Sceptres of Power.

As the tumult died away and the cries of the stricken went up in the stillness of the air, the members of the Sacred Band came to the Tower. They took their Emperor, for though he still breathed they saw that he was dying. And the body of Eldhoril they covered up and bore away, for he seemed already dead. The Sceptres also were taken from that accursed place. But the body of Ral they left there.

Dying, Talmond the Man was lain in the Tombs. With him was lain Eldhoril the King, and he was amidst all the Kings of the Peiri and all of them were dead. The last act of the Emperor was to give the lifeless Sceptres into the hands of Nine Guardians. The Guardians and the Lords of Wenyaltrir went out from that place into the ruins, nor was Talmond ever seen in the world again, as all Werendilren died about him.

The Fourth Age — Age of Ruin. Ral, the Witch, was not dead as the Sacred Band had thought her to be. She awoke in the empty Throne Room in the midst of the destruction she had wrought. She looked out on the broken spires and wept, for she was one of the Peiri, and Werendilren the Golden was fallen. She looked on the broken spires and laughed, for now her vengeance was won. Then she took thought to her plight. By the Witch Voice she summoned the Black Lords to her. Heedless of danger she ran through the ruined city. Eager and fearful she scrambled and sought in the rubble within the Tower of the Sword. And there she found the Sword of Doom again.

At night the Black Lords fell upon the remnants of the High Race in the city with great slaughter. The Empire of Telmirandor crumbled that night. The Black Lords triumphed in the thrall of their Great Goddess. The survivors of the fallen Peiri fled as they might among the ruins, but the new Guardians of the Sceptres still lived, and Delwen the Empress and her son Talarnidh and Elandril her daughter.

The Empire of Telmirandor did not fall in a day when Werendilren the Golden was broken. In the ancient Kingdoms of the High Race there was long battle when the Black Lords came in their panoply. But the Kings were gone and the Sceptres were scattered. New warlike kingdoms arose, made by men glad to shake off the dominion of the High Race. Cruel little empires were carved out by the Black Lords from the body of the old Empire. Goblin cities grew up maggot-like amidst the ruins of the cities of the Peiri, and the Goblins and the creatures of evil and the warlike men of the new kingdoms all in some measure served the Black Lords, and the Black Lords served Ral.

Nothing was left of the power and dominion of Telmirandor in the Northlands, and much of the West was desolated in strife. Further south some at least of the High Race of old resisted, with loyal Men and Elves and other races also. They built what they could amid the downfallen splendour, and the Goblins and the Black Lords never wholly had the mastery over them. Of these, greatest was Parvaloril, son of the King of Morena, who returned to Morena and there his kingdom survived. Some of the Peiri stayed in the stricken West and they fought the bravest fight. Among them was Talarnidh son of the Emperor. But many of the Peiri fled out of Tharang into the Overworld, and those who remained to fight were few. These were the great years of triumph for Ral, the Witch Queen, the Great Goddess.

For five thousand years Ral was supreme. For four thousand of those years Eldhoril the King, the Wizard of Wenyaltrir, lay as dead in the vaults of the Peiri. But he was not dead. When he awoke, Niaherz the Black Lord had betrayed his Goddess and stolen the Sceptre Spiritual from its Guardian to dwell as Banatem, last of the High Magicians, with Delwen and Elandril in the Underworld. Eldhoril sought and found his Sceptre, Elemental, — and then began his search for the Empress and her daughter. Long he sought and at last he found them there in the phantom palace of Banatem. But Black Lords had followed Eldhoril to that palace. They siezed Delwen, and when Banatem and Eldhoril went up against them, they taunted Eldhoril, saying: 'Why does the Wizard of Wenyaltrir ride with Niaherz the Hooded One, the Black Lord?' Then Banatem loosed the Monsters of the Mind upon them and slew them. And Delwen, Empress of Telmirandor, High Queen of Wenyaltrir, died at the hands of Banatem the false who loved her. Eldhoril now saw that Banatem was truly Niaherz, but Eldhoril too was defeated by the power of the Sceptre. Thus it came to pass that Niaherz planned his vengeance for the death of Delwen on Ral who had been his Goddess.

He went to the Peiri that dwelt now in the Overworld, and found them still a strong and valiant race. He came before them as Banatem, last of the High Magicians. But now he took a third name, and that was Selenthoril, which means 'White King'. Then Selenthoril led the hosts of the Peiri down into Tharang, and the War of the Sceptres was fought against Ral. Many men deserted the Witch Queen and many fought for the Peiri. For, though Ral was not Sagoth, many now hated her and all hated the Black Lords. And because Ral was not Sagoth so her evil was less mighty.

The War of the Sceptres went ill for Ral and for the false Selenthoril alike. Ral was defeated in her very strongholds and fled to the Forest of Sorcery, broken for a thousand years. But as Selenthoril and the Sceptre Bearers sat in the castle of Ral on Nyaroth Khrathril in the North, so Eldhoril came to haunt the triumph of the White King. Strange tales are told of what befell in those times, nor are the Elves or Men or the High Race sure of what befell. This much only they knew, that the host of the High Race was lost out of the world, and that was the end of all the dreams of the Peiri and the last of their hopes. For the Sceptres were vanished away, as if they had never been, and out of the mists and twisted ways that surrounded the island of Nyaroth Khrathril none ever came forth, and Selenthoril too came no more.

While Selenthoril was lost to the world in the fastnesses of Nyaroth Khrathril, Eldhoril, unknown to the world, for all his paths had been secret, lay in the Forest of Sorcery. There the power of Selenthoril had cast him. Again it was as if he was one dead, but the years brought healing to him, and as the years went by he perceived that another dwelt nigh to him in the forest.

Away from the ruined north, Parvaloril made again a great realm in his Kingdom of Morena. From Alban in the Western Ocean Talarnidh tried to restore some of the lost power of the High Race in the Northlands. But the days of the Peiri were gone. It was Men who had fought in great armies across the lands in the War of the Sceptres. It was Men who had defeated the Black Lords and Goblins in battle, and Men who founded the new nations.

In the Northlands the Men of Chamley were the new force, who had come from the South to fight against Ral and her servants. A new state arose in Torondidh whose lords had once served Ral. And in later years out of this ancient kingdom came Melatin and the rich republic of Amray. East of Torondidh the Kingdom of Aroth rose and declined, while in Khirkhan, out of the Goblin chaos a new empire of Men was founded on the shores of the Sif Oumeid. To the west was Mindrim and in later days the wide realms of Azantul and Alnaron. All these were mighty nations and, though for the most they held the Peiri in honour, they gave but little heed to the forgotten pomps and power of fallen Telmirandor.

Eleven hundred years went by, and then the past awoke. Men of the First Race trod the soil of Tharang again. And in the Outer Worlds the Stars went out.